DATE DUE

5-2-07			
12-6-07			
9-19-09			
1-13-10			

Demco No. 62-0549

Lazo's War

Don Kuzma

Copyright © 2004 by Don Kuzma

All rights reserved. No part of this book shall be reproduced or transmitted in any form or by any means, electronic, mechanical, magnetic, photographic including photocopying, recording or by any information storage and retrieval system, without prior written permission of the publisher. No patent liability is assumed with respect to the use of the information contained herein. Although every precaution has been taken in the preparation of this book, the publisher and author assume no responsibility for errors or omissions. Neither is any liability assumed for damages resulting from the use of the information contained herein.

This is a work of fiction. Names, characters, places, and incidents either are the product of the author's imagination or are used fictitiously. Any resemblance to actual events or locales or persons, living or dead, is entirely coincidental.

ISBN 0-7414-2113-5

Published by:

INFINITY
PUBLISHING.COM

1094 New Dehaven Street, Suite 100
West Conshohocken, PA 19428-2713
Info@buybooksontheweb.com
www.buybooksontheweb.com
Toll-free (877) BUY BOOK
Local Phone (610) 941-9999
Fax (610) 941-9959

Printed in the United States of America

Printed on Recycled Paper

Published August 2004

ACKNOWLEDGMENT

I met Mitzi Kannitz in Vienna, Austria, in 1946, while serving with the U.S. army of occupation. I had just turned 19 when I met her and though she must be dead, I feel obligated to recognize her for the part she played in the development of this novel. She had left Poland in early 1945 to escape the oncoming Soviet army and ended up in Dresden, just in time to experience the terrible bombings of the Old City. Some of what she told me of that horrible event has been incorporated in the chapters describing the bombing of Dresden.

I must also acknowledge the tireless efforts of my wife, Yvonne, for without her help, this novel would never have reached the publishers.

CHAPTER ONE

A few miles west of Benghazi, in a tent village called Tokra, a soldier, wrapped in a G.I. towel, made his way between the long monotonous rows of fluttering canvas. He was a tall man and it was quite amusing to see him tripping gingerly over the hot desert sand, now and then hopping on one foot so that he might comfort the other with a gentle slapping of his hand. Each morning for the past several weeks he had made his way to the latrine and each morning he paused just before entering and raised his face toward the East.

One could only guess the words he used to address the hot African sun but two years of army life must have, more than adequately, prepared his vocabulary for such occasions. After completing his ritualistic exercise in profanity, he turned and one might notice that his face had become less agitated. He smiled gently; his teeth seemed blanched against a face turned rusty by the hot desert sun. He brushed the flies from the screened door, opened it and dashed in.

"Oh, good morning Yank!"

Lazo squinted and turned.

"Oh, Hi Sarge! How the hell are you?"

The sergeant brushed away some lather that had collected on his upper lip. "Just fine Lazo, just fine." Then he pointed his razor at Lazo. "And you? Weren't you supposed to ship out last night?"

Lazo moved his fingers through his shortly cropped hair, leaving it parted gently to the left. Then without turning replied, "The flight was scrubbed again."

"How so?"

"Inclement weather over the Adriatic, was the way they put it," replied Lazo, not trying to conceal his disappointment.

"Cheer up, lad. It's not all that bad." Replied the Sergeant.

Lazo squeezed some lather from a large tube of Barbasol and began to cover his face with the foamy mist. "Looks like I'll never get out of this damned hell hole!"

The Sergeant turned and chuckled, "I see you don't care much for our British hospitality." He ran the palm of his hand over his face several times, to ascertain the quality of his shave. "Why is it?" he asked, his eyebrows raised, "that you Yanks are always so bloody impatient? You must learn to become a little more sportive."

Lazo did not intend to offend the Sergeant for he truly admired these British soldiers. After all, they were the men who had crushed the vaunted Afrika corps.

"Didn't you hear me, Lazo?"

"What?" asked Lazo, pretending that he had lost track of the conversation.

"I merely suggested that perhaps you did not look with favor upon our British hospitality."

"Oh, that's not it at all. But tell me, how the hell do you get used to this boredom?"

"You don't, Lazo. At least, I never have. It does kind of make one long for the excitement of battle."

Lazo looked up askance, "You can't be serious!"

"I do, Lazo. So help me God, I do, I really do."

"I could believe you if you were a rookie but hell, you fought all the way from Dunkirk to Alamein."

"And some places in between. A lot of my friends are buried out there," interjected the Sergeant pointing eastward.

Lazo couldn't help but notice that the old Sergeant's face became less rigid and his voice became almost reverent when he mentioned Alamein. Lazo remained silent for a moment, so as not to interrupt the old soldier's reminiscences. "You're just pulling my leg, Hell, I have heard of cases where soldiers have deliberately maimed themselves to avoid combat."

"That may be true," replied the old Sergeant, "but most of the men I served with were not at all like that. No sir, Lazo, not at all."

The Sergeant picked up his hair brush and shook his head. "No, Lazo, you've got it all wrong." Then he ran the brush through his hair ever so gently so as not to dislodge any of the precariously few strands, which remained. "For example," he continued, "when we were pinned down at Dunkirk waiting to be rescued, some of the men in my platoon amused themselves by deliberately raising their helmeted heads above the sconse to draw German sniper fire."

"What the hell for? Is that what you mean by being sportive?"

"Perhaps," replied the Sergeant, "but I rather believe it was the ultimate form of defiance."

"Defiance, hell!" remarked Lazo, they were just submitting to the inevitability of their own destruction."

"No, my young friend," replied the old Sergeant, trying not to appear condescending, "that is not the case at all. The urge to live dangerously does not necessarily connote a death wish. The soldiers, by facing death, have in effect conquered it. In combat, a soldier is so totally immersed in the present. There is no past and no future. It may sound absurd to someone who has never been in combat, but see, Lazo, the source of all fear is ego and in the confusion of battle the soldier's attention is so completely fixed outward, that all consciousness of the self disappears. Don't you see, Lazo? Instinct keeps us alive!"

The Sergeant paused briefly, then continued, "We all must die; it's only a matter of time. In combat, all sense of time disappears, hence no thought of tomorrow. Consequently, the combat soldier does not feel the sting of death because for him death no longer exists."

Lazo did not respond. He just stared at the floor.

"Did you ever kill a man?" asked the Sergeant, quite matter-of-factly.

Lazo remained silent, pretending not to hear the question.

"What's wrong, Lazo? Did I embarrass you?"

Still, Lazo made no reply. His eyes remained fixed on the fly-studded floor. He was about to speak when the Sergeant, sensing Lazo's discomfiture, endeavored to change the subject. "By the way, Lazo, did they reschedule your drop for tonight?"

"Yes, they have, weather permitting. If everything goes well, I should be in Yugoslavia by tomorrow morning."

"You lucky bastard. I'd give anything to get out of this bloody place. This heat, these flies and the damnable sand are getting to me."

Lazo stared at the old Sergeant and for the first time he noticed the deep lines which time and worry had carved on his otherwise almost youthful countenance. The Sergeant gathered up his toiletries and meticulously placed them in a much weathered cigar box. He then threw his towel over his shoulder and started for the door. As he was about to exit, he turned and in words compassionate yet not indulgent wished Lazo God speed.

"Wait, Sergeant! If you have some time to kill, I would like to answer the question which I had previously ignored."

"Which question?" queried the Sergeant, pretending forgetfulness.

"You had asked me if I had ever killed a man."

"Oh, yes, but you need not tell me."

"But I want to. I have never told this story to anyone. I was so ashamed of what I had done that I couldn't. I want to tell you because I think that you will understand."

"Well, Lazo, I do have time, as you very well know." He chuckled and winked at Lazo.

"Then make yourself comfortable for the story I am about to relate will take some time."

The Sergeant sat down on a bench; much maligned by careless knives and bayonets and rested his head against the wall. Then Lazo took a seat next to the Sergeant. He removed a beat-up pack of Camels from his shaving kit, offered the Sergeant one, and then nervously lit both cigarettes. Lazo took a long drag and allowed the smoke to slowly slip from his nostrils:

"My parents," he began, "immigrated to the United States from Yugoslavia when I was just a young child, I was too young to remember the place of my birth, but my mother, whom I love very much, described the little village to me so many times that when I close my eyes, I can actually picture myself walking down its quiet, dusty streets. Well, my parents finally settled in a small mining community in northern Minnesota. Here they planned to save enough money so that they might some day return to their native land and live a life of ease. But fortunes were not that easily made and though my father worked hard, he barely made enough money to keep our bodies and souls together. Still, my mother clung desperately to her hopeless dream. Perhaps she honestly thought that it would come true because she devoted a great deal of time teaching me German and Slovenian. She would not permit me to speak English and when I was old enough to attend school, I could speak and read both German and Slovenian, but knew very little English. Oh, how I hated school the first year. Not so much because of my inability to communicate with the other children, but because I was considered to be a dummy. Many times I had to defend myself and frequently came home quite bloodied up. My mother would dress my physical wound and massage my damaged ego but much to her credit, she never went to school to plead my case."

"Always remember," she said, "a transplanted tree takes time to establish its roots but once the roots have taken hold, no force is strong enough to foreclose its destiny."

My father was not quite so idealistic. Upon returning home one evening after an especially hard beating, he looked up from his newspaper, shook his head and said, "Wo gehobelt, sind fallen Spanne."

"What does that mean?" asked the Sergeant.

"Where there is planing, there are shavings."

"In England, we have a similar saying, I believe it goes something like, 'As the river flows, it casts the debris along its banks.'"

"Needless to say," continued Lazo, "I flourished and in 1942 graduated from high school at the top of my class and that, Sergeant, was no minor accomplishment."

Lazo paused, took one last drag from his now shrunken cigarette and carefully dropped it through a large knot hole in one of the floorboards.

"Two days after my graduation from high school, I received my greeting."

"Your what?" asked the sergeant.

"My induction notice," replied Lazo. "I was commanded to report to Fort Snelling on June Twenty Sixth. I was happy because I wanted to fight the Germans who had visited such havoc on my native land. God, how I wanted to get even with those bastards. After basic training, I was certain that I would be assigned to some infantry unit and shipped overseas but that was not to be. I was assigned to counterintelligence and sent to Elright Field, Nebraska. I objected quite heatedly, but you know the army."

"They must have had a good reason."

"Oh, but they did," replied Lazo, quite vehemently. "Apparently, my command of foreign languages was impressive enough to condemn me to a life of hopeless inactivity."

"Hopeless inactivity!" laughed the Sergeant. "Why I thought that cloak and dagger stuff was bloody well exciting."

"Well, it wasn't," replied Lazo, "at least not at first. My assignment at Elright was quite simple. I was ordered to keep under surveillance, one Private Werner Krebs. It seems that prior to our entry into the war, a number of German families came to the United States to escape the Nazi tyranny. Many of the families were sincere but some with teenage sons were sent by the Nazi to serve as spies. The young men were to join the army and serve as sources of information for the German Abwehr. It was thought that Private Krebs was one of them. I was assigned to a bunk adjacent to his and for the next two months we were inseparable, and indeed became very close friends."

"He must have been an engaging sort."

"Oh, yes. All of the men in the barracks liked him. No one considered him to be an enemy. Hell, one evening he jumped up on his footlocker and began to imitate Hitler. He was perfect. He kept the barracks in stitches for the better part of an hour."

"He sounds like an interesting chap."

Lazo paused for a moment. He left the bench and walked over to the window. A German POW was washing kettles behind the mess tent. He was singing Lili Marlene and Lazo began to sing along:

Und sollte mir, ein Leid geschehen,
Wer wird bei der Laterne stehen,
Mit dir Lili Marlene,
Mit dir, Lili Marlene.

"Where in hell did you learn the words?" asked the Sergeant.
"Werner taught them to me. It's quite beautiful, don't you think?"
"Yes, quite."

Lazo returned to the bench, lit another cigarette and continued, "Well, one night after taps, Werner got out of bed and left the barracks. I waited a moment and then followed him.The night was as quiet, as dust settling on a summer road. A bright full moon made it possible for me to follow him at a safe distance. As I followed him, I remember thinking to myself, "What the hell am I doing? I should be back in bed." But I continued, perhaps more from curiosity than from a sense of duty. He eventually stopped before a hanger door marked, AUTHORIZED PERSONNEL ONLY. He calmly looked over his shoulder and satisfied that no one had followed him reached into his pocket and removed a rather small object. It was difficult for me to discern the nature of the object but I was almost certain that it was a key of some sort. He managed to open the door. Then he looked over his shoulder once again, waited a second or two and entered. I waited until he was safely in. Then I moved toward the hangar, as quietly as I could. My heart was pounding and I could feel beads of sweat forming under my nose. God, how I wanted to turn and leave, but I couldn't. Honest, Sarge, I could not turn and leave. It was as if some unseen hand was tugging on my shoulder. I entered the hangar and nervously fumbled for the light switch. After what seemed like an eternity I found it and switched on the lights. I had caught him completely unawares, his hand in the cookie jar, so to speak. It was almost comical. Then, and I still do now know quite why, I shouted, in German, "Was machst du da!" He didn't answer. He reached into his shirt, pulled out a knife and jumped down from the wing of the B-17. He bounded toward me and I remember thinking that it couldn't be true. It was just a dream. He came straight at me, knife in hand and before I could move, I felt a sharp sting in my right shoulder. I don't quite remember what happened next. It was all too confusing. All I remember is that he was behind me and I could feel the sharp edge of a knife blade on my throat. Instinctively, I guess, I swung my elbow full force, into his stomach. He fell back, gasping for air, but he did not release the knife. I leaped at him and we both slammed into the fuselage of the giant aircraft. We struggled desperately, for God knows how long. Finally, I managed to pin him to the concrete floor. He continued to struggle with all of his strength. I had a good grip on his wrist but somehow he managed to free his arm and once again the knife was coming toward me. I parried his thrust with my forearm and managed somehow, to grab his wrist. I forced the knife blade down to his throat and with all my remaining strength, drew the blade across his throat. The blood gushed forth. It was awful. I tried to cover up the ugliness with my hand but the blood oozed from between my fingers. He seemed to be looking at me. I cradled him tenderly in my arms and held his hand. By now, my tears were gently dropping to his face. I saw his lips move but no sound came. He squeezed my hand. He died in my arms. I couldn't tell precisely when. There was no convulsed movement, no final gasp. He just silently slipped away.

    I sat there with Werner in my arms until the awful stillness was interrupted by a strident voice.

    "What the hell is going on here?"

    I looked up and saw the O.D. and several military policemen standing in the doorway. They had obviously been attracted to the hangar by the lights.

    "Is anybody in here?"

    All of the anger that had been welled up within me erupted and I shouted, "No, you stupid son of a bitch!"

    Then the timid bastard ordered two M.P.'s to move forward and investigate. I watched the two men approach but said nothing. When they finally saw me, they turned white. One of them stepped on some of the congealing blood, slipped and almost fell.

"Over here, Lt.!" Shouted one of the M.P.'s.

I watched the Lt. approach. God but he was a cautious man. When he reached the spot where I was seated, he took one look, turned and ran for the door. Then I heard him retching. The poor bastard was puking. I remember whispering, "Wo gehobelt, sind fallen Spanne." I don't know why. After that, I don't remember anything. I had lost a considerable amount of blood from the gash in my shoulder and I must have passed out.

When I awoke the next morning, I was in a hospital bed and there were two large M.P.'s at the door. Some "ninety day wonder", named Kaplan, came in and began to question me. I was in no mood to answer his stupid questions and I told him to go to hell.

"Look, "he said, "I don't know exactly what the fuck happened last night but I mean to get to the bottom of it, and mind you, soldier keep a civil tongue in your damned mouth."

Now, I am not by nature, a truculent person but I was in no mood for military courtesy. I looked squarely into his eyes and shouted as loudly as I could, "Go to hell, Sir!"

The Lt. turned crimson and I thought that the fat bastard was going to have an attack of apoplexy. I was sure that he was going to strike me and I was preparing myself to duck.

Just then a portly, bald headed Colonel came into the room to remind us that we were in a hospital and that he would not tolerate any further commotion. Then he looked directly at the Lt. and quietly but deliberately said, "Lt. Kaplan, you should know better."

I thought that the Lt. was going to shit. He looked at me and his face turned purple. If looks could kill, I would have been twice dead. Then the Colonel came over to my bed. He gave my chart a perfunctory glance, set it down and asked me how I felt.

"You lost quite a bit of blood, soldier. Looks like they got you here in the nick of time."

I told him that I was feeling better but I would feel much better if he would tell the "goddam kike" to get out of my room.

"Now, now, soldier, that's no way to talk to a superior officer," he shouted, his voice becoming quite menacing.

"The hell you say, sir," I retorted. "Here he is safe and secure, playing amateur detective while his whole race is being systematically slaughtered by the Nazis. Please sir, get him out of here before I vomit."

The Lt. was deeply stung by my callous tirade. He made no attempt to reply. Beads of sweat trickled down his chin and disappeared in the ample folds of his neck. The Colonel walked over to Lt. Kaplan, put his arm around his shoulder and in a voice accustomed to command exhorted.

"Alright, Lt., do you think that you can tell me what the hell is going on around here?"

The Lt., in a voice somewhat acquiver replied, "Colonel, sir, that man lying there, did a knife job on a fellow soldier last night and I am trying to find out what happened. I'm just doing my job but that insubordinate bastard won't cooperate."

"Is that correct?" asked the Colonel, looking directly at me.

"Yes sir, Colonel. That is correct," I responded, as politely as I could. "Yes, I killed a man and no Colonel, I will not cooperate with the Lt."

"And why not, may I ask?"

"Because sir, it's none of his business."

"What do you mean, it's none of his business," replied the Colonel, now quite peeved with my apparent insolence. "Are you bucking for a court-martial?"

"Look, Colonel sir, I am not at liberty to reveal a damn thing to anyone but my commanding officer."

"And who the hell is he?" queried the Colonel.

"Major John Kovach, sir."

"Do you know the Major?" asked the Colonel, looking directly at Lt. Kaplan.

"Yes sir. He is in charge of counterintelligence." Replied the Lt..

"Well, Lt., get him over here and let's get to the bottom of this mess."

The Lt. left the room and returned about fifteen minutes later with the Major. Needless to say, I was extremely happy to see him. He walked up to my bed, casually sat down rested his boots on my bed.

"Hi Lazo! Some young bitch give you a dose?" he asked, in his usual insensitive manner.

I wanted to laugh but it hurt too much.

"Well, Lazo, what did happen?"

"I killed Werner last night."

I obviously caught him unawares for he quickly put his finger to his lips then politely asked the two officers to leave. After they had departed I quietly told him what had transpired and he was very sympathetic, He knew that Werner and I had become close friends and sensed that I was deeply troubled.

He slowly raised his lanky frame from the chair and walked to the window. Then he turned and looking directly at me said, "War is hell! Do you know Lazo, not one great thinker has had the courage to tell the truth about it. Men kill and destroy, not because they are commanded to do so but because they love the killing and destroying. God help us Lazo but we do. If that was not so, wars would have ended long ago. F. Scott Fitzgerald once said that men go to war because the women are watching.

He was not entirely correct. We go to war because we are watching and we are intoxicated by what we see and feel."

Then, as if oblivious to my presence, he turned and left the room. I heard him tell the Lt. to take his men and leave. The Lt. must have been reluctant to obey because I heard the Major say.

"Look damn you, there is a boy dying in that bed and your presence disgraces his birth."

After that I fell asleep. I must have been exhausted because when I awoke it was morning again and there, standing beside my bed was Major Kovach, but he was not alone. The Major bid me a jaunty good morning and I smiled. Then he said, "I want you to meet General Huntley, base commandant."

The General stood erect and saluted me. I tried to return the salute but my right arm was so stiff I could barely move it. He must have sensed that my failure to respond was not a rebuff because he smiled and said, "Lazo, the Major told me what you did and I wanted to personally commend you for your courage. I know that it must have been extremely difficult, but remember, you did what you had to do. Incidentally, I wanted to recommend you for the Soldier's Medal but the Major tells me that the sensitive nature of your work would be compromised if any of this were made public. The best I can do to show your country's appreciation is to grant you a thirty-day convalescent furlough. Is that agreeable?"

I politely thanked the General. He smiled and departed. After the General had left, the Major sat on my bed and quietly, almost in a whisper said, "Lazo, you are not to tell anyone what happened. It must remain a secret."

"How in hell is that possible?" I asked. "His family must be informed."

"Oh, we can handle that easily enough," he responded. "We will just put the body in a sealed coffin and ship it home."

"But how do we explain his death to the family?" I asked.

"Oh, that's no problem," he replied. "We'll just put it down as a suicide. Those things happen you know."

"You people think of everything, don't you?" I responded.

The Major must have been offended by my sarcasm because in words quite blunt, he said, "See here, soldier, quit wallowing in self pity. It could be your body going home in a sealed casket. You won and he lost and that's what the hell it is all about. In war there are only winners and losers and the dead, and they don't count. So be thankful that this time you were a winner. Pray that you may always be so fortunate." Then he turned and left the room. I never saw him again.

Lazo reached down, picked up his shaving kit and placed it in his lap. He tossed the half empty pack of Camels into it and pulled the zipper shut. Then he turned to the Sergeant and said, "And that, Sergeant was my first and only encounter with death."

"That's a rather grizzly story, Lazo. I can appreciate why you were somewhat reluctant to talk about it. It must have been hellish."

"It was, Sarge. I feel a little better but I don't think I'll ever wash the stain away."

"Perhaps not Lazo, but I am certain that this will not be your only encounter with death and though you may never develop a fondness for killing, you will become less and less unsettled by it." He smiled and added, "Your Major Kovach must be one helluva soldier."

Then both men left the latrine and walked squint eyed into the bright sun.

CHAPTER TWO

The sun had just crested and a few scattered clouds moved gently against an otherwise azure sky. It was so very still that one could almost hear the birch leaves as they twisted to avoid the burning sting of the summer sun. The tall pine trees perched awkwardly on the lichen covered ledges, dropped their shriveled shadows downward in a seemingly desperate attempt to reach the cool waters that brushed the shore below. Off in the distance a faint cloud of moving dust was just barely visible above the tree tops. A screen door slammed. The noise punctured the silent serenity of the northern wilderness and wore itself out against the rocks on the far side of the lake. A young girl, tall and sun-tanned, appeared from among the trees and walked slowly toward the mailbox that stood lonely beside the road. She did not stop at the mailbox but continued until she reached the center of the dusty, gravel road. She turned and looked in the direction of the moving dust. Then she reached down, picked up a few pebbles and began to toss them into the lake. Soon a model-A Ford speckled with red dust, came into view and made its way to where she stood. She stepped back onto the grassy shoulder of the road and waited for the car to stop. Then she ran over to the driver's side and in a voice, barely above a whisper, asked, "Did it come?"

"Oh, hello, Ilse! No, there is no mail for you today. I'm sorry."

She dropped her head and a veil of mist clouded her brilliant blue eyes. She began to walk toward the lake, a picture of delicate misery.

"Wait, Ilse, is this what you were waiting for?"

Ilse stopped but she did not dare to turn. She was too upset to participate in any game.

"It has a New York APO number!"

She turned and bounded toward the car, snatched the letter from his hand and clutched it to her heart. Then she threw her arms around his neck and settled a big kiss on his bewhiskered face.

"Thank! Thank you!" she yelled, as she crossed the road and ran up the path that led to a hilltop covered with tall virgin white pines; her bare feet scarcely touching the sun tanned pine needles that nature had strewn along the way. When she reached the top of the hill she fell breathless to the ground and whispered, "Gott sei Dank! Gott sie Dank!" She took a few deep breaths and settled herself against the trunk of one of the huge white pines. Then she carefully removed the letter from the envelope and began to read.

My dear one:

Forgive me for not writing sooner. The events of the past, few days have been so tumultuous that I have scarcely had time to collect my thoughts. The nature of my new assignment is so highly secret that I can tell you nothing except that this new adventure will take me to the land of my ancestors. But know, my dear one, that in the midst of this frenzied activity, you were never out of my thoughts. From the moment I first saw you, I knew that I loved you. I know it must seem strange but it is as though I have known you forever and have loved you from the first light of my life. From this moment forward, I promise to unlive my life for you and if destiny should see fit to close my eyes before we meet again, do not sorrow over me for I have known that love of which the poets speak. And so my love, I bid you good night and in my thoughts, I embrace you and hold you close.

Adieu, Lazo

Ilse was deeply moved by Lazo's confession of love for she had felt the same way about him and had likewise told him of her love in the many letters she had sent to Elright Field.

"Is it possible," she thought, "that my letters have not yet reached him. That he might go to his death without knowing how deeply I love him?" Tears began to fill her eyes and soon she was sobbing pitifully.

But let us leave this beautiful and pathetic creature for a while so that I might take you back in time and relate to you how it was that these young lovers chanced to meet.

You will recall that Lazo had been promised a thirty day furlough and when his wound had healed, he departed Elright Field for his home in northern Minnesota. His homecoming was a very joyous occasion but try as he might, Lazo could not quite get over the death of Werner. The memory of that event came back to hurt him, especially during the early hours of morning when sleep had left him and he lay in bed, unable to re-enter that insensate realm of nothingness.

It was on one of these mornings that he made up his mind to leave home before his furlough was to expire and journey to northern Wisconsin, to visit Werner's family. He thought, perhaps, that seeing and talking to Werner's parents might somehow still the storm that raged within him.

So it was that Lazo found himself, standing before the door of a rather rustic cottage, situated in the beautiful lake country of Wisconsin. It was late afternoon and the sun was barely visible above the trees. The shadows were slowly blending into darkness. Lazo raised his hand and was about to knock, when suddenly, seized by indecision, he lowered his hand, turned and began to walk slowly up the narrow path that led to the road. He was so preoccupied that he didn't notice the girl bounding down the path toward him. She saw him but she was running so rapidly that she could not stop. He looked up just in time to brace himself before she collided with him sending both sprawling to the ground. She slowly untangled herself from him and they sat on the ground facing each other. She began to giggle and he, unable to control himself, joined in. Soon they were both laughing so loudly that they could scarcely hear the voice calling from the cottage door.

"Ilse! Is that you out there?"

"Ya, mama," replied Ilse, trying to stop laughing but with little success.

"Well come in now. Papa will be home soon."

"Okay mama, we'll be right in."

"What do you mean? Who is out there with you?"

"I don't know, mama. I'll ask him."

"My name is Lazo, Lazo Krall."

"Very pleased to meet you," responded Ilse, reaching out her hand. Then she shouted, "He says his name is Lazo Lazo Krall, mama!"

Lazo took her hand in his and whispered, "Not Lazolazo. Just Lazo."

"Well bring him in with you so that I might meet him."

Lazo, still holding her hand in his, got up and gently helped her to her feet. Then hand in hand, they walked up to the cottage door. They stopped before entering and she turned to him and said "By the way, I'm Ilse."

"Yes, I know," replied Lazo. "Werner talked of you so often that I feel that I have known you for a very long time."

"You knew Werner, then!"

"Yes, I knew him very well. He was my best friend."

"Then you know."

"Yes, I know." replied Lazo as he walked to the far end of the porch and sat on the railing. "I'm so sorry, so terribly sorry."

Ilse walked over to him, took his hand and sat beside him. He turned toward her but said nothing. He reached out and removed a pine needle that had settled in her soft, blonde hair. She smiled and was about to speak when the stillness was jarred by the beautiful, poignant cry of a loon.

"Oh, Ilse, it's so lovely and peaceful here, and I almost walked away from it. I have never felt so alive. It's almost frightening. I don't understand what's happening."

Ilse looked directly into his eyes and whispered, "'Verveille doch, du bist so schon."

"Is that an invitation?" asked Lazo with a smile.

"Oh, you! You understand German, don't you," retorted Ilse, her face turning crimson. She covered her face with her hands to conceal her embarrassment. You must think me terribly forward."

"Not at all. That's the nicest thing that anyone has ever said to me."

"Ilse, what's keeping you?" shouted her mother.

"We'll be right in mama." she took Lazo's arm and pulled him off the railing and together, they walked into the cottage.

"Mama, this is Lazo. He was a friend of Werner's". Mrs. Krebs wiped her hand on her apron and extended it. Lazo received it and said, "Es freut mich sehr, sie kennen zu lernen, gnadige Frau."

"Danke. So you were one of Werner's friends. It is so nice to meet you. Please sit down."

Lazo walked over to the couch and sat down. Ilse took a seat next to him.

"And how was it that you came to know Werner?" queried Mrs. Krebs.

"We were bunk mates at Elright Field," replied Lazo, quite matter of factly, his eyes fixed on Ilse.

"Funny that he never mentioned you in any of his letters."

"Oh, mama," Ilse remarked, "you know that Werner never wrote much about anyone or anything. His letters were never more than one page long."

"Ya, I know," replied Mrs. Krebs, "and now he will write no more." She removed a handkerchief from her apron pocket and wiped her eyes.

"When do you have to report back?"

"I have three more days," replied Lazo.

"Then you must spend some time with us. You can have Werner's room."

"Oh, I couldn't," replied Lazo. "I don't want to impose on you. I just wanted to come to pay my respects and express my deeply felt sorrow."

"But you must stay. You wouldn't be imposing," pleaded Ilse.

"Ya, Lazo, please stay. It is so lonesome here. It will be nice to have a young man around the house again. It will be so good for papa."

"Alright, if you insist," replied Lazo, pretending capitulation but knowing that he really wanted to stay.

"Good, then it's settled," responded Mrs. Krebs. "Now Ilse, go and get the young man a cold beer. He must be thirsty."

The two women went into the kitchen and Lazo was left alone in the dimly lit living room. He had come here, he thought, because of Werner, but now the image of Ilse so completely filled his mind that all thoughts of Werner had been erased by the thought of her beauty and there was no room for ugliness. He was, for the moment at least, at peace with himself and the world.

"Do you want a glass for your beer or do you drink it from the bottle?"

"I'll have it from the bottle."

"Good," responded Ilse, entering the living room. "That's the way papa drinks it too."

She handed him the bottle and sat down beside him. He raised the bottle to his lips and took several swallows. "That was good," remarked Lazo as he set the bottle on the small table that stood next to the couch.

"Don't you drink beer?" he asked.

"Once in a while, when mama isn't looking. She believes that women who drink beer become fat and unattractive." She paused and looked toward the kitchen. "May I have a small sip?"

"Certainly," replied Lazo, as he handed her the bottle.

She took a small sip and returned the bottle to Lazo. "I really don't like it that much. It has a bitter taste."

Lazo smiled gently, "You're right, it does have a bitter taste." He took another swallow and was about to set the bottle down when footsteps sounded on the porch.

"Oh, that must be papa!" exclaimed Ilse and she rushed to the door to meet him. The door opened and a very large man entered. He must have been six and a half feet tall and his shoulders were so broad that they brushed against the door frame as he entered. And though Ilse was quite tall, she was virtually dwarfed by her father. He effortlessly lifted her off her feet and kissed her forehead.

"Put me down, papa. You are embarrassing me. Can't you see that we have company?"

Ilse's father looked over at Lazo and asked "And who might you be?"

Lazo raised himself from the couch and walked over toward Mr. Krebs, extended his hand and said, "I'm Lazo Krall."

"And I'm Hermann Krebs," replied the father, shaking Lazo's hand vigorously. "And what brings you here?"

"He was Werner's friend, papa. Mama has invited him to stay with us for a few days."

"Krall, that's a Slavic name, isn't it?"

"Yes," replied Lazo, "my parents and I came to this country from Slovenia."

"That's beautiful country."

"Yes," agreed Lazo. "My mother often spoke of its beauty but I don't remember. I was much too young."

"Well sit down Lazo," and turning to his wife said, "bring us some beer."

Lazo watched the big man lower himself into the over stuffed chair that stood in the corner by the window and wondered if the chair could sustain his huge bulk. They were no more seated when Ilse entered the living room, holding two bottles of beer. She went over to her father and handed him one. Then she walked to the couch, sat down next to Lazo and handed him the other.

Lazo took the bottle and said, "Thank you Ilse."

"Ya, Liebchen, thank you," said Hermann, and he raised the bottle to his lips. Lazo noticed that Hermann's enormous hand almost concealed the bottle from view. It looked quite humorous and he could not hold back a smile.

"Well, Lazo, how do you like our little cottage on the lake?" asked Hermann, setting his empty bottle on the much weathered window sill.

"It's very nice and peaceful," replied Lazo.

"Ya, it is so very peaceful that I sometimes forget that we are living in a world gone mad, a world run by lunatics and gangsters."

Hermann paused briefly. Then he turned to Lazo and in a voice conveying some sadness said, "I will never understand why Werner hated this place so much. Perhaps it was too peaceful for his raging vitality. Did you know that he didn't even wait to be drafted into the army?"

"You mean that he volunteered?" asked Lazo. "He didn't tell me that."

"Ya, he enlisted on the day of his eighteenth birthday. He just couldn't wait. Sometimes I wish that he had waited until he was drafted."

Hermann paused briefly, looked up at the ceiling and added, "Perhaps things would have ended differently. Ach, but there I go again, thinking like a woman."

"I wish he had waited also," whispered Lazo.

"What?"

"Oh, I was just agreeing with you, but why did you say, just like a woman? Is it wrong to wish?"

"No, it is not wrong to wish, Lazo but to believe that Werner could have behaved differently is to believe that he could have been that which he was not."

"What do you mean?" asked Lazo, his voice expressing more than a little interest.

"Oh Papa," interrupted Ilse, "'must you always involve people in these senseless conversations?"

"No, Ilse, let him continue. I do not find his remarks to be senseless. On the contrary, I find them to be quite interesting."

"You see, Lazo," continued Hermann, pretending not to have heard Ilse, "some people believe that we are what we do, but that is not the way it is. We always do what we are. Werner could no more help what he was than Ilse can help being a young beautiful woman, that she is."

Lazo did not respond immediately. His thoughts silently slipped back to that unfortunate night. He remembered how he had wanted to return to the barracks and how he had been drawn as if by some irrestible force to the hangar, and that dark episode that had so clouded his life. He put his bottle down, turned to Ilse and said, "Perhaps your father is right."

"Oh you can't be serious," replied Ilse. Then looking straight at her father, she said, "The fault dear papa is not in the stars."

"But look, Ilse," replied Lazo. "It is because of Werner's death that I am here tonight and because of him, our lives, yours and mine are now inextricably intertwined."

"Precisely," replied Hermann, "and there is nothing on heaven or earth that could have changed the course that has drawn you to us. For better or for worse, as you have suggested, our lives are now intertwined." He paused for a moment. "Have you stopped to consider, Lazo," he continued, "that Werner must have had some other friends at Elright Field and yet not one of them has written to us regarding his death. You are the only one who has shown any consideration for Werner and for us. We will always be indebted to you." Then he shouted, "Erika, when will supper be ready? Our young friend must be famished."

"Ya," replied Erika. "Supper will be ready in a few moments. Ilse show the young man where he may wash."

Ilse took his hand and said, "Come, I will show you to the bathroom."

Lazo jumped up, slapped his forehead and exclaimed, "Oh, my God! I forgot all about my duffle bag! I left it at the bus depot. I'll have to go back and get it."

"Oh, is that all!" exclaimed Ilse. "I thought that something was seriously wrong." Then she yelled, "Mama, doesn't Otto Warmke live out this way?"

"Ya, Ilse, he does. Why do you ask?"

"Lazo left his duffle bag at the depot."

"Well, why don't you call him and tell him to drop the bag off on his way home."

"I'll do that!" shouted Ilse, as she ran to the phone.

"I'm sure that Otto will be quite happy to drop your bag off," said Hermann. "He is such a nice man."

"Now come Lazo, I will show you where you may wash up."

Ilse went into the kitchen and waited for Lazo to return. When he returned, Ilse assured him that Otto was a very dependable man. She took his hand and led him onto the huge screened porch which seemed to be suspended over the lake.

"Oh, this is breath taking," remarked Lazo. "I have never seen the stars shine so brightly."

"Yes," whispered Ilse. "I know no picture more spell binding. I often come here to dream."

"Now sit down and eat before the food becomes cold," exhorted Erika.

Lazo tended to Ilse's chair and seated himself next to her.

"Good, now let's eat," said Hermann, "Ich habe einen grossen Hunger."

After the dinner was completed, Ilse helped her mother clear the table. Lazo made a gesture to help, but Hermann would not permit him to.

"That is woman's work, Lazo. We Germans do not believe in spoiling our women. Remember that well, Lazo." Then he shouted, "Erika, bring me my pipe and tobacco!"

Lazo looked out over the lake. The full moon was rising above the trees. Its light played on the gently moving water and transformed the lake into a shimmering garden of light. He was so impressed that he didn't notice Erika standing in the doorway.

"Here's your pipe, mein Herr."

Lazo looked up and for the first time since he arrived, really noticed her. She had removed her wrap around apron and was wearing a spotless white peasant's blouse and a pair of khaki colored walking shorts. In the dim of the evening, the traces of gray in her hair were not visible and she looked much younger than her years should indicate. "Hermann was indeed, a lucky man," thought Lazo.

Hermann took the pipe and filled it with tobacco. Then he struck a match against the bottom of his chair and lit it. The pleasant aroma of burning tobacco soon filled the room. Lazo, prompted by the smell, unconsciously reached into his shirt pocket and removed a pack of cigarettes. He lit one, took a deep drag, inhaled it and watched the smoke pass through the screen and into the darkness.

"Mama," came Ilse's voice from the kitchen. "I've scraped and stacked the dishes. Do we have to wash them tonight?"

"No, Ilse," replied Erika, "let's leave them until tomorrow. They'll keep. Now come out and sit with us."

"Ilse," shouted Hermann, "bring that bottle of wine from the refrigerator and some glasses!" Then he turned to his wife and said "I think it appropriate that we toast our new friend."

"Bring the good glasses, the ones we use for very special occasions," added Erika. "And do be careful with them."

"Oh, quit fussing mama," retorted Hermann. "They're only glasses."

"Oh, Liebling, quit teasing. You know how I treasure those glasses."

"Ya, I know," replied Hermann with a big smile. Then he turned to Lazo and said, "When we left Germany, we were allowed to take only the barest necessities, but somehow she managed to bring her glasses along. To this day I do not know how she managed it."

"And you will never know," responded Erika, a little smugly. "Ilse and I are the only ones who know and it will always remain our little secret."

"Is papa still trying to find out how we smuggled the glasses out of Germany?" asked Ilse, as she entered the room.

Hermann took the tray from Ilse and carefully set it on the table. Then he filled the glasses with the cool wine. Ilse took one of the glasses and handed it to Lazo. "Papa always makes light of these glasses but down inside, he really treasures them as much as we do. They were given to mama's great, great grandfather by Frederick the Great."

"Ya," interrupted Erika, with a hint of pride in her voice. "My great, great grandfather saved Frederick's life at the Battle of Leuthen. These glasses have been in the family for about two hundred years and some day, they will be Ilse's."

"Aren't they beautiful, Lazo?"

"Yes," replied Lazo, "but how can something so fragile endure for such a long, long time?"

Hermann stood up, raised his glass and said, "To Lazo, may fortune always treat him gently. And now, as they say in America, bottoms up."

They emptied their glasses and returned them to the table. Hermann filled them once again. Then he set the bottle down and said, "On the other side of the ocean, Slavs and Teutons are killing each other but here in a lonely cottage by a quiet lake, Slav and Teutons drink together in peace. It is a splendid bit of irony and deserves to be celebrated."

Ilse had seated herself next to Lazo and after her father had spoken, she quietly moved her hand until it touched his and gave it a gentle squeeze. He turned and looked at her but said nothing. He sensed that words would only confuse the moment. The room fell into silence; not the kind of uncomfortable quiet that so often occurs when a group of people have run out of conversation but the kind of silence that brings with it a sense of well being and unity. And so they remained, until the quiet was interrupted by a loud persistent banging on the front door.

"Is anybody home?"

"Ya, Otto, come in," shouted Hermann.

"I brought the duffel bag. Where shall I put it?"

"Put it in the living room, then come out to the back porch and have a glass of wine with us."

"Okay, Hermann, but just one drink. I can't stay long," replied Otto.

"Ilse get a glass for Otto."

"Oh, so this is the young soldier who left his duffel bag at the depot," said Otto, extending his hand to Lazo.

Lazo stood up, took Otto's hand and shook it.

"This is Lazo Krall," said Hermann. "He will be spending a few days with us."

"It is so good to meet you, Lazo," replied Otto. "My name is Otto Warmke."

"How do you do, and thank you very much for bringing my duffel bag. It saved me a trip into town. Danke viemals."

"Ach, du bist auch ein Deutscher!" exclaimed Otto, enthusiastically.

"No," interjected Hermann, "he is a Slovenian."

"But he speaks German," replied Otto with a bewildered look on his face.

"Sit down Otto," urged Hermann and he filled Otto's glass with wine.

Otto took a sip of wine, wiped his lips with the back of his hand and asked? "Where are you stationed?"

"At Elright Field."

"Will you be going overseas?"

"I hope so Otto. I'm getting tired of state side duty."

"Well, let's hope that you don't have to go to Europe to fight," said Otto.

"Why?" asked Lazo, with a puzzled expression on his face.

"Because we should be helping the Germans kill those damn Jewish Bolshevists; that's why. We are fighting the wrong war. Hitler may have his faults but he is not all wrong. Mark my word, Lazo, the day will come when we will realize that our real enemies were not the Germans but those damn Russians. But then it will be too late. Is that not right, Hermann?"

Hermann did not respond immediately. He seemed to be steeped in thought. Then he lifted his glass and said, "Earlier this evening, Lazo wanted to know how something so fragile as this glass could have endured for two hundred years. I did not answer him then but I have been pondering his question." He put his glass down and filled it again. Then looking directly at Otto, asked, "Have you ever heard of Krystal Nacht?"

"No," replied Otto.

"Then I will tell you about that Night of Broken Glass. Perhaps it will rid you of your illusions regarding that maniac in Berlin."

Hermann paused again. He took a sip of wine and continued.

"Before coming to America, Otto, I was a teacher of philosophy at the Gymnasium in Leipzig. My best friend was a Jew named Lev Goldberg. He taught chemistry. He was a very intelligent and decent man. If he had not been a Jew, he would have received a chair at one of the major universities. Oh, how many evenings we sat together discussing philosophy and politics. And how many times I told him to get out of Germany before it was too late. But he would only laugh and say, 'Their anti-Semitism is only propaganda. They wouldn't dare do anything to us. They wouldn't risk world condemnation. No, Hermann, he would say, they need us too much and in the end it will be the very things they hate us for that will save us.'

"But he was wrong. On November 7, 1938, a young Jew, named Hershel Grynspan went to the German Embassy in Paris, entered the office of a minor functionary named vom Rath, and shot him. Two days later, vom Rath died. His death was used by the Nazis as a pretext for launching the most lamentable pogrom against the Jews that the world had ever witnessed. I had never seen anything like it. The good citizens of Leipzig, divested of their humanity, ran through the streets and committed the most barbarous acts that their perverse ingenuity could invent. They entered Jewish residences and subjected the occupants to the worst kind of indignities imaginable. Before the night had ended, every Jewish shop in Leipzig was ransacked. The sidewalks were strewn with broken glass. Three Jewish Synogogues were put to the torch. Hundreds of Jews were rounded up and eventually shipped to Dachau."

Hermann paused again and took another sip of wine. Then he turned to his wife, took her hand and said, "But that was not the worst. On that evening, Erika and I were visiting Lev and his wife. They lived in a third story flat, in the Jewish section of the city. Lev and I spent the evening playing chess while our wives visited. Just about the time Erika and I were about to leave, it must have been about eleven o'clock, we heard a loud commotion on the street below. We went to the window to see what was happening. About three blocks down the street, we saw a wild torrent of humanity moving toward us. I remember Lev saying, quite sarcastically, "Another demonstration to honor our Austrian Messiah."

"It was quite a spectacle. Torches were everywhere. Men, women and children were marching and singing the infamous, Horst Wessel Lied. Erika and I, not wanting to get caught up in the demonstration, bid the Goldbergs a hasty good night and departed. We didn't know it then, but it would be our last evening together.

Erika and I walked to the corner and waited for the tram. We watched the crowd move toward us. When they reached the building occupied by the Goldbergs, they stopped and shouted, "Juden sind hier nicht erwunscht! Juden sind hier nicht erwunscht!" Then a large number of men and young boys, led by brownshirts, went into the building. They were shouting and cursing like madmen. It was horrible. We wondered what they were going to do but we didn't have to wait long. Soon, we could see the apartment residents being unceremoniously ushered into the street. Erika and I unconsciously, I guess, began to inch slowly toward the apartment building, so that we might see what was happening. Once the residents reached the street, the mob preyed upon them like crazed animals. They kicked and beat them. Some of the younger men pulled the clothing off the young Jewish girls. The girls pleaded with them to stop but their pitiful screams only served to whet their appetites and spurred them on to deeds of greater depravity. They took one of the young girls, she couldn't have been more than fifteen years old, and ripped her clothes off. Then some of the boys pinned her to a lamp post. She tried desperately to free herself but they were too strong. One of the boys casually took a pair of pliers from his pocket and began to pull out her pubic hair. She let out a series of agonizing screams but her tormentors continued until, her energy spent, she began to whimper pitifully. An old Jew pushed through the throng and tried to cover her with a blanket. The boys threw him to the pavement and kicked him savagely. Then they spread the blanket on the street and threw her into it. They used the blanket to catapult her into the air. Each time she landed, they threw her higher. Higher and higher they threw her, then as if by a prearranged signal, they collapsed the blanket and let her splash to the pavement. She must have died instantly.

It was at this point that Erika pleaded with me to leave as she could bear no more. Tears were streaming down her face and she was shivering, not so much from the cold, as from the intense emotion brought on by the horrible spectacle. We turned and were about to walk away when we heard a loud voice bellow, "Look what we have here! Look what we have here!"

All eyes turned and looked up at the open window on the third floor of the building, from whence the voice was coming. We also looked up and Erika screamed, "Oh my God! It's Lev! It's Lev!"

Two men were holding him before the open window. One of them shouted, "Here is the Jewish professor! What shall we do with him?" Someone in the crowd answered, "Throw the bastard out!"

The crowd immediately echoed the same words and the two men, intoxicated by the mob's enthusiasm, responded by hurling Lev through the window. We saw him tumble erratically through the air while the crowd chanted its approval. We did not see him land because the crowd stood between us and the building but we both knew that the fall must have killed him.

The two men left the window and returned with Lev's wife pinioned between them. "What shall we do with this Jew loving German whore?"

One of the brownshirts shouted, "Bring her down and we'll show her what happens to Germans who marry Jews!"

By now Erika was beside herself. She was shaking violently. I held her close and tried to calm her. She looked up at me and asked, "What will they do to Geli?"

Before I could respond, the two men and Geli appeared in the doorway.

Someone shouted, "Bring some torches so that we all may see!"

Several men, carrying torches ran up the steps and positioned themselves behind Geli. Then they stripped her to the waist. She didn't struggle. She stood there motionless as if in a daze. I will never forget the way she looked. It seemed that in that instant, all life had left her face. Then a man painted a yellow star of David on each of her breasts, while the crowd shouted obscenities at her. This done, they released her and she slumped to the cold gray concrete.

Erika remained in the shadows until the mob had moved down the street. When they were at a safe distance, we slowly walked over to the apartment building. Geli was still huddled before the door. Erika knelt beside her and tried to comfort her. I walked over to the center of the street and covered the dead girl with the same blanket that had served as the instrument of her death.

Then I heard Geli scream, "Where's Lev?" She ran over to me, half crazed and began to beat on my chest. "They've killed him! Those bloody bastards have killed him!" She screamed and collapsed in my arms. I carried her to the steps and seated her next to Erika. Then I walked over to where Lev had landed. It was grotesque. He had landed on a spiked, steel fence and one of the spikes protruded from his stomach. He must have died instantly because there was an expression of terror frozen on his gentle face.

My recollection of what happened next is not too clear. Grief and anger can cloud a man's perceptions and render them unreliable. I know that I removed him from the fence and remember talking to him as if he were still alive.

He paused, "Do you know Otto, this is the first time that I have ever talked about that night. We have tried to blot it out of our memories. Do you remember what happened next, Erika?"

"Ya, I remember," replied Erika. "I watched you walk away from us. Then I heard you shout, not in anger, because I could feel the tears in your words, "Oh you kind and gentle fool! Why didn't you listen to me? Why didn't you leave when I told you to?"

Hermann got up and walked over to the far end of the room and looked out over the lake. The recounting of that horrible night had left him emotionally spent. Then without turning said, "And that Otto, is the new German order and that is why I am almost ashamed to call myself a German."

Otto set his glass down. He walked over to Hermann and put his hand on his shoulder. "I didn't know it was that bad," he said, in a voice that did not conceal his embarrassment. "Please try to understand."

"I don't blame you," replied Hermann. "You had to be there to really understand. No words can describe what it was like. It was because of this, that we decided to leave Germany and come to the United States."

"What happened to Geli," asked Lazo.

"We tried to persuade Geli to come with us but she wouldn't hear of it," replied Hermann.

"To leave," she said, "would only serve to betray the memory of my dear husband. Lev's death cannot go unanswered. I will fight them even to my death. There is no other way for me."

"Have you heard from her, since you left Germany?" asked Lazo.

"Ya," replied Erika, "we received just one letter from her. In it, she told us that she had left Leipzig and had gone to live in Dresden. She said that she had received employment in the Office of the Nazi Archivist. She told me not to worry, and that she was honoring the pledge she had made."

"We knew what she meant, but the censors obviously did not."

"Mama, do you think we will ever see Geli again?" asked Ilse.

"Of course, Liebchen, of course we will," responded Erika, trying not so much, to convince Ilse, as to reassure herself.

"Would you like another glass of wine, Otto?" asked Hermann.

"No, it's getting late and my wife will begin to worry. You know how women are."

"Ya," responded Hermann. "I don't know what we would do without them."

"Or with them," laughed Otto, as he got up and prepared to leave.

Lazo got up, extended his hand to Otto and said, "Thank you again for bringing my duffel bag. It was most kind of you."

Otto took the outstretched hand and replied, "It was my pleasure, Lazo. If it had not been for you, I would not have learned what I have learned here this evening. For that I must thank all of you." Then he shook Hermann's hand vigorously and said, "Thank you dear friend." He turned and walked out. The screen door slammed against its withered frame and the room became silent.

Hermann struck a match against the bottom of his chair and relit his pipe, which had become quite cold during his lenghty disquisition on Nazism. He pulled the smoke deep into his lungs and with a sigh, blew the smoke upward. He watched it intently, until hitting the ceiling, it flattened and drifted out into the night.

"Some more wine, Lazo?" he asked.

"Bitte," replied Lazo, reaching out his glass.

"And now Liebchen, is it not time for your bed?"

"Oh papa, must I? Please, can't I stay up a while longer?"

"Ya, papa, it is afterall, a rather special night. You said so yourself," interjected Erika.

"Well, alright, but just for a short while longer." Then turning to Lazo, said, "You see how it is. Out there, I am considered to be a giant among men, but here, in my own house, I am like putty in their hands."

Lazo chuckled and said, "I would consider it good fortune to be molded by two such beautiful women."

"Ya, Lazo, but it can bruise the ego a little," replied Hermann with a smile.

It was quite obvious to Lazo that Hermann was very devoted to them and they to him, "It was nice," thought Lazo, "just to sit in this house and be touched by the love of these gentle people."

"You know Lazo, we too often make light of women, perhaps unwittingly, but it is true none the less. We are so busy trying to be men that we occasionally lose sight of our humanity. We need them to remind us of what we ought to be and these gentle awakenings can be so precious. I will never forget such a moment. Now mind you, I have never discussed it with anyone, not even Erika. I guess I was too ashamed to tell her. It happened on the night that Lev was killed. I have already mentioned that Erika and I were waiting for the tram but I did not tell you that for a brief moment, I found the madness of the moment exhilarating and was in fact, drawn toward it. If it had not been for Erika, I do not know what might have happened. Perhaps I would have participated in the undoing of my friend. But because Erika was watching I held on to my reason and remained civil. So now you know why I had to leave Germany. I was not afraid of Hitler and his mob. I was afraid that in that atmosphere, I might have in a moment of weakness, done something that would lose, for me the love of my wife. I could not bear that. For without her love, I knew that my life would be only a succession of mornings . So I want you to know Lazo, that it was not cowardice that brought me to this wonderful land."

Erika got up and walked over to where Hermann was seated. She took his hand and said, "Thank you, my dear husband." Then turning to Lazo, she said, "My husband is no coward. He lived through the bloody battle of Paschendaele in World War I, and anyone who lived through that hell and did not lose his love for humanity, is not only a hero, but a man as well. I am so proud of him."

"Ach, Erika, quit embarrassing me. I was just a man doing what a man must do."

"See, how he shrinks from praise," teased Erika. "He's just like a little boy."

Hermann, now feeling somewhat uncomfortable under the shower of praise, said, "Let us end the evening with a toast." He filled the glasses and said, "Here's to this moment. Let us cherish it for there will never be another quite like it."

They raised their glasses and drank. Then they bid each other a good night and went to bed. Lazo slept well that night. It may have been the wine or it may have been Ilse, but in any case, he fell asleep with a smile on his lips

CHAPTER THREE

Lazo waited until the Sergeant had disappeared behind the billows of camouflaged canvas, then he turned and slowly walked back to his tent. The hot sand and the flies, which had earlier been such an irritant to him, no longer seemed to matter. As he neared his tent he noticed the outline of a person moving about within. He slowed down and moved forward, ever so quietly. He had heard that the camp was beset with thieving Arabs but he had not encountered any.

He paused before entering. Then he let out a loud bellow and rushed in. He tackled the intruder and pinned him face down, to the floor. The towel which had been wrapped around his body, fell off during the struggle and to some casual observer, it might appear that he was to have his way with a fellow soldier. It was almost comical. "What the hell did you do that for!" came the muffled voice from beneath him. "Now get off me or I will have you court- martialed."

Lazo slowly loosened his powerful grip. The man turned and displayed a collar adorned with a set of captain's bars. Lazo jumped up and came to a full salute.

The officer slowly raised himself and with his back to Lazo, said, "You had better have a damn good explanation for your stupid behavior."

"I'm sorry, sir, I truly am. I thought you were one of those thieving Arabs."

The officer turned slowly, and began to chuckle. By the time he was facing Lazo, he was roaring with laughter.

Lazo was at a loss. He didn't know what to think. The officer apparently knew him but Lazo could not place the Captain.

The officer, still doubled up and laughing, asked, "Don't you remember?"

Lazo took a closer look. His eyes were still not fully adjusted to the light in the tent. "No, can't say that I do. Sorry, sir."

"I met you in the hospital at Elright Field. I'm the Jew bastard that you berated so mercilessly. Do you remember?"

Lazo paused. He remembered being interrogated by a Lieutenant Kaplan but this man didn't look at all like him. "I remember a Lieutenant Kaplan," replied Lazo, "but hell, you don't look anything like him. He was at least thirty pounds heavier than you. Nah, you can't be that man." insisted Lazo.

"But I am," replied the Captain, equally insistent. "And the Lieutenant you speak of was not thirty pounds heavier. He was more like fifty pounds heavier," averred the Captain with more than a modicum of pride.

"Well, I'll be damned!" shouted Lazo, scratching his head, "It is you. God, do you look fit. I would never have guessed it. Not in a hundred years."

Lazo rushed forward and extended his hand to the Captain. Then remembering that he was nude, he stopped abruptly, and became quite embarrassed. He quickly gathered up the towel and wrapped it around his body, securing it tightly to his waist. Then he shook the Captain's hand enthusiastically.

The Captain responded, "It's good to see you again."

The genuine sincerity of the Captain's greeting seemed to move Lazo, and remembering some of the unkind remarks he had made at Elright Field, said, "Look Captain, I'm awful sorry for the rotten way in which I treated you."

"Forget it, Lazo. It was the best thing that ever happened to me. It is because of you that I am here. I want you to know that no matter what happens to me, I will always be indebted to you. You see Lazo, you were the instrument of my resurrection."

"What the hell do you mean?" asked Lazo, still gripping the Captain's hand.

"Some other time," replied the Captain. "Right now, I want you to get dressed so we can go to breakfast. I haven't eaten since noon, yesterday and I'm famished."

"Okay," responded Lazo, "but damn it anyway Captain, I want you to know that it's good to have another American around. I feel better already."

"Thank you, Lazo, and I'm glad that you feel that way because you and I are going to be spending a lot of time together. Hell, we may even die together."

"Now hold it right there Captain, don't go rushing things. I don't intend to die, at least not yet."

"I'm not exactly in love with the idea myself, but in war, one must at least consider the possibility. Incidentally, since we will be going on a mission together, I think you had better stop referring to me as captain. And while we're at it, let's drop the sir bullshit also."

"What shall I call you?" asked Lazo, tightening the belt on his poplin jumpsuit.

"Just call me Sam. That will do just fine."

"Okay Sam, now let's get some breakfast and on the way, you can tell me about the mission."

"I'm not quite sure myself," remarked Sam, as he turned the tent flap back and ushered Lazo out into the morning sun.

"But I already have a mission."

"That's been scratched."

"What in hell for?"

"I don't know but they say that this mission was organized by 'Big Jim' himself. I don't know much about it but it has something to do with a guy named Tito. Have you ever heard of him?"

"Oh yes," replied Lazo. "He is the head of the Partisan forces in Yugoslavia. He's a bloody communist."

"But an ally, nonetheless."

"My sentiments lean more toward the Chetniks," declared Lazo.

"Haven't you heard?"

"Heard what?" asked Lazo.

"Why hell, I thought everybody knew that Draza Mihailovic had fallen from grace."

"I don't believe it," protested Lazo.

"Believe it or not, it's true. They say he's been dummying up to the Nazis and the Italian Fascists."

"Well, why in hell don't they send someone in to investigate? If he's a goddam traitor, we'd better damned well know about it."

"We've been trying," replied Sam, "But the bloody British seem to deliberately frustrate our efforts. Our top brass in Cairo just couldn't seem to get anywhere with them. That is, until 'Big Jim' went over and had a little chat with them. I was told that a feverish exchange took place, but he finally convinced them that we were fighting on the same side and White Hall had better damn well start cooperating with us, or else."

"And are they now cooperating with us?"

"You're enjoying British hospitality, aren't you?"

"You mean, I owe all of this good living to 'Big Jim'? I'll have to thank him the next time I see him."

"That might be a little sooner than you think," replied Sam, with that I know something you don't expression on his face.

"Jim, here! You've got to be the most gullible soldier in this man's army. Why Jim wouldn't be caught dead out here."

"You've got to learn to trust me," replied Sam, pretending to be a little offended. "I got the information straight from the desk jockeys in Cairo."

"I don't get it," replied Lazo. "Why would he come out here when all he has to do is snap his fingers and dozens of Ivy League lawyers will jump up from behind their safe mahogany desks and kiss his arse."

"You're right," replied Sam. "Those goddamn sissy Bastards would do anything to save their asses and Jim knows it. Don't believe for one minute that he doesn't. Hell, if he had it his way, he'd send the whole kit and kaboodle to New Guinea."

"Then why the hell doesn't he?"

"Because their fathers have too damned much political clout and that my good friend, is no shit."

Lazo tried to keep a straight face and though the smile on his lips was ever so gentle, Sam detected it and began to blush.

"Why you son of a buck! You're putting me on. Hell, you've been in the OSS longer than I and here I am, telling you the facts of life. Well, it's the truth, anyway."

"You're right," replied Lazo, "but you left out something."

"What's that?"

"When this war is over, those sissy bastards to whom you referred, will end up running the country."

Sam nodded his head. He knew that Lazo was correct.

After breakfast, the two men returned to the tent and plopped down on their cots.

"What does one do to kill time around here?" asked Sam.

"Not a helluva lot."

"There must be something to do. We may have to be here a week or more before the drop."

"What!" exclaimed Lazo. "Another week! Hell, I've been here too damned long already."

"Well, there's gotta be something we can do to fritter away the time."

"Oh yes, you can read your mail, if it ever comes. You can lie on the beach. You can get drunk. You can write letters or you can kill flies. That about covers it."

"Well, what do you do?"

"I spend a lot of time killing flies," replied Lazo, "and when you do that, time really flies."

"Oh, that's funny," replied Sam, "but let's get serious."

"All right Sam. I'll tell you what we'll do. We'll get some beer and spend the day on the shores of the beautiful Mediterranean. But first I'll have to check the mail tent. It just may be that the Army Post Office has found out where I'm stationed."

"That would be a stroke of good fortune," replied Sam. "By the way, Lazo, Are there any broads about?"

"Oh yes." replied Lazo. "Several spiritual descendants of Florence Nightingale, occasionally parade their ugliness along the shores, and quite a few native girls from Benghazi, of course. I'm given to understand that they are not particularly fond of your race."

"Are they pretty?" asked Sam, his interest mounting.

"Oh yes," replied Lazo, "very pretty. There's only one thing wrong."

"What is that?" asked Sam.

"They still rinse their hair with camel urine."

Lazo barely had time to avoid the pillow that sailed over his head.

It was thrown with such vigor that the tent ropes strained as the pillow hit the canvas and fell harmlessly to the ground.

"Take it easy!" shouted Lazo. "I am not exactly fond of their cosmetic practices either but you've got to learn to adapt.

"I should live so long," retorted Sam.

It was obvious that Sam would not rest until he had seen the native girls and to make him wait any longer would just serve to strain his patience, so Lazo raised himself from the cot and said, "You really want to go to the beach, don't you."

"Of course, I do."

"Very well, I'll drop by the mail tent to see if I have any mail. Then I'll pick up the beer and meet you there."

"How do I get there?"

"Just keep walking north and when your feet start feeling damp, you'll know," replied Lazo jokingly.

"All right," shouted Sam as he walked out of the tent. "I'll see you there."

Lazo followed him out and began to walk toward the mail tent. He had not received any mail since he left ElrightField and began to wonder if Ilse had forgotten him. He entered the mail tent almost reluctantly.

"Any mail for me?"

"I believe so, Lazo," responded the mail Sergeant, as he reached under the counter and came up with several letters. "I believe these are yours," said the Sergeant, handing them to Lazo.

Lazo looked at them, but did not reach out, "You wouldn't kid a desperate man?"

"I might Lazo, but in this case I could never do anything so devilishly cruel."

Lazo, convinced of the mail Sergeant's sincerity, reached out and took the letters. He fingered through them, looking carefully at each envelope and each time he turned one over, the smile on his face grew in extent. There must have been ten letters and they all bore the same Wisconsin address. He thanked the Sergeant, turned and pretending nonchalance, walked out of the tent. Once outside, his contrived composure gave way to untrammeled exuberance, he let out a yell that announced to the camp that Lazo Krall was present and for the moment, at least, he was a king.

He carefully placed the letters into his pocket and secured the flap. Then he ran to the camp exchange, picked up the beer and headed for the beach. It was only a matter of minutes before he deposited the beer in the sand beside Sam and continued on down the beach.

"Where the hell are you going?"

"The army post office has found me!"

Sam watched Lazo move away. He made no comment because he realized that Lazo had to be alone.

Lazo continued until he found a deserted spot on the beach where he fell to the warm sand and began to read. He read each letter. Then he read them over and over again until he had consumed every word and every punctuation mark. He was especially drawn to the letter, which she

30

had written on the evening after they had taken their farewells. In it, she had written:

"I have always loved you. Not just since the moment of our first collision but from the beginning of time. I know this because I have seen you over and over again in the secret memories of my soul."

She ended the letter and all of the others with the same postscript"Verweille doch, du bist so schon."

Lazo remembered how she blushed the first time she had used the quotation and a smile came to his lips. He put the letters down and settled back on the warm sand. He closed his eyes and permitted his thoughts to retrace the last day they had together. It was a beautiful morning that greeted him on that last Saturday. The sky, freshly laundered by an early morning rain, presented itself to Lazo in all of its splendid arrogance. The savory smell of bacon caressed his nostrils as he walked into the kitchen and sat down opposite Ilse. They greeted each other warmly. Then came the usual admonition from Frau Krebs, as she heaped his plate with bacon and scrambled eggs, "Eat Lazo, we have a long day ahead of us."

"Yes, I can hardly wait to get started," replied Lazo.

"Shall I get the coffee? Mutti."

"Ya, Liebchen, please."

Lazo's eyes followed Ilse as she moved toward the large stove. Her long blonde hair, bleached by the summer sun, was pulled back into a tight ponytail. A loose white sweatshirt, and grayish leather hosen covered a body that was almost boyish in appearance. As she turned, the straps, which supported her leather hosen, pressed gently against her body, revealing the graceful contour of her womanhood and bringing a faint blush to Lazo's forehead.

After breakfast, the four set out for a day of hiking and blueberry picking. Each of them carried a rucksack and a pail. Hermann and Erika, walking arm in arm, led the way down the gravel road. Ilse and Lazo followed at a short distance.

About five miles down the road, they turned left and headed up a narrow trail. It was not quite wide enough for two to walk abreast, so Hermann led and Lazo brought up the rear.

"Remember Lazo," cautioned Hermann, "you are carrying the wine so be careful."

"Don't worry Hermann," laughed Lazo, "I will guard these bottles with my very life."

They climbed higher and higher up the trail and as they ascended, the scent of pine and balsam became ever more pronounced. Lazo could not remember a time when he felt such exhilaration and he burst into song.

"Mein Vater war ein Wandersman, und mir stecht auch in Blut.
Drum wander ich froh so lang ich kann and schwenke meinen Hut."

They all joined in on the chorus and the forest echoed their Valleries and Valleras. Ilse followed with the second stanza:

"Drum trag ich Ranzlein und den Stab weit in die Welt hinein und werde bis and kuhle Grab, Ein Wanderbursche sein."

And again they sang the chorus, filling the wilderness with their happiness. They continued to sing until they reached a place where the land flattened and the white pines stretched higher than he had ever seen. As they approached the carefully prepared campsite, which overlooked a small lake, Hermann asked, "Was it worth the trek, Lazo?"

He didn't wait for Lazo's reply. He shook off his rucksack and carefully hung it on a branch of a tall tree. He admonished the others to do likewise so that their provisions would be out of the reach of the brown bears that frequented the area.

Once unburdened, Lazo took Ilse's hand and they walked to the edge of the cliff, which fell precipitously into the lake. "Isn't it lovely? I don't think that I will ever tire of this place."

"Yes," replied Lazo, almost spellbound, "it is magnificent."

"Come," she said, pulling him along, "I want to show you something." She led him to the face of another cliff. "Are you thirsty?" she asked, pointing to a place where a stream of water issued from the granite. Above the spring, carved into the rock, Lazo read,

"Let us drink, rejoice and step aside, for we are only moments, carved not in granite, but in whispers."

H. Krebs, sojourner, A. D. 1940

"That's beautiful but tell me Ilse, why is a man of such obvious talent, content to live out here, as a handyman and woodcutter."

"I once asked my father that very thing and he told me that there was more honest philosophy to be learned in this silent wilderness than in the entire university lecture halls, taken together. I didn't quite believe him then, but now I am beginning to see what he meant."

The two had become so involved with each other that they didn't hear Erika and Hermann approach. Erika put her arms around the couple and gave them an affectionate squeeze. Hermann reached out and allowed the cold water to splash against his hand. "There is an old Indian saying", he said, "that they who drink from this spring will understand the secret poetry of the heart."

He took the cone like vessel, which he had made from birch bark and held it under the stream until it was half full. He handed it to Erika. "Hold this, and I will get the wine."

"Why the wine?" asked Ilse.

"I honestly don't know," responded Erika.

Hermann returned, carrying a bottle of red wine. He removed the cork and carefully poured the wine into the clumsy vessel until it reached the brim.

"Good. Now let us drink to the legend."

"Why the wine, papa?"

"Can't you guess, Ilse?"

"No papa, I cannot."

"It's quite simple, Liebchen. If the water can unlock the secret poetry of the heart, the wine will insure that that poetry will be only happy poetry. Besides, it tastes much better this way." He smiled, winked at Lazo and raised the vessel to his lips. The vessel was passed around until it was empty. As he hung the vessel back on the wooden peg, he said, "Someday we will do this again."

"Yes," replied Erika, "and let us pray that it be very soon."

Lazo's reverie was momentarily interrupted by a large fly that settled upon his nose, he swept it away and a flow of mild expletives issued from his lips. Then he closed his eyes once again and in thought, returned to Ilse's side. They were picking blueberries amid the slashings of a logged out forest. It was not far from the campsite.

The blueberries were unusually large and plentiful, making the picking quite easy. He marveled at the ease with which Ilse gathered the berries. She filled her pail very quickly and then helped Lazo with his. When both pails were full, she reached over and took his hand.

"Come."

"Where?"

"Never mind. It's a surprise."

"Okay, I'm game, but how far is it?"

"Not too far. Maybe a mile."

Then she began to run, pulling him behind. They came to a brook and followed it until it entered a part of the forest that had not been logged out. They continued to run until they came to a place where the sun's rays warmed the soft, green grass and the brook fell into a small pool of cool water. It was so clear, that the brook trout, swimming on the bottom, were clearly visible, even though the pool was quite deep.

Ilse put her pail down and fell back on the lush grass. She folded her arms beneath her head and closed her eyes. Neither of them spoke. Lazo sat down beside her and watched the sun's rays caress her long elegant legs. She discarded her beaded moccasins and stretched her toes. The hem of her loose sweatshirt had followed her arms upward until it came to rest high on her browned midriff. He had never been this alone with a girl in his entire life and he blushed slightly. Still, he was unable to remove his eyes from that area of her nakedness, where the sun brushed against the tiny golden hairs that graced her bronzed, smooth skin. A droplet of perspiration appeared from under her sweatshirt and wandered slowly downward until it disappeared beneath her loose waistband. Lazo, unable to bear the distance any longer, leaned forward and gently, ever so gently, rested his face against the smoothness of her skin. Her stomach, naturally concave yielded further to the weight of his head, and permitted him a glimpse of the silken whiteness that the sun had not touched. She ran her fingers through his hair, and he responded by gently touching his lips to the softness of her body. He had never experienced anything like it. Her stomach began to quiver under his lips as he moved ever closer to her distended waistband. When his face touched the rough leather of her shorts, he paused and waited, thinking that he might be embarrassing her.

What might have happened next will never be known because her passion was abruptly dampened by the approach of her parents. She hastily moved to the edge of the pool and plunged her feet into its coolness. "There will be other times," she whispered.

Lazo's reminiscences were once again interrupted. This time, not by the flies but by the sound of Sam's voice, as he yelled, "Hey, Lazo, is it going to take you all the Goddamned day to read those letters! Get your damned butt over here and help me kill these beers!"

Lazo picked himself up, brushed the sand from his clothing and began to walk slowly toward Sam. If one looked carefully, one could detect a smile on his face and a new buoyancy in his stride. Lazo was happy and when he reached Sam, he picked up a can of beer and holding it at arm's length removed the cap. He watched the beer erupt and spill over, causing his hand to disappear under a cascade of foam. He held it out until he was sure that the beer's fever had abated. Then he transferred the can to his other hand so he could shake the foam off his right hand.

"Does she still love you?" asked Sam.

Lazo put the can to his lips and took a drink.".

"Well, does she?"

"Yes, Sam, if you must know, she loves me very much."

"Good. Without passion, there can be no love."

Lazo blew the mound of foam from the top of the can and sat down. He scooped up a handful of warm sand and allowed it to trickle slowly through his fingers. "Is it true?" he asked. "Do men, in love, really make poor combat soldiers?"

"I don't know. Why do you ask."

"Well, in the movies, you always hear the commanding officer haranguing his men about the dangers of love."

"Oh yes, I know what you mean. They always have an actor who looks like he played fullback at Notre Dame, play the part."

"Yes," interrupted Lazo, "and they always start out with something like: mennnnn, war is a selfish mistress. She commands your absolute attention and will tolerate no distractions or side excursions. Remember men, a soldier who is worried about his girl friend's fidelity, does not have his mind fixed on the enemy. His pre-occupation might, very well, cost him his life, or even worse, the life of a comrade."

"That's very good," responded Sam, who was now laughing quite loudly. "But you forgot something."

"What's that!"

Sam got up and in a voice, deliberately lowered by one octave, said, "Now soldiers, I do not mean to diminish the importance of sex. You and I both know that sex is good. Sex is healthy, but a good soldier never confuses sex with love. One is entirely possible without the other. A smart soldier takes his pleasure wherever and whenever he can find it and he never gives it a second thought. Why even I have been known to indulge a little, that is, of course, when my adorable wife isn't around."

By the time Sam got to the last sentence, they were both laughing uncontrollably.

"All kidding aside, Sam, doesn't it frighten you a little, knowing that you will be going on a dangerous mission with a man who is head over heels in love?"

"Not at all, Lazo. I want you to know that I volunteered for this mission. I did so, because I knew that I would be going with you."

"Why me?"

"I'm not absolutely sure but I have this strong urge to prove to myself and perhaps to you, that I am not a coward."

"You don't have to prove a damned thing to me, Sam."

"Oh, but I do. You see, Lazo, your malediction back at Elright, was quite correct. I was aware of what was happening to my people. My father, you see, is one of those so-called 'influence peddlers' in Washington and he is privy to a lot of secret information. He told me what was happening to our people, but I, like a fool, tried my damnest to put it out of my mind. That is, until you reminded me of what I was. I'll never forget that day."

"I really didn't mean what I said, Sam. After I left the hospital, I tried to find you, to apologize, but I was told that you had been transferred."

"Nevertheless," continued Sam, "you and Kovach did a hellava job on my self respect. I walked out of the hospital that day, feeling dirty, crawling dirty. I don't know if you can understand what I mean but I had the feeling that I was covered with vermin. Soon, I was no longer walking but running. I felt this urgent need to scrub myself clean. A block away from my quarters, I was already undressing. By the time I reached the door, I was carrying my shirt and undershirt in my hand. I kicked off my shoes and ripped off the rest of my clothing and ran into the shower room. Then I began to scrub myself, over and over again. I scrubbed and rinsed, scrubbed and rinsed, until my skin began to smart. After each rinsing, I looked down at the drain to see if all of the 'Masadas' and 'Good Fridays' had been scrubbed away. I was trying to scrub away my Jewishness." He paused for a moment, and then continued

"That's what I was trying to do. I was ashamed of being a Jew. I was ashamed of my people. Can you understand the absurdity of it? I was ashamed of my people. The same people who gave to this piss ass world the most precious of all gifts; the belief in the universal brotherhood of man. Then it dawned on me. Do you remember what Kovach said to me that morning, in the hallway?"

"I think so," replied Lazo.

"Well, I remember it, word for word because it stung me so deeply. He said, 'Look damned you, there is a boy dying in that bed and your presence disgraces his birth.' I didn't know what he meant then, but standing in the shower, his words came back to me. They didn't seem to hurt anymore because I realized what he meant."

"That's good, because I was never quite sure what he meant."

"I think he was saying that there comes a time in every man's life when the boy in him must die to make room for the man. For you it was the hangar; for me it was in that shower room. Can you think of a more unlikely place to find one's manhood."

Lazo made no reply. The trenchancy of Sam's remarkable insight would only be blunted by any response he might make. He now understood what Sam meant when he referred to him as the instrument of his resurrection and Lazo no longer felt ashamed.

The two men remained on the beach until the sun was low on the horizon and as it dropped out of sight, Lazo closed his eyes and for a brief second the scent of pine touched his sensibility and a strange new warmth filtered through his body. He raised himself up from the sand, extended his hand to Sam and with a quick jerk, pulled him up. The two remained, hand in hand, for a second or two, and then they turned and walked silently away.

CHAPTER FOUR

The next morning Lazo arose earlier than was his habit and being careful, not to awaken Sam, stepped out into the cool dawn. The sun had not yet appeared but the red drenched horizon, foretold that it would soon force its presence on the African continent as it had done since the dawn of man. He seated himself on the cool concrete apron and lit a cigarette. His thoughts were yet with Ilse. Her letters had so intensified his ardor that he seemed no longer in possession of himself. The words of love that she had written, were permanently etched on his memory and for the first time in his life, the fear of death had seized him. Then remembering the words that Hermann had carved into the cliff, he muttered out loud, "But damn it, I will not step aside to make room for another. "

"What the hell is going on out there! Can't a fellow get a little sleep around here!" Sam stepped out on to the concrete, clad only in his olive drab shorts.

"Sorry, Sam, I didn't mean to disturb you."

"No need to apologize, Lazo. You really didn't awaken me. I didn't sleep well at all. These damnable cots were designed by the army to make sleep virtually impossible." He arched his back and scratched at his chest quite vigorously.

"You'll get used to them."

"I don't plan to be here that long," responded Sam. "The way I see it, we'll be out of here in a couple of days."

"I hope you're right, but I wouldn't bet on it."

Sam sat down next to Lazo. He took the pack of cigarettes that was lying at Lazo's side, removed one and returned the pack. He lit it, took a couple of quick puffs, then quietly, almost in a whisper said, "Lazo, I'm going to tell you something and I want you to promise never to tell a soul."

"Okay Sam, anything you say." replied Lazo, matter of factly.

"You've got to swear, Lazo."

"If that's the way you want it, you've got it. I swear on the graves of all of my ancestors and everything holy, that I will never reveal what I am about to hear from one, Captain Sam Kaplan. Is that okay?"

"Damn you Lazo, get serious."

Lazo quit smiling and said, "Look Sam, you can trust me and remember, if there's anything that I can ever do for you, just ask and you've got it."

"I'm aware of that Laz. I feel the same way, but this is so damned important to me."

Sam paused long enough to grind out the partially consumed cigarette on the concrete and like a good soldier, field stripped it. Then he looked squarely at Lazo and said, "I volunteered for this mission because I wanted to get to Eastern Europe. It wasn't easy but my father pulled the necessary strings."

"Why Eastern Europe?" asked Lazo.

"Because that's where the Nazi death camps are located," replied Sam, his voice cracking.

"What death camps?"

"Auschwitz, Treblenka, Maidanik and a half dozen others."

"How do you know that?" asked Lazo, his forehead becoming fluted.

"The State Department knows about them and my father knows what the State Department knows. That's how."

"I had heard some rumors regarding the extermination camps that the Nazis had erected to make Europe 'Judenrein', but I thought that they were somewhat exaggerated."

"Exaggerated, hell!" exclaimed Sam, his anger beginning to tell. "There are no words in the English language that can adequately describe the crimes that are being committed against my people. Men, women and children are being systematically slaughtered by the thousands and this, only after they have been subjected to every kind of degradation and humiliation. The things that I have heard make me want to kill every one of those Nazi sons of bitches."

"What the hell can you do about it? Do you think that you can crush those bastards single handedly?"

"I must do something, Lazo. I wouldn't be able to live with myself if I didn't try. The men responsible, must be punished."

"Why the hell doesn't our government do something to stop it?"

"That's a laugh," responded Sam. "Hell, they've known about it for a long time. Some officials find it convenient to pretend that the reports are not true, or if true, greatly exaggerated. Others, some who occupy very important positions in Washington, are of the opinion that the only good Jew is a dead one. They are the ones who believe that every Jew is a damned Bolshevik and Hitler is making the world safe for capitalism."

"You can't mean that," replied Lazo. "I cannot believe our government could be guilty of such blatant stupidity."

"You've got a lot to learn," replied Sam, miffed by Lazo's incredulity.

"Look Sam," responded Lazo, "I don't mean to make light of the suffering which your people have endured but there is not a hell of a lot either of us can do about it."

"Perhaps not, but I intend to try and that is why I want you to keep the promise you made to me."

"How can I keep it if I don't know it?"

"After we complete our mission in Yugoslavia, I will not return with you."

"What do you mean?" asked Lazo, somewhat amazed.

"I will be heading north."

"What the hell do you mean? That's occupied territory. You'll never make it. I can't believe that you can be so utterly naive."

"I know that my plan is fraught with danger. I'm not stupid, you know. I plan to go to Poland. I want to see those death camps, first hand. I want to be able to tell the world about them. God willing, I am going to make such a loud stink that no one will ever again do what they are doing. I want to be able to look my children, straight on, and know that they will never have to suffer that kind of agony. Do you understand Lazo?"

"Of course, I understand but what you plan is impossible. Why risk it, when you know that those responsible will be tried and punished, once the war is over."

"Fat chance," replied Sam. "Oh, they'll be punished all right but only if it is politically convenient to do so. Besides, the camps are located in territory that will be liberated by the Russians and they don't give a damn about Jews. Hell, they've been persecuting us longer than the Germans."

"I still think that it would be wiser to allow the law and the lawyers to take care of it. The law must ultimately prevail," replied Lazo, his voice conveying a heightened quality of urgency.

"Now, who the hell is naive? Haven't you learned that where there are lawyers there are laws but no law," replied Sam, his voice becoming more and more strident. "Every outrage against humanity can be ultimately attributed to the odious designs of some damned attorney. Who the hell do you think drew up the Nuremberg Laws? Give them a dollar and they will frolic and gambol through the labrynth of legal verbiage until they have so perverted the meaning of justice that any crime can be committed in its name. I only hope that some day soon, they will all suffocate on their own legal muck."

"My God, you really mean it, don't you!" exclaimed Lazo, his face contorted in disbelief. "You really plan to desert the army and carry on a one man crusade against those bloody bastards!"

"You're damned right I do," replied Sam, "and there is nothing anyone might say that could dissuade me. I have thought about it for a long time but you are the first person that I have ever confided in. So please, Laz, don't give me away. This is more important to me than my very life."

"Don't worry, I won't," replied Lazo. "But what if you get killed?"

"I've worked that out too."

"How?"

"After this bloody war is over, I will get in touch with you and then we can have one hellava reunion."

"But what if you get killed?"

39

"If I don't contact you within three months after the war has ended, you must consider me dead. In that event, I want you personally, to contact my father in Washington and tell him what I tried to do. Try to make him understand why I did what I did. Try to make him understand, Laz."

"Fine." replied Lazo, "I will. But if I get killed? Then what?"

"In that case, it won't matter much, will it? But let's not bury each other yet. Chances are that we will both survive this war and someday we will be able to tell our grandchildren about our noble endeavors."

"I hope so Sam. God, I hope so."

"Good, now let's shake and be done with it," said Sam, extending his hand to Lazo.

Lazo took the hand and with renewed confidence, said, "I think you're right. We'll survive. You're damned right we will and in the meantime, let's settle a few scores with those sons of bitches who call themselves supermen."

"Nothing would pleasure me more," said Sam, nodding his head and smiling.

"Good," replied Lazo, "now let's get ready for breakfast."

CHAPTER FIVE

A week had passed since Sam had arrived and Lazo could sense that he was becoming more and more peckish each day. On this particular morning in late August, Lazo awakened Sam with a loud,

"Hey, Buddy, are you getting used to the cot yet!"

Sam, half asleep, rose up and hurled his pillow at Lazo and a few well chosen, four lettered Anglo Saxon words issued from his lips.

"Stay loose, Buddy! Stay loose! Maybe today's the day."

"Maybe, hell," responded Sam, pulling his blanket over his head. "They've forgotten about us. This war will end and we'll still be rotting here."

"Hell, you should complain, I've been here a lot longer than you," replied Lazo, returning the pillow to Sam, with equal fervor.

Sam was about to reply when the tent flap was thrown back and someone shouted, "Is anyone home?" But before they could respond, a man wearing the uniform of an American officer entered the tent. Lazo spotted the Major's insignia and immediately came to attention. Sam, still not quite awake, responded in a similar fashion.

"At ease, men!" commanded the Major, as he sat down on the footlocker next to Lazo's cot. "I'm Major Featherstone of the O.S.S. Which one of you is Captain Krall?"

"My name is Krall, sir," responded Lazo, "but I'm just a private in this man's army."

"Not anymore. Headquarters has decided that this mission is much too important to entrust to a private. They felt that you would be able to speak with greater authority if you were wearing the bars of a captain. Where you are going, the people have a profound respect for rank."

Lazo, taken by surprise, was not able to respond immediately, but when he had finally collected himself, he said,"Well I'll be damned. I'll be god damned."

"Perhaps you will, Lazo. Perhaps we all will be but in the meantime, we've got a job to do." Then he turned to Sam and said, "You must be Captain Kaplan."

"Yes sir, I am."

"Well, I was in Washington last week and your father asked me to give you this." He reached into his valise and pulled out a big bottle of scotch. He looked at the label and handed it to Sam.

"Thank you, sir. Thank you very much. How was my old man?"

"He seemed quite fit for a man of his age," responded the Major.

"Did he say anything else?"

"Yes, as a matter of fact, he did. He asked me to tell you to take good care of yourself because your mother is going to hold him personally responsible, should anything happen to you." The Major removed his hat and mopped his head with his neatly folded pocket handkerchief.

"The poor bastard, and she will too." Replied Sam. "I wonder how she found out about the part he played in my assignment."

The Major stood up and moved toward the entrance. When he reached the aperture, he turned and said, "By the way, gentlemen, there will be an intensive briefing at eleven hundred hours at headquarters. We will expect you to be prompt. I must warn you that the Colonel is an impatient man and will not tolerate any tardiness."

"We'll be there," replied the two, in unison. "We'll be there."

When the Major had left, the two jumped up and embraced each other enthusiastically, shouting, "We're going! We're going! By God, we're finally going!"

"Did you hear what he said?"

"Yes, Lazo I did. Don't be tardy! What a joke!"

"Son of a bitch, it's been so long that I can hardly believe it. We're going, Sam. We're going to make some history."

Their celebration was cut short by the sound of voices outside the tent.

"Did you hear that?" asked Lazo.

"I think so but it's been so long, I can't be sure. It sounded like women."

"Nah, it can't be," replied Lazo, "not out here."

"Does a certain Captain Krall reside hereabouts?" came a distinctly feminine voice from the other side of the canvas.

"Yes, yes he does," responded Lazo, after a slight hesitation. It was still not easy for him to respond to the title of captain.

"May we enter, suh?"

"Please, please do, ladies."

The two women entered. The soldiers, startled by the sight of two such uncommonly beautiful women, stood there with their mouths and eyes agape. The women were attired in well-fitted khaki shorts and blouses. The blonde, wearing captain's bars, had hiked up her shorts in such a way, that little was left to the imagination.

"What seems to be wrong?" asked the Captain, "Haven't you evah seen O.S.S. agents befoh."

She walked up to Sam, extended her hand, and said, "I'm Virginia Lee, and this is June Janasek."

Sam shook her hand and replied, "It's so good to see you." He meant it. Oh, how he meant it. "My name is Sam Kaplan and this is Lazo Krall."

They shook hands and exchanged pleasantries. Sam suggested that they sit down and make themselves comfortable. He had been so transported by their beauty, that he had forgotten that he was attired only in G.I. shorts. His face reddened and he quickly covered himself with the terrycloth robe that lay crumpled at the foot of his cot.

Lazo, unaware of Sam's predicament, was still shaking June's hand. He had never seen an upper torso like hers; not in his entire life. It seemed almost incongruous. "How could a girl be so slender and yet so abundantly endowed?" Each time he shook her hand, her upper arm brushed against her breast, causing it to plash about and strain against the fragile buttons of her blouse.

"Look, Captain, let's not overdo it." she uttered as she tried to pull her hand free.

"Oh, I'm sorry, June. I guess I kind of got carried away."

He released her hand and she smiled. "Thank you, I do hope it's not bruised."

"So do I," responded Lazo, and from the position of his eyes, it was obvious that his concern was not directed to her hand.

Virginia reached into her blouse pocket and drew out a pair of captain's bars. She walked over to Lazo and said, "The Colonel sent these ovah for you. He wants you to wear them to the briefing." She handed them to Lazo, stepped back and said,"Well, boys, we all must go now."

"Will we see you again?" asked Sam.

"Oh, certainly," responded June. "We'll be present at the briefing."

"I don't mean that way. Couldn't we get together this evening?" "Look," pleaded Sam, "I just received this bottle of perfectly good scotch and I should very much like to share it with you. Perhaps the four of us could go to the beach and have a picnic of sorts."

"Tell you what," responded Virginia, "if we are still here this evening, we all, will try to join you. Now we all must go, or our beloved Colonel will have our collective hides."

As they turned to leave, June's foot got tangled up in the blanket which was lying on the floor. It caused her to lose her balance and she stumbled into Lazo's out stretched arms. All of her softness pressed against him. She looked into his eyes and thanked him effusively. Then one of her large green eyes closed and a smile came to her lips.

Our young soldiers said nothing until they were quite certain that the women were well on their way, then their youthful exhuberance, held in check, until now, erupted and their unbridled enthusiasm manifested itself in such eloquent expressions as, "Hot damn!" and "Did you see them?" "Did you see those boobs?"

Sam threw himself on his cot and began to beat his pillow with his fists. Lazo sat down on the floor, picked up the blanket and kissed it. He was still pondering the generous dimensions of a certain portion of June's anatomy.

Soon the tempest in the tent abated. It ended as abruptly as it had begun and a momentary silence filled the tent.

"Do you think they will show up?" asked Sam.

"I know they will," replied Lazo.

"How can you be that sure?"

"Trust me, Sam. Put your faith in me and the unbounded curiousity of the female species. They'll be here."

"I hope you're right."

"Well, let's get ready, Sam. We don't have a helluva lot of time, you know. Like the women said, the Colonel has a penchant for punctuality."

They arrived at headquarters a full fifteen minutes before the appointed time and were ushered into the briefing room. Lazo seemed to be somewhat uncomfortable. Perhaps his newly acquired status caused him to feel a little self-conscious. He had never, after all, entertained any desire to become a commissioned officer and as a matter of fact, was not overly fond of officers. They waited impatiently and when the appointed time arrived, the door opened and Major Featherstone shouted, "Attenhut!"

Lazo and Sam rose to attention. The Colonel entered followed by an entourage comprised of one civilian, two British officers and two American women. They filed in until the Colonel was immediately in front of Lazo. He stopped. Major Featherstone stepped forward and in a manner bordering on sycophancy, said,

"Colonel Lee, may I present Captains Krall and Kaplan."

The Colonel shook hands with both of them. Then he beckoned to the civilian. "And this gentlemen, is Milovan Vrak, representative of the Yugoslavian Government in exile. He is here at the express request of King Peter."

Milovan stepped forward, shook their hands and greeted them quite cordially.

"I believe," the Colonel continued, "You have already met these two officers."

"Yes we have," replied Lazo, smiling.

"And this is Colonel Roundtree of the British S.O.E., and his aide, Lieutenant Townshend. And now, ladies and gentlemen, let us be seated."

"Major Featherstone, you may begin."

The Major stood up, mopped his forehead with his pocket handkerchief and began. "As you probably are aware, there are two factions competing for the control of post-war Yugoslavia. The Chetniks, under Draja Mihailovich and the Partisans, under Josip Broz, more commonly known as Tito. At the beginning of the war, the allies had given their blessing and support to the Chetniks, but as time moved on, it seemed that the Partisans were more resolute and effective in their campaigns against the Nazis. There was even some cause to believe that the Chetniks were openly cooperating with the Nazis, to thwart the efforts of Tito. In 1943, a top British S.O.E. agent headed up a group that was parachuted into Yugoslavia, with the express purpose of finding out more about the Partisans. His reports concerning their activities were so glowing that by the summer of '43, the British government was overtly cooperating with Tito. At the Teheran Conference that November, the allies agreed that they must support the group that was killing the most Germans and that meant, Tito's Partisans. King Peter urged Mihailovich to cooperate with the Partisans so that a civil war might be averted. Mihailovich has repeatedly rejected these overtures. The allies also suggested that Mihailovich leave Yugoslavia and take up residence in the United States. This too, was rejected by him, out of hand. Needless to say, we are enmeshed in a situation, rife with peril. At this very moment, the Partisans are amassing their forces on the Serbian border and a civil war appears to be imminent." The Major poured some water in a glass and began to sip.

"Thank you, Major. You may be seated."

"And that ladies and gentlemen," said the Colonel, "is the raison d'etre, of this mission. We simply must find out what this fellow, Tito is up to. We know that his sympathies lie with Moscow but we must ascertain how deeply he is committed to a Soviet takeover of Yugoslavia. The British have assured us that they have not bartered away Yugoslavian independence in exchange for the Soviet Union's guarantee of British hegemony in Greece and the eastern Mediterranean. Am I correct, Colonel Roundtree?"

The British Colonel cleared his throat and said, "You have my absolute assurance that the British government has in no way compromised the sovereignty or integrity of Yugoslavia. We have not and let me repeat, have not given the Soviet Union any cause, tacit or otherwise, to believe that the British Government will countenance any such Soviet ambition."

"Are you getting this all down, Virginia?" asked the Colonel.

"Yes, daddy, I mean, Colonel suh, every word," responded Virginia.

Colonel Roundtree cleared his throat and the flesh immediately above his tight collar took on a purplish tint. At the same time, Lazo received an elbow in the ribs. He turned and saw Sam's eye directing him to the scratch pad upon which Sam had scribbled, "Looks like I'm gonna have me a spoiled Colonel's daughter."

Lazo smiled and whispered, "It's your funeral."

The Colonel then turned to Milovan and asked, "Would you like to make a statement regarding the official posture of your government?"

"Yes, I would." He paused to collect his thoughts. Then in a voice of unquestionable sincerity, said, "King Peter has asked me to convey to you his best wishes for a successful mission. He hopes that the mission will result in the establishment of cordial relations between the two factions. The saving of human lives has become his primary concern and he has told me that he would gladly relinquish his throne, if it would bring about a prompt and equitable peace. Thank you very much."

"And thank you," said the Colonel.

Lazo could not help but feel a surge of sympathy for Milovan. It was obvious, even to him, that the "Yugoslavian Government in Exile", had been sacrificed by the Allies on the very brittle altar of political expedience. He looked to where June was seated. She had been staring at him and when his eyes met hers, she screened her face with her hand and winked at him. He smiled and the thoughts of politics evaporated from his mind, making room for pleasant hopes.

"And now," said the Colonel, "we come to Captain Lazo Krall and the part he will play in this mission. I suspect that the Captain is somewhat bewildered. Afterall, it is not customary for someone, in this man's army, to be catapaulted from the rank of private to that of captain, in the space of one day. Am I not correct, Lazo?"

"Yes sir," replied Lazo. "I am still dizzy. Are you quite certain that a mistake has not been made."

"Believe me, Lazo, a mistake has not been made. Our research staff has gone over your background with a fine toothed comb and believe you to be the only one who can bring this mission to a successful conclusion."

"And what is my mission, Sir?"

The Colonel paused, then turning to Major Featherstone, asked, "Do you have the picture, Alfred?"

"Yes Sir, I do." The Major reached into his briefcase, removed a photograph and handed it to the Colonel.

The Colonel looked at it, then handed it over to Lazo and asked, "Do you recognize this man?"

Lazo looked at the picture very carefully and said, "It's not very clear but the man in the picture does bear a resemblance to my uncle Blaz."

"That is your uncle Blaz and the man pictured with him is Tito. That is the reason you have been chosen to head the mission."

"But he was killed by the Nazis, early in the war. How can he be of any use to us?"

"He was a friend of Tito's."

"Are you quite certain, Colonel?" asked Lazo, somewhat bemused.

"Quite certain. Are you familiar with a place called Lepo Glava?"

"No, I don't think so."

"Well, it's the name of a notorious prison, situated on the outskirts of Belgrade. It was in this prison that your uncle Blaz and Tito became friends." "During the twenties," he continued, "Tito was involved in a labor movement. As a labor organizer, he was often at odds with the police. In 1929, he attempted to organize the employees in the plant where your uncle worked. Your uncle was one of the first to join the movement and when the police arrested Tito, they also arrested some of the workers whom they considered dangerous. Blaz was one of them. They were placed in adjacent cells and were able to communicate with one another quite freely. During the seven months that Blaz was incarcerated, he and Tito became close friends. Their discussions, we have been told, were quite extensive, ranging from politics to women. On the day that Blaz was released, Tito told him that the hours of the Monarchy were numbered and that soon Yugoslavia would be looking for a new krall. He supposedly asked Blaz, perhaps jokingly, if he would help him put on that crown. We have been told that he embraced Tito warmly and said, 'Dear friend, when the time arrives, you need only call and I will be at your side.' Tito then kissed him and they parted."

The Colonel paused and reached for the glass that had been placed in front of him. Major Featherstone jumped up, grabbed the pitcher of water and filled the Colonel's glass. The Colonel took a sip and set the glass down. "And that, Lazo, is where the story ends. We do not know what happened after they parted but we have every reason to believe that they remained in touch with one another."

"How do you know all this?" asked Lazo.

"Their conversations at the prison were monitored and recorded. We have also been in touch with your mother and she has been very helpful. With her assistance, we were able to craft a rather complete dossier on your uncle."

"May I see it?" asked Lazo.

"Certainly. Do you have it with you, Major?"

"Yes Sir, here it is."

The Colonel took the dossier and handed it to Lazo. "You may take it with you. We want you to memorize all of the pertinent data. It will come in handy where you are going."

"And where is that?" asked Lazo, with a rather devilish smile on his face.

"You are going to have a little chat with this fellow they call Tito."

"Does he know we're coming?"

"He knows that someone is coming but for security reasons, we decided it was best that we not tell anyone about you."

"Why the hell not?"

"Actually Lazo, there are two very good and pertinent reasons why we decided not to." He took another sip of water, paused and in a voice that seemed to convey some reluctance, said, "There are those, Lazo that would like to see this mission fail and in fact, would do anything to sabotage our efforts. I will not elaborate but believe me, they do exist. We also believe that you will make a more credible representative if Tito discovers, for himself, that you are a relative of Blaz Dolanz. If he knew beforehand, he might believe that you were a fabrication created by the

O.S.S., for the express purpose of deceiving him. No, Captain, it is best that Tito discover for himself, your relationship to Blaz."

"Precisely," added the Major. "Learn everything that the dossier contains but when you speak with him, mention only the things that your mother would have told you about Blaz. Do you understand?"

"Yes I do sir. An innocent demeanor will serve to disarm him."

"Absolutely," remarked the Colonel. "He will thus be somewhat more candid with you and might even reveal the true nature of his intentions. At least, that is our hope, and that is why we chose you to lead the mission. And now, are there any further questions?"

The Colonel waited and satisfied that no questions were forthcoming, said, "Major Featherstone."

Major Featherstone arose and said, "This concludes today's briefing. The final briefing will be scheduled for tomorrow. Those involved, will be notified as to time and place." Then he shouted.

"Tenhut!"

Before anyone could respond, Colonel Lee shouted, "At ease!"

Then looking at the Major, "Let us dispense with the formalities. Then he stood up and walked toward the door. The others followed, leaving Lazo and Sam all alone.

"Do you know what this means, Lazo?"

"No, I don't think so."

"It means that we will be going on a picnic tonight."

"Oh that," replied Lazo, "I had almost forgotten about that."

"Like hell you did. I saw the way she was ogling you during the briefing. Did you wink back?"

"You don't miss much, do you Sam?"

"No, Lazo, I don't and that is why I'll make a damned good agent."

"Well, we'd better get going. I have a lot to do before this evening."

"What do you have to do?"

"Memorize this dossier and you are going to help me."

"It will be my pleasure," replied Sam, as the two walked toward the door.

"Hold it fellahs," came a voice from behind them.

They turned and saw Virginia standing in the other doorway. She walked up to them, smiled and asked, "When do we meet you all?"

"You mean you all will be there tonight?"

"Yes Sam, that's exactly what I mean."

"That's great! Why don't the two of you come to our tent around 1800 and we can walk to the beach together."

"That sounds good, Sam." "By the way, Sam," she continued, "you don't have to bring any food."

"We've got to have food," replied Lazo.

"We will Lazo, and it will be the best."

"Who is going to bring it?" asked Lazo.

"June and I will manage, don't worry your little heads ovah it. Afterall, my daddy is a colonel in this man's army and he'll do anything I ask."

As she was about to leave, Lazo said, "Remember now, 1800 hours."

"We won't forget," replied Virginia. "By the way, what shall we wear?"

"Wear something comfortable," replied Sam.

"Doesn't it get quite cold around here at night?"

"If it does, we'll build a fire."

"That sounds fine, Sam" replied Virginia, as she turned and walked toward the door.

Lazo and Sam carefully surveyed the superbly contoured seat which moved so gracefully with each step. When she disappeared, they turned and left the room.

Sam, smiling quite devilishly, said, "I sho do like her southern accent."

"Yeh," replied Lazo, "and those tight shorts sure do accent her southern frontier."

CHAPTER SIX

The day passed slowly for Sam. The army, to be sure, had habituated him to the wait, but this was different. "It might very well be," he thought, "the last opportunity I will ever have to enjoy the company of beautiful women."

Now Sam was not the kind of man who spent his entire life with one eye canted on death. No, not Sam. As a matter of fact, he had hardly given it any notice at all. Perhaps it was because death had always been so proximate to the Jewish people. What began to trouble Sam was the thought of dying without a son. He muttered something like, "That mustached son-of-a-bitch, I'll fix him."

"What's that?" asked Lazo, who was occupied with Blaz's dossier.

"Oh, nothing," replied Sam. "I was just thinking out loud, I guess. Have you memorized the material?"

Lazo scratched his head. "I think so. What time is it?"

Sam looked at his watch, "It's about five-thirty."

"Oh hell, I didn't think it was that late."

"What do you have to do?" queried Sam.

"I've got to shave and shower before they come." replied Lazo, running his hand against his cheek.

"You've got plenty of time. You know women. They're never on time."

"Maybe, but if they get here before I return, don't let them get away," replied Lazo, as he ran out of the tent.

"Don't worry, buddy. They won't get away."

Lazo had not been gone five minutes, when Sam heard the sound of women's voices. He tidied up the cots and quickly ran a comb through his dark, coarse hair.

"Hey in there, can you give us some help?"

"I sure can, June," replied Sam. He rushed out of the tent and beheld the women, holding between them, the largest picnic basket he had ever seen. It was so heavy that they could not straighten out and consequently, the basket swayed but a few inches above the ground.

"Where did you get it?" asked Sam, unable to conceal his excitement.

"Nevah mind Sam," retorted Virginia, "give us a hand befoh we all collapse."

"Yes," added June, trying to stand on one foot, "grab this damned basket before my feet burn off!"

Sam took the basket, and the women, now relieved of the overwhelming burden, hopped into the tent and fell upon the cots. Sam followed them and set the basket on the floor.

"Hurry!" admonished June. "There's a bucket of ice in the basket. Get us some, please."

"You ought to know better than traipse over these hot walkways, barefooted."

"Nevah mind the lecture, just get us some ice," implored Virginia.

Sam reached into the bucket and grabbed a couple clusters of ice cubes which had been fused together by the heat. He handed the first one to June, since her need seemed to be the most urgent. She took the clump of ice, fell back upon the cot and began to run the ice, ever so gently, against the soles of her burning feet. As she did, she kept repeating, "Oh, that feels so good, so very good."

She was wearing a green halter top and when she raised her feet, the force of gravity acted upon her extravagant bosom in such a way that part of the deep crimson wreaths, which accented her breasts, became quite visible.

"Have you forgotten poor little me so soon, sugah? The ice will be melted befoh you get to me."

"What? Oh no," replied Sam, as he turned and handed the half melted cluster to Virginia.

"Thank you evah so much, Sam. Would you?"

"Of course, I will," replied Sam. He sat down on the cot and began to caress the bottoms of her feet with the ice.

"Oh, that feels so soothing. Do the othah one also."

As she raised the other foot, it became obvious to Sam that she was wearing absolutely nothing under her khaki shorts. It so distracted him that he unwittingly began to press the ice against her foot much more vigorously.

"Not so rough! Please, Sam, not so rough!"

"Oh, I'm sorry Virginia. Did I hurt you?"

He bent down and gently kissed the sole of her foot.

"Don't do that! "I'm ticklish." pleaded Virginia.

"Oh, is that so?"

Virginia, saw the devilish look in Sam's eyes and she screamed, "You wouldn't dah!"

"Oh, wouldn't I!" and before she could utter another word, Sam grabbed her foot firmly and began to move his lips along the bottom of her foot.

"Please don't, Sam! Please don't!" she beseeched, half laughing and half screaming.

Sam was so amused by what he was doing that he did not notice Lazo sneak into the tent.

"Tenhut!" he shouted.

The three revellers jumped to attention before they realized who had issued the command.

"Let's get him!" shouted June and the three pounced upon him and brought him to the floor.

"The ice! The ice!" shouted June. "Hand me some ice!"

Virginia reached into the bucket, took out a large clump and handed it to June but before she could drop it down his back, he managed to free himself. He took the ice cube from June's hand and dropped it down into the front of Virginia's shorts.

She screamed and jumped up. She began to shake her hips but the cluster of ice was too large to slip through. She was too embarrassed to reach in and remove it, so she began to jump up and down, hoping that the ice would slip out.

"Lie down and raise your hips!" shouted June.

Virginia quickly complied and the ice slipped out from beneath her belt and fell to the floor, but not before the front of her shorts were quite well drenched.

"Someone hand me a towel."

Lazo threw his towel to her and she began to wipe the front of her shorts. The more she wiped the more her shorts clung to her body. Finally, realizing that her efforts were to no avail, she draped the towel around her waist and sat down on Sam's cot.

"This calls for a drink," said Sam, groping for the bottle he had stashed under his cot.

June reached into the basket and took out the four silver goblets. She filled them with ice and handed them to Sam, who poured a generous portion into each glass.

Lazo took his goblet and asked, "May I propose a toast?"

"You certainly may, you rascal, you," declared Virginia, "but you will forgive pooh little me if I choose not to stand."

"I understand and I'm sorry."

"Don't be sorry. It was all in good fun and I really quite enjoyed it, you know. It cooled me off considerably."

Lazo raised his goblet and said, "Here's to friends and friendship."

"Here, here," responded Sam.

The four raised their goblets and emptied them.

Sam filled the glasses again and said; "Now it's my turn. Here's to love, may it always triumph."

"I'll drink to that," declared Virginia. She raised the goblet to her lips and emptied it. "Now," she continued, "is it really necessary to go to the beach for our picnic? May we not, in deference to a young lady with wet shorts, picnic right heah in this little old tent? I'll be beholding to you all."

"I don't see why not."

"Oh thank you evah so much, Lazo," declared Virginia, as she leaped up and planted a big kiss on his lips. As she did so, she reached behind and dropped an ice cube down the back of his jump suit.

"You sneaky devil!" shouted Lazo, as he wiggled his body until the ice cube fell down his pant leg and came to rest on the floor. "Why I thought you loved me?"

"But ah do, Lazo, ah sincerely do." protested Virginia.

Lazo reached down, picked up the ice cube and put it into his goblet. "Here's to the devil in all of us. May she always have cause to laugh."

"That's beautiful," said June, recovering from her fit of laughter. She walked up to Lazo and gave him a prolonged kiss.

"Don't I get one?" asked Sam.

"You sure do, doesn't he, Jinny?" The two girls rushed over to him and each gave him a big kiss. "Now, how's that?"

"Terrific, Virginia. I never felt better. And now, how in hell do we set up a picnic in this tent?"

"It will be easy," responded June. "All we have to do is put the blankets on the floor, here between the two cots. You get that one Jinny and I'll get this one."

They removed the blankets from the cots and spread them neatly on the floor, one on top of the other.

"What about a backrest?" asked Sam. "I like to rest my back against a tree when I picnic."

"We could use the footlockers."

"That's a splendid idea, Lazo. We can put them on this side," said June, as she walked over and indicated with her hand, where the lockers should be positioned.

"Hop to it, Sam, we don't have all night, you know."

"You're a born commander, Ginny, I mean mam," replied Sam, as he saluted her, quite correctly.

"You get the basket, Lazo."

"Consider it done," replied Lazo, as he picked up the heavy basket and set it down on the blanket.

"Now that looks great," declared June, as she sat down and tested one of the footlockers with her back.

"Pour us another drink, Sam, before we get too comfortable."

"Okay, Laz, coming right up."

While Sam poured the drinks, Lazo sat down next to June. "This isn't half bad. As a matter of fact, it's better than the beach."

"Do you really think so, or are you all just saying that to make me feel better?" asked Virginia, seating herself on the other side of Lazo and pressing her thigh against his.

"No, I really mean it," insisted Lazo. "The flies on the beach are a terrible nuisance. They would drive you insane."

"Here they are," said Sam, as he walked over, holding the four goblets in one hand and the bottle in the other.

"Be careful, Sam," cautioned Lazo. "We don't want to waste any of that expensive booze."

"Don't worry Laz. Just watch this." He walked over to the side of Virginia, crossed his legs and slowly eased himself downward, sans arms, until his seat made contact with the blanket.

"See, I didn't spill a drop."

Each of them took a goblet and began to drink.

"Do you know something," declared Sam, "I can't remember ever being happier than I am at this moment."

"You don't mean that. It's just the liquor talking."

"I really mean it, June. You'll never know how lonesome the life of a fat, friendless Jew boy can be."

"You fat? That's impossible!"

"It's a fact, June. Just ask Lazo."

"Is that true?" queried June.

Lazo seemed a bit reluctant to respond.

"Ah, go ahead Lazo, tell her about our first meeting."

"It's true June. When I first met Sam, he was a fat slob."

"You didn't have to put it quite so indelicately," retorted Sam, pretending to take umbrage.

"How did you two meet?" asked June.

"I thought this was to be a party," replied Lazo. "Let's drink and be happy."

June, sensing that her question was out of line, raised her glass and said, "Here's to the moment, may it last forever."

Lazo touched his goblet to hers and whispered, "Will tiefe, tiefe Ewigkeit."

"What in tarnation are you talking about?"

"It's nothing," replied June, "Lazo simply commented on the eternal dimensions of joy."

"Where did you learn German?" asked Lazo.

"At college," replied June.

"Do you mean to tell me that I am sitting next to one of those spoiled college brats."

"Yup, Laz, you are. As a matter of fact, you are sitting next to two spoiled and pampered college brats."

"You mean .... "

Before he could finish, Virginia shouted, "Universuty of Kentucky, class of '42!"

Lazo then turned to Sam, "Not you too?"

"Yup, Columbia, 1940."

"Don't feel bad," said June. "We still love you. Now what say we eat."

June carefully removed the contents from the basket and placed them on the blanket.

"I declah, have you evah seen anything so exquisite? I'll have to give daddy a big kiss."

"Where in hell did he get all of this food?"

"He had it flown in from Cairo. Wasn't that nice of daddy?"

"It certainly was," replied Lazo. "I'll bet there's enough food to serve ten."

"That's what you think," retorted Sam. "Hell, I bet I could eat half of it myself."

"What's that stuff in the little jar?" asked Lazo.

"You really don't know!" exclaimed June. "Your education has been sorely neglected." She reached over and spread some of the stuff on a cracker. "And now, my dear, open your mouth and allow me to introduce you to caviar." She put the cracker into his mouth and waited for a response. "Do you like it?"

"Not really. It's a bit salty for my blood." He took a drink to rinse away the taste. "You know," he continued, "I can't imagine why people are willing to pay so much for so little."

"Nor can I," replied June, "but perhaps our tastes are not sufficiently cultivated to appreciate such delicacies."

"Perhaps you're right."

Then the four stacked their beautiful china plates with the splendid food which the Colonel had so generously provided. It was a repast, sumptuous enough to titillate the palate of the most discriminating gourmet. When their hungers were sufficiently sated, the few morsels which remained, would not have been enough to cloy the appetite of a humming bird.

"See, didn't I tell you, Laz?"

"What did you tell me?"

Sam ushered the only surviving grape to his mouth and as he bit into it, some of its sweetness managed to elude his tongue and stroll down his chin. He brushed his chin with the fine linen napkin and said, "Didn't I tell you that we would be able to devour the contents of the basket."

"Yes you did," replied Lazo, "and if I hadn't seen it with my own two eyes, I never would have believed it."

"I guess we're just a bunch of gluttons," declared Virginia, as she dabbed at the corner of her mouth with her napkin.

"I don't feel like a glutton," proclaimed June, reaching into the basket and removing an oddly shaped bottle.

"What is it?" queried Sam.

"It's called Slivovitz."

"Oh, I've heard of it," remarked Lazo. "It's a brandy distilled from plums."

"Yes," replied June, as she broke the seal and removed the cork. "Now before I pour," she continued, "I would like you to wipe out your goblets so that you may enjoy the pure flavor of the brandy."

"May ah pour?" asked Virginia.

"Of course you may, but first, don't you think we ought to switch on the lights? It's getting a little dark in here."

"Not the lights," replied Virginia. "Let's light the candle."

"What candle?"

"The one ah put into the basket, of course."

Virginia removed the candle and closed the basket. She placed her plate on the basket and asked, "May I have a light?"

"Of course," replied Lazo, as he flicked his lighter and extended the flame to Virginia.

She lit the candle and held it so that the melting wax fell upon the plate. When enough of the wax had collected on the plate, she placed the candle into it and held it firmly until the wax had hardened, fusing the candle to the plate. As she removed her hand from the candle, she said, "Now that's much more romantic, isn't it?"

"May Ah have your goblet, Sam?"

Sam handed his goblet to Virginia and she poured a goodly amount into it. Then she poured about the same amount into June's goblet.

"How about me?" asked Lazo.

Virginia turned and held the bottle over Lazo's goblet for what seemed to be a very long time, pretending to pour him a very generous amount of brandy.

"Not too much now," cautioned Lazo.

"Don't worry, I'll take good care of you," she replied, as she withdrew the bottle.

"Aren't you going to have any?" asked June.

"Ah certainly am," replied Virginia, pouring some into her goblet.

Lazo looked into his goblet and could scarcely believe what he saw. Perhaps the dim light was blunting his otherwise perfect vision. There wasn't enough Slivovitz in his goblet to cover the bottom.

"Hold my glass while Ah replace the cork."

"Sure," replied Lazo. He looked into her goblet and saw that hers contained even less than his and he began to wonder what kind of devilish prank she was up to.

"May Ah have my drink?"

Lazo returned it to her and she raised it and said, "May this brandy serve to bind us together forevah." Then she turned to Lazo and said, "Bottoms up."

They raised their vessels and quickly dispatched the brandy. Now, none of them had ever tasted Slivovitz and were not prepared for the harsh strength of the liquor.

"Some water, please!" cried June, frantically waving her hand before her mouth.

"Me too," pleaded Virginia, pretending that her throat was on fire.

Lazo hastily took the ice bucket and filled his goblet with the water that had been produced by the melting ice. He handed it to June, knowing that Virginia was only acting. June filled her mouth with the cold water and then handed the glass to Virginia.

"Wow! That's potent stuff," remarked Sam. "I didn't realize that plums could be so devastating."

"Ah guess we just drank it too rapidly," announced Virginia, as she extended the vessel to Lazo. "Care for some watah?" she asked.

"Not really, Ginny, but I will have some more of that brandy."

"You mean you really like it?" asked June.

"As a matter of fact, I really do."

"I'll have some more also," said Sam, holding out his goblet.

"Why don't we all have anothah," suggested Virginia, quite solicitously.

"Okay, but this time I'm just sipping it. No bottoms up for me," replied June. "My mouth is still numb."

"Good," said Virginia as she poured generous portions into June's and Sam's glasses. Lazo held out his goblet and again received a very small ration. Then she poured a few drops into her glass and pretended to sip. As custodian of the bottle, she continued to pour in the same manner, until both Sam and June were quite drunk. They were sipping the brandy quite rapidly and Virginia knew it would not be long before the two would be terribly drunk or terribly ill. She did not have long to wait before her diabolical scheme came to fruition. Sam was the first to succumb. He slowly rose to his feet and said,

"I feel sick." He fell upon his cot, and was heard from no more.

"Where is Sam?" asked June. "Where did he go? I want Sam." She began to rise but before she was upright, she mumbled, "I feel sick. I think I'm gonna throw up."

Virginia jumped to her feet and steadied June. "Ah, better help her find her way back. In her condition, she'd probably end up in the sea."

"Yes," replied Lazo, "you had better see her to bed."

"I'll take good care of her. Don't worry your lil ole head ovah it."

See you tomorrow," said Lazo, as he watched the two stumble out of the tent.

When he was certain that they were well out of hearing range, he walked over to Sam and said, "It's safe now. You can get up."

"Are you quite sure?"

"Of course, I'm sure."

Sam rolled over on his back and began to laugh. Lazo joined in and the tent became alive with their laughter.

"We've got to hurry if we're going to pull this off," said Lazo, pulling Sam off from his cot.

"Thanks buddy, for warning me about the drinks."

"It was nothing. By the way, what did you do with the brandy you didn't drink?"

"I poured it into the canteen cup that I keep under my cot."

"Well, I'll be damned."

"Look here," said Sam, as he reached under his cot and picked up the cup.

"Oh my God, she really wanted you out, didn't she?"

"Yeh, but we'll get even with her won't we all?"

Lazo took the canteen cup and raised it to his lips.

"What the hell are you doing!"

"I'm having a drink. I don't know about you, but I'm still thirsty as hell."

Lazo took several large swallows and handed the cup back to Sam. "The way I figure it, Sam, we've got about a half hour to prepare our revenge."

"Do you really think that she will be back that soon?"

"You bet your sweet ass I do. I'll clean up this mess while you get yourself a real close shave and don't forget to use my after shave lotion."

"But I just shaved this morning," protested Sam.

"I know," replied Lazo, "but your beard is much coarser than mine and we don't want her to recognize you, do we."

"Okay, I guess you're right. Where's your aftershave?"

"Right there, on the shelf, now get going."

"Okay, okay. I'll be back before you can say Hitler's mustache," remarked Sam, exiting the tent.

While Sam was gone, Lazo tidied up the tent. Then he carefully placed his duffle bag and some sorted laundry on Sam's cot and covered the cot with a blanket. Then he picked up his pillow and the bottle of Slivovitz and waited for Sam to return. "Hitler's mustache!" shouted Sam as he entered the tent.

"Did you douse yourself with the aftershave?"

"Sure did. Can't you smell it?"

Sam returned his gear to the shelf and sat down on Lazo's cot. "Well Buddy," said Lazo, "it's all up to you now." As he exited the tent, he turned and whispered, "Good hunting."

Sam fell back upon the cot and closed his eyes, pretending to be asleep. Soon the tent flap was thrown back and the much awaited event began to unfold. Virginia tiptoed over to the candle and gently blew it out. Then she unbuttoned her shorts and allowed them to fall softly to the floor.

"You were expecting me, weren't you, Lazo," she whispered, as she put her body on top of his. Then she put her lips to his and pressed downward, until consumed by desire, she began to move her hips back and forth, over him. Then she raised herself upward and delicately ushered herself downward, until her hips pressed fully against him.

It was well after midnight when Virginia departed the darkened tent and made her way back to her quarters. Sam, exhausted and happy closed his eyes and was asleep.

CHAPTER SEVEN

The morning broke quite splendidly but Lazo was not at all taken with its beauty. His senses, usually acute, were numbed by the lack of sleep and it took him several minutes to determine his bearings. He painfully raised himself from the bench upon which he had slept. His pillow fell to the floor. He bent down to retrieve it but half way down, his head began to pound and he became very dizzy. He cautiously righted himself and propped his body against the wall. He remained in this precarious position until his body had partially regained its equilibrium. Then feeling more confident, he stooped down, still retaining his head in an upright position, and ever so carefully picked up the pillow, muttering, "There you little bastard, I've got you." Then making certain that the pillow was securely tucked under his arm, he picked up the blanket and with carefully measured steps, walked out into the morning freshness. As he neared the tent he wondered if Virginia was still there and so to avoid any unnecessary embarrassment, he stopped before entering, yanked on the tent rope and shouted, "Are you decent?"

"Yeh, come on in, Lazo."

"Is Virginia there?"

"No, she left quite some time ago."

Lazo entered the tent, dropped his bedding to the floor and fell face downward on his cot.

"What's the matter, buddy? You look like hell. Didn't you sleep well?"

"You know damned well I didn't," replied Lazo.

"Where did you spend the night?" asked Sam.

"In the damned latrine!"

"You mean you slept in the goddamn latrine," remarked Sam, trying not to laugh!

Lazo reached out, grabbed his pillow and said, "You're damned right I did."

"Well, I'll be a son of a gun."

Lazo rolled over on his back and carefully positioned his pillow under his head. Then looking directly at Sam, asked, "How did it go for you?"

"I've never been so happy."

"You can't be serious."

"I've never been more serious. I love that girl and I'm going to tell her so."

"After what we did! You've got to be out of your mind! Hell, we'll be lucky if we don't get court maritaled!"

Sam stood up and walked to the far side of the tent. Then he turned. "What the hell should I do?"

"Leave it alone! Just leave it alone!"

Lazo rolled over and buried his head in the pillow. He closed his eyes and was about to drop off when he heard the sound of footsteps outside the tent.

"Jesus H Christ, you don't suppose they've scheduled the briefing at this ungodly hour do you?"

"You can never tell, Laz. After all, this is the army," responded Sam as he walked toward the front of the tent and looked out.

"Who in hell is coming?"

Sam did not reply. He ran out of the tent and shouted, "Good morning, June!"

"Good morning, Sam. I came to pick up the basket. Is Lazo in?"

"Yeh, June. He's in the tent but he is not in the best of moods. It seems he slept in the latrine last night and beside that, he has a peach of a hangover.

The two entered and saw a rather distressed Lazo, hunched over in a sitting position. He had managed, with some difficulty, to right himself and from the pained expression on his face; it was obvious that he was not feeling at all well.

"Good morning, Lazo," pealed June, "too much slivovitz last night?"

Before he could respond, she sat down and gently put her arm around him.

"She's come to get the basket."

"I heard her, Sam! I'm not deaf, you know!"

"Do you want me to leave?" asked June, apologetically.

"No June, I'll be okay. Just give me a couple of minutes."

"Maybe what you need is a good slug of scotch," declared Sam, reaching under the cot and picking up the almost empty bottle.

"Maybe you're right. I've got to try something. It can't make me feel any worse than I do right now."

Sam handed him the bottle. Lazo raised it to his lips and took a healthy belt.

"God, that tastes awful. I don't know if I can keep it down."

"Just sit quietly and if it feels like it's going to come up, swallow and keep swallowing until it settles," prescribed June and she gave him a gentle squeeze.

"I think it's going to work! It's actually going to stay down. Hell, I feel a little better," declared Lazo shaking his head to dislodge the cobwebs that were numbing his sensibilities.

"Then perhaps you will begin acting with some civility," taunted June. "After all, you are supposed to be an officer and a gentleman."

"Gee, I thought I behaved like a real gentleman last night." Lazo swallowed and grimaced.

"What do you mean by that?" asked June.

"Oh nothing, nothing at all," replied Sam, "he's not at all himself."

"Well, that's what you get for drinking too much," taunted June.

"You should talk," replied Lazo. "You should have seen yourself. Why you were a veritable glutton."

"Did I do anything foolish or stupid?"

"Of course you did," replied Lazo. "Haven't you ever been that drunk before?"

"Just once, Lazo, when I was a junior in high school. A friend and I drank a quart of gin, sans any mix. I was in bed for two days with what my mother dismissed as the flu. Boy was I sick." She paused and seemed to relive that moment's painful indiscretion. Then she turned to Lazo and beseeched, "Now be honest with me. Did I really make a fool of myself, last night?"

"You really don't remember, do you?"

"No, Lazo, I don't remember anything after the Slivovitz."

"Then allow me to enlighten you. After all, it was you who suggested that we play the game."

"What game?" asked June, almost in a whisper.

"Why, 'hold-your-breath' of course."

"I've never heard of that game."

"You haven't!" exclaimed Lazo, with feigned incredulity. "Why it was you who taught us how to play it."

"Me! How can that be possible when I have never heard of the game? How do you play it?"

"It's quite simple," replied Lazo. "You suggested and we all agreed that we each take a small piece of tissue paper, and after taking a deep breath, put the paper to our lips, making sure that our lips were moist enough to guarantee that the paper would cling to them."

Lazo watched as Sam leaned forward attentively. He was amazed at Lazo's inventiveness and didn't want to miss a word.

"Would you like to take it from here, Sam?" asked Lazo with a devilish grin.

"No, Ah think not. You all are doing splendidly."

"Okay, but hand me the bottle, I feel a slight thirst."

It was obvious that Lazo's request was just a ploy. He needed some time to fabricate the rest of the game.

"Go on," urged June.

"Alright, I will," responded Lazo, returning the bottle to Sam. "After we had all taken a deep breath and fixed the paper to our lips, we pinched our nostrils to prevent the air from entering."

"Oh, I see," remarked June. "Eventually we would have to exhale and the papers would fall from our lips."

"Precisely," replied Lazo. "You see, you are beginning to remember."

"Then, what happens?"

"She doesn't remember," yelled Lazo, as he laughed and slapped his thighs in pretended disbelief. "The loser had to divest himself, or in this case, herself, of one article of clothing."

"You meant that one article of clothing would be sacrificed for each loss?"

"That's the way it was," responded Lazo. "And besides losing an article of clothing, you had to bottoms-up one inch of Slivovitz."

"And who, pray tell, lost the first round."

"Virginia did." replied Lazo.

"And what article did she sacrifice?" asked June.

"Her hair ribbon, of course. She lost her ribbon, but after that, it was all your game. You kept losing quite convincingly ."

"You mean..... "stammered June.

"Yup," uttered Lazo, "you lost the next three games in a row."

"But that was all I had on."

"We noticed that," said Sam. "After your third loss, you stood on the footlocker to drink the Slivovitz."

"I didn't," whispered June, with the kind of reluctance that suggested that she really didn't wish to know.

"Yes," shouted Sam, with a diabolical laugh. "Then you gingerly slipped off your panties and tossed them to Lazo."

June did not respond. She folded her arms atop her upper torso in an unconscious attempt to conceal herself but she could not conceal her embarrassment. She kept backing up until her body pushed against the canvas, signaling the end of her retreat. Then she stopped and raised her face upward to conceal the film of moisture that was already developing under her closed eyelids.

Lazo, embarrassed by the pain he had inflicted, raised himself from his cot and walked up to her. He put his arm around her shoulders and tried to console her. She grabbed his arm and pushed it away. Then she turned from him and said, "I don't need your sympathy, so please get the hell away from me!"

"You are right," replied Lazo. "You really don't need my kindness but I need yours. We all do."

"What do you mean?"

"You tell her, Sam."

"Yes, tell me, Sam."

Sam looked down at the floor and said, "We didn't play any game last night. And no, you didn't doff any of your clothing."

June turned to face the two conspirators, "You mean I didn't make a fool of myself!"

"Of course not," replied Sam, "unless you consider passing out to be foolish."

"I did pass out, then."

"You sure did," laughed Lazo, "colder than a picnic lunch."

"And the rest was plain malarkey!"

Before anyone could respond, she grabbed Lazo's pillow and began to pelt him about the head. "You think you're pretty damned clever, don't you? I'll fix you!"

Lazo beat a hasty retreat and fell upon his cot, face down. He covered his head with his arms to ward off the blows, which rained down upon him.

"Stop it!" pleaded Lazo. "I give up! I give up! I surrender, honest I do!"

"Unconditionally?"

"Yes, unconditionally."

June dropped the pillow but after only a brief pause, decided that he had not paid sufficiently for his mischief. She swooped down upon him and began to tickle him, mercilessly.

Sam, sensing that it would be only a moment before June would have cause to regret her breech of the truce, turned and said, "I'm going to the latrine so that you two can enjoy your little war, in peace."

Sam had no sooner left than June found herself on the defensive, with her arms pinned firmly above her head. She responded by kicking and turning her hips back and forth, trying to shed her indomitable adversary but his strength was overpowering and soon he had her hips firmly pinioned between his knees. Her exertions became futile pretensions.

"Do you surrender?"

"I do! I really do!"

Lazo carefully withdrew his hands from her wrists. She shook her hands vigorously, not so much to restore circulation, as to disengage his attention.

"Now, would you kindly get off of me," she exhorted.

But before he could respond, she dug her fingers into his ribs and began to tickle him again.

"So this be your womanly honor!" He grabbed her arms and pinned them to her sides.

"Please let me go!" she pleaded. "I'll quit! I'll quit!"

"Do you promise?"

He didn't wait for her response. He bent down and secured the zipper tongue of her jumpsuit with his teeth and began to pull it downward, ever so carefully. She struggled but her efforts were in vain. She pleaded but the devil in him was now, so completely aroused, that he was not about to stop.

"Please, I'm not wearing anything under these coveralls. Someone might come in."

Lazo tugged at the zipper until the poplin fell away, completely exposing her ample breasts. He began to caress them with his lips. As he did so, he noticed that she was no longer struggling but indeed, seemed to be enjoying his attentions. Soon he had the zipper tongue in his mouth once again and pulled it downward until he felt hair spring out against his lips. Her stomach began to pitch feverishly and he knew that she was his.

"Please," she whispered, "let go of my hands so I can get out of this suit."

He released her hands and she raised herself on one elbow and began to wriggle and tug on the sleeve until one of her arms was completely free. She was about to remove the other arm when she heard the sound of footsteps. Lazo jumped up from his cot. June quickly returned her arm into its sleeve and hastily restored the zipper to a more dignified position.

"Who is there?" yelled Lazo.

"Major Featherstone," came the reply. "You've got exactly one half hour until your final briefing. Now don't disappoint us."

"Very good sir," replied Lazo. "I wouldn't miss it for the world."

"By the way, you haven't seen the girls, have you? The Colonel has been looking for them. Something about a picnic basket."

"No," replied Lazo, "but if I see them, I will tell them that you had inquired as to their wherabouts."

"Good. We'll see you in half an hour then."

The two waited until the Major's footsteps were no longer audible, then June said, "My God, I've got to get out of here. The Colonel will have my hide."

She arose from the cot but about half way up, she let out a scream and began to giggle.

"What's the matter?" asked Lazo.

"Can't you guess," replied June, holding her body in a bent position, daring not to straighten out.

"No," replied Lazo, "is it your back?"

"No, you damned fool, can't you see!" retorted June pointing to her zipper.

Lazo looked where she had directed and beheld a number of auburn strands extruding from the teeth of her zipper. He fell back upon the cot and began to chuckle.

"It's not that amusing. Now give me a hand," she exhorted. "This damned zipper is stuck!"

Lazo quickly positioned himself on the edge of the cot. "Turn around and come over here," he directed, trying desperately to stop laughing.

She, obedient to his command, shuffled over to him. He leaned forward to investigate the source of her discomfiture. As he did he chuckled and asked, "Now tell the gut doktor, ver it hurts."

"Oh, you're funny, aren't you?"

"Vell vat vil you have me do? Shall I pool them aus?"

"You do and I'll clobber you, so help me."

"Well, I see two alternatives," said Lazo. "One embarrassing and the other painful."

"What do you mean?" asked June.

"Well," mused Lazo, stroking his chin, while reaching for the zipper with his free hand, "I could unzip you, but someone might walk in. That could be embarrassing for both of us."

"And the other?"

He looked up at her and she beheld a kind of sadistic grin, etched on his otherwise gentle countenance.

"You wouldn't! You wouldn't dare!"

She tried to shuffle back, out of his reach but before she could do so, his fingers made contact with her ribs and he began to tickle her. She let out a scream and reached down with both hands to massage the area of pain, but she stopped short of embarrassment and squeezed her thighs together to ease the sting.

"Thank you, Doctor," whispered June, removing the strands from her zipper. "You really are a devil, you know."

"Aren't you going to inquire about my fee?"

"Of course. And what might you be exacting for that devilishly clever procedure?"

"I would like a lock of your hair."

She looked directly at him, and with reddened face, said, "You don't mean..... "

Before she could complete the sentence, he said, "No, I don't mean that. No, I want a lock of hair from your head."

"Oh, is that all," replied June, quite relieved. "I thought you meant the other."

"Come here," he directed, with feigned paternalistic exasperation.

She walked over and settled herself on his knee. He kissed the top of her head and said, "Do you know something, I think I'm becoming terribly fond of you."

June pulled her head back and looking quite wistfully, said, "I feel the same way." She gazed at the floor and asked, "Is there someone else?"

"Yes," replied Lazo, "there is."

"Is she beautiful?"

Before he could respond, she placed a finger on his lips and said, "No, don't tell me. I had no right to ask you that."

He gently removed her finger and kissed the tip of her nose. "You had every right to ask. Yes, she is beautiful, very beautiful and until I met you, she was the most beautiful girl I had ever touched."

"Damn this war anyway," she cried, "I do so want to be with you." She threw her arms around his neck and gave him the most passionate kiss he had ever experienced. Then she jumped up from his lap and ran out of the tent, leaving Lazo in a state of complete bewilderment. He began to feel that he had betrayed Ilse's love yet he felt no real sense of guilt or remorse. "How very strange," he thought. "How very strange."

His musings were cut short by Sam, who entered the tent and deposited himself on his footlocker.

"Well, what do you have to say for yourself, buddy?"

"What do you mean?"

"I met June, running back to her quarters."

"Well?"

"She was crying. Why was she crying, Lazo?"

"Look Sam, I don't have time to explain it to you now. We have less than a half hour before our final briefing."

"Hell, Lazo, that means we'll be leaving soon."

"That's what we've been waiting for, isn't it?"

"I guess so," replied Sam, "but I sure would like to tell Virginia about last night."

"Look, you'll have plenty of time to tell her when this war is over, so let's get our asses in gear. We wouldn't want to disappoint the Colonel, would we?"

"Why the hell not!" retorted Sam, conveying his displeasure. "By the way, I told June about last night."

"You did what?"

"I told her about Virginia,"

"How did she react?"

"She wiped her eyes and began to smile."

"She wasn't angry with us?"

"No, but as she left she said that she now understood why you slept in the latrine."

"She's one helluva gal," remarked Lazo. He put his arm around Sam, smiled and said, "Well, let's get going. Afterall, we do have a rendezvous with destiny. "And in the words of Allan Seeger," replied Sam, "we shall not fail that, rendezvous."

With that, the two left the tent and went forth, into the morning of adventure.

CHAPTER EIGHT

The day that they had so anxiously awaited had finally arrived. The two young soldiers silently climbed up and dropped into the belly of the aircraft that would carry them away. Even as they sat down upon the canvas benches, the crew of the B-24 was preparing the plane for takeoff. Lazo's sojourn in North Africa was at an end and would soon be transformed, as if by some sleight of hand, into that memory where all of our yesterdays meld into that one collective timelessness, we call history. Neither of them spoke. Perhaps they had still not fully recovered from the shock of their hurried departure. Lazo kept unfolding and folding a small piece of paper, upon which had been scribbled the number, 887-4145.

After having secured the number in his mind, he rolled the paper into a tight ball and with a deft flip of his wrist, sent it to the other side of the ship, where it collided with the metal skin and dropped to the floor. Its feeble whisper was marked only by Lazo and soon, even for him, it would shrivel and die. "Oh how the events betray each other," he thought, as he reached into his pocket and drew out a cigarette. He was about to light it when he noticed Sam pointing to a sign which read, "No Smoking While the Aircraft is Taxiing."

The pilot gunned the engines and the plane began to rush down the runway, gathering speed until it was pulled skyward by its four powerful engines. Lazo waited until satisfied that the plane had succeeded in its bout with gravity, lit his cigarette. He took a long drag and as he removed the cigarette, a bit of paper had adhered to his upper lip. He chuckled softly as he pulled it away.

"What's so funny?"

"Oh nothing, I was just reminded of how June reacted when we told her about the game."

"Oh that," replied Sam. "She's quite a gal."

"Boy, that's an understatement if I've ever heard one!"

"I guess you are right. They were wonderful. Do you think we'll ever see them again."

Lazo drew on his cigarette and blew the smoke upward. He watched it until it flattened against the ceiling and disappeared.

"I doubt it."

"What do you mean?" asked Sam.

"We've got as much chance as a snowball in hell."

"I don't know about you," replied Sam, "but I promised myself that I was going to survive this war and I intend to do just that."

"Who the hell do you think you're kidding! If the Germans don't get us, the Chetniks, or the Partisans or the USTASHI will."

"It's not funny," retorted Sam, in a voice which did not mask his perturbation. "Who the hell are the Ustashi?"

"Oh, all right, I'll tell you. The Ustashi is a group of Croatian Nazis headed up by the sadistic Ante Pavelich."

"Thanks for nothing."

Lazo let the half consumed cigarette drop to the floor. He crushed it under his boot, closed his eyes for a moment and would perhaps have fallen asleep; for the previous night's revelry had left him quite exhausted.

"Are you afraid to die?" asked Sam.

Lazo opened his eyes and said,"No, I'm not afraid to die, but I don't want to die."

"Same difference," replied Sam.

"We all die, Sam, but it is how we die that lends significance to our lives . Thomas Mann said, 'that it is only after we lose our fear of death that living becomes possible'."

"And death," added Sam.

"That's a goddam cynical point of view."

"Not any more than yours, Lazo. Not any more than yours."

"Then really, there's no reason for living."

"Perhaps not," replied Sam, "but in a little while, we'll both find out, won't we."

Lazo did not respond. He folded his arms behind his head and leaned back against the fuselage. He looked upward then closed his eyes and pretended to go to sleep.

"You tired?"

Lazo did not reply. He hoped that his continued silence would indicate to Sam that he wished to be alone with his thoughts. He knew that Sam would understand and soon Lazo's thoughts began to overflow with images of Ilse. He was back in Wisconsin, walking down a country road. Ilse was at his side. He could almost feel the strap of his duffel bag digging into his shoulder. It was a brilliant day.

Erika had offered to drive him to the bus depot but Ilse would not hear of it. She insisted that the two of them walk into town. Lazo pretended to demur but he was genuinely happy with Ilse's suggestion.

He wanted, very much, to be alone with her. There were so many things to talk about and so little time. It was, after all, only a three mile walk.

He remembered Hermann saying, "That's a very long walk and your duffel bag must weigh at least fifty pounds."

"Oh let them be, papa. Don't you see that they want to be alone," scolded Erika. "Remember when you were young?"

"Ja, I guess I'm just an old fool. I forgot that love can ease the pain of any burden."

Lazo remembered the blush that came to Ilse's face and he began to smile. "Don't worry about me" he remembered saying, "I could easily run that distance with a full field pack on my back."

And so the two walked up the path, the very same path upon which their destinies first intersected, he remembered Erika shouting, "Come back to us! Lazo, please come back!" He was deeply moved by her words but he could make no reply. He was afraid that the lump in his throat would betray his manhood. He followed Ilse up the path and it pleasured him immensely to watch the elegant grace with which her long, slender legs carried her up the path. Her oversized sweat shirt and blue jeans, rolled up to her knees did not detract from her natural beauty.

Then without warning, she bent over and picked two Indian Paintbrushes that grew along the path. As she did, the hem of her sweatshirt fell down toward her chin. Sensing what had happened but without embarrassment, she straightened up and tucked the sweatshirt into her jeans. She turned and pressed one of the flowers against Lazo's lips and the other against hers. Then she deftly spliced the stems together and said, "I will hide these near the deep pool where once we sat and when you return, we will seek after them together."

Lazo's musings were cut short by Sam's voice, "This is it."

"What?"

"We have five minutes until we reach the drop zone."

"That can't be," replied Lazo, looking at his watch. "We're at least an hour away. What the hell's going on?"

"The limey sergeant, said something about favorable winds."

"Oh," replied Lazo, "I guess the gods are favoring our mission, after all."

The two men checked their equipment, as they moved toward the open cargo door. The sergeant checked them over quite carefully and said, "Well, gentlemen good luck and God speed."

The green light went on. Lazo stepped forward. Then he turned and looked at Sam, "This is a helluva way to drop in on my native land."

"See you down there!" yelled Sam

Lazo did not hear Sam. He was already plummeting through space. Sam waited until Lazo's chute had opened and then he too jumped out, following Lazo to the ground. Upon alighting the two scrupulously buried their chutes and began to move in a westerly direction.

"Are you sure that we are heading in the right direction?" asked Sam, looking over Lazo's shoulder.

"Of course,""replied Lazo, "I do know how to read a compass, you know."

"This is too damned easy."

"What do you mean?" asked Lazo.

"It's too damned casual."

"What the hell did you expect?"

"I don't know but it can't be this easy."

"Well, easy or not, let's put some distance between us and the drop zone."

"Do you think we were spotted?"

"You can never tell," replied Lazo. "Someone may have heard the plane."

"Well," replied Sam, "if someone did hear or see us, let's hope that it was the Partisans and not the Chetniks."

"Right," agreed Lazo, quickening his pace.

"How far will we have to go before we reach the Partisans?"

"As near as I can reckon, about twenty-five miles. We'll know for sure when we reach the Drina River."

The two men kept walking until the darkness forced them to discontinue. They settled down for the night and tried to get some sleep. Lazo didn't sleep much. The strange sounds of the forest and Sam's constant snoring were sufficient to guarantee him, a restless and interminable night.

At long last, the night gave way to dawn. Lazo grabbed Sam by the shoulder and shook him. The vigor with which he applied his hand could be attributed more to the frustration of a sleepless night than to the desire for a successful mission.

"What the hell are you doing!" shouted Sam, as he pushed Lazo's hand away. "Just trying to awaken you. It's time to go on."

"Oh, is that all? I thought, from the way you were shaking me, that we were beset by the entire Chetnik army."

"No, but if you continue shouting, we very well may be," replied Lazo, quite sarcastically.

"What's for breakfast?" queried Sam. He slowly raised himself to his feet and tried to reduce the stiffness of his body by swinging his arms and arching his back. These gestures, accompanied by a series of facial grimaces and contortions, served to bring a smile to Lazo's face.

Lazo reached for his musette bag and removed two K-ration boxes. He threw one of them to Sam and said, "Here, eat hardy. God only knows when we will eat again."

"Is this all we have?" asked Sam, in a voice that matched the expression on his face.

"Yup, that's all we have but don't fret. By midday, we should be devouring some damned good Slavic sausages."

"Do you think so?"

"Of course I do. We should reach the Drina River just about noon."

"Well, what the hell are we waiting for? Let's get cracking," said Sam as he munched on one of the stale crackers.

"Good," replied Lazo, "we can eat as we go along."

The two soldiers resumed their pilgrimage, eager to reach the Partisans lines before noon. Lazo led the way and Sam could not help but admire the ease with which Lazo moved through the forest. Lazo, taken with the beauty of the breath-taking landscape, began to wonder about the sanity of his parents. "How could anyone," he thought, "leave this almost idyllic wonderland for the rather harsh environment of northern Minnesota.

The two proceeded, without incident, for about two hours, when suddenly Lazo stopped, turned and put his finger to his lips.

"Listen," whispered Lazo, "Do you hear it?"

"Hear what?"

"The water."

"I don't hear anything."

"Are you deaf, man?"

"Of course not but I don't hear any water."

"You will," declared Lazo, as he quickened his pace, eager to see the rushing waters of the Drina.

"I hear it! I hear it!"

"Thank God," retorted Lazo, "you had me frightened."

They advanced about a hundred yards when Lazo pointed and shouted, "There it is! The Drina!"

Sam hurried to catch up, eager to see the river and its promise of safety.

"I think you're right. I really think you're right."

"What do you mean?"

"I think we're going to make it."

"I didn't doubt it for a minute," declared Lazo. "It is a rather beautiful sight, nevertheless."

"Yes it is. It's so very peaceful that one might easily forget that there is a war going on."

The ugliness of war did not interfere with the joy that our two adventurers were experiencing as they rushed to the river's edge. To the casual observer, they might have been two young school boys rushing to refresh themselves in the cool water, on this very warm September day. Their youthful enthusiasm had carried them beyond the river's edge but they did not heed the water lapping at their ankles. Sam was the first to retreat from the water. As he did, one could discern a certain calmness on his face.

"What do we do now?" he asked.

"Huh?"

"What do we do now?"

"Oh," replied Lazo, as he stepped back out of the water. "I guess we'll have to reconnoiter the area and find a safe place to cross into Bosnia."

"How far is it?"

"You've been looking at it," replied Lazo, with a chuckle.

"You mean ...."

"Yup, that's it. Let's get cracking."

The two followed the river, downstream, keeping their conversation to a minimum. They both knew that they would not be safe until they reached the opposite bank. They walked along the bank, looking for a place to ford but the river was too wide and the current too strong.

"What's that, over there?"

"Where?"

"There, in the bushes."

"I see it. It looks like the prow of an old row boat."

The two ran over to the greying, half hidden boat and pulled it out of its concealment.

"Not a bad discovery," declared Sam, his voice conveying more than a modicum of pride.

"Not bad. I think we can cross with it, if only …"

"If only what?" asked Sam.

"If only we could find the oars," replied Lazo.

"Aren't they in the boat?"

"Give me a hand and we'll see."

The two of them turned the wreck of a boat over. "They're not here," said Lazo, almost in disbelief.

"Where the hell can they be?" asked Sam, his voice losing some of its earlier enthusiasm.

"I couldn't tell you, but the owner must have hidden them near by."

"Why would he do that?" asked Sam.

"I can't be sure but perhaps he was insuring against theft. I know they do it back home."

They searched the area and as usual, Lazo was correct. The owner had hidden the oars in the branches of a nearby tree. They gathered the hand-hewn oars from their precarious perch and hastily returned to the boat.

"Well, here goes," said Lazo, as the two ushered the boat into the water. They waited for a moment or two. Then, assured of the boat's seaworthiness, they carefully, almost gingerly, stepped in and seated themselves. Lazo positioned the end of one of the oars against a rock and pushed against it. Soon the boat was free and adrift. Sam began to paddle with the oar.

"Here, give me that oar before you kill both of us," exhorted Lazo.

"What the hell are you laughing at! Haven't you ever seen anyone paddle a boat!"

"A boat, no! A canoe, yes!" replied Lazo still laughing.

Sam handed the oar over and watched as Lazo placed them between the thole pins and began to row toward the opposite shore.

"And this, my friend, is how we do it in northern Minnesota."

Sam made no reply. He rested his back against the bow of the boat and allowed one hand to drag through the cool, refreshing water. When they reached the western shore, Sam jumped out and pulled the boat in.

"We won't be needing these anymore," shouted Lazo, as be threw the oars out into the river. Then unable to restrain his excitement, he leaped out, threw his arms around Sam, shouting, "We've made it! Hot Damn, we've made it, Sam!"

It was clear that our young celebrants had forgotten the peril, which accompanied their mission, and had the enemy been within a mile of that place, the mission would have been compromised, or at least, placed in serious jeopardy.

Lazo was the first to recover his equilibrium. He grabbed Sam by the arm and said, almost in a whisper, "Let's go on. We've got to make contact."

"Right," said Sam, as he followed Lazo up the embankment.

The two walked about half a mile, when suddenly the forest gave way and a highway appeared. Lazo stopped, took out his map and placed it on the ground. Then using his compass, he oriented it, and began to study the map very carefully.

"Well, what's the verdict?" asked Sam.

"There's something wrong. According to this map, this highway shouldn't be here."

"Are you sure?"

"Look for yourself."

Sam bent over to scrutinize the map.

"Do you see any highway on the map?"

"No," replied Sam. He paused a moment and looked at the map once again. "Maybe the map is incorrect."

"No chance," replied Lazo.

"Then where the hell are we?"

"I don't know for sure, but I think we'll find a railroad about half a mile further on."

"And if we do?"

"Then we'll know," said Lazo as he folded the map and placed it into his musette bag. "Well, let's find out."

The two walked on and as Lazo had predicted, found the railroad. Then unable to conceal his disappointment, Lazo whispered, "We've been screwed."

"Are you certain?"

"Yes, I am. The river we crossed was not the Drina. It was the Morava."

"Then we're ..."

Before Sam could finish, Lazo said, "Ya, we're in the middle of Serbia. Chetnik country."

"Oh, goddam! Let's get the hell out of here before we're discovered."

"Yeh," replied Lazo, and they bounded across the tracks and disappeared into the forest.

CHAPTER NINE

Our two courageous but hapless warriors did not stop when they entered the forest. They continued to run, motivated perhaps, more by a sense of anger than by fear. Both wondered why they had been dropped a full one hundred and fifty miles short of the designated area. Neither wanted to believe that their present plight was the result of a political conspiracy. "Yet to believe," thought Lazo, "that it was the result of a navigational error, would be even more incredulous." The more he thought about it, the angrier he became. Finally, he fell to the ground and in a sense of utter frustration, began to strike it, full force, with his fists, and kept repeating, "Son of a bitch! Some bastard wants us dead! They want us dead!"

Sam, who was in the lead, did not see Lazo drop to the ground. He kept running until, he too was brought down not by exhaustion or anger, but by a fallen tree that lay in his path. One of its dead branches caught his foot and he plummeted through the air, coming to rest on a rounded rock. The force of the impact caused the air to gush from him, leaving him breathless and writhing in pain.

Lazo did not see him fall and was quite astonished when he heard Sam shout, "Lazo, help me! Help me! I think I've broken something!"

Lazo leaped to his feet and rushed to Sam's side. "Can you move your legs?"

"I think so," replied Sam, with a pained expression on his face. "Well, what the hell are you waiting for? Move them!" shouted Lazo.

Sam, with some reluctance, moved both of his legs. Then satisfied that they were not broken, moved his arms likewise.

"You bloody faker!" cried Lazo, as he settled down against the very tree that had felled his comrade. "You aren't hurt!"

Sam raised himself to his feet and began to walk about.

"We have a lot to talk about."

"I know," replied Sam, as he carefully lowered himself and sat down next to Lazo. "What do we do now?"

Lazo removed the map from his musette bag and unfolded it with unusual care. He now knew that the map was essential to their future well being, if indeed, they had a future. He placed it on the ground, between his legs and said, "As I see it, we have only one choice."

"And what is that?"

"I think that our best bet is to move north to Belgrade."

"Why Belgrade?" asked Sam, somewhat dumbfounded. "Why can't we head west, as we had planned?"

"Because," replied Lazo, "we would have to pass through some very rugged terrain and a torrent of Chetniks and Nazis." "No," he continued, as he removed a cigarette from a K-ration packet, "as near as I can figure, we are less than a hundred miles from Belgrade. We can follow the railroad tracks and if we push ourselves, we could be there in two days, three at the most."

"Hold it a minute! So we can't carry out our original mission. Why can't we make our way back to the Adriatic and get to the Island of Vis. Once there, we'll be home free."

"What chance do you think we'll have?" queried Lazo. "Do you really believe that those bastards who dropped us here would help us?"

"Okay, maybe you're right, but why Belgrade?"

"Because it's a large city," replied Lazo. He lit his cigarette and took a long drag. "It will be easier to lose ourselves in a big city."

"Then what?"

"Then we'll get a job on a barge going up the Danube. We've got to get to the American lines and that means getting to southern Germany." Then, almost as an afterthought, added, "We've got to get out of here before the Russians arrive."

"What the hell do you mean? The Russians are our allies, aren't they?"

"Oh yes! At least for the time being. Karl Marx once said that the Russians have always coveted a western border extending from Stetin on the Baltic to Trieste on the Adriatic. And that my friend, includes Yugoslavia."

"Do you believe that?"

"I don't know what I believe anymore, but I wouldn't stake my life on their innate generosity or their love of humanity."

"Well, I hope that you are wrong." He paused, looked upward and added, "For the sake of humanity."

Lazo field stripped his cigarette, then stood up and carefully folded the map. He placed it in his pocket and said,"Let's get on with it. We can't afford to waste anymore of today."

Sam carefully raised himself up and followed Lazo. There was a hint of a limp in his walk but he was able to keep up.

"What will we do if we meet someone?" asked Sam.

"Well, let's hope to hell that doesn't happen until we can get some native dress."

"Won't that be dangerous?"

"Why?"

"We could be shot as spies."

"I know," replied Lazo, "but I speak Slovenian like a native and if we cover ourselves with native garb, it shouldn't be too risky. That is, if you let me do the talking."

"Don't worry," laughed Sam. "If we encounter anyone, you can be sure that I will remain speechless."

"Good, then let's find us some native clothing."

And so the two pressed on, in the direction of Belgrade. They stayed within eye's reach of the railroad, yet far enough in the forest to make detection quite difficult. They were so absorbed by their quest that they did not notice that the bright blue sky was beginning to shed some of its brilliance, nor were they cognizant that their shadows were straying farther and farther from their aching feet. At about sunset, they spotted a small cottage, half hidden among the trees, and halted.

"Wait here," whispered Lazo. "I'll go over and check it out."

"Be careful," admonished Sam, as he sat down and rested his back against the trunk of a large pine tree.

"Don't fret," replied Lazo, walking quite boldly toward the cottage. When he neared it, Sam noticed that Lazo's steps became more measured and his arms, which usually moved quite freely, were now pressed against his sides. When he reached the building, he carefully peered through the large window, using his hand to screen out the shadows. Then with his back pressed against the wall, he moved along its length until he reached the corner. He paused, then rounded it and disappeared from Sam's view. Sam remained seated until unsettled by curiosity, he quietly raised himself to his feet and contrary to Lazo's admonition, began to inch slowly toward the cabin. Suddenly Lazo reappeared, swinging his arms in a beckoning motion. Sam, forgetting his pain, bounded up to Lazo.

"Is it occupied?"

"No, there doesn't seem to be anyone here."

"Are you sure?"

"Come and see for yourself," replied Lazo as he grabbed Sam by the arm and ushered him to the front of the cottage. When they reached the door, Lazo threw it open and said, "See."

Sam walked in, surveyed the room and said, "Well I'll be damned! It's not much, but it's better than nothing."

"It certainly is," agreed Lazo.

"What's behind the door?"

"I don't know," replied Lazo, "I haven't had time to look."

"Well, let's find out," said Sam, walking over and grabbing the doorknob. "Should I?"

"Go ahead. If anyone was in there, they would have come out by now."

Sam turned the knob ever so cautiously and slowly pulled the door open.

"Do you see anything?"

"No, it's just a bedroom."

Lazo put his "forty-five" back in its holster and said, "For a moment there, you had me scared."

"I know," replied Sam, with a big grin. "I just wanted to see if you were human. I'll check out the bedroom."

"Good, and while you're doing that, I'll check out the kitchen. Perhaps they have some food stashed around here," replied Lazo, rummaging through the drawers of what appeared to be an old homemade kitchen cupboard.

"Jesus H. Christ!" shouted Sam as he rushed out of the bedroom.

"What the hell's the matter, now?"

"There's an S.S. uniform hanging in the closet."

"Are you sure?"

"Come and have a look."

Lazo followed Sam into the bedroom. "It's over there," directed Sam, pointing to the closet.

Lazo walked over to the closet and looked in. "It is an S.S. uniform and not only that, but it is a Major's uniform."

"What do you make of it?" asked Sam.

"I don't know but we'd better get the hell out of here before he gets back. It wouldn't do to have him find us here now, would it?" Lazo closed the closet door. Then he turned and said, "Well, Sam, do you still think it's too damned casual."

The two men retreated to the kitchen. The uniform reminded them that they were in the midst of a war and from now on; their survival would depend upon how well and how courageously they could conduct themselves.

"Where in hell do they keep their food?"

"I don't know," retorted Sam. "You look around and I'll go outside and stand guard."

Lazo continued his search. He was careful not to do anything that might betray their presence to the Germans. His search through the cupboard proved to be fruitless. He was about to give up when he noticed a trap door on the opposite side of the room. He rushed over and pulled it open. It was too dark to see, so Lazo used his lighter and beheld what appeared to be an old fashioned root cellar. He carefully descended into the darkness. Each step caused the old stairs to groan loudly. When he reached the bottom, he held the lighter up and surveyed the cellar. The shelves were well stocked with tins of food. Lazo removed several of them and placed them into his bag. He was careful not to take too many, as it might alert the German officer. He was about to leave when he noticed some smoked sausages hanging on a pole. Then remembering the promise he had made to Sam, he broke off about fifteen links, draped them over his shoulder and walked up the stairs. After closing the trap door and double-checking to make certain that nothing was amiss, he rushed out into the dimness of the declining day.

"Did you find anything?"

"Here," shouted Lazo, "Catch!" and he threw the heavily scented sausages to Sam.

Sam did not react quickly enough to avoid them and the sausages wrapped themselves around his neck. "What the hell are they?" asked Sam, as he hurriedly pulled them from his neck.

"I think they're Polish Sausage," replied Lazo. "At least they smell like the ones my mother makes."

"Talk about smell!" exclaimed Sam. "Hell, they reek of garlic. The Chetniks could smell these a mile away."

"I didn't promise you caviar. I promised you Slavic sausages and there they are."

"Do people actually eat these or do they use them to ward off evil spirits?"

"Originally, they were used to keep the vampires away," replied Lazo, half smiling.

"Vampires, hell!"

"No shit," replied Lazo. "Yugoslavia was the original home of the vampires. I thought every college grad knew that."

"Transylvania, Lazo, not Yugoslavia," retorted Sam, holding the sausages as far from his nose as possible.

"Not really," replied Lazo. "In some places of Yugoslavia, the chemical structure of the soil is such that the bodies buried in it remain intact for long periods of time."

"You mean, the bodies don't corrupt!"

"Precisely," replied Lazo "and that is why they say that there are places in Yugoslavia where the natives are truly incorruptible." As these words ushered from Lazo's lips he could no longer remain sober and he burst into a fit of laughter. The laughter was short lived. It ended when Lazo felt the long string of sausages coil themselves around his neck.

"Let's cut the bullshit and get the hell out of here."

"Okay," replied Lazo, unraveling the sausages from his neck. "We've got at least half an hour before darkness sets in. Hell, we can be a couple of miles away from here by then."

With that, the two moved back into the forest. They did not seem to be too worried even though they both knew that the Germans could be very near. When the darkness finally descended and the forest became enveloped in a moon checkered veil, the two soldiers settled down by a little brook which gurgled softly as it gently caressed the rocks in its downward slide toward the Morava.

"Are you hungry?" asked Lazo.

"Of course I am, but we can't eat those sausages."

"And why the hell not?"

"Because we would have to cook them and you know damned well that we can't start a fire."

"Wrong," replied Lazo. "These sausages were boiled and then smoked. We can eat them as they are."

"Are you certain?"

"Not completely, but I'll chance it." With that he took his knife and cut one of the sausages from the string and began to eat.

Sam watched intently. What he expected was difficult to ascertain. Perhaps he expected Lazo to succumb or at least, to double up in pain. He waited and when nothing happened to Lazo, he said, "Throw one of them over here."

Lazo cut another off and tossed it over to Sam. Sam took it and wiped it carefully on his sleeve. Then he raised it to his mouth and gingerly bit into it. He quickly spit it out, and yelled, "Jesus H. Christ! There's pork in this damned thing, isn't there?"

"Of course, but not much. They add a little for flavor."

"Why didn't you tell me?"

"I forgot about it, I guess."

"You know I can't eat pork."

"Why in hell not. Do you really believe that in the midst of this war, while thousands of people are dying, God has nothing more pressing to do than check up on the dietary habits of one insignificant schmuck."

"That's not the point," retorted Sam.

"Then what the hell is the point?" asked Lazo, somewhat irritated.

"Self discipline," rejoined Sam, "self discipline."

"What are you going to eat then?"

"Nothing, I guess."

Lazo did not respond. He cut off another sausage and was about to raise it to his mouth when he jumped up and hit his forehead with his fist, "Porka Madonna, I was so preoccupied with the sausages that I completely forgot about the tins!"

"What tins? Have you gone nuts?"

"No," replied Lazo, as he turned his bag upside down, allowing the contents to spill to the ground.

"You're not going crazy!" shouted Sam as he reached over and grabbed one of the tins. "I suppose these are all filled with ham," uttered Sam, sarcastically.

"Not all of them. Some have cheese and some, beef."

"Which are which?" asked Sam.

"Can't the college boy read German?"

"You know I can't."

Lazo knelt down beside the tins. He tried to read the labels but it was too dark. "Do I dare use my lighter?"

"I suppose you could but be careful," urged Sam.

Lazo flicked his lighter and trying his best to conceal its brightness. He searched out a tin of beef and threw it to Sam.

"I hope no one saw the light."

"If they did," replied Lazo, "it will be the most expensive beef you will ever eat. Eat heartily, my friend."

Sam opened the tin, and then as if starved, hastily devoured its contents, scarcely stopping to breathe.

"Is it that good?"

"Better than that. It's excellent."

"How could you tell?" laughed Lazo.

"What do you mean?" queried Sam, wiping the grease from his face with his sleeve. Then realizing that Lazo was referring to the haste with which he dispatched the beef, added, "Funny, aren't you?"

"Well, now that we've eaten, what say we hit the sack."

"Good idea. We've got to get going at the crack of dawn," replied Sam, as he walked over to the brook and rinsed out the empty tin. Then he filled the tin with the cool water and drank it down.

"How does it taste?" asked Lazo.

"Not bad. Do you want some?"

"Please," replied Lazo, "the sausages made me very thirsty."

Sam filled the tin and handed it to Lazo. As the two settled down to sleep, the scent of pine caressed the night, filling Lazo with thoughts that gentled and warmed his heart.

CHAPTER TEN

It was not quite dawn when Lazo awakened to a loud call of a bird. It was the most exotic bird call he had ever heard. He looked over to see if Sam was awake to the song but Sam's snoring had deafened his ears to the beauty of the call. Lazo listened intently, then drawn by some inexplicable urge, he arose and moved pensively in the direction of the sound. The bird's call drew him farther and farther away from the encampment but Lazo, so thrilled by the prospect of seeing the bird, was not cognizant of his straying steps. The bird's call became stronger and just when Lazo thought the bird near at hand, the sound would grow faint. This happened several times. "The damned bird is mocking me," thought Lazo as be continued his search for the illusive songster. The song stopped. Lazo waited patiently for an encore, but none was forthcoming. Finally, realizing that the concert had ended, he turned and began to walk back to the encampment. He glanced at his watch. The luminescent hands, dulled by the coming light, indicated that he had strayed for almost half an hour. His steps began to quicken and he wondered how Sam would regard his absence.

He ran along until the quiet splashing of the brook became audible, then he slowed down so as not to awaken Sam, if perchance, he was still asleep.

"Where the hell have you been?"

"Chasing a bird," replied Lazo, with quiet nonchalance.

"Oh, that's good!"

"Did you miss me?"

"No, I didn't miss you, but what the hell were you thinking of?"

"What do you mean?"

"Here we are, our lives in peril, and you go about chasing some goddam bird. What's wrong with you?"

"I was going to awaken you but you were sleeping so soundly and snoring so loudly that I thought better of it and decided to go it alone."

"Well, next time, try to remember that I don't speak Slovenian, Croatian, Serbian or any other Slavic language. What would have become of me if someone happened by?"

"You didn't have to worry. The way you were snoring, no one would dare come near."

"And why the hell not?"

"Because," replied Lazo with a smile, "when you snore, you sound like the grunting of a love starved boar, during mating season."

"There you go again."

"I'm sorry," replied Lazo, in a somewhat subdued voice, "I'll try not to place you in harm's way."

"I hope not. My dad would never forgive you if you allowed anything to happen to me."

Lazo knelt down beside the bag, took out a sausage and bit into it. Then shouldering his musette bag, he raised himself to his feet and said, "Let's go. We have a long way to walk."

"Righto," replied Sam, "we won't get to Belgrade, sitting on our arses."

The two resumed their trek northward, being careful not to stray too far from the comforting sight of the railroad right of way. Conversation was kept to a minimum. At about noon, Lazo's visage became noticeably troubled. He was not certain, but he felt that they were being watched. He said nothing as he did not want to alarm Sam unnecessarily. And so they went on until they came to a narrow, dusty country road. Lazo stopped, looked at his map and shook his head.

"What's wrong?"

"The map doesn't indicate any road," came Lazo's reply.

"So what. Jerry probably built it so that they would be able to move troops with more efficiency."

"You're probably right. I guess I worry too much."

They crossed the road without incident. Lazo was still not able to rid himself of the feeling that they were being watched. He kept looking back over his shoulder but his efforts were futile. If someone was following, that someone was very careful not to reveal himself.

"I hate to mention it but what are we going to do about these clothes?" asked Sam.

"I don't know," replied Lazo.

"Well, perhaps we'll soon stumble upon some small village."

"I hardly think so," replied Lazo. "The map does not indicate any village in the immediate area."

"The map could be wrong, you know."

"Perhaps, but I wouldn't want to bank on it. According to this map, we should be coming into Veliki Plana at about sundown."

"How large is this Veliki Plana?" asked Sam.

"No population figures are indicated but I would guess that the population is not too substantial."

"That's too bad," responded Sam. "It would have been much easier to move about in a larger city."

"You may be right, but right now, I would prefer a small village."

"Why?" asked Sam, somewhat mystified by Lazo's incongruence.

"Because, my good friend, the Germans do not garrison small villages. I know that we might have to contend with Chetniks. They're bad enough, so let's try to keep the Germans as far from us as possible."

Sam did not respond immediately. He brushed the perspiration from his forehead with a deft sweep of his hand. "I didn't think about that but small towns do trouble me."

"Why?" asked Lazo, as he stopped and took a quick glance at his map.

"Because people in small towns are very bored and readily seize upon every opportunity to paint some excitement into their otherwise shallow existences. And that Lazo, can be very dangerous."

"I never thought about it in that fashion, but now that you, mention it, you could be very right." He folded the map, which he had been holding and put it back into his pocket and very softly, repeated, "You could be very right."

"Were your parents born around here?" asked Sam, perhaps attempting to change the subject.

"No," replied Lazo. "My parents were born in a little village near Ljubjana, called Butroi."

"Where's that?"

"In the province of Slovenia, of course."

"Is that very far from here?"

"About three hundred miles, as the crow flies," laughed Lazo, trying to make light of Sam's utter ignorance of Yugoslavia.

"Wouldn't we be better off going there?" queried Sam.

"We no doubt would but Butroi is not on our itinerary."

They continued on in silence and couldn't have gone more than a few kilometers, when they spotted a church steeple protruding, quite abruptly from the tree tops.

"What the hell's that?" asked Sam, in a whisper.

"Damned if I know. I know that it can't be Veliki Plana. We haven't come far enough."

"Are you quite sure?" asked Sam, with a kind of raspiness in his voice that Lazo had not heard before.

"I'm sure, Sam. This village is situated too far from the railroad. According to the map, Veliki Plana is situated along the right of way."

"What do we do now?"

"Beats the hell out of me," answered Lazo. He did not try to conceal the sense of futility which he was presently experiencing. He ran the back of his hand across his upper lip and wiped away the glistening bubbles of perspiration that had collected there.

"Well, do we go around or do we sneak in and try to find some clothes?" queried Sam.

"I don't know. An hour or so ago, there wouldn't have been any doubt in my mind, but now I'm not certain of anything.

"What do you mean?"

"What you said about small towns, troubles me."

"My perceptions may have been wrong."

"They could have been correct and that is what troubles me." Lazo turned his head and as he did, he saw what appeared to be a human form disappear into the thicket above them. He was about to alert Sam, but then thought better of it. "No sense troubling him" he thought. "Besides, it could very well have been a wild boar or some other animal."

"Well, I think that we ought to chance it, we've got to get out of these clothes before someone spots us."

"Okay," replied Lazo, "but I'll chance it and not we."

"What the hell do you mean? If you think that I'm gong to stay here, all alone, you're crazy."

"You will remain here," insisted Lazo, "and I mean right here. I don't want you to stray one inch. When I return, I might be in a goddam hurry and I won't have time to look for you. Do you understand?"

"Okay, I won't move from this spot but you had better be damned careful that no one spots you."

"Don't worry. I'll try to keep to the outskirts of the village. Some family will have its wash hanging out on this bright and sunny day."

"Ya, it wouldn't do to wear soiled clothing now would it," replied Sam with a chuckle.

Lazo did not reply. He was already running toward the village. When he reached the edge of the forest, he dropped to the ground. He took a few deep breaths, then raised himself on his elbows to survey the clearing which lay between him and the village. Beyond the meadow, stood a frame house, well apart from the others. It had a rather careless look about it. Its color, once white, was now grey and mottled. The result of years of inattention. "It was not unlike some of the frame houses which one frequently sees on the poorer farms in northern Minnesota," thought Lazo, as he slithered forward to get a closer look. The pasture grass was high enough to provide ample cover. Lazo looked back over his shoulder and seeing no one, began to crawl toward the house. At first, he moved very slowly. He did not want to call attention to his presence by causing the grass to sway, unnecessarily. But soon emboldened, either by the thought of success or impatience, I know not which, he began to move with greater alacrity. When he reached the low stone wall which surrounded the house and the out buildings, he breathed a sigh of relief. Then using the wall as a shield, he crawled along until he reached a point, just behind the house. He slowly raised his head so that he might peer over the wall and into the farm yard. As he did, something like "holy cow," issued from his lips, for there, not quite five yards away, stood a large tawny milch cow. On the far side of the cow, sat a young girl. Only the lower half of her body was visible but that half was sufficient to cause Lazo's mouth to fall open and his eyes to round out. She could not see him but he could and did see her.

The stool, upon which she was seated, was very low and the young girl, so as not to soil the hem of her long skirt, had it pulled up high over her well parted thighs. She wore nothing beneath the skirt and Lazo's eyes became fixed upon the area which nature had so endeared him to.

It was fortunate for Lazo that she did her work well for had she been less attentive to her labors, Lazo would have been in great danger of being detected, so carried away was he by the pleasantness of the moment. When Lazo saw that she was preparing to leave he quickly dropped down, out of sight. His face had become quite flushed but not as a consequence of his encounter with the bright summer sun.

He waited a few seconds then carefully raised himself up and looked in the direction of the house, but she was not to be seen. Somewhat disappointed, Lazo turned and saw her walking toward the large barn.

She was close enough for Lazo to see her face which though unkempt was not entirely without beauty. Her long brownish hair hung loosely about her shoulders and she was wearing a faded, red blouse, whose buttons, though present, were left undone. "Such obvious disregard for modesty," thought Lazo, "could only be attributed to the absence of men in the vicinity."

Lazo began to feel more at ease, for the absence of men would make his search for clothing much less perilous. He watched as she entered the enormous barn, which at some earlier time, most assuredly, symbolized substantial wealth. It had of late, due to prolonged neglect, taken on the appearance of some lost or crippled monster. It leaned heavily to the left and might have already fallen had it not been propped up by several unshorn timbers.

He waited impatiently for her reappearance, knowing that he could not continue his search until she had returned to the house. He did not wait well. He watched the butterflies as they flitted about on brittle wings and remembered that once Ilse referred to them as worms turned into music. A smile softened his frenzy and for a moment at least, he again left the anxious world of Chetniks, Germans and Partisans. But his sojourn from reality was soon curtained by strange noises coming from the barn. He raised himself and peered over the wall hoping to discover the source of the strange utterances. He listened carefully but was unable to determine their nature, since they were somewhat obscured by distance. Curiosity soon gained control of him and he decided to move to the rear of the barn. The danger involved would be minimal and besides, he really wanted to see the young girl, once again. He moved quickly along the wall and when he was near the rear of the barn, he hurdled it and began to move toward the barn. When he reached it, he searched for a knothole that would not endanger his presence. He found one near the ground and looked in. There in the center of the barn, seated on the earthen floor was the girl. Next to her, with its head cradled softly in her lap, lay a beautiful brown and white nanny goat. Suddenly the goat's body convulsed and it let out an almost human cry. Lazo now knew from whence the sounds had issued. The young girl held the head securely and when she turned, the long shaft of light, which prowled through a crack in the wall, lit up her face, causing her tears to glisten as they journeyed slowly down her nose. It was a pathetic sight but Lazo's sympathy was directed more at the young girl than at the goat.

She seemed so helpless. Then the quiet was again insulted by another cry and the girl leaned forward. This time her eyes brightened and a smile came to her lips. Lazo could not see what had transpired but he surmised that the nanny must have dropped her kid. His speculation proved correct, for soon the girl raised the kid to her bosom in a gentle embrace. The little goat responded by tugging on one of her nipples. The girl burst into laughter and quickly placed the kid down beside the nanny. The tiny goat soon found a more profitable pap and began to suckle noisily. The girl gracefully raised herself from the dusty floor and began to walk away. When she reached the door, she turned to look at the nanny and her kid. She smiled and ran her hand across her breast. She picked up the bucket of milk and left the barn.

Lazo waited until he heard the door slam. Then he began to disengage a loose board. The nails which held it in place were almost rusted through so it broke away quite easily, sending forth a small cloud of reddish brown dust. The opening was still not large enough to allow his passage, so he removed still another board. He crawled in and began to search for clothing. He seemed not too hurried in his quest.

Perhaps he wished for the girl's return. Even so, he took time to run his hand over the little goat's head. He smiled and continued his search but found nothing. Then he directed his attention to the loft and moved over to the well worn wooden ladder. His feet searched out the smooth indentations on the rungs, which had been carved by generations of feet. The ladder moaned under his feet but it did not break. When his foot reached the last rung, he reached for a beam and effortlessly pulled himself into the loft. The air was heavy with dust, reminding him of the times when he and his friends were called by a neighbor to pack down the hay that was being forced into a loft, not unlike this one.

He looked around but held little hope of finding clothing. He walked over to an old trunk which was covered with hay. He opened it but it contained nothing that would be of use. He turned away without bothering to close it, and moved over to the trap door. He was about to descend when he heard a girls' voice shouting,

"Franzka! Franzka! Where are you?"

Lazo retreated and stiffened, waiting for the girl to enter the barn. The girl bounded in and again shouted,

"Franzka, are you here? Where are you hiding?"

She waited for a response and when none was forthcoming, she shouted, "Are you hiding in the loft again?"

Lazo was certain that she would search the loft and was about to take cover when he heard the loud slam of a door and another voice shouting,

"What do you want, Olga?"

"Come here. I've got something to tell you. Hurry! Hurry!" she urged.

Franzka rushed into the barn. "Well, what do you want?" she asked, in a voice that did not hide her irritation.

"They caught a German spy."

"Who caught a German spy?"

"The Chetniks, of course, who else?" shouted Olga. "They caught him hiding in the woods, just east of town."

"Are you sure?" queried Franzka.

"Of course, I'm sure. I'm not stupid, you know."

"Who told you?'

"My brother told me, so there. He is a Chetnik, you know," replied Olga, quite smugly.

"Where are they holding him?" asked Franzka, her interest piqued.

"They have him tied to the church wall."

"You mean the men are all back in the village?"

"Some of them are but most are still looking for the other one."

"Which other one?" asked Franzka, as she buttoned her blouse.

"The other German spy. There were two of them, but one disappeared."

"That's a laugh. What would a German spy be doing around here anyway?"

"I don't know. My brother told me that the one keeps insisting that he is an American, but no one believes him."

"Didn't he have any identification?"

"Of course, he did, silly. You know that spies always have fake identification papers."

"How do you know that?"

"He was carrying a bag containing tins of German food."

"I see," replied Franzka, "and an American wouldn't be carrying German food."

"That's what my brother said."

"What are they going to do to him?"

"My brother said they were going to execute him tonight."

"What if he really is an American?" asked Franzka. "It would be terrible to execute an American."

"What's the difference? My brother told me that the American were now backing Tito and you know how the Chetniks hate the Partisans."

Franzka reached down, picked up a piece of straw and began to chew on it. "Is he handsome?" she asked.

"I haven't seen him yet. That's why I rushed over here. I want you to come with me so that we can go and see him."

"Okay," replied Franzka, "but first, I'd better tell my mother. You know how she worries."

"Let's hurry then," shouted Olga, as she ran out of the barn, pulling Franzka behind.

After the girls had left, Lazo walked over to the trunk. He closed the lid and sat down upon it. He was so angry with himself that he could scarcely think. Images came and left, leaving his mind in a state of hopeless and utter confusion.

"Those damned tins of food! Those damned tins of food!" he kept repeating. "If only I had not found them. It's my fault and I've got to do something."

He looked at his watch and saw that it was almost six o'clock. He decided that he would wait until dark when he would be able to move about with less fear of discovery. "In the meantime," he thought, "he might devise some plan for rescuing Sam. But first, I've got to get out of here. I'll be safer outside the wall."

He left the barn and took cover on the shadow of the low stone wall. The sun was just barely visible above the trees and the grass upon which he lay, was already beginning to cool. He closed his eyes and waited for the darkness.

CHAPTER ELEVEN

"Have you found him yet?"
"No, we haven't."
"Why have you returned, then?"
"Because it's hopeless."
"What do you mean, hopeless?"
"Look for yourself, Vaso. Can't you see? There's no moon to light our way. It's impossible."
"So, Milosh, you and your men have given up, have you?"
"It's not a question of giving up, Vaso, it's just a question of judgment. Besides, we have one, don't we? It's been so long since we have had anything to celebrate and we are tired. Did you hear me, Vaso? We are tired! Dammit, what do you expect?"
"Ya, perhaps you are right," replied Vaso, putting his hand on Milosh's shoulder, a gesture of paternalistic solicitude. Then he stepped back, inserted his thumbs into the armholes of his sheepskin vest and pushed them forward, trying to create an aura of authority.
"What shall we do with our German friend?"
Most of the villagers had gathered at the church and when they heard Vaso, one of them shouted, "Kill the fuckin son of a bitch!"
The others, upon hearing this, echoed, "Ya, kill him! Kill the bastard!"
"All right! All right!" shouted Vaso, gesturing for silence.
They would not listen so he took one of the flambeaus which bad been positioned on the top of the stone wall and began to brandish it wildly, hoping that this gesture would serve to silence the mob.
They paid no heed to his maneuverings so Milosh took the torch, jumped to the top of the wall, shouting, "Silence! Let Vaso be heard!"
Still they would not be silent so Milosh drew his pistol and fired several shots into the air. The crowd, startled by the reports, came to a sudden quiet.
By this time, Lazo had managed to make his way back to the church yard and when he heard the shots, his heart began to pound mercilessly against his chest. He was about to turn and run, when he heard Vaso's strident voice, shouting, "All right! You have pronounced judgment and your wishes will be done, but first, bring on the wine and let's celebrate."
A small group of men rushed into the church and returned with several casks of wine. They placed the casks atop the stone wall, not more than five feet from where Sam sat, bound, hand and foot.
Upon hearing Vaso's voice, Lazo's breath became more settled and he began to move, very slowly, toward the festivities. He wanted to be near enough to take advantage of any opportunity that might arise as a

consequence of the drunkenness that most assuredly would follow. He had developed no plan but he was confident that a combination of darkness and Slavic debauchery would provide them with the needed avenue of escape.

"Where's Josa?" thundered Vaso.

"Over there," replied Milosh, pointing to the rear of the crowd.

"Go and get him."

Milosh pushed through the crowd and returned with Josa.

"Come here, Josa."

"Ja, Vaso, what do you want?"

"What do I want?" shouted Vaso, bursting into laughter. "I want you to remove the bungs from these casks, so that we may drink."

"Ah, is that all," replied Josa, as he raised his fist and with a mighty swing drove the bung down into the cask.

The crowd shouted its approval as Josa raised the cask and began to drink directly from it.

"That's enough!" shouted Vaso. "That's enough!"

Josa set the cask down and then struck each of the other casks with his gigantic fist and the festivities were begun. The villagers stampeded to the casks and began to drink, as only Slavic people can.

Men, women and children partook of the churchly spirits. The more they drank, the more they taunted Sam. Even the children participated in the baiting. At first, they were careful not to come too close but when they realized that he was well tethered, their jeers became less distant and were often accompanied by kicks.

Lazo could not see Sam so he did not know what was happening to him. Yet he dared not approach too closely, for fear of discovery and he honestly believed that the Chetniks would not execute his friend.

So he remained in the shadows of the low stone wall, waiting for the crucial moment. Then he could make his move.

The merriment continued until all of the casks were empty. Then Vaso climbed to the top of the stone wall, assisted by Milosh. He was quite drunk and had some difficulty maintaining his balance.

"Have you all seen the bloody Boche!" he shouted.

"No!" some of them shouted. "Show us the Boche!"

"Josa, show them the Boche!"

Josa walked up to where Sam was seated. He lowered his gargantuan frame over Sam and placing one hand on Sam's neck, the other on one of his thighs. Then he raised Sam over his head, laughing coarsely, as he displayed Sam like some well deserved trophy.

Vaso then shouted, "I give you, the Boche!"

Lazo watched as Josa held Sam over his head. The anger he was experiencing wanted to erupt in some act of blind courage, but he knew that neither Sam nor he would be well served by such impetuosity, no matter how gallant.

"And now that you have seen him, let us begin!" shouted Vaso.

Josa lowered Sam and placed him on top of the wall. Vaso cut the ropes that bound him and four of the men, Josa included, gathered around Sam. They removed the gag from Sam's mouth. Sam responded immediately, shouting as loudly as he could, "I am not a German spy! I am an American! I have come to help you, you stupid assholes!"

His tirades were futile. Only Milosh had some little understanding of the English language and even if he did believe Sam, he was not about to deprive the bloodthirsty villagers of their pleasure.

Vaso removed one of Sam's boots and threw it into the crowd. They fought over it like crazed animals.

"Who got the boot?" he asked.

"I have it," came a loud reply from the crowd.

"Oh, it's you, Ludmilla. Bring it here and you shall have the other."

Ludmilia pushed her way forward, her prize held high over her head. When she reached the wall, she brought the boot down, full force, upon Sam's balls. Sam screamed in agony but his screams were dwarfed by the deafening roar of the villagers.

"Take it easy, Ludmilla," cautioned Vaso. "We have better things in store for him. It won't do to render him unconscious."

Ludmilla took the other boot and turned to leave. "Wait Ludmilla, now you must remove his clothing."

Ludmilla tied the laces of the boots together and draped them around her neck. "Now give me your knife."

Vaso removed his knife from its scabbard and handed it to Ludmilla.

She pressed it against Sam's chin and Sam instinctively drew his head back. "Don't worry, Boche, I won't kill you. That would be too easy. Then she proceeded to cut off his clothing until only his G.I. shorts remained. Then she paused.

"What the hell are you waiting for?" shouted Vaso, impatiently.

"I like his underwear."

"Well, take them then."

She bent over to undo his shorts. Her black greasy hair brushed against his nakedness and he sucked in his stomach; so repulsed was he, by the hideous appearance of the Slavic hag.

She removed his shorts and brandished them over her head for all to see. Then she disappeared into the crowd.

"Have you got the rope?"

"Ya," replied Milosh.

"Then do your job, and do it well."

Milosh took one end of the rope and threw it over a branch of the huge tree that grew next to the wall. He took the other end and busied himself over Sam.

"Hurry now, we don't have all night."

"There, it's done," declared Milosh, as he walked over to the tree and grabbed the other end of the rope.

"All right. Now raise him up," commanded Vaso.

The four men raised him up about three feet above the top of the wall and held him there while Vaso bound Sam's hands together. Milosh then methodically fixed the rope to the tree, allowing about a foot of slack.

"Bring more torches!" bellowed Vaso. "We want them all to see." The torches were immediately brought up and the area around Sam was lit up like noonday. Lazo was now able to see what they had contrived. Unable to bear the sight, he turned away and tried to blink away the tears.

"Are you ready, Milosh?"

"Ya, Vaso, I have tied it well."

Vaso reached down and grabbed Sam's hands, now bound firmly together and raised them upward until they made contact with the rope. Sam clung to the rope as firmly as he could. He did not scream or lament. Perhaps he had already accepted his death.

"Let him go then!" commanded Vaso, with a diabolical grin.

The men obediently stepped back and the crowd screamed hysterically as they watched Sam trying desperately to sustain the few inches of slack that separated him from oblivion.

The crowd had begun to count. At first their utterances were slightly louder than whispers but as they progressed, the volume intensified, so that by the time they reached thirty, they were shouting so loudly that Lazo pressed his hands against his ears. When they reached one hundred, they stopped. The silence was deafening.

Lazo, thinking that it was all over for Sam, raised himself upward to look. As he did, Sam shouted, "Lazo, where the hell are you? Why don't you tell them? Why don't you help me? Please Lazo!"

Then, unable to sustain the rope any longer, he let go. Lazo watched him fall until the slack was used up and the branch pitched downward. A pitiful agonizing scream issued from Sam. This was followed by a series of moans. A pistol rang out. Then there was silence and Lazo knew that Sam was gone forever. He slumped to the ground. He had never felt so all alone and so ashamed in his entire life. There were no tears in his eyes, only anger and when the numbness finally departed his body, he raised himself up and quietly made his way toward the forest. He didn't know what to do but he knew he had to get away from this place. When he reached the forest, he broke into a run; the anger in him kept calling for revenge. The more he thought about Sam, the angrier he became. The low hanging branches beat against his face as he ran along, but he heeded them not. No amount of physical pain could assuage the mental agony which he was now experiencing, and when his legs had carried him far from that accursed place, he stopped and shouted, "No man should have to die that way!" He fell to the ground, utterly exhausted. The crying which he had held back began to spill over into tears which rolled down his sweated, grimy face. The scent of pine covered his tortured body and soon, he too, was asleep.

CHAPTER TWELVE

It was six o'clock in the morning. The sun's light had already begun to erase the darkness. A sliver of brightness settled on Lazo's peaceful countenance, causing the stubble on his face to glisten golden. A greenish fly settled on his sweat stained collar and slowly made its way to Lazo's ear. Lazo brushed it away but did not awaken. The fly, emboldened by its own agility, settled on Lazo's lip. This was more than the young soldier could suffer. He jerked his head and swung wildly with his hand. Unfortunately, his hand did no damage to the fly but the abruptness of the movement caused Lazo to awaken from his slumber. He sat up and pressed his arms heavenward. Several of his joints cracked loudly as the stiffness of sleep began to depart his body. The fly which had awakened Lazo continued to flit about and finally lighted on one of Lazo's boots.

"I'll get you, you little bugger," whispered Lazo, as his hand came down heavily upon the irksome insect. "There, that'll fix you."

He reached down and picked up the dead insect. The smug expression that had marked his victory was now gone. He stared at the dead fly for a long time. His eyes became tender as he made a small furrow with the heel of his boot and gently placed the fly into it. Then he covered it and caressed the grave with his hand, whispering, "Die immer fliegt und fliegen springt und gleich im Gras ihr altes Liedchen singt." Then he jumped to his feet, yelling, "I'll get those bastards for you Sam! I'll get them, every goddam one of them. You can bet on it."

He shouldered his bag and began to run through the forest. He took one of the remaining sausages from the bag and was about to bite into it when the forest gave way and in the clearing, he could see the hunting cottage that Sam and he had visited the day before. He stopped. The bag, hanging from his shoulder, continued to swing forward spilling some of its contents to the ground. He hastily retrieved them and began to walk boldly toward the cottage. When he reached the door, he pounded on it and waited. There was no immediate response, so he pounded again. This time even more severely. He waited. Still no response. Then in perfect German, he yelled, "Is anyone home?"

"Ja, ein Moment!" came a response, in a loud, throaty voice.

Lazo stepped back from the door and waited. He began to have second thoughts about the pistol he had thrown away, kind of wishing that it was still hanging on his side. The door opened. "What do you want?"

Lazo did not respond immediately. He looked at the rotund, chalky complected German and almost chuckled. He looked into the man's blood tangled eyes and said, "I am a German officer on special assignment. I need help."

"Well, why did you come here? How could you have known that this cabin was not occupied by the enemy."

"We were here earlier."

"You were?"

"Yes, but no one was here. We saw the S.S. uniform and helped ourselves to some food, Herr Major," replied Lazo, as he clicked his heels together and gave a snappy Nazi salute.

The Major returned the salute and said, "Heil Hitler." "Who is there, Karl?" came a voice from the other room. "What is your name, soldier?"

"Heinz Frick," replied Lazo.

A young woman, dressed only in scanty night clothes, walked up to the Major's side.

"This is Heinz Frick, Hedda. He is a German soldier on special assignment."

"Well, come in, Heinz," exhorted Hedda, in labored German.

"Danke," replied Lazo, stepping in. "You are too kind." Lazo clicked his heels. Then he took Hedda's hand and politely kissed it.

"I am Karl Kranz," said the Major, scratching his hairy chest. "By the way, you keep saying we and yet I see only you. What do you mean by we?"

"There were two of us," replied Lazo, releasing Hedda's hand.

"What do you mean, were?" asked the Major.

"May I sit down?"

"Certainly," replied the Major, pointing to a chair near the battered old table.

Lazo walked over and sat down. "It's like this, Herr Major. My partner Klaus and I were to make our way into Chetnik territory. We were to enlist their support for our mission."

"Which was?"

"To make our way to Ravno Goro and either capture or kill Tito."

"Oh, I see," replied the Major, walking over to the cast iron stove, upon which a large greying coffee pot was steaming. "Would you like some coffee?"

"Ja," replied Lazo, "I haven't had any for several days."

"Get him a cup, Hedda!"

Hedda walked over to the make-shift cabinet, removed one of the rusting tin cups and handed it to the Major.

"And how were you to accomplish such an impossible mission?" asked the Major, pouring the thick brew into the cup. He handed it to Hedda.

"Do you take sugar?" she asked politely, as she offered the steaming cup to Lazo.

"No," replied Lazo, raising the cup very carefully to his lips. "It was like this, Herr Major. Klaus was to be the key to the whole venture. He was to pose as a Soviet agent."

"Oh, I see," replied the Major. "you were to make it appear like a Soviet conspiracy."

"Ja, Herr Major, quite brilliant, don't you think?"

"Indeed! It was a master stroke of genius."

"Ja, we thought so too. If we would have succeeded, we would have turned the Partisans against the Russians."

"I can see it now," responded the Major, gleefully. "Just think, Germans, Chetniks, Ustashi and Partisans, all fighting together. Hell, we could drive the Russians right back to Kiev."

"And win the war," replied Lazo. He got up and walked to the window. Then he turned and with a contrived sadness in his voice, said, "But it won't happen."

"Why the hell not?"

"Because the sons of bitches killed Klaus."

"Who killed Klaus?"

"The Chetniks, of course. The buggers hung him by his balls."

"The Chetniks are our friends. Why would they do such a terrible thing?" asked Hedda. She walked over to Lazo. "It must have been awful."

"It was," replied Lazo, "and I will never forget Klaus' agony. No, not so long as I shall live, will I forget."

"Can't we go ahead with the mission, anyway?" asked the Major.

"No," replied Lazo, "Klaus had lived in Russia as a young man and could easily pass as one of them. Without him, the mission had no chance of success."

"That's too bad."

"Yes it is, and that's why I am here. We've got to make them pay. We've got to teach those bastards a lesson."

"Well, what do you want me to do?" asked the Major.

"How many men can you get?"

"As many as you want," replied the Major.

"Good," replied Lazo. "I think that twenty-five armed men will do."

"You're way ahead of me, Heinz. What would you have me do with the men?"

"We must go back and kill the Chetniks responsible for Klaus' death."

"But I can't do that without first consulting higher authority. Afterall, the Chetniks are our friends."

"We can't wait. If we do, those responsible for Klaus' death, will disappear into the forest and we'll never find them."

"But I can't assume responsibility for this kind of mission," pleaded the Major. "I don't have the authority."

"All right. You get me the men, Herr Major, and I will assume full responsibility. I cannot let them get away with the murder of a soldier who served the Reich so courageously and died so ingloriously. He deserved much better. He was a true German patriot."

The Major, moved by Lazo's patriotic ardor and not wanting to appear lacking in his loyalty to the "Fatherland", threw his arms outward in a sign of submission and said, "All right. I will do it. I will get you the men and equipment and I will accompany you." He paused, scratched the back of his head and said, "Who knows? It might be fun. I haven't done anything like this since Kralljevo. Get me my brief case, Hedda!"

Hedda rushed into the bedroom and returned with a smart leather case and carefully set it on the table. The Major opened it and removed several maps. He fingered through until he found the one he was looking for. "Ach, Ja! This is the one." He unfolded it and placed it on the table. He smoothed out the folds with his chubby, meaty hands.

"Show me where it happened, Heinz."

"I don't know the name of the village."

The Major, startled by Lazo's reply, threw his arms upward and shouted, "How do you expect me to find it then!"

"Ein moment, Herr Major, you musn't upset yourself. I don't know the name of the village but I can find it for you." He walked over and studied the map. It happened not far from Veliki Plana. Ja, right here." replied Lazo, putting his finger on the spot.

"That's better, Heinz. I know that area very well." He turned to Hedda and beckoned. Hedda rushed over to the table.

"What is the name of the little village just south of Veliki Plana?" asked the Major.

"You mean Cherni Lukno?"

"Ja, that's the one. Thank you Hedda, I can always count on you."

Then he looked at Lazo and said, "Well, Heinz, it won't be long now."

"Right, Herr Major. We must hurry. There is no time to lose."

"May I come too?" asked Hedda.

"Why not," replied the Major. "You might enjoy it."

"Ja, why not," echoed Lazo. "You will witness how the Third Reich deals with the so-called Untermenschen."

Hedda turned toward Lazo. There was fire in her brilliant green eyes. Lazo had never seen anyone express their anger so discreetly. She turned abruptly and followed the Major into the bedroom.

While the Major and his mistress were busy getting dressed, Lazo walked to the door. There was a smile on his face. He had not, even in his most sanguine moments, believed that it would be so easy. It seemed, that for once, at least, dame fortune was dancing about him. "Is it really possible," he thought, "that the Germans could be so easily duped?" As he waited, he began to have second thoughts. Then the fully uniformed

Major opened the bedroom door and walked into the kitchen. "Hurry Hedda, we don't have all day!"

"Ja, Karl, I am hurrying."

"How long will it take to assemble the men?" asked Lazo.

"Not too long," replied the Major. "There is a company of S.S. billeted about ten kilometers from here."

"How do we get there?"

Before the Major could respond, Hedda emerged from the bedroom. "I am ready, Karl," she said, as she walked up to the Major. "Would you button my blouse?"

"I have my hands full," replied the Major, somewhat embarrassed.

"Here, let me do it," said Lazo.

"Thank you Heinz, it's very nice of you."

Then the three of them left the cottage and walked down a well worn path.

"Are we going to walk all the way?"

"Don't be foolish Heinz," laughed Karl. "I have a lorrie up ahead."

"Oh, that's good. For a while, I thought we would have to walk the whole distance."

"Don't be so impatient Heinz. We'll get there in plenty of time."

"And then you can have your fun," added Hedda.

"Don't be so sarcastic, Liebchen," admonished the Major. They walked in silence for the next few minutes. When they reached the gravel road, Lazo saw the lorrie parked on the shoulder. The Major quickly entered on the driver's side. Lazo opened the other door for Hedda and assisted her into the vehicle. He was about to slam the door when the Major shouted, "No, Heinz, there is plenty of room up front. Sit next to Hedda. She won't bite."

Lazo, happy to oblige the Major, replied, "It will be my pleasure."

The Major started the vehicle and soon they were moving down the road. A huge cloud of reddish dust trailed behind. As the lorrie picked up speed, the wind played with Hedda's long, flaxen hair, tossing it about so that it brushed against Lazo's face.

"Isn't this refreshing?"

"Ja, Hedda, nothing like an early morning drive through the country side to get the blood flowing again," remarked the Major, as be patted Hedda's thigh.

"Or the passions," responded Hedda, pushing the Major's hand away.

Lazo wondered why the gesture of modesty. "Was she actually embarrassed?" he asked himself. A lock of her hair brushed against his face leaving a soft trace of lilac. The delicate aroma caused him to stir. He wanted to move closer but he was afraid that she would be repulsed by his state of uncleanliness. He had not bathed for several days. He almost unconsciously pushed himself away from her until he felt the door handle dig into his ribs.

"What's the matter, Heinz? Don't you like me? Perhaps you prefer those big, buxom German girls." taunted Hedda.

"Quit teasing him, Liebchen," admonished the Major. "He has other things on his mind."

"Ja, I'll bet he does," whispered Hedda, her lips barely parted.

"How much further?" asked Lazo, impatiently.

"A couple more kilometers."

There were no more words until the lorrie approached the gate of the German military compound, sequestered among the pines. The sentries were familiar with the Major's lorrie, so they opened the gate and flagged him through. Once inside the compound, Lazo began to feel less secure. So far, his plan was working splendidly but if the Major should take it upon himself, to contact some higher authority, not only his plan but his very life would be in peril. The Major parked in front of the orderly room.

"Wait here," he said, as he got out of the lorrie. "It won't take me very long."

He bounded up the steps and entered the building. The door slammed sharply behind him.

"Why do you hate my people so deeply?" asked Hedda.

Lazo did not respond immediately, for indeed, there were more crucial questions occupying his mind.

"I know that some Chetniks killed your friend," she continued, "but is that any reason to hate all of us? You know, as well as I do, that terrible things happen during wartime. No one knows that better than you Germans. You are the experts."

"Perhaps you are right," replied Lazo, "but if you had to witness what I did, I am certain that you would feel much as I do."

"Why do you say that? Don't you think that I have seen death? Does it matter so much to you, how a man dies?"

"You don't understand. You're a woman. How could you understand?"

"Oh, now I see," replied Hedda. "We don't understand because we are, by nature, weak and cowardly. Is that it, Heinz?"

"You said it."

She paused. Then she threw her head back in a gesture of defiance and said, "You men, you make me sick. You wouldn't even be here if your friend Klaus had been executed by a firing squad, would you?"

"Perhaps not."

"I thought so. His death was not nearly so important as how he died. The hero must die with honor. Ach, that's it, isn't it Heinz? Ehre! Ehre! Immer Ehre! God help us all." She looked directly into his eyes, "And now, you think that you can remove the stain by killing his killers."

"Perhaps, but that doesn't matter. What really matters is that we teach them a lesson that they will never forget."

"I see. You must insure against it ever happening to you. That's it, isn't it? And it will make you feel so good, won't it Heinz? You must get your licks in, musn't you?"

"Yes, I must. We must do what we must." A certain air of disgust marked his reply.

"Well, that's it then. We must do what we must," replied Hedda, quite sarcastically. "I'm sick to death of heroes. I'm sick of them because they honor death. I prefer the coward who hides under the skirts of women. They too get in some licks, but more important, they honor life."

Lazo chuckled and was about to reply when the door of the orderly room opened and the Major appeared, carrying a small package under his arm. "It's all set, Heinz. A truck carrying twenty men will follow us."

"Good, Herr Major. I knew you could to it."

"Ach, it was nothing," replied the Major, as he entered the lorrie. "A German officer knows his duty, right Hedda?"

"Ja wohl, Herr Major, and now we will have some fun. After all, we must do what we must. Right Heinz?"

As the lorrie pulled out of the compound, Lazo somewhat perplexed, asked, "Where is the truck? Shouldn't we wait for it?"

"Ach, don't worry, Heinz. They will catch up with us before long. They don't like to eat dust."

Karl had placed the package on the floor of the vehicle and when the compound disappeared from sight, the Major reached down, picked up the package and dropped it on Hedda's lap.

"There, Liebchen, a present for you."

"For me, Karl?"

She removed the wrapping from what was a large bottle of French cognac. "Oh, you shouldn't have done it," replied Hedda, clutching the bottle to her bosom.

"Well, don't just sit there! Open the bottle! We are thirsty, right Heinz?"

"Ja wohl, Herr Major! Nothing like good cognac to quench one's thirst and raise one's spirits."

Hedda removed the cork and asked, "May I?"

"Of course, you may," replied the Major. She put the bottle to her lips. Lazo watched her throat move as she swallowed the cognac.

"That's good," said Hedda, handing the bottle to Lazo.

"To your continued good health, Herr Major."

"Danke, Heinz."

Lazo put the bottle to his lips and took a large swallow, he wiped his lips with his shirt sleeve and handed the bottle to the Major. They passed the bottle around until it was empty and they were all, quite tipsy. The Major took the bottle and threw it against a huge rock which rested on the shoulder of the road. As he did, the car veered and almost left the road.

"Easy, Herr Major," cautioned Lazo as he lunged to steady the wheel, his left hand came down quite heavily on Hedda's lower abdomen. The Major quickly regained control and Lazo removed his hand from the wheel.

"That was close, Herr Major!" Then removing his hand from Hedda's lap, he said, "I'm sorry, Hedda. I hope I didn't hurt you."

Hedda straightened out her skirt and said, "No, you didn't hurt me. As a matter of fact, you probably saved my life." She leaned over and gave him a kiss on the cheek. As she did, she whispered, in perfect Slovenian, "Perhaps, some day, I can thank you more appropriately."

Lazo's face turned color and she knew that he had understood.

"What are you two whispering about?"

"Oh, nothing Karl. We were just making small talk."

"Well," replied the Major, "it looks like we have company."

Lazo turned and saw a large grey troop carrier bearing down upon them. "You'd better step on it, Major. It looks like they want to pass us up."

"Don't worry, Heinz. We're not going to eat their dust." The major pressed the accelerator down to the floor and the lorrie surged forward.

The three laughed and waved, as the distance between the two vehicles increased, substantially. "There! There!" shouted Lazo. "There's the church steeple!"

"Ja, that's Cherni Lukno, straight ahead," remarked the Major, removing his foot from the accelerator, allowing the lorrie to slow down.

"Why are we slowing down?" asked Hedda.

"We don't want to alert them," replied the Major, as he brought the vehicle to rest on the grassy shoulder. "I think it best that we proceed on foot from here."

"I agree, Herr Major. We must catch them unawares," replied Lazo, stepping out of the vehicle.

The Major dismounted and flagged down the truck. Lazo assisted Hedda out of the lorrie. As the Major walked over to the truck, Hedda turned to Lazo and said, "You are not a German. Who are you?"

"Of course I'm German," insisted Lazo. "Who the hell do you think I am?"

"You can fool the Major, but you can't fool me, Heinz, or whatever your name is."

"I am a German soldier," protested Lazo, as he turned and began to walk toward the truck.

Hedda took his hand and whispered, "Wait. Don't go. I won't give you away. I don't know what you are up to but I trust you and I will even help you. Remember, you can trust me." Then she gave Lazo's hand an affectionate squeeze and said, "Alright, now let's join the Major."

The two walked toward the truck. "Heinz!" yelled the Major. "Come here! I want you to meet an old friend of mine. We have been together since the beginning of the war."

"Any friend of yours is a friend of mine," replied Lazo.

"Heinz, this is Lance Corporal Willie Zimmerman. Willie, meet Heinz Frick."

Lazo shook his hand with pretended cordiality. "Well, what are we doing here?" asked Willie, surveying the landscape.

"We've got to teach a few Chetniks a lesson," replied the Major.

"Do you know who they are?" queried Willie.

"No, I don't but Heinz knows them. He knows them very well. Right Heinz?"

"Ja wohl, Herr Major. I could never forget their faces."

"Well, let's get started then."

"Right, Willie," replied the Major. "Assemble the men!"

"All right men, get out of the truck and form down here!" ordered Willie.

The men quickly filed out of the truck and fell in on the shoulder of the dusty road. Each of them was equipped with a machine pistol and a full field pack.

"Well, Heinz, what do you think of these men? Will they do?"

"Ja, Herr Major. I wouldn't want them chasing me."

"Nor I," echoed the Major.

Lazo walked over to Willie and asked, "Do you have a spare weapon? I lost mine last night and I could sure use one now." "Here," replied Willie, "take mine. I have my trusty old Manlichler in the truck."

Lazo took the weapon and pulled back the lever.

"Be careful, Heinz," cautioned the Major, "those damned things are very tricky."

"I know, Herr Major."

Willie walked up to the Major, saluted smartly and said, "We are ready, Herr Major. What are your orders?"

"You take three of the men and assume positions on the west side of the village. Now be careful. They must not know that you are there. We will take the rest of the men and enter the village from the east. We will not attempt to secret ourselves."

"I see, Herr Major. Just like we did at Kralljevo, last year."

"That's right Willie. If they decide to run when we enter, you can surprise them. Now go!"

"Ja wohl, Herr Major!"

He turned to the men and yelled, "You three, in the back, come with me and be careful. You heard what the Major said."

Lazo watched and when the last man disappeared into the forest, he turned and said, "Well Major, I guess it's time."

"Right Heinz, it is time."

"Will Hedda be coming with us?"

"Of course she will," replied the Major.

"Won't it be dangerous for her?"

"I don't think so."

"But what if they start shooting?"

"They won't Heinz. They have no reason to suspect anything. They don't even know why we are here."

"I see," replied Lazo, "I was just concerned about her safety."

"Ach, thank you Heinz. It's nice to know that you don't hate all of us," replied Hedda.

"All right men," commanded the Major, "follow us!"

"What time is it, Herr Major?" asked Lazo, as they walked into the sun.

"I have exactly eight o'clock."

"Good, I hope that they are still asleep."

"If what you say is true, they will be. I know these people and when they celebrate, they drink and when they drink, they sleep."

They entered the sleeping village without incident. The quiet was accented by the persistent barking of a dog. "See Heinz, did I not tell you that it would be easy."

They approached the church. Lazo looked at the tree which had served as the instrument of Sam's death. He pointed to it and said, "There, Herr Major, there is where it happened."

The Major looked to where Lazo was pointing and replied, "Good Heinz. Then this is where they will receive their retribution."

The Major halted his men and with arms clasped behind his back, said, "All right men. I want you to pair up and search every house in the village. You will collect all of the male inhabitants and assemble them in the village street. If any should resist, shoot them immediately. When you have searched every house, you will march them here. Do you understand? And leave the women and young girls alone, at least for the time being. Now go!"

The three watched as the men marched, quite smartly, down the village street. "Well, all we can do now, is wait," remarked the Major. "We may as well make ourselves comfortable."

The three walked over to the stone wall and sat down on the soft green grass. The Major removed his hat and placed it at his side. Then he lowered himself until his head came to rest on Hedda's lap.

"Ach, this is better. I think I will catch a few winks."

"Good, Karl. We will awaken you when the men return." She turned to Lazo and asked, "What will you do after we finish here? Will you remain with the Major?"

"No, I can't do that. I must get to Belgrade as soon as possible."

"May I go with you?"

"What do you mean, go with me? Won't he have something to say about that?" asked Lazo, pointing to the Major who was already fast asleep.

"He will not object. I think he would be glad to rid himself of me."

"Are you sure?" asked Lazo, scarcely believing what he heard.

"Of course, I'm sure. Do you think ich bin ein dummkopf?"

"Well then, with the Major's permission, of course, it will be my pleasure."

"Good," replied Hedda, with a warm smile. "Now as they say in American, let's shake on it."

Lazo took her hand, shook it gently and said, "It's a deal.Together, we will march to Belgrade."

Then the two leaned back against the low stone wall. "Do you mind?" asked Hedda, as she lowered her head to his shoulder.

"No, of course, I don't mind. I rather like the smell of your hair."

And so they remained. To a passerby, it might seem that the three were just happy sojourners on summer holiday, resting briefly, before pressing on.

Lazo placed his hand on top of hers and whispered, ever so softly, "Linger a while."

"What?" asked Hedda.

"Oh nothing," replied Lazo. "Nothing at all. I was just thinking out loud. How long do you think it will take them?" asked Lazo."Not long," replied Hedda. "They have done this so often that they have become very efficient."

"I think I hear them," remarked Lazo, as he jumped up to his feet.

"Ja, I hear them too." She shook the Major and said, "Get up Karl. They are coming back."

"What? What? What's going on?"

"They are coming back," replied Lazo, extending his hand to the Major.

"Gut. The hour of retribution is at hand." He grabbed Lazo's hand and Lazo jerked him to his feet.

"Danke, Heinz, danke."

"Where's my cap?" asked the Major.

"Here it is," replied Hedda, handing it to him.

He carefully positioned his cap upon his head and asked, "Is it on straight, Hedda?"

"Ja, Karl, it is straight."

The Major waited until the column was within shouting distance, then he bellowed, "Bring them over here and line them up against the wall!"

As the column approached the wall, the Major asked, "Where's Willie?"

"He went to get the truck."

"What for?"
"He thought you might need some rope."
"I don't think we'll need the rope, but we'll wait for him anyway."
The soldiers lined the hostages up against the wall. Lazo counted them as they passed by. There were fifty three. Some dressed only in night shirts, others in their underwear. Not one of them was properly attired. They had been caught completely unawares. "But why were there no signs of apprehension on their faces? Mighty peculiar," thought Lazo.
"Well, Heinz, do you see any of the guilty here?"
"Ja wohl, Herr Major. They are here. Every mother's son of them."
"Well then, you point them out for us."
Lazo was still mystified by the lack of fear displayed by the hostages. "What kind of men are these, who face death so stoically?"
Milosh stepped forward and in perfect German, yelled, "Herr Major, what is the meaning of this? Have we not always cooperated with you?"
Now Lazo knew why these men acted so unconcerned. "So these were his kinsmen," he thought, as he walked up to Milosh and struck him with all of his might, on the point of his jaw. Milosh did not anticipate the blow and he took it full force. His head bounced back and he slumped to the ground.
"Easy Heinz!" yelled the Major. "We'll take care of him for you."
Then Vaso stepped forward to address the Major. He was attired only in his underwear, but somehow he had managed to put on his sheepskin vest. He inserted his thumbs into the armholes of the vest, as he was wont to do, and asked, "What is the meaning of this? We have done nothing."
Lazo watched Vaso's bald head glisten as the sun played on the drops of perspiration that were beginning to accumulate.
"How about the German spy?" asked the Major.
"What are you talking about? We know nothing about a German spy," protested Vaso.
Lazo bounded forward until he came face to face with Vaso. He pulled the lever of the machine pistol back and pressed the muzzle against Vaso's balls. "You son of a bitch! So you know nothing about a German spy? Perhaps this will refresh your memory."
"You can't do this! Major ... "
Vaso's sentence was cut short by a loud burst of the machine pistol. Vaso screamed in agony, as he fell to the ground, clutching at his blood soaked underwear.
"You can't leave him that way!" screamed Hedda.
"Why the hell not?"
"For Christ's sake, you can't let him suffer like that. Finish him off! Finish him off!" she screamed. Then without hesitation, she removed the Luger from the Major's holster, ran up to Vaso and fired two shots into

his temple. Then she turned to Lazo. Tears were streaming down her cheeks. You are becoming just like them! You are worst than animals. Damn you! Damn you!" She turned and walked up to the Major and handed him his pistol.

"What the hell is going on here?" asked Willie, stepping down from the running board of the truck which had approached, unnoticed. "Have you started without me?"

"**Ach** ja, Willie, but there is still plenty to do," replied the Major.

"Do you want the rope?"

"No, Willie, we won't need it now." The Major put his arm around Willie and walked him a short distance away. Lazo could not hear what they were saying, as they spoke in whispers. It didn't matter anyway. He was still suffering the sting of Hedda's tirade. He walked up to where Hedda was standing and put his hand on her shoulder.

She jerked away and said, "Get away from me! I can't stand to have you touch me!"

"Don't say that. You don't understand. I had to do it."

"You had no right! You are not God," she remonstrated.

"He deserved what he got. You know that. Don't make me feel dirty." He reached out his hand but before she could respond, Willie said, "Ja wohl, Herr Major!" He saluted smartly, then turned to his men and ordered them to take up positions in a straight line, facing the captives.

"What are they going to do?" asked Lazo.

"You don't know? Don't pretend with me, you know damned well what they are going to do."

"They're not going to shoot all of them! They can't!"

"They must," replied Hedda. "You killed their leader. What do you think they will do if the Major allows them to go free?"

"They can't do that," protested Lazo. "That would be criminal."

"Look who's talking," replied Hedda, quite abruptly.

"I want no part of this. I'm leaving right now," declared Lazo. "Are you coming with?"

"Ja, I'll come with, but we've got to be careful," admonished Hedda.

"There's nothing to worry about. They're too preoccupied with their dirty work." He took Hedda's hand and slowly made their way to the opposite side of the truck. Then certain that their retreat went unnoticed, they threw all caution to the wind and began to run toward the forest. Hedda had difficulty keeping up with Lazo so he took her hand and pulled her along. "Not so fast Heinz! My dress keeps catching on the bushes!"

Lazo slowed down and said, "By the way, you don't have to call me Heinz anymore. My name is Lazo, and I'm an American officer, attached to the O.S.S."

"I knew it! I knew it!

"How could you tell?"

"I've been around Germans for four years and believe me, I can tell," she replied, still gasping for breath.

"Well hurry now. We don't have all day." He had barely finished the sentence when the stillness was punctuated by the loud burst of machine gun fire. The firing could not have lasted for more than five minutes but to Lazo, it seemed like forever. He clasped his hands to his ears to shut out the noise.

Hedda grabbed one of his wrists and jerked it away from his ear.

"Look," she cautioned, "we don't have time to lament. We've got to get to the lorrie before the Major. Remember, they have a truck."

Lazo followed her. He kept saying, "I didn't know. I didn't know. So help me, I didn't want it to end like this."

"Oh shut up!" snapped Hedda, in English, thinking that the shock of hearing English would bring him back to his senses.

He said nothing for the rest of the way and when they reached the lorrie, he asked, "Do you have a key for it?"

"Yes, I have a key and please don't speak German anymore. I can't stand that language."

"What language then?" asked Lazo.

"English, Lazo. I need the practice." She jumped in on the driver's side and got behind the wheel.

"Are you going to drive?"

"Of course, I'm going to drive. Do you think that I would allow you to drive? In your condition, you would kill us both. No Lazo, I'll drive. Now get in so we can get going."

Lazo jumped in and watched as she put her hand into her blouse and removed the key. She started the vehicle and the two were on their way.

"Will the Major follow us?" asked Lazo.

"No, he won't follow us. He knows that for him it is already too late."

Lazo was about to ask her what she meant, when she shifted the lorrie into high gear. As she did, her skirt, which had been severely treated by the underbrush, fell away, exposing most of her right thigh. Lazo's eyes strayed. She turned toward him, her large green eyes sparkling. Then she adjusted the hem of her tattered skirt and began to laugh. "We are free!" she shouted. "We are free!"

She gave Lazo a peck on the cheek and the scent of lilac, once again filled his thoughts, but only for a moment. He looked back and watched the dust rising behind them. He shouted, "Yes, Hedda, we are free!" Then he whispered, ever so softly, "So long Sam, so long."

CHAPTER THIRTEEN

It was just dawn. A large reddish brown rooster climbed to the top of a huge pile of manure, reached out his neck and crowed loudly. A woman, perhaps in her late forties, opened the door of the house and walked into the farmyard. She wore no shoes and was careful not to step on the droppings which the chickens had so generously deposited in the yard. She carried a shallow basket in one hand and the other held a large crust of black bread, which she munched on as she walked along. When she reached the barn she put the crust into her mouth and held it fast with her teeth, while she threw the door open and entered. The door closed behind her. The noise of the door slamming shut served as a cue for the chickens who were now racing toward the barn. Soon the door opened and the woman emerged, the crust of bread still in her mouth. The basket was filled with dry corn. She walked among the chickens, tossing out handfuls of corn and calling, "Here chickie, chickie. Here chickie, chickie."

The sound of her voice could scarcely be heard above the chorus of cackling chickens. Each of the chickens rushed about, frantically trying to devour as much corn as possible. When the basket was empty, the woman turned it upside down, shaking it vigorously, to dislodge any kernel that may have stuck to the bottom of the basket. Then she walked over to an old chopping block which had been placed adjacent to the barn. She wiped it off with her apron and sat down. As she surveyed her feathered domain, her feet played in the soft sandy soil, creating a series of unintentional scribblings. When the last of her bread had been eaten, she slowly raised herself up and began to walk toward the house.

Not far from this pastoral scene, Lazo and Hedda were desperately making their way through the forest which surrounded the farmstead. They had been on the run since they left Cherni Lukno. The two of them had foolishly driven back to the hunting lodge so that Hedda might retrieve some of her prized possessions. Her trust in the Major had been almost tragically misplaced. He did follow them and they had no sooner collected her belongings, when they heard the roar of the approaching troop carrier. They dashed out of the lodge and headed for the forest. When they reached the forest, Hedda stopped and threw the satchel which she had been carrying, as far as she could.

"Hurry," cautioned Lazo, "we don't have any time to waste."

"I know," replied Hedda, "but I've got to tuck my skirt into my panties so I can run faster."

"Well hurry, we don't want to lose our lead."

She made no response until she had passed him by. Then she turned and taunted him with, "What are you waiting for? Can't you keep up?"

Lazo, astonished by her agility, shouted, "Just keep running! I'll follow!"

The two ran along for a solid hour before Hedda fell to the ground. She tried to say something but only a hollow rasping sound issued from her parched throat.

"Don't try to talk, Just relax."

He sat down beside her. She was lying on her side with her knees pulled up tightly against her stomach. He watched her body heave as it instinctively tried to satisfy its desperate need for oxygen. He caressed her forehead ever so gently, hoping that it would help her to relax and bring an end to the spasms. His prescription worked. Soon she was breathing quite normally. She sat up and said, "Let's go. I'm sure they must be close behind."

"Just relax for a while. We've got time."

"Are you sure?" she asked.

"Quite sure. And besides, it seems that I've been running ever since I got here. I'm getting damned tired of it."

"How could I have been so wrong?"

"What do you mean?" asked Lazo.

"I didn't think the Major would follow us. He had no reason to."

"Perhaps not," replied Lazo, "but remember, desperate armies are made up of desperate men. Right now, I can't think of an army more desperate than the German army."

"Yes, I know. I was counting on just that."

"You were?"

"Of course. Desperate men need friends and they need them desperately."

She raised herself to her feet. Her skirt was still tucked in her panties. Her legs were covered with reddish welts and scratches.

"Don't they look awful?"

"The bruises don't look so good but your legs; your legs look just beautiful." He winked at her and smiled.

"Do you really think so?"

"Yes, I really think so," replied Lazo, "and no, I'm not just saying it to make you feel good."

Buoyed by Lazo's remarks and enjoying a renewed sense of exhilaration, she said, "Well, let's get going." She broke into a run.

"Just relax," urged Lazo. "We're not going to run any more. We're going to walk and when we get tired, we'll rest. Do you understand?"

"I hear," replied Hedda, "but I don't understand."

"There's nothing to understand. The worst that they can do is kill us. Besides, I've been listening and I haven't heard anything remotely akin to the sound of moving soldiers."

"You think we've lost them then."

"That's exactly what I think."

"Okay then, let's walk. Do you want me to lead?" asked Hedda.

"Yes," replied Lazo. "You know this country better than I and I rather do like to look at your legs."

And so they walked along, pausing occasionally to listen for any alien sound. On one such occasion, Lazo asked, "Was he really your friend?"

"Who?"

"The Major, of course, who did you think I meant?"

"Oh, the Major! No, he was no friend of mine."

"Well, were you lovers?"

"No, we weren't lovers either."

"Then what?" asked Lazo, his impatience beginning to tell.

"I think that you have already arrived at some conclusions about me, haven't you? Remember, things are not always what they appear to be."

"Then why in hell were you sleeping with him?"

"Oh, so that's it. I don't think that that is any of your damned business."

"It isn't," replied Lazo. He paused, trying to find the right words. "You can sleep with whomever you wish and you are right. It isn't any of my damned business."

"Then why the questions?" asked Hedda, tucking the part of her skirt that had fallen loose, back into her panties. She looked directly into his eyes and asked, "Would you like to sleep with me?" She smiled as she watched his face turn crimson.

"Let's get going," replied Lazo, quite curtly.

"What's the matter? Did I embarrass you?" Then she whispered, "I'd like to sleep with you."

Lazo was already walking so he did not hear her last utterance.

"Wait a minute," she exhorted.

Lazo turned and before he could speak she was pulling her blouse from her skirt. Then she undid the lower three buttons and tied the tails together under her gracefully contoured breasts. "There, that's much more comfortable," she said, as she hastened to catch up.

They walked along in silence. She had plucked three daisies and was now braiding them together. When she finished, she tugged on Lazo's shirt and asked, "Will you do something for me?"

"Now what?" asked Lazo, pretending impatience.

"My hair. It's a mess," replied Hedda, as she pulled it back into a pony tail. "Here, take this," she added, handing him the plaited daisies.

"What do you want me to do with this?"

"Come back here and tie my pony tail with it."

"I can't believe it," replied Lazo.

"Can't believe what?" asked Hedda, with a big smile.

"Here we are, enemies all around us and you are concerned with the state of your hair. You know what you are? You're nuts, that's what you are."

He walked behind her and with feigned reluctance, proceeded to tie the pony tail.

"Tighter."

"I don't want to break it," replied Lazo, "especially after all the work you did."

"It's a lot stronger than you think."

"There, is that better?"

"Yes, much better. How does it look?"

Lazo did not reply. His eyes had wandered down the front of her blouse.

"Well, how does it look?" she repeated.

"They look .... I mean it looks great." He put his hands on her shoulders and was about to kiss her behind the ear, when his cheek brushed against the daisies, reminding him of the Indian Paintbrushes that Ilse had hidden. Instead of kissing her, he slapped her bottom and said, "Let's get going. We have a long way to go."

"Don't you want to kiss me?"

"No," he replied, as he jumped ahead of her.

"I thought you wanted me to lead."

"I'll lead. We've lost too much time already."

"All right," she replied, undoing the buttons of her blouse above the knot.

They continued to press on. The beauty of the landscape impressed itself upon Lazo. For the first time since he landed in Yugoslavia, he seemed less than frenetic.

"Do you know where we are?"

"I really can't tell," she responded.

"Then we're lost, aren't we?"

"Not necessarily."

"What do you mean, not necessarily? Either we are lost or we are not."

She smiled and said, "We know that we are in Yugoslavia, so we are not hopelessly lost."

"Oh, that's funny. I didn't know that I had a comedienne on my hands."

"Quit being such a grouch. In peace time, people pay a lot of money to vacation in this wonderland and it's not costing us a penny."

"Not yet, it hasn't."

She did not respond. She walked up to him and kissed his cheek.

"Why did you do that?" he asked.

"Because I feel good. For me the war is finally over and I feel like a woman again. I want you to notice me, that's why."

"Oh but I have," replied Lazo, somewhat embarrassed. "Now button that blouse before you catch cold."

"Oh, you're nothing but an old fuddy duddy."

"Where in hell did you learn that?"

"At the cinema, that's where," she replied quite smugly, pretending to button her blouse. "Before the war, I went to see every American movie that played in Ljubjana."

"Why did you do that?"

"To learn English, of course."

"Well, you've succeeded."

"Do you really think so?"

"Of course I do." he replied, taking her hand into his. He pulled her to his side and together, they continued their trek through the forest.

"How old are you?" she asked.

"How old do you think I am?"

"Oh, I'd guess about twenty. Am I close?"

"Yup, I'll be twenty-one in February."

"And how old are you?" asked Lazo.

"Now it's your turn to guess," replied Hedda.

"Oh, I'd guess about thirty-five or maybe forty."

She made no reply. She simply pulled her left hand back and landed a punch to his mid section. It caught him completely unawares, causing him to double up in pain.

"Did I hurt you?" she asked, her teeth clenched.

"Of course you hurt me," replied Lazo, still doubled up.

"Please forgive me! I didn't mean for you to suffer so." She put her arm around his waist. Lazo was enjoying her attentions, but try as he might, he could no longer pretend and a soft chuckle slipped from his closed lips. This was soon followed by an eruption of loud laughter that completely surprised Hedda. She pulled her arm away in anger but soon she too was laughing loudly. He straightened up and gave her a big hug.

"Do you really think that I look forty?" she asked.

"Of course not," replied Lazo. "I was just teasing. You don't look a day over eighteen." Then as an afterthought he asked, "How old are you, actually?"

"I shouldn't tell you. You know how it is with women. We don't like to reveal our ages."

"Ah, come on," pleaded Lazo, giving her a squeeze.

"Okay," she replied, "I'll be twenty-eight next November." She looked up at him and asked, "Do you like older women?"

"I don't know. I have never been with an older woman, but if you are old, I think maybe I like older women." He kissed her forehead and stepped back.

"See, I knew it!" she exclaimed. "You kissed me just like you'd kiss your mother."

"That's not it at all," protested Lazo. "It's just that we're not out of danger yet and we ought to get going."

"Okay," replied Hedda and before Lazo could reply, she darted swiftly ahead, yelling, "now let's see if you can keep up with an older woman!"

"Go ahead, I'll try to keep up!" he snorted.

And so they continued, until they came to a small lake. It was almost dusk and the beautiful crimson sky was reflected in the water. Hedda ran to the water's edge, dropped down and began to drink the cool, refreshing water.

"Is it safe to drink?" asked Lazo, dropping down beside her.

"I don't know but I'm so thirsty, I don't care."

Lazo put his mouth to the water and began to drink. When he had satisfied his thirst, he pushed himself up and said, "I don't know if it is healthy, but it's the best water I have ever drunk."

"It was good but now I feel hungry. Do you have anything to eat?"

"I don't think so," replied Lazo. "I left my bag at the cottage. Wait just a darn minute," he shouted as he remembered the sausage he was about to eat when he came upon the cottage. "I think, yes, I know I have it."

"Have what?"

Lazo did not reply. He reached down into the huge pocket of his trousers and removed the one remaining sausage. "Voila, a feast!"

At the sight of the sausage, Hedda leaped up and pounced upon him, knocking him over on his back. The force of her unexpected enthusiasm almost caused the sausage to leave Lazo's grip. She settled upon him and gave him a long passionate kiss. Then she jerked the sausage from his hand, "May I have the first bite?" she asked, and without waiting, she bit into the sausage.

"Take it easy," admonished Lazo. "It may have to last us a couple of days."

She made no reply. She was too busy, chewing the mouthful of sausage.

"Well, may I have a bite?"

"Of course you may. Open your mouth."

Lazo opened his mouth and she shoved the sausage between his teeth. He bit off a piece and began to chew. "Now isn't that good?" Then she took what was left of the sausage and broke it in half.

She gave one of the pieces to Lazo and said, "Don't worry Lazo, we won't starve. There are many small farms in these valleys and we should run into one of them any time now."

"I hope so," replied Lazo, enjoying the press of her body against his.

When she finished her part of the sausage, she placed both of her hands against the ground and raised her shoulders upward, causing the lower part of her body to press heavily against him. She held the position for a few seconds then got up and walked toward the water.

"What are you doing?"

"I'm going for a swim before it gets too dark."

"Mind if I join you?" asked Lazo.

"Be my guest. You do smell quite awful, you know."

He watched as she kicked off her shoes. "What are we going to use for bathing suits?" queried Lazo.

She laughed and pulled the hem of her skirt from her panties. She looked at him, teasingly and began to unbutton her skirt. Lazo turned his head before the skirt fell to the ground.

"What's the matter? Are you bashful? This is Europe not America."

"Of course not," replied Lazo, somewhat embarrassed. "It's just the way I was brought up, that's all."

"Oh I see. It's alright to kill people, but it's not right to look at the human body. Boy, are you mixed up." Then she undid the knot of her blouse and slipped it off her shoulders.

Lazo turned toward her and watched as she removed her panties. "Will you help me with my bra?" she asked.

"Why? You seem to be doing just fine."

"I know but the clasp is bent and it won't come off."

Lazo got up and walked over to her. She turned her back toward him and he, with fumbling hands, undid the clasp. "It wasn't bent at all. You were just trying to embarrass me."

"Not true," she insisted. "I just wanted you to touch me."

She removed her bra and turned to him. "Well, what are you waiting for?"

"What do you mean?" stammered Lazo, his face now quite red.

"We can't go swimming until you get undressed, can we?"

"I guess not," replied Lazo, as he sat down and began to untie his boots.

"Do you want me to help?" She seemed to enjoy making him feel uncomfortable.

"No, thank you. I can manage quite well," came Lazo's rejoinder.

"Well hurry then." She turned and ran toward the water. When her feet touched the cold water, she let out a scream that resounded through the forest.

"Quiet," beseeched Lazo. "Do you want to alert the whole German army?"

"I'm sorry. I couldn't control myself. The water is so cold." Then she looked over her shoulder and shouted, "Hurry up!"

"Here I come!" warned Lazo, as he entered the water with a big splash.

"Don't splash me," pleaded Hedda. "Please don't."

She just finished the sentence when he swooped down upon her, cradled her in his arms and ran out into the deeper water.

"Put me down! Please put me down!" she urged.

He paid no attention to her plaints and continued until the water reached his waist. He kissed her and with her still in his arms, plunged headlong into the water. Once under water, he released her and she rose to the surface. He stayed under water for a minute or so, then he too surfaced.

"Now that wasn't so bad, was it?"

She made no reply. Her teeth were chattering so loudly that Lazo began to feel sorry for her. "Come out here, where it's deeper," he implored. "The water will feel warmer than the air."

"Are you quite sure?"

"Yes, I'm very sure."

"Okay, I'll trust you." She began to walk toward him but very cautiously.

"Here, take my hand," urged Lazo.

She took his hand and he pulled her over to him. "Doesn't that feel better?" He put his arms around her shivering body and locked her in a tight embrace. "Do you feel any warmer now?" he asked.

"Much warmer, but I know how we can get even warmer." She didn't wait for him to respond. She locked her legs around his hips in a tight scissors and began to rub her hips against him in an up and down motion. "I'm beginning to feel warmer already. How about you?"

"I've never felt better," he whispered.

"Good," she said and she released her legs, pulled away from him and began to run for the shore. When she reached shore she turned and yelled, "Where's the towel?"

"Oh, that's funny!"

"Aren't you coming out? It will be dark soon and you should build a fire for us."

"Build a fire! Are you nuts? The Germans aren't blind, you know."

"Don't be silly," she replied. "There aren't any Germans within twenty miles of this place. Besides, this is farm country and chimney smoke is quite common around here."

"Okay, if you say so. I'll be right out but first turn around."

"What in heaven's for?" she laughed. She picked up her skirt and began to dry herself.

"Well, what are you waiting for?"

"Oh, all right, but please hurry. It's very cold, you know." She slipped on her panties and smiled. She was enjoying his embarrassment but she finally turned her back to him and said, "Men, if I live to be a hundred, I'll never understand men."

Lazo ran in as fast as he could and quickly donned his coveralls. Then he walked over to her and gave her an affectionate slap on the seat. "Put your blouse on so you don't freeze."

"Where are you going?" she asked, as he began to walk toward the forest. "You're not going to leave me, are you? I was only teasing."

"Of course not. If you want a fire, we'll need some wood, won't we?"

"Oh, is that all, I thought that you were angry with me."

"I am, but I'll get over it." He disappeared and she finished putting on her clothes and sat down on the cool grass. She tried as best she could to dry her hair and was about to give up when Lazo reappeared, carrying an armful of dry wood. He dropped the wood beside Hedda and asked, "Did you miss me?"

"Of course I missed you," she replied. "Can I do something?"

"Ya, go over there and get me some birch bark."

"What do I use to get it off with?" she asked.

"Nothing, just pull it off with your hands. It comes off real easy."

Lazo began to lay the wood for the fire and when Hedda returned he placed the birch bark under the wood.

"How are you going to light it?" she asked.

"I'm going to rub a couple of dry sticks together."

"Will it take long?" she asked.

"I don't think so," he replied. Then he took his lighter from his pocket and ignited the birch bark. "There," he said, "that didn't take too long, did it."

"Rub two sticks together, eh?" And before he could brace himself, she gave him a push and he rolled over backward. "There," she said, "that'll teach you to make fun of me."

Soon the fire was raging and Hedda was no longer shivering. She knelt down by the fire and began to dry her hair. "Careful now," cautioned Lazo. "I don't like bald headed, older women."

She laughed and said, "Come here and sit by me. You make me feel good to be a woman."

Lazo sat down next to her. He put his arm around her and together they watched the fire until only glowing embers remained. Then the two, exhausted by the day's ordeal, settled back on the grass and were soon asleep. They did not stir until their slumber was interrupted by the persistent crowing of a rooster.

"Is that what I think it is?" asked Lazo, raising himself upward and resting on one elbow.

"You mean the rooster?"

"How far away do you think it is?"

"About half a kilometer, I would guess," replied Hedda, rubbing the sleep from her eyes.

"Well then, we'd better hurry. We don't want to miss breakfast, do we?"

"Must we go so soon?"

"I'd like to stay, but we had better get moving. Belgrade is a long way off."

"Oh, all right," she replied, reluctantly raising herself from the ground. "You'll have to excuse me now," she said, as she disappeared behind a clump of bushes.

Lazo, feeling some embarrassment, turned and walked off in the opposite direction. When he returned, she was splashing the cool water against her face.

"Do you have a handkerchief?"

Lazo reached into his pocket, removed his handkerchief and handed it to her. Then he knelt down next to her and began to wash his face. When he finished, she handed him the handkerchief so that he too might dry his face. He wiped his face and was about to get up, when she took his head and pressed it against her thigh. "Can't we stay awhile? Must we leave?"

"We do, if we want to eat," he replied, extending his hand. "Here, help me up."

She pulled him to his feet and the two began to walk in the direction of the rooster's call. As they disappeared into the hemlock forest, Lazo smiled and seemed happy with the thought of what might have been. The dry twigs snapped under his heavy boots as he hurried to catch up with Hedda.

CHAPTER FOURTEEN

The two reached the farm just as the sun appeared above the hill tops. The air was so very still that the white smoke seemed to cling to a chimney, bent and disfigured by time and history. They walked up to the barbed wire fence that surrounded the meadow and Lazo carefully passed between the rusted strands. Once through, he pulled the top strand upward so that Hedda could pass without mishap.

"Do you think we'll be safe here?" asked Lazo, his face turned back toward the forest.

"I don't know but let me do the talking."

"Why? Don't you like the way I speak?"

"Of course, I do but remember, we are now in Serbia and you might experience some difficulty with their language."

"Do you speak Serbian?"

"Of course I do. I spent a lot of time in Belgrade, before the war."

"How come?" asked Lazo, his curiousity piqued.

"My father was a member of the Yugoslavian parliament, that's why."

"Okay then. You do the talking and I'll play the strong silent type."

"Good. Now let's get moving. I'm famished and I do believe that I smell fresh bread baking."

"Your father was important, then."

"Of course he was," replied Hedda as she grabbed his hand and hurried him along. "He was so important that the Nazis arrested him as soon as they entered Belgrade."

"Where is he now?"

"I don't know. The damned Nazis do not permit prisoners to write letters."

"Haven't you heard anything?"

"Not a word for three years," she replied, as she squeezed his hand.

"It must be hell for you, not knowing whether he is dead or alive."

"It is but you learn how to survive." She turned and very softly, said, "Do you realize that you are the first person that I have touched in almost three years."

"How do you know that I am not a Nazi?"

"Believe me, I know. As I told you before, it's not as difficult as you might think."

"Well, you seem to have gotten along with him quite easily."

"Some day, when we have more time, remind me to tell you about him. I assure you, it will be most interesting."

Lazo stopped and pulled her to him.

"What's the matter?"

"Oh nothing. I just want you to know that you can depend upon me."

She put her arms around him and said, "I know I can. Now come on," she urged, as she pulled him along.

"Are you going to leave your skirt like that?"

"Why? Don't you like it that way?"

"I do but what about the owner of this farm?"

"Oh no! I can assure you that he will not think it strange."

"Well, I just thought ..."

"Oh, do I detect a hint of jealousy?" she asked, and with a smile, said, "That's nice."

As the two approached the farmyard, the sounds of the chickens became more pronounced and Lazo's pace quickened. He began to imagine a large plate of steaming, scrambled eggs and his mouth began to water. He hadn't tasted fresh eggs since he left Wisconsin and the thought of them was almost more than he could bear.

"Hurry," he muttered, as he surged forward, pulling her along.

"I didn't mean to get you angry. I'll pull my skirt out, if it will make you feel better. I will."

"It's not that," he replied as he began to laugh. "No, I see a vision of fresh eggs and maybe some ham."

"And fresh bread," she cried. "Oh what I wouldn't give for some fresh bread."

Soon they were off and running and when they reached the house, Lazo paused and asked,"Do you think my clothing will frighten them?"

"Oh no," she assured him. "They probably can't tell one uniform from another. Besides, I will do the talking, remember?"

She rapped gently on the screen door. It was very old and did not fit well and even her gentle rapping made the door strain on its hinges.

"Who is there?" came a loud feminine voice from within.

"A friend!" shouted Hedda, brushing her hair back from her forehead. "May we come in?"

"Yes, of course!" she yelled. "I haven't heard a friendly voice or seen a friendly face for such a very long time."

The smell of freshly baked bread wafted through the screen. She took a deep breath, then opened the door.

"After you," whispered Lazo.

The two entered the large room which served as the kitchen. The light was not too good but Hedda noticed four loaves of bread, cooling on the table and her mouth began to water.

"In here," came the voice from the next room.

Hedda took Lazo's hand and said,"Remember, I will do the talking."

They entered the room and were greeted by a shrill scream. It seemed to shake the very walls of the house. They stopped in their tracks. For there, in the center of the room, standing in a tub made out of an old wine barrel, was a woman of more than average proportions, sponging herself.

She tried to conceal her breasts with her arms while Lazo beat a hasty retreat into the kitchen.

"Get me that towel!" she screamed, pointing to a chair, upon which a faded blue towel was draped.

Hedda took the towel and helped the woman out of the tub.

"I didn't know there was a man present," she stammered. "Why didn't you warn me?"

"How could I know that you were taking a bath," replied Hedda.

"Well," she replied, "there haven't been any men around here for such a long time that I no longer have any cause to practice modesty."

Hedda could not help smiling. It was, after all, quite humorous, and she would never forget the look on Lazo's face, when he saw the woman. "My name is Hedda Pulash."

"And mine is Franzka Fantich." They shook hands and Franzka asked, "The young man. What's his name?"

"His name is Lazo Krall," replied Hedda, "and he is a very good friend of mine."

"Good, it will be nice to have a man around the house again." Then looking at Hedda, "You will be staying for a while, won't you? It gets so lonesome here."

"Of course we'll stay, that is, if we are welcome."

"You are welcome," she replied, as she slipped a somewhat soiled, cotton shift over her head and pulled it down until it covered her well tanned body.

"Where is your husband?" asked Hedda.

"My man? God only knows where he is. I haven't seen the son of a bitch for over a year now," replied Franzka, with anger in her voice. "And there is so much work to do around here before winter comes."

"Perhaps we can help."

"Perhaps you can," replied Franzka, "but now, let's go and have a look at that young man of yours."

"Of course," answered Hedda, as she followed Franzka into the kitchen.

"Oh, there you are, you devil, you."

Lazo did not reply. His mouth was full of bread.

She walked up to him and gave him a big hug. "Welcome to my home and my bread."

Lazo looked at Hedda who held her hand over her mouth to muffle the laughter that wanted release.

"Do you like my bread?" asked Franzka, releasing her hold and stepping back so she could get a closer look at Lazo.

Lazo did not speak. He understood her and was certain that he could have made himself understood but he decided that he would continue to allow Hedda to do the talking.

"My, you are a handsome one, aren't you?"

"Yes he is, isn't he," agreed Hedda, walking over to Lazo's side.
"Doesn't he know how to talk?" asked Franzka, somewhat mystified.
"Well, yes he does, but he only speaks Slovenian," replied Hedda.
"Oh! Is that all? I thought he was, you know, a little slow."
"Oh no, he's not slow. That's one thing he is not."
"Have you eaten breakfast yet?"
"No, we haven't. We haven't had anything to eat since yesterday morning and we are famished."
"What would you like?" she asked.
Before Hedda could respond, Lazo replied, "Eggs, fresh eggs. Lots of them."
"Yes, we would like some eggs," said Hedda, "and some coffee, if you have any."
"I have plenty of eggs and there is some hot coffee on the stove."
"That's wonderful," cried Hedda. "I could eat a horse."
"Now Lazo, you sit down at the table over there and Hedda, you pour the coffee, while I begin breakfast. Do you want your eggs scrambled?"
"Yes, scrambled," replied Lazo, sitting down at the table.
"Where are the cups?" asked Hedda.
"Over there, in the cupboard, top shelf," replied Franzka, as she removed a huge cast iron skillet from the oven and placed it on top of the stove.
"Do you want some coffee, Franzka?"
"Yes, please," replied Franzka.
Hedda removed the gray porcelain cups from the shelf and placed them on the table. Then she walked to the stove to get the coffee pot. She filled the three cups and returned the pot to the stove.
"Before you sit down, you had better get some plates and forks for yourselves. The eggs will be ready very soon."
"Will you be needing a plate?"
"No," replied Franzka, "I have already eaten."
Hedda got the plates and forks and set them on the table. Lazo was sipping the hot coffee and seemed very comfortable in his new surroundings. Hedda sat down next to him and placed her hand on his knee. He squeezed it affectionately. The warmth of the kitchen, the smell of the frying eggs, reminded him of home and a look of contentment shown on his face.
"There," said Franzka, "they are done." She wrapped a towel around the handle of the skillet and brought it to the table. "Here, help yourselves and don't be bashful."
Lazo filled both plates with the steaming eggs and began to eat.
"Do you want some bread? I baked it fresh this morning."
"Yes, please," replied Hedda. "I'm dying for some fresh bread."
Franzka broke off two large pieces from one of the loaves and gave a piece to each. She sat down next to them and began to slurp her coffee.

"How is it that the two of you are in this area?"

"Luck, I guess," replied Hedda. "We are running away from the Germans and just happened upon this place."

The expression on Franzka's face became very sober. "Do you mean to tell me that the Germans are nearby?" She seemed quite frightened.

"No," replied Hedda, "we lost them yesterday afternoon. They won't be coming here."

"Are you sure?"

"Yes, I'm very sure. They have more urgent things to do than chase a couple of harmless people."

"I hope that you are right," replied Franzka. "I don't like the bloody Germans."

"Have you ever seen any of them around here?" asked Hedda.

"No," answered Franzka, "but I have heard of the terrible things that they have done and it scares the hell out of me."

Lazo looked up from his plate and said, "Don't worry about the Germans. They will soon be gone. You had better worry about the Russians because they will soon be here." He spoke very slowly so that she would be able to understand him.

"What does he mean?" she asked, looking directly at Hedda.

"He means that the war will soon be over."

"Yes, I know he said that, but what did he mean about the Russians?"

"Oh nothing," replied Hedda. "He was just joking." With that, she kicked Lazo in the shin.

Lazo got the message and said no more. He continued to devour the eggs with a fervor that brought delight to Franzka's face.

When the two had finished breakfast, Hedda thanked Franzka effusively and aked, "What can we do to help you prepare for the coming winter? We can spare a day or two, can't we Lazo?"

"Well," replied Lazo, "we ought to be getting to Belgrade but I guess a couple of days won't matter. What would she have us do?"

"You could help me with the haying," suggested Franzka.

"We could do that, couldn't we, Lazo?"

"Of course. It might be fun."

"Can one of you handle a team of horses?" asked Franzka.

"I can't," answered Hedda, turning to Lazo.

"Don't look at me. Hell, I've never been near a horse."

"Do you mean to tell me that neither of you can handle a team of horses!" She laughed coarsely and slapped her thigh.

"That's right," replied Hedda, with a hurt expression on her face.

"Then I'll have to drive the team. You two do the dishes and I'll hitch up the team. I'll pick you up in front of the house in about twenty minutes!" she shouted as she left the house.

"Let's get started," said Lazo, getting up from his chair.

"I'll wash and you wipe. Is that alright?"

"That's fine."

Lazo collected the dishes while Hedda took the large kettle of hot water from the stove and placed it in the sink.

"What's that you're holding?" asked Lazo.

"What? Do you mean to tell me that you have never seen home made soap?"

"I guess not," replied Lazo.

"Well, live and learn," said Hedda, as she began to wash the dishes.

"How do we rinse them?" asked Lazo.

"There's more hot water on the stove, use that."

It didn't take very long for the two to finish the dishes and tidy the kitchen. "What do we do now?" asked Lazo.

"Empty the kettles."

"Where do I empty them?" asked Lazo.

"In the yard of course, and then fill them with fresh water."

"What?" asked Lazo.

"Fill them with fresh water and put them on the stove."

"Why?"

"Because we'll need hot water for baths."

"And dishes I suppose," uttered Lazo.

"Yes and dishes. While you're at it," she added, "you may as well carry in some wood for the stove."

They had no sooner completed their chores, when they heard the sound of approaching horses.

"She's here! Let's get going," said Hedda, rushing to the door.

Lazo followed her out, allowing the screen door to slam shut. They jumped on the hay rack and the horses headed for the field. The late summer sun shone brightly, making it a perfect day for haying. When they reached the field, Franzka brought the horses to a stop.

"Have you every hayed before?" asked Franzka.

"I haven't," replied Lazo, jumping down from the rig.

"Nor I," said Hedda, with a smile.

"Well, I guess we'll have to do the best that we can. "Lazo," she said, "You take the fork and load. Hedda, you pack the hay down and I'll handle the team."

Thus began Lazo's first experience with farming. His great strength enabled him to stack the hay very high, so high indeed, that he began to fret about Hedda's safety, as she stomped back and forth, packing down the hay. She was at least ten feet above the ground and should she slip she could have been injured quite severely.

"Be careful, up there!" he shouted. "I don't think I could catch you, should you slip."

"Don't worry about me. I'm a pretty good mountain climber. Just keep the hay coming," she laughed. "How come you're sweating so much?"

"Because I'm working, that's why."

"Why don't you take off your jumpsuit?" she asked.

"I'd like to," replied Lazo, "but not with her around."

"Why not? She won't mind," taunted Hedda.

"Is that right?" he shouted, and he put as much hay on the fork that he possibly could and pitched so high that it came down on top of her.

"You bastard!" she screamed, as she tried to brush the hay from her hair and upper torso. "It's gotten into my blouse!"

"Why don't you take your blouse off?" he shouted. Then pointing to Franzka, "she won't mind."

"What's all the yelling about?" shouted Franzka, bringing the team to a halt.

"Oh nothing," replied Hedda, "we're just having a little fun."

Franzka, stood up and looked at the load. "You two have done very well, for beginners. Ya, I think we have a load. Jump on Lazo, and we'll head for the barn."

"Look out, Hedda!" shouted Lazo, as he threw his pitch fork to the top of the hay. Then he scrambled up and joined Hedda, who was still trying to shake the hay from her blouse.

"Do you want me to help?" asked Lazo and he reached toward her just as the team surged forward. They lost their balance and fell into the warm hay. He gave her a quick kiss and she dug her fingers into his ribs and began to tickle him.

"So that's the way you want to play," he yelled. Then he began to run his fingers back and forth over her bare midriff. He thought that she would object but she seemed to be enjoying his attentions. He untied her blouse and pulled it away from her body.

"What are you doing?" she asked.

"Don't you want me to get the hay out from under your blouse?"

"Fine," replied Hedda, as she sat up and removed her blouse. She shook it vigorously, to cleanse it of the hay and dust that had accumulated on it. Then she turned her back to him and said, "Now brush the hay from my shoulders and back."

Lazo gently brushed her back and when he finished, he asked, "Is there any under your bra?"

"Yes," she replied, "there is, but it can wait until tonight." She put on her blouse and sat down to enjoy the ride.

Lazo fell down beside her and rested his head on one of her thighs. This is the life." he said.

"Yes, it is." She paused briefly, then said, "I wonder if the Major is still looking for us?"

"I doubt it. I don't think we'll ever see him again."

"I hope not," replied Hedda. She bent over him and gave him a kiss. "I never want to see him again."

"Me thinks the lady doth protest too much," rejoined Lazo.

"Don't be foolish. I hate the son of a bitch more than you will ever know. She pulled her thigh away and climbed on top of him. She placed her hands on his shoulders and pressed her hips against his, rocking from side to side.

"What are you doing?" he whispered. "Have you no shame?"

"No. As they say in the American movies, I'm just a wanton hussy." She lowered her lips to his and gave him a long, passionate kiss.

"You're just trying to take my mind off the Major," said Lazo.

"Am I succeeding?" she asked.

"Yup, you certainly are." Lazo moved his hands downward until they made contact with her thighs. He was just about to pull her skirt from her panties, when the team came to a stop and Franzka yelled, "Here we are! Everyone down! We've got work to do."

Hedda reluctantly got up, brushed herself off and slid downward until her feet made contact with the ground. Lazo followed her down and then brushed the hay from his hair.

"What do we do now?" asked Lazo.

"What we have to do now," replied Franzka, "is get the hay up there in the loft."

"How do we get it up there?" asked Hedda.

"It's simple," she said, "Lazo will pitch it up through the door and you and I will carry it back and pack it down."

And so they went to work. They continued the routine until the sun lay heavy against the horizon and the loft, whose appetite for hay, seemed insatiable, was now so full that its door could not be closed. It was a good day's work and Franzka thanked them over and over again. So much so that Lazo felt somewhat embarrassed. "It was, after all," he thought, "just another day's work. He was tired and that made him feel good. The two walked arm in arm toward the house, while Franzka unhitched the horses and led them into the barn to be unharnessed.

Once inside the house, Lazo sat down beside the table and lit the lamp. "Will you please get me a glass of water. I'm too tired to move. My arms feel like they weigh a ton."

Hedda walked to the sink and pumped until the water was very cold. Then she filled a glass and handed it to Lazo. He drank it very quickly and handed it back to her. "Another." he said.

"You really are thirsty, aren't you?" She pumped another glass and he downed it. He placed the empty glass upon the table.

"Now would you please hand it to me," directed Hedda, pretending to be exasperated.

"Oh sure, I didn't know you were thirsty," replied Lazo. He took the glass and said, "Here, catch."

"You wouldn't dare!" she screamed.

"Oh no?"

And before she could reply, he tossed the glass to her.

She let out a scream and having no choice, managed to catch the glass. "You're crazy!" she exclaimed.

"Of course, I am. Aren't you glad that I'm not sane."

She did not reply. She pumped until the glass was full. Then she sat down beside him and drank the cold, refreshing water.

"What are you two up to now?" came Franzka's voice from outside the door. She obviously wanted to make her presence known to them so that they would not be embarrassed. She then presented herself to them, carrying a clay jug in one hand and a large ham in the other.

She set both on the table.

"What do you have in the jug?" asked Hedda.

"Homemade Slivovitz. We are going to drink and then we'll eat. After the work we have done today, we deserve to celebrate. Right!"

Lazo's eyes moved from the jug to the ham and back again. He was hungry, but he also remembered the slivovitz he drank back at Tokra and he became quite thirsty again. Franzka got the glasses and filled them to their brims.

"Now let's drink a toast to tomorrow." she said, as she raised the glass to her lips and drank about half its contents. "Well, what are you two waiting for?" she asked. "Don't be bashful. There's plenty more where that came from." She slapped the table and laughed loudly.

Hedda raised the glass to her lips and swallowed a large portion. "Oh my God! If I continue to drink this, there will be no tomorrow for me."

Lazo, not wanting to appear timid, raised his glass and quaffed about the same amount that Franzka had drunk, perhaps a little more. After all, he did not relish the thought of being beaten by a mere woman. He brought his glass down heavily upon the table and shouted, "Prost!"

Hedda began to laugh heartily and Franzka slapped him on the back and said, "It's so good to have a man around again." She raised her glass. "To the men! May they never know how much we miss them!" She emptied the glass and set it on the table. "Now I will make supper."

"Can I help?" asked Hedda.

"No, I can handle it. You enjoy yourself. Remember, life is so very short."

"What are you going to make?" asked Hedda.

"Fried ham, scrambled eggs, hot peppers and fresh bread. How does that sound?"

"And slivovitz!" shouted Lazo.

"Ya, and slivovitz," echoed Franzka, laughing heartily.

"That sounds great," remarked Hedda. "I believe that I could eat a horse."

Soon the smell of frying ham filled the dimly lit kitchen as Franzka busied herself over the hot stove.

"Bring me a glass of slivovitz, please."

Lazo filled her glass and carried it over to her. She took it and began to sip. Lazo returned to the table, put his arm around Hedda, quite affectionately, and asked, "Would you like some more?"

"No, I haven't finished what I have."

"What's the matter? Don't you like it?"

"Of course I do," she replied, "but I don't want to lose my sensibility. And you, you'd better go easy, else you'll be no good to me tonight."

He did not reply. Not being accustomed to such talk, it tended to embarrass him, even though her candor excited him. He sat down and placed his hand on her thigh. She put her hand on his and moved it slowly until it came to rest between her legs.

"There," she whispered, "that should keep your mind off the Slivovitz."

"That's what you think," he replied, as he gave her a very gentle pinch.

She giggled and drew her legs together, tightly. "You devil," she whispered.

"What's the matter?" asked Franzka.

"Oh nothing," replied Hedda, "I just spilled some slivovitz on my blouse."

"Is that all? Well, you'd better set the table. Supper will be ready in just a few minutes."

"Did I hurt you?" whispered Lazo, apologetically.

"A little," she replied.

"Do you want me to rub the hurt?" asked Lazo. There was that devilish smile on his face and Hedda gave him a sharp jab to the ribs. He pulled his hand away and said, "God, you have a wicked left."

"My right isn't too bad either, so just watch it, Buster!"

She stood up and emptied her glass. Then she walked over to the cupboard and got the dishes.

"Be careful," cautioned Lazo, "you look a little wobbly."

"Why don't you help then?"

"I thought you would never ask." replied Lazo, setting his glass down.

They set the table and waited for Franzka to finish with her preparations. Lazo refilled the glasses and placed the jug on the floor, so that there would be more room on the table. Franzka loaded the platters with the ham and eggs and carried them to the table. Then she sat down and said, "Let's eat."

"Where are the peppers?" asked Lazo.

"Oh, I forgot," replied Franzka. "You'll find them in the cupboard, bottom shelf."

Lazo jumped up from the table and returned with a large jar of peppers. "There," he said, "and now let's eat."

And they ate. They ate until both platters were clean. The day's labor and the slivovitz had whetted their appetites like never before. "Who wants the last pepper?" queried Franzka, holding up the jar.

"Not I," replied Hedda. "I'm about to burst." She looked at Lazo and said, "But I will have some more slivovitz."

"I'll take that pepper," said Lazo, as he filled Hedda's glass.

"I'd like some too," pealed Franzka. "I haven't felt this good for a very long time and I have you to thank for this good feeling."

Lazo filled her glass and put the jug down. Then he broke off a piece of bread and put the remaining pepper on it. He raised the make shift sandwich toward the light and said, "Here's to good food, good booze and good women." He devoured it as though it was a mere tidbit. He wiped his mouth with the back of his hand, then rubbed his palms against his thighs.

"That was an interesting toast," remarked Hedda, "but are you sure of the order?"

"What do you mean?"

"You placed women last, in order of importance, didn't you? Why did you do that?"

"I always save the best for last," replied Lazo, without hesitation.

"I see." Hedda took a swallow of slivovitz and said, "I'm glad that you did not slight us."

"Careful now," admonished Lazo, with a smile. "You don't want to get drunk. Remember, we have more work tomorrow and it won't do to have a hang over. Besides, we've got to do the dishes."

"No," said Franzka, "we won't do them tonight. I'll get up early and do them before you two are awake. Let's just sit around and talk. There's still a lot of slivovitz left."

Neither of them demurred. They were enjoying the serenity of the evening very much. Hedda continued to down large amounts of slivovitz, in spite of Lazo's admonitions.

"I want to offer a toast," said Hedda. "Here's to the Major. If it had not been for him," and looking directly at Lazo, "we would never have met."

"I'll drink to that," said Lazo.

"Who's the Major?" asked Franzka, in a voice that suggested that the liquor was beginning to take its toll.

"He's the .... "

But before Lazo could complete the sentence, Hedda interrupted, "No Lazo, allow me to tell her."

"If you insist."

"I do," replied Hedda. She set her glass down and began to toy with it.

"You really don't have to do this."

"I want to, Lazo. I want you to know the truth about the Major." She looked up at the ceiling and continued, "When the Nazis occupied

Belgrade, they arrested my father and me. The Major was in charge of the unit that arrested us and when he found out that I could speak several languages, including German, he suggested that I become his interpreter. Of course, I refused. I wanted nothing to do with those bloody bastards. Then he made me an offer that I had to consider. He assured me that if I were to accept his offer, he would see to it that my father would not be executed. Of course, I accepted. I would have done anything to secure the safety of my father. Thus began a relationship that was to last until two days ago, when I met you, Lazo."

"Did you love him?" asked Franzka.

"Oh, no," replied Hedda, "I hated him, but I had to pretend that I didn't."

"You poor girl. It must have been hell for you."

"It was. If you only knew the half of it."

"Did you have to sleep with him?" asked Franzka.

"Yes, eventually. He insisted on it." Then she laughed and said, "But not in the way you think."

"What do you mean?" asked Lazo.

"Can't you guess?"

"No," replied Lazo, "I can't."

"He was a homosexual," yelled Hedda. "He only liked young boys. He kept me around for appearances only. After all, the Fuhrer did not look kindly upon homosexuals."

Lazo laughed and said, "So that's what you meant when I asked you about him." There was a sense of relief in his voice.

"Yes, that's what I meant, Lazo. Now don't you feel foolish?"

"A little," replied Lazo. Then as an afterthought, "But what if he had not been a homosexual? Would you have slept with him?"

"Of course not," replied Hedda. She laughed and added, "You know me. I only love good looking men." She took Lazo's hand and gave it an affectionate squeeze. "Perhaps when this war is over and sanity returns to Europe, the three of us could meet here again."

"I'd like that," echoed Franzka. "I'd like that very much." She raised her glass and said, "Let's drink to that. Perhaps, by then, my old man will return and he could join us. He's not as bad as I said he was. You two would like him."

"If you like him, we'll like him," declared Lazo. "Now let's do some serious drinking." He filled each of the glasses. Then he raised his and said, "Here's to us, may this day stay with us forever."

They continued to drink and talk until the jug was empty. Then Franzka showed them the bedroom, where they were to sleep. She bid them a good night and as she departed, said, "See you tomorrow, bright and early."

"Not too early," said Lazo, as he closed the door. Then he turned and fell heavily upon the bed. The old bed protested loudly, under his bulk, but it did not collapse.

"Aren't you going to undress?"

"I'm too damned tired."

"You are, are you? We'll see about that." She slowly removed her blouse and set it on the chair. Then she reached back and undid her bra, allowing it to fall to the floor. "Will you brush the hay from my back?"

She sat on the edge of the bed. Lazo reached over and gently brushed away the bits of hay that had lodged under her bra and were clinging to her skin. Then he pulled her over and kissed her breasts.

"Are you going to get undressed?" she asked.

"Oh, alright, if you insist."

He sat up and quickly removed his boots, allowing them to fall to the floor.

"Not so loud," cautioned Hedda. "You'll wake up the dead."

He stood up and removed his jumpsuit. "Is this better?" he asked.

"How about those?"

"What do you mean?"

"You know what I mean."

Lazo turned his back to her and undid his shorts, allowing them to fall to the floor. He fell back upon the bed and pulled her on top of himself. His hands reached downward and he removed the hem of her skirt from her panties.

"Wait," she said, and she rolled over on her back. She unbuttoned her skirt, raised her hips and slipped it downward until she was able to kick it off.

Lazo extinguished the lamp and soon they were lost in each others arms. A new surge of energy filled his body and it was spring again; a spring like none he had ever known.

CHAPTER FIFTEEN

Barely a week had passed since Lazo had dropped into Yugoslavia, yet during that moment of time, he had tasted more than most men will experience in a life time. He had seen a friend die, in shameful agony. He inadvertently participated in the elimination of the male populace of a small village and finally, for the first time, he had experienced the absolute joy of lying with a woman. All of this could not erase his boyish innocence. Buoyed by the thought of returning to Ilse, he remained ever sanguine. There was in him, no sting of guilt, no feeling of betrayal. During the several days which he spent on Franzka's farm, Hedda had clung to him and he to her, but they both knew that the pleasures shared, were only for the moment. They would soon take leave of each other, never again to feel the raging torrent of passion that spills over only to those fortunate enough to make danger their occupation.

It was early on the fifth morning after their arrival that the three friends climbed up into an old landau and began their journey to Belgrade. Franzka had become so fond of the young couple that she insisted on seeing them safely to Belgrade. Their protestations, though protracted and emotional, were for naught.

"How do you expect to get to Belgrade, walk?" she would ask.

"Yes," they would reply, "we will walk."

Then she would break out into laughter and say, "You will never get there alone. I know the way and together, we can succeed."

"But who will look after the livestock? Who will feed the chickens?"

"Oh Lazo, don't be a dupa. I will only be gone for three days, four at the most. I will get one of my neighbors to look after the livestock. They will be only too happy to return the many favors that I have done for them."

Lazo and Hedda, sensing that any further debate would be futile, gave in to the stubborn woman they had come to love.

"Good," she retorted, "it will be such fun. I haven't been away from this damned farm for almost a year. A change will do me good."

And so the three headed down the dusty road that led to the highway. Franzka had prepared a huge sack of food for the journey and she did not forget to include a jug of slivovitz. It was almost as if she was taking them on a summer picnic. She had no notion of the possible dangers they might encounter on the way to Belgrade and Lazo was not about to worry her. She seemed so happy and guileless. When they reached the highway, Franzka turned the team and headed north.

"How far is it to Belgrade?"

"Well Lazo, I've made this trip several times since we bought this farm and as near as I can figure, it's about seventy kilometers."

"How far is that in miles?" asked Lazo.

"Oh, I'd say about fifty miles," replied Hedda.

"That's not very far. We should be able to get there by nightfall."

"Then what will you do?" asked Hedda.

"I'll try to get a job on a river barge that's heading up the Danube. I believe that will be the easiest way to get to the allied lines. What do you think?"

"It shouldn't be too difficult," remarked Hedda. "With your command of languages, you should be able to deceive the authorities."

"Do I look like a native Yugoslavian?"

"Certainly. You are, after all, a Yugoslavian, aren't you?"

"Of course," replied Lazo, "but what about these clothes?"

"They'll do," replied Hedda. "If they were good enough for Franzka's husband, they should be good enough for you. By the way, I do like the Tyrolean hat. It makes you look like Helmut Dantine."

"Who the hell is he?"

"You don't know him?" laughed Hedda. "He's an Austrian movie star that acts in American movies. You must have seen him." she insisted.

"If I did, I don't remember," replied Lazo. "Is he handsome?"

"Of course he is," replied Hedda with a smile,"but not as handsome as you."

Lazo blushed a little and then adjusted his hat.

"What are you two gabbing about?"

"Oh nothing, Franzka. We were just making plans," replied Hedda.

"Well, we'll soon be coming to Veliki Plana," remarked Franzka. "Shall we visit the monasteries?"

"No, not today," replied Hedda. "Perhaps some day, after the war is over, Lazo and I can visit them together. After all, some of us are in need of redemption, aren't we, Lazo?"

Lazo felt the sting of Hedda's remark and he became silent. The color left his face and beads of perspiration began to form on his upper lip.

Hedda took his hand and squeezed it. "Easy now. I'm sorry Lazo. It really wasn't your fault. After all, how could you know the kind of beasts they really are."

"I know," replied Lazo, "but I feel so rotten whenever I think about it."

"You'll get over it, but I'm glad that it troubles you." Then she kissed his cheek and whispered, "You are a good man, Lazo and I do love you very much."

Lazo did not answer. He placed his arm around her wasit and drew her closer. Soon he was warm again.

"My man and I visited the Koporin Monastery, once," remarked Franzka.

"Did you like it?" asked Hedda.

"I did," replied Franzka, "it was so nice and peaceful." She paused briefly, then added, "But my man thought it was a lot of bullshit." She laughed heartily. "My man! You'd like him." Then she slapped Lazo on his back and said, "Give me the jug. I need a drink."

Lazo reached back and picked up the jug. He pulled out the cork and handed the jug to Franzka.

"Here, take the reins, Hedda!" yelled Franzka, handing them to her. Then she took the jug and raised it to her lips.

"Hey, you're getting to be a pretty good teamster, aren't you?" remarked Lazo.

"It's easy. When this war is over," she continued, "I might just become a farmer."

"You, a farmer," chortled Franzka, "you're much too delicate for that kind of life. No, you stick to the city life, else you will become hard and crusty like me." She slapped Hedda on the thigh and laughed loudly. Then she handed the jug to Lazo.

Lazo took a few sips. He wasn't thirsty but he did not want to hurt Franzka's feelings. Then he turned to Hedda and asked, "Would you like some?"

Hedda shook her head and said, "Not while I'm holding the reins."

"What are your plans for after the war?" asked Hedda.

"I don't know," he replied. "My mother wants me to go to college and become a professor."

"That sounds like a good idea. You will make a charming professor," replied Hedda.

"And what does your father want you to be?" asked Franzka.

"Pa doesn't say much," replied Lazo, "but once when we were cutting wood for the winter, he stopped to watch me as I was notching a very large tree. When I had finished, he tugged at his long mustache and asked, "Do you really want to be a college professor?"

"I told him that I was not sure and that I had not made up my mind. Then I asked him what he thought I should become."

"My wishes for you are of no consequence," he replied. "Only you can know what you must be and you must never be less." Then as he turned to pick up the saw, he added, almost in a whisper, "A happy zigan is better than an unhappy gospodar."

Franzka slapped her forehead with the palm of her hand. "Oh, yoi!" she exclaimed. "Your father must be a very good man. I wish that my father had told me that. If he had, I wouldn't have married that no good man of mine."

"What did you want to be?" asked Hedda.

"Promise you won't laugh."

"Of course," replied Hedda.

She took the reins from Hedda's hands and urged the horses to a quicker gait. "When I was seven years old," she began, my aunt took me to Vienna. While there, I visited the ballet for the first time in my life and I had never seen anything so beautiful or so extravagant. I was so moved by the spectacle that when the ballet ended, I would not leave. I clung to the seat and refused to budge. I wanted to remain in that theatre forever. My aunt was a very kind person and when I told her that I wanted to become a ballerina, she encouraged me with a big hug. On the day that we left Vienna, she presented me with a carefully wrapped box. I eagerly opened it and there in the box was a pair of pink ballet slippers and a length of beautiful blue ribbon. I clutched them to my heart, as only a child could. Then I gave my aunt a hug that she would never forget." Franzka paused. She looked up at the blue sky, then turned to Lazo and asked, "Would you please pass the jug. I don't want to become too sentimental." She took a long drink and handed the jug back to Lazo.

"What happened then? Please tell us," urged Hedda.

"When I got home, I showed my parents the ballet slippers and told them that I wanted to become a ballerina. My mother said nothing but my father, oh my father! He laughed coarsely and told me that I must rid myself of such silly notions. Then he took the slippers and threw them into the stove. I screamed, no pappa, no! Please no! I reached in to get them but the flames were too hot." She paused again and seemed almost reluctant to go on.

"Then what happened?" asked Hedda.

"I told him how much I hated him. Then I took the blue ribbon and ran to my bedroom and cried myself to sleep. When I awoke the next morning, I vowed that I would never cry again." Franzka looked at Hedda and added, "And do you know what? I haven't cried since that day." Hedda threw her arms around Franzka and gave her a kiss.

"Careful now," she yelled. "Do you want us to go into the ditch?"

"What happened to the blue ribbon?" asked Lazo.

A faint blush came to Franzka's cheeks.

"You still have it, don't you?" said Hedda.

"Oh yes, I still have it. I saved it so that if I ever I had a daughter, I would give it to her. I never had that daughter, so the ribbon is of no use to anyone, now."

"I'll just bet that you would have been a beautiful ballerina," remarked Hedda.

"Me!" laughed Franzka. "Are you out of your mind! Hand me the jug, Lazo. I need another drink."

And so they continued on their journey. It was almost noon when they came upon a small brook, cascading over the rocks toward the Morava.

"This looks like a good place," said Franzka, as she brought the horses to a stop.

"What for?" asked Lazo.

"Well," replied Franzka, "the horses need a rest and we should have some lunch. I'm hungry."

"But that will cost us time. We must go on," insisted Lazo.

"What's a half hour more or less," laughed Hedda. "It's so beautiful here," and she jumped down and ran toward the stream.

"Will you unhitch the horses and lead them to the stream? They need a drink."

Lazo jumped down and quickly unhitched the team and led them down toward the water. Then he ran down to join Hedda who had kicked off her shoes and was now wading in the stream.

"How's the water?"

"It's nice and cool. Come on in."

"Nah," replied Lazo. "I'll just sit here and get some sun."

He leaned back against a large rock and pulled his hat down over his eyes. Hedda quietly moved to where he was sitting. She bent over and was about to splash him, when he leaped up, shouting, "Oh no you don't!" he ran into the water, grabbed her in his arms and began to walk out toward the deeper water.

"You wouldn't! You wouldn't dare!"

"Oh, wouldn't I?"

She clung to his neck and shouted, "If I go in, you go in too, so help me!"

When he reached the deep water, Lazo lowered her until her bottom made contact with the water and held there until he was sure that she was well moistened. Then he turned and with her still in his arms, began to walk to the bank. When he reached it, he leaned over and kissed her. Then he set her down on the soft green grass.

"Why did you do that?" she asked.

He sat down, next to her but made no reply.

"Now, how do I dry off?" She pulled her skirt around and began to wring it out.

"Hey, you two! Lunch is ready!"

Lazo took her hand and together, they began to walk toward the landau. "Where will we spend the night?" asked Hedda.

"Don't they have hotels in Belgrade?"

"Of course they do," replied Hedda, "but they cost money and I don't have any."

"I've got plenty. Uncle Sam is a generous banker."

"Well, how much do you have?"

"About fifty thousand dinars."

"You're not lying, are you?"

"No, I'm not lying and I also have about five hundred dollars, American."

She threw her arms around his neck and gave him a big kiss.

"Can I buy some new clothes? Oh, how I'd love a new dress."

"Of course you can, but first we will have to find a hotel."

"One with a bath and a large bed!"

"Are you two coming?" shouted Franzka.

"Ya, we'll be right there," answered Hedda and they ran over to where Franzka had prepared the picnic.

The food was delicious, especially the fried chicken. "Eat, eat," insisted Franzka. "It will only spoil and God knows what kind of food you'll get in Belgrade." Their protestations were of little avail against the pleas of the lovable woman who could not repress her motherly impulses. Lazo realized that the only way he could get Franzka back on the road again, was to eat and he ate with gusto. Franzka was, after all, a very good cook and eating her food was not exactly a chore. It took them at least an hour to resume their journey. The traffic was almost non-existent, so they made excellent time.

Still, they did not arrive in Belgrade until nine o'clock and it was close to eleven before they could find a place to shelter the horses.

"Now where do we find a hotel?" asked Lazo.

"Well, my father and I stayed at the Balkan, whenever we were in Belgrade."

"Is it a good hotel?" asked Lazo.

"Very good, and it's not far from here, on Prizrenska Street."

"Well, let's get going. We don't have all night."

They walked out into the dark street and headed for the hotel.

They had walked about half a block when Lazo noticed that Franzka was not with them. "Where the hell is she?" asked Lazo, somewhat exasperated.

"Who?" asked Hedda.

"Franzka, of course."

Hedda turned and not seeing Franzka, said, "she must still be in the stable." She took Lazo's hand and the two ran back to see what had happened to their errant protectress.

When they arrived at the stable, Lazo threw the door open and yelled, "Franzka, where the hell are you?"

"Over here!" came her loud reply.

They walked over and found Franzka sitting on a bale of hay and next to her was the stable attendant, with the jug of slivovitz held to his lips.

"Are you coming with us?" asked Lazo, not trying to conceal his impatience.

"No," came her reply. "I'll stay here with Drago and help keep an eye on the horses."

"Will you be all right?" asked Lazo, his voice touched with concern.

"Of course she will," remarked Hedda, tugging on his arm.

"We'll see you tomorrow, then?"

"Ya, Lazo. Bright and early. We're not planning to go anywhere, are we Drago?" There was a sneaky grin on her face and Lazo knew that she would be just fine.

They left the stable and ran, until they got to Prizrenska Street. "I think we should turn left, here," said Hedda.

They stopped on the corner. She looked up and down the street and said, "Yes, we turn left here."

"Do you think Franzka will be all right?"

"Of course she will," replied Lazo, "but if she hasn't been with a man for over a year, I feel sorry for Drago. He may not last the night."

"He didn't look especially strong, did he?"

"No, he didn't, but looks are sometimes deceiving. How far is the hotel?"

"Just a few blocks," replied Hedda.

"Will it be safe there?"

"I think so. The manager was a good friend of my father."

"Do you think he'll still be there?"

"He might be," replied Hedda. "He was too old for the army, so unless he died, he should still be there."

"Kiss me," whispered Hedda.

"Why?"

"Don't ask silly questions. Just kiss me."

Lazo took her in his arms and kissed her. "Why are you shivering?" he asked.

"Can't you see them?"

"See what?"

"The German soldiers, coming toward us."

"Where?" whispered Lazo.

"Look to your right."

Lazo turned. "Now I see them. How do you know that they are German?"

"I know," whispered Hedda. "Believe me, I know."

He squeezed her more strongly and when the Germans were almost upon them, Hedda said, "Let me do the talking."

Lazo could feel her heart pounding against his chest. "Don't be frightened," he whispered. "If it comes to it, I think I can handle both of them."

"Don't be a muton!" she whispered. "You have no weapons. You wouldn't stand a chance."

They waited until the Germans were only a few steps away, then Hedda greeted them with, "Gute Nacht!"

"Was machen Sie hier?" asked the taller of the two.

"Wir sind vorloren, Herr Major. Bitte, Konnen Sie mir sagen ob die Hotel Balkan in der Nahe ist?" Her German, though not perfect, was passable.

The German corporal, flattered by being called a major, replied, pointing up the street, "Ja, sie ist da druben."

"Vielen Dank, Herr Major. Laku noc."

Neither of them spoke until the two Germans disappeared into the darkness. Then Hedda kissed him passionately and said, "I feel an overwhelming urge to make love with you."

"Here?"

"Right here, on this very corner," she replied.

"You're nuts!" He took her hand and they began to run toward the hotel.

"Not so fast!" she yelled, "you're pulling my arm off!"

"Then behave yourself," he admonished.

"I'll try," she replied, and kissed him more passionately than before.

When they reached the hotel, they were both gasping for air. They paused for a moment then entered the lobby and walked up to the desk. It was difficult to see, since the hotel was very dimly lit. Lazo looked around and seeing no one, rang the bell.

"I'm coming," came a raspy voice, from the small room adjacemt to the desk.

"It's him," whispered Hedda. "I'd recognize that voice anywhere. Then she bent down so that she could not be seen from behind the desk.

"What are you doing?"

"Shhh," whispered Hedda. "I want to surprise him."

"I wonder what's keeping him?" asked Lazo, becoming impatient.

Hedda did not reply. She was running her hand along his inner thigh.

"Cut that out!"

"What?" came the voice from the other room.

"Nothing," replied Lazo, "I was just talking to myself."

"Oh, I'll be right there."

Lazo reached down and removed Hedda's hand. "Now behave yourself," he whispered.

"Now, what is it you want?"

Lazo looked up and there stood the fattest man he had ever seen. He must have weighed four hundred pounds or more. If he had not been so dark complected, he could have easily passed for Sidney Greenstreet.

"We would like a room, if you have one."

"What do you mean, we? I see only you."

"I'm expecting company," replied Lazo.

"Oh," remarked the man. "Will you want twin beds or a double bed?"

"We want two double beds and a bath!" shouted Hedda, as she jumped up and made herself visible.

The man, startled by Hedda's sudden appearance, jumped back and almost lost his balance. "What do you want to do, give me a heart attack!" he shouted.

"Don't you remember me, Janos?" asked Hedda, as he bent over the desk so that he might better see her face.

"No, it can't be!" he exclaimed. "They told me that you were dead!" He reached over and grabbed her by the waist and with little or no effort, lifted her over the counter. She threw her arms around his neck and the two embraced. Neither of them spoke for the longest time. Finally, he set her down on the counter. Then he removed a handkerchief from his pocket and dried his eyes.

"Have you heard from your father?" he asked.

"No," replied Hedda. "I haven't heard from him since he was arrested. Have you heard anything?"

"No, not a thing. But don't give up." He put the handkerchief back into his pocket. "Your father is a survivor and we need him. Yugoslavia needs him."

"I know," replied Hedda and she swung her legs over the counter and jumped down.

"Janos," she said, "I want you to meet Lazo Krall, he is an American agent and a good friend."

Janos reached over the counter and extended his hand to Lazo.

They shook hands and Janos said, "Any friend of Hedda's, is a friend of mine."

"Thank you," replied Lazo, touched by Janos' obvious affection for Hedda.

"How did you get here, anyway?"

"What do you mean?" asked Hedda.

"It's way after curfew. Didn't the Nazis see you? You could have been shot."

"Ya," replied Hedda, "we saw two of them but they didn't stop us."

"You were lucky. Those bloody bastards have taken to shooting anybody out, after dark."

"Why are they doing that? The war is almost over."

"True, Lazo. The war is almost over but they can't believe it. They still have some mistaken notion that the Herrenvolk will ultimately prevail and they will continue their 'Drang nach Osten'."

"But why shoot innocent people?"

"They're not taking any chances, Hedda. They believe that the Russians are sending agents in advance of the army."

"Are the Russians really that close?" asked Lazo.

"Yes, Lazo, they are that close."

"You don't sound very happy," said Hedda.

"They're as bad as the Germans," replied Janos, as he banged the counter with his fist.

"What do you mean?" asked Hedda.

"They've been looting and killing. They rape anything wearing a skirt."

"But they are our allies," protested Hedda. "They wouldn't do that."

"They wouldn't eh? Let me tell you something. They are doing those things and more. Their agents have a list of political leaders and they are sparing no effort in tracking them down."

"To what end?" asked Hedda.

"To what end she asks! How can you be so naive? Didn't your father teach you anything about politics?"

"Do you mean to tell me that they are killing them?"

"Of course, they are killing them. They want to dominate Eastern Europe after the war. They can do that only if leaders sympathetic to Russia come to power."

"I can't believe it," protested Hedda. "The other allies won't stand for it."

"Believe it, Hedda, believe it. The allies are in no position to stop them. Ah, but you two must be tired. We can talk politics tomorrow. Now let me see. You want two rooms with double beds."

"No," interrupted Hedda. "We want one room with two double beds. Isn't that right, Lazo?"

Lazo blushed, "Ya, that's right. And it must have a bath."

"Let me see," mused Janos. "No, I don't have a room like that, but I do have two adjoining rooms, each with a double bed. Will that do?"

"Oh yes," replied Hedda, with unabashed enthusiasm. "That will do just fine."

"Well, here's the key. It's on the second floor."

Lazo took the key and the two began to walk toward the staircase.

"Would you like some food sent up?" asked Janos. "The kitchen is closed but I'm sure that I could scrape up something for you."

"That would be nice," replied Hedda, "but give us a little time to freshen up. And, oh yes, bring up some wine, also."

"Fine," replied Janos, as he turned and walked into his office.

The two bounded up the stairs and ran down the hallway.

"Here they are!" shouted Hedda.

Lazo nervously turned the key and flung the door open.

"Isn't it grand!" cried Hedda, as she ran over to the bed and fell into its softness.

"This is elegant," declared Lazo, walking about the room. "I just can't believe it. Where's the bathroom?"

"Over there," replied Hedda.

"I thought that was the closet," remarked Lazo, walking toward the door. He stopped abruptly and asked, "How did you know where the bathroom was?"

"Because this is the room my father used, whenever he was in Belgrade." Then she smiled and added, "That sly devil. He wants me to feel guilty."

"What do you mean?" asked Lazo.

"You wouldn't understand," replied Hedda.

"Who gets to take the first bath?" asked Lazo.

"We both do," replied Hedda. "Turn on the hot water and get undressed."

"That's what you think," replied Lazo, as he ran into the bathroom and locked the door behind him.

"Why did you lock the door?"

"Because I bathe alone," replied Lazo, his voice barely audible above the roar of the running water.

Hedda ran to the door and banged on it. "Let me in! Let me in!"

"You'll have to wait your turn!" shouted Lazo. "By the way, what the hell is this flat thing, next to the toilet?"

"Haven't you ever seen one of those?"

"No, I haven't," replied Lazo, "and what the hell are you laughing at?"

"Open the door and you'll find out."

"Okay, I'll open the door but I still bathe first."

"Alright, if you insist," answered Hedda.

Lazo slowly opened the door. Then pointing to the object in question, "What the hell is it?"

Hedda burst into laughter.

"What's so funny?"

"You are," replied Hedda. "That's a bidet. Do you want me to demonstrate for you?"

"No, that's all right. Now get out of here so I can take my bath." He turned to undo his trousers and in that moment, she jumped into the water, clothes and all.

"You little bugger!" he shouted.

"Come on in, the water's perfect. There's room for the two of us." She reached her hand toward him. "Come on now, you can wash my back."

Lazo took her hand and carefully stepped into the tub. Then he sat down, facing her. She quickly removed her clothes and threw them on the floor. "Now hand me the soap."

Lazo reached back, removed the bar of scented soap from the tray and handed it to her. She wrapped her legs around his waist, gave him a kiss and began to rub the bar of soap, ever so gently, over his back. "How does that feel?" she asked.

"Great," replied Lazo, "I never believed that taking a bath could be so much fun."

"Now do mine," said Hedda, handing the bar of soap to him.

And so they continued, until the bar of soap had touched every part of their bodies and they were very clean.

"How about your hair?" asked Hedda.

"What about my hair?"

"It's dirty," and before he could respond, she reached over and with both hands, pushed his head downward until it was totally immersed. She held it under for a moment, then allowed Lazo to surface.

"You little brat!" he shouted and without any hesitation, grabbed her head and returned the favor. "Now, we're even." He took the bar of soap and began to scrub her hair.

"Not so hard!"

"I'm sorry. I guess I got carried away." When he had finished soaping her hair, he said, "Now do mine."

When she finished scrubbing his hair, she stepped out of the tub.

"Where are you going?"

"You'll see," she replied. She took the huge porcelain pitcher and filled it with fresh water. Then she ordered Lazo to stand up as she poured the water over his head until his hair was thoroughly rinsed. "Now do mine."

Lazo got out and filled the pitcher. Then he slowly poured the water over her.

"Are you finished?" she asked.

"Not quite." He filled the pitcher again and began to pour it over her body.

She screamed loudly and shouted, "You bastard! That water is ice cold!"

He watched as her nipples hardened and she began to shiver.

"Come here and I'll warm you up."

She stepped out into the huge towel which Lazo was holding. He wrapped it around her and pulled her to him. "What are you going to wear?" asked Lazo, pointing to her wet clothing, lying on the floor.

"I'll wear this," she replied, tucking the loose end of the towel over her breasts. "See, doesn't this look good?"

"Yes, but what will Janos think when he brings the tray of food?"

"Don't be so puritanical. This is Europe and not America. Now throw me the other towel."

"Don't they say 'please in Europe? We do, in America."

"All right. Please throw over the other towel."

He tossed it to her and said, "That's much better."

She wrapped the towel about her head like a turban, then sat down on the bed.

"Do you want me to wring out your clothes and hang them up to dry?" asked Lazo.

"No, I never want to see them again."

"But what will you wear tomorrow?"

"You will have to go shopping for me. You promised that I could have some new clothes."

"That I did," replied Lazo as he wrapped the towel around his waist and sat down next to her. "How do you know that I will buy the right things? I've never shopped for a woman before."

"I trust you, Lazo." She was about to kiss him when the door opened and an older woman entered, carrying a huge tray, ladened with sandwiches and a bottle of wine. She set it on the table and left, without as much as a word.

"Don't they ever knock?" asked Lazo. Her sudden appearance had obviously made him feel uncomfortable.

"What for?" asked Hedda. She fell back upon the bed and pulled him on top of her.

"What about the tray?"

"You talk too much," whispered Hedda, putting her finger to his lips. "Now kiss me." She pulled the chain of the table lamp and the room fell into darkness. When the first hint of dawn shown upon the tray, it was still untouched and our two lovers were fast asleep, in each other's arms.

CHAPTER SIXTEEN

Frau Bischof left her desk and slowly walked over to the window. The clock on the Frauenkirche showed the time to be three-thirty. She glanced at her wrist watch, nodded her head and then returned to her desk. She carefully removed some large photographs from an envelope and began to study them. A lock of her auburn hair fell forward and came to rest on one of the photographs. She brushed it back with her pale, delicate hand and looked up at the crack in the ceiling which she had done so many times in the past. Her blue eyes sparkled as they caught the yellow of the winter sun.

"Frau Bischof! Come here, please!" came a heavy voice from the next room.

"Ja wohl, Herr Major." She hastily returned the photographs to the envelope and placed it in the top right drawer of her desk. Then she covered the envelope with some nondescript papers and closed the drawer. "I'll be right there!"

She stood up, straightened her skirt and walked into the Major's office.

"Well, Frau Bischof, I suppose you have heard the news?"

"What news, Herr Major?"

"Yesterday, Marshall Zhukov and his Russian army crossed the German border. They are now, less than 200 kilometers from Berlin."

"I had heard something to that effect, Herr Major," replied Frau Bischof, "but I thought it was just one of those rumors that seem to abound during these times."

"No, Frau Bischof, I can assure you that this time, it is no rumor." He got up and slowly walked to the window, his hands tightly clasped behind his back. "Please be seated, Frau Bischof."

Frau Bischof sat down, pulled her skirt down over her knees and said, "Then all is lost." The corners of her mouth moved upward and if one looked carefully, one could almost detect the trace of a smile.

"Not exactly," replied the Major, his voice regaining some of its lost stridency. "The Fuhrer has assured us that the German army will hold. And if they should fail, the Fuhrer believes that the Americans approaching from the west, will ultimately collide with the Russians and together, we will destroy Bolshevism, once and for all."

"You really don't believe such nonsense, do you Herr Major?"

"Why not? Everyone knows that the Western Allies hate Bolshevism as much as we do. They are bound to clash." He shook his finger at her. "You mark my word, Frau Bischof, when they meet, there will be plenty of fireworks."

"And that, Herr Major, is just wishful thinking."

"Perhaps you would rather see the Russians enter Dresden," sneered the Major, running his fingers over his flabby jowls.

"Are you questioning my loyalty, Herr Major?"

"No, I think not," replied the Major. "We have been together too long for that."

"Ja, six years is a rather long time. I don't believe that we have any secrets." She turned her head and smiled.

"Well, anyway, I called you in because I think that we must prepare for the worst."

"What do you mean?"

"During these past several years, we have been collecting a lot of information regarding our activities on the Eastern Front. Some of this information could be quite damaging to us if it should happen to fall into the wrong hands. Ja?"

"You mean the Russians."

"Precisely," replied the Major.

"They're not that close, are they?"

"I'm afraid so. Word has it that Konev is headed for Breslau and after that, well, it's only a stone's throw to Dresden."

"Perhaps the Americans will be here first. Is that not a possibility?"

"Ja, it is but we must still prepare for the Russian occupation."

"Well," replied Frau Bischof, "perhaps the Russians are not so bad as we have made them out to be."

"Now, who's wishfully thinking," rejoined the Major. "Haven't you seen the long queues of refugees coming in from the East I have heard from reliable sources, that they now number well over one hundred thousand."

"Ja, I have seen some of them and what a pathetic lot they are. Some of them are barely alive. They are so hungry and cold. We really should do more for them."

"Well, why do you suppose they are coming west?" The Major did not wait for a reply. "Because they want to be as far west as possible when the war ends. They will do anything to avoid being occupied by those damnable Russians. They know that the Russians are nothing but savages. They know because they have witnessed some of the beastialities, first hand."

"Well," replied Frau Bischof, "from the information we have, right here in our own archives, I would suggest that we have nothing to be proud of either." There was more than a hint of sarcasm in her voice.

"Perhaps we have been somewhat over zealous at times," retorted the Major, "but as bad as we may have been, those refugees still prefer us to them. Do you believe that these refugees are only German? No, no, Frau. They come from all parts of eastern Europe. I have been told that even a number of Russians are among them.'"

He walked back to his desk and sat down. He picked up a document that was lying on his desk and pretended to study it. Then he looked up at Frau Bischof and said, "You know, if I wasn't an S.S. officer, I think, perhaps, I would be heading west. Ach, but we must remain and do our duty, musn't we?"

"Ja wohl, Herr Major. We must all do our duty."

"Well, what do you plan to do when the Russians come?" asked the Major.

"They are not here yet," replied Frau Bischof, "and if they do come, I will remain right here. Dresden is my home and not even the Russians will drive me out."

"I admire your resolve, but perhaps you will change your mind when you witness their exploits, first hand." The Major paused, then added, "And then, there's the Mongolian Clap."

"What Mongolian Clap?" asked Frau Bischof, her interest piqued.

"Oh, then you haven't heard yet," laughed the Major. "Allow me to enlighten you. It is a social disease, not unlike the western variety, but our drugs have little or no effect upon it. Even penicillin doesn't seem to work."

Frau Bischof crossed her legs tightly and squirmed. Then wishing to direct the conversation elsewhere, asked, "What do we do with the thousands of documents we have collected? Do we destroy them?"

"Not yet, Frau Bischof. That would be somewhat premature, but I do believe that we ought to sort them out."

"What do you mean?"

"I would like you and your assistants to collect the most damaging of them so that they could be destroyed at a moment's notice. Do you understand?"

"And where would you like us to store them, once they have been collected?"

"Use your discretion. I trust your judgment. And now, Frau Bischof, I have an early engagement, so I must leave now. Will you please see that all is secure when you leave?"

"Ja wohl, Herr Major. I will see to it personally."

She helped the Major with his leather great coat and walked him to the door. "Aufwiedersehen, Frau Bischof," said the Major, as he clicked his heels together, quite smartly and departed.

Frau Bischof closed the door. There was a large smile on her face as she walked back to her desk and sat down. She removed the envelope from the drawer and once again began to examine the photographs. As she did, she tapped the desk with her fingers. Then she slowly turned and yelled, "Otto, are you still here?"

She waited for a reply and when none was forthcoming, she yelled, "Otto, come here!"

Soon an older man, with long unruly, gray hair and big round eyes, appeared in the doorway.

"Did you call, Frau?"

"Ja, I called. Were you sleeping again, Otto?"

"Ja, I guess I dozed off. After all, an older man requires his sleep, you know."

Frau Bishof smiled and said, "Come here, old man, I want you to see something."

Otto walked to her desk and leaned over her shoulder.

"Have you ever seen this man before?"

Otto picked up the photograph and examined it very carefully. Then he set it down.

"Well, Otto?"

Otto put his hand to his lips and began to tap his teeth with his thumbnail, a habit which Frau Bischof found quite irritating.

"Must you do that, Otto?"

"I'm sorry, Frau, but it does help me to concentrate."

"Well, do you recognize any of them?"

"I think I recognize this one," mused Otto. "I believe we have some other pictures of him in our files."

"You mean Major Karl Kranz?"

"Ja, Frau Bischof."

"What about the other man?" asked Frau Bischof.

"You mean, Heinz Frick? No, I am sure that I have never seen him before."

"Are you quite certain?"

"I can't be absolutely certain," replied Otto, as he ran his fingers through his hair, "but we could check our files."

"I have already done so," retorted Frau Bischof.

"And?"

"We have nothing on him. I can't find any mention of his name whatsoever."

"What have they done?"

"It says here, that they wiped out the male population of a village in Yugoslavia, called Cherni Lukno."

"Where in Yugoslavia?"

"In Serbia," replied Frau Bischof. She got up and began to pace about the room. "We must make a special effort to get them."

"What makes you think that we will be able to find them?" asked Otto, as he sat down in her chair and leaned back, causing the chair to complain loudly under his bulk.

"Where else can they go? The Russians are already in Yugoslavia and will soon be moving northward."

"Oh, I see," replied Otto, "and you think that the rats will return to the sinking ship."

"Oh, yes, Otto. They will return to that part of the sinking ship which will be occupied by the Americans. They want no part of the Russians."

"But the Americans are still so far away."

"It makes no difference. Our brave S.S. officers will run to the west, as fast as their polished jack boots will carry them. Why, it would not surprise me to see our beloved Major abandon us in the very near future."

"You don't mean our courageous Major 'fatbottom', do you?"

"Ja, that's who I mean."

"Well, what do you want me to do?" asked Otto, clasping his hands behind his head.

"First, I want you to go to the darkroom and make about ten reprints of this picture, so that we may distribute them among our friends. Then I want you to contact as many of them as you can, and tell them that we must have a meeting tonight at eight o'clock."

"At the usual place?" asked Otto.

"Ja, at the usual place. And tell them to be careful. We could be watched."

"Ja wohl!" snapped Otto, as he sprung to his feet with an alacrity that surprised even Frau Bischof.

"We are doing the right thing, are we not, Otto?"

"Ja, Frau. We are doing the right thing. History will, in all probability, never hear of our exploits but we are doing that which is right."

"Good, Otto. I sometimes feel like a traitor and I need someone to reassure me."

Otto walked over to her and affectionately placed his arm around her waist. "You are like a daughter to me, so please be careful. It would be unbearable for me, if something should happen to you.

Especially, now, when the war is almost over. Who would nag me then?"

"Don't fret, Otto. Nothing will happen to me, so long as I have friends like you." She kissed his cheek and said, "Now get to work. We don't have much time."

"Do you want me to lock up for you?"

"Ja. Would you do that for me, Otto?"

"Of course, I will," replied Otto, as he turned to leave.

"Aren't you forgetting something?"

"Ach, what a Dummkopf I am!"

She smiled and handed him the photographs. "And don't drink too much schnaps," she admonished.

She put on her coat and left the office. The chilly waters of the Elbe streamed northward like a silver lanyard, threading its way through the topless tunnels of stone. There was a look of tranquility about her and as she descended the steps, she sang, "dann loesch aus das licht, mein Herz vergisst dich nicht. Schlafe, schlafe, ein."

CHAPTER SEVENTEEN

On the morning of October eighteenth, just two days before the Russians entered Belgrade, Lazo left the city that he had grown very fond of and headed north on the Danube. He wanted to remain longer but the approach of the Russian army, foreclosed any such inclination. Janos had taken an immediate liking to Lazo and saw to it that every hospitality which the city could provide was extended to him. The money that had been given to Lazo by the army, especially the American dollars, made it possible for him to purchase anything Hedda or he desired. For the first time in his life, Lazo had experienced what it felt like to be wealthy and he liked it very much.

Janos had secured passage for him aboard a barge that travelled between Belgrade and Vienna. The man who owned the fleet of barges was a very close friend of Janos', so Lazo was able to embark on this new Odyssey with little or no trepidation. When the barge pulled away from its moorings, Hedda, standing on the dock with Janos, shouted, "We will meet again! We will be together again, you'll see!"

There was so much confidence in her voice that Lazo felt compelled to answer in kind and he yelled, "I will see both of you again! Soon!"

But as the barge slipped through the murky waters of the Danube and headed north toward Vienna, Lazo's attention became fixed on the gun fire that could be heard in the distance. The flickering show on the horizon, reminded him that battles were still being waged and men were dying. The war, that had been so remote during the past several weeks, had finally caught up with him.

The barge reached Budapest on the first day of December. The day was very heavy and quite cold. The journey had been rather uneventful and even dull. They had encountered several German patrol boats along the way but they were not the least bit troublesome. There had been several long delays but that was to be expected. The advancing Russian armies demanded the full attention of the Germans and a Yugoslavian barge was of little moment to them.

"Hey, Fraino, catch this rope!"

"Ja, Choma! Throw it! Careful now!"

"Any news?" asked Choma.

"Haven't you heard?"

"Heard what?" asked Choma.

"The Russians have crossed the Danube."

"Cut the bullshit," replied Choma. "We've been on the Danube for a month and we haven't seen any bloody Ruskies."

"That's odd," replied Fraino. "Tolbukhin's army crossed the Danube, near the Drava River, almost two weeks ago, and Malinovsky is threatening Budapest from the East."

"How far away is Tolbukhin?" asked Choma, who was now beginning to show some concern.

"Oh, about one hundred kilometers. It won't be long now and Budapest will be surrounded," responded Fraino, with a chuckle.

"How far away are the Americans?" asked Lazo.

"Oh, I see you have a new man with you," remarked Fraino.

"Ya," replied Choma. "His name is Lazo Krall. He has relatives in America."

"I see. Well, he'll have a long wait. The Americans haven't even crossed the Rhine yet and they say that the Germans are preparing a major offensive in the west."

"How long do you think before the Russians get here?" asked Choma.

"It will be quite some time. The Germans have thrown in over one hundred and fifty thousand men to defend Budapest."

"How about in the north?" asked Choma.

Fraino removed his cap and scratched his head. "Well," he replied, "this morning's paper said that Warsaw will fall to Zhukov in less than two weeks and after that, who knows."

"We've got to get to Vienna as soon as possible. How much petrol can you spare?"

"Not much. The Germans are confiscating every liter that they can get their goddam hands on." He paused briefly, then added, "Ah, but it is so nice to see those blonde, blue eyed beasts squirm."

"How much can you let us have? Can you give us enough to get to Bratislava?"

"Ya," replied Fraino. "I can let you have that much but what can you give me in return?"

"I've got plenty of dinars," replied Choma, as he reached into his pocket and pulled out a huge roll of bills.

"Dinars!" laughed Fraino. "What good are they? Have you got any American cigarettes? That's what we want, American cigarettes."

"No," replied Choma, "I don't have any cigarettes at all."

"Well, what do you have?"

"I've got fifty dollars, American!" shouted Lazo, reaching into his pocket.

"Where did you get fifty dollars, American?" asked Fraino, his eyes bulging.

"Never mind where I got it. Is it enough?"

"For fifty American dollars, I can sell you enough fuel to get you all the way to Vienna," replied Fraino, with a big grin on his face.

"Good," said Lazo, "and now, where can we get a good hot meal?"

"You are hungry, uh? I know just the place but there will be German soldiers there."

"That would be dangerous," whispered Choma. "What if they should ask for your papers?"

"Don't worry," replied Lazo. "Janos saw to that. I have a set of papers that would fool Himmler, himself."

"Alright then, but first let us get the petrol before that son of a bitch raises the price. Now that he knows about your American money, he will try to squeeze you."

"Don't you trust him?" asked Lazo.

"Trust him!" laughed Choma. "Do you take me for a fool? Hell, he'd sell his own sister if the price was right."

"What are you two talking about?"

"Oh nothing, Fraino," replied Choma. "Lazo wanted to know if there were any good looking women in Budapest."

"Well, you tell him that the best looking women in Europe, are found right here, in Budapest."

"Is that so? Then you'll have to show me."

"When can we load the petrol?" asked Choma.

"Right now, if you like but I must have the money up front."

Lazo reached into his pocket and removed his billfold. Then he carefully counted out fifty dollars and handed them to Fraino. "Here, now let's get the fuel on board."

Fraino took the money and without counting it, put it into his pocket.

"Aren't you going to count it?" asked Lazo, somewhat perplexed.

"No," replied Fraino. "If I can't trust you, whom can I?"

"Good," replied Lazo, "let's get started."

Fraino went into the warehouse and soon five men, each carrying two jerrycans, walked up the gangplank.

"Where do you want them?" asked one of the men.

"You had better pour them right into the tank. We're almost empty," replied Choma.

"Aren't you going to check it first?" asked Lazo, his voice subdued.

"No," answered Choma. "He knows that he got the best of the deal."

"I hope you are right," said Lazo, as he watched the men empty the cans into the tank.

By the time the men had filled the tank, darkness had already enveloped the barge. The sullen waters of the Danube seemed to irritate the vessel as it flinched to avoid each oncoming swell. Lazo pulled his arms tightly about his chest, trying to prevent the damp chill from seeping through the pores of his heavy woolen sweater.

"Well, gentlmen, now that you've got your fuel, what say to a good stiff drink to warm up the insides."

"What have you got?" asked Lazo.

"I've got some good French cognac, four star!" He chuckled and said, "A prize from the Germans."

"That sounds good to me," replied Choma, rubbing his hands together.

"Then come on in and we'll celebrate the imminent collapse of the 'Thousand Year Reich'."

"Why not," said Lazo, running down the gangplank.

Fraino led them into a small, dimly lit cubicle, that served as his office. "Sit down, gentlemen. It's not very elegant, as you can see, but it is warm and safe. The Germans seldom come down here."

"And why is that?" asked Lazo.

"Well," replied Fraino, as he twisted one end of his mustache, "let's say that they are very well compensated for shirking their duty."

Lazo, warming his hands over the kerosene lamp that sat on an empty crate, looked up just in time to see the bottle of cognac which Fraino had tossed to him. He nervously trapped the bottle in his hands and yelled, "I could have dropped it!"

"Don't worry, Lazo, I've got plenty more. Now drink."

Lazo removed the cork and raised the bottle to his lips. He took several big swallows, then wiped the bottle with his hand and handed it to Choma. "That really warms up the old gut," declared Lazo, as he sat down on a bale of old rags that Fraino had assembled for God knows what reason.

"Well, Lazo," asked Fraino, "how do you like working on a barge?"

"I like it. It's a bit lonely at times but I do like it."

"I was wondering why a big strong man like you is not fighting with the Partisans."

"I did fight with them for a while," replied Lazo, "but I saw no future in it."

"But there is a future on the barges, huh?"

"No, Fraino, there's no future on the barges, but the farther west I go, the better are my chances of meeting up with the Americans. Then who knows? Maybe they can help me get to America. But enough about me," said Lazo. "Tell me, Fraino, why is it, that a man who is so obviously well educated, is spending his life here, on these dingy docks?"

"Oh, that's a long story, Lazo," laughed Fraino. "It would bore you to death."

"No it wouldn't," insisted Lazo, "Besides, I've got nothing better to do. We can't leave until day break."

"I thought you said you were hungry."

"I was," replied Lazo, "but the cognac has made me feel better. I feel very comfortable."

"I'll tell you what. I'll send for some good sausage and bread and we'll have a feast."

"Isn't it hard to get good food?" asked Lazo.

"Not if you've got what they want," replied Fraino, raising the bottle to his lips. "I learned a long time ago that the unprincipled, seldom starve." He handed the bottle to Lazo. "In this Christian world," he added, "it is the moral chameleons who always survive and prosper."

He left the room and Lazo heard him yell, "Hey Bela! Go and get some good bread and sausage!"

"What do I use for money?" asked Bela.

"Just tell the bastard that I will settle with him tomorrow!"

Fraino removed one of his well worn sweaters and threw it to the floor, then he sat down next to Lazo. For some reason, he too, had taken a liking to this young man from America. He brushed his hair back. "Now where were we?" he asked.

"You were going to tell me how it was that you ended up here."

"Ah, it would only bore Choma."

"Never mind me," said Choma, with a chuckle. "You two talk and I'll just get drunk. How's that?"

Fraino put his feet up on the crate and leaned back against the wall made of roughly hewn planks. "You see, Lazo," he began, "I was born in a little village, a few kilometers from Belgrade. The village was peculiar in that the people were predominately Roman Catholic. A kind of island of Catholics in a see of Serbian Orthodoxy. My parents were poor but excessively devout and they had decided early on, that I was to become a Catholic priest. I liked the idea very much. Ah, but I was young and so very naive."

He took the bottle in his hands and pretended to read the label. Then he raised it to his lips and emptied it. "I'll have to get another," he said. He got up and walked over to the cabinet and removed two bottles of cognac. He placed them on the crate and said, "This should be enough."

"More than enough," said Lazo. "Now sit down and tell me the rest of the story."

He made himself comfortable and continued with his story. "My older sister had married a very wealthy Serbian merchant and he was willing to underwrite the cost of my education, even though he was not Catholic. When I was nine, I was sent to a Seminary in Ljubjana. It was quite lonesome, at first, but there were several other boys my age so I did not want for friendship. Time passed quite slowly for me and had I not been able to visit my family during the Christian holidays, I doubt very much that I could have endured the rigors of seminary life."

He reached for the bottle and took a big swallow. Then he handed it to Lazo. "The turning point in my life," he continued, "occurred when I was sixteen years old. It was the Christmas season and I had just arrived at my village. I had to walk from the station to my home. It was snowing ever so gently. I felt so warm and happy that it almost frightened me. My pace quickened as I neared my home. I so looked forward to seeing my family that soon I was off and running. As I turned into the yard, it suddenly occurred to me that they might not be at home. I ran up the steps, threw open the door and yelled, Merry Christmas! I heard a loud scream. There, standing in a tub, next to the kitchen stove, was my sister, Klara. My mother and father were out, so she thought it safe to bathe. She was two years older than I and very beautiful.

"Oh, it's only you," she remarked, and she continued to bathe as though no one was present.

"Would you like to wash my back?" she asked, and she threw the wet wash cloth to me. I did not speak. It was the first time that I had seen a nude woman and even though she was my sister, I was overwhelmed by her beautifully contoured body. I walked up to her, closed my eyes and began to scrub her back.

"Not so hard!" she implored.

I complied with her wishes and continued to run the wash cloth, ever so gently about her back. When I had finished, she turned to me, threw her arms about my neck and shouted, "Merry Christmas, brother!" Then she gave me a big kiss.

"Now throw me that towel," she directed, and once again, I complied with her wishes. I don't know why I didn't leave. I should have. I remember saying to myself, "If thine eye offend thee, pluck it out and cast it from thee," but as you can see, I did not yield to the scriptures. He chuckled loudly and once again raised the bottle to his lips.

"What happened then?" asked Choma, quite eagerly.

"Oh, I thought you weren't going to listen," taunted Lazo.

Fraino put the bottle down. Lazo noted that with each successive drink the bottle came down upon the crate with greater force.

"Then," he went on, "she stepped out of the tub and began to dry her feet. As she did, she revealed her most secret part to me. I kept wondering why she was doing this to me. She obviously believed that priests were bereft of any sexual inclination. Needless to say, I blushed and had I not been wearing my great coat, she would have noted the bulge in my trousers. I was so embarrassed that I ran out of the kitchen and didn't stop until I was safely in my room."

"Was it then that you decided to leave the seminary?" asked Lazo.

"No," replied Fraino. "At first, I thought that I should. Then I began to feel that God was just testing me, you know, to see if I had the courage and the strength to overcome these new feelings that were overwhelming me."

"Well, when did you decide to leave?" asked Lazo.

"Don't be so eager," admonished Fraino. "We've got all night." He scratched his moustache with his thumb and said, "I wonder what's taking that damned Bela so long. He should have been back by now. I'm getting hungry."

"Forget the food," beseeched Choma, "and get on with the story."

"Alright, if you insist." Fraino leaned back and continued. "Shortly after that incident, the Pastor of our village church asked my parents if they would allow my sister, Klara to become his housekeeper. Well, my parents, trusting souls that they were, considered it a great honor and eagerly gave their consent. I never did know how my sister felt about it. She never told me. Well, anyway, two years later, I came home for my gandfather's funeral. It was a very hot summer day and as I got off the bus, I decided to go to the village inn and get a glass of beer. I sat down at a table in the far corner of the room, so that I would not be noticed by any of the townspeople. I was not in the mood for any protracted conversation. I had loved my grandfather dearly and was deeply saddened by his death. As I sipped my beer, I could not help but hear the conversation of a group of men seated in the center of the room. They were not cognizant of my presence, and one of them asked, "Did you hear about beautiful Klara?"

"No." replied the others.

"At that moment, I should have left but my interest was aroused and like a fool, I remained."

"Well," the first man continued, "my sister, Olga, is a close friend of Klara's. She visits with her several times a week. Well, two weeks ago, my sister borrowed Klara's electric curling iron. On the very next day she went back to the parish house to return it and finding no one at home, she entered and put the curling iron on Klara's bed. The next week, Olga went back to visit Klara and was quite surprised when Klara asked her why she had not returned the curling iron. My sister ran to Klara's bedroom and returned with the iron."

"Here it is," she said, "I put it on your bed last week, when you weren't home."

"The room was filled with laughter. I was so embarrassed that I left without finishing my beer."

"And it was then that you decided to leave the seminary," declared Lazo.

"What in hell would a curling iron have to do with his leaving the priesthood?" asked Choma, somewhat befuddled.

"You're dumber than I thought," uttered Lazo and he began to laugh.

"What the hell do you mean?" asked Choma, who was now becoming somewhat unsettled.

"Well, you see Choma," Lazo explained, "if she had been sleeping in her bed, she would have found the curling iron."

"You mean," replied Choma, "that she had been sleeping with the priest. Well, I'll be a son of a bitch!"

"Ya," replied Fraino, who was by now, becoming drunk. "The old bugger was screwing my sister."

"What happened to her?"

"Well, Lazo, the gossip almost destroyed her. She left the village and went to live in Belgrade."

"Is she still there?" asked Lazo.

"I don't know. I returned to the seminary and tried to forget the incident, putting it down to human fraility. I still wanted to become a priest and would have, had it not been for Monsignor Stepan."

"Who in the hell is Monsignor Stepan?" queried Choma.

"I'll tell you," replied Fraino.

"Can you wait a minute?" asked Choma, as he got up and began to walk toward the door.

"Where in hell are you going?" asked Lazo.

"If you must know," replied Choma, without hesitation, "I've got to take a leak."

He almost collided with Bela, who walked into the room with a huge package of food, held tightly to his barrel chest. "Where do you want it?" asked Bela.

"Put it down here, on the crate," said Fraino. "Did you bring any horseradish?"

"Ya, Fraino, I brought the horseradish. Now can I go home. My wife will be worried."

"Ya, Bela, you can go home. Good night and we'll see you tomorrow."

"Where's he going?" asked Choma, as he returned to the room. "Isn't he going to stay for lunch?"

Fraino removed the food from the package and spread it out on the crate. "Help yourselves, gentlemen. It isn't much but it is tasty."

Each of the men helped themselves with huge slices of the sausage and bread.

"Have some peppers?"

"Are they hot?" asked Lazo.

"Not too," replied Fraino, with a smile. "They're good for you. They stimulate the flow of digestive juices."

Lazo bit into one of the peppers. "It's not too bad." He had barely finished the sentence, when he began to wave his hand before his gaping mouth. "Where's some damned water?" he screamed.

"We have no water," replied Fraino, laughing heartily. "Here, take this." He handed Lazo the bottle of cognac.

Lazo, not realizing what he was doing, took a huge swallow, then yelled, "Oh my God! That's worse!"

"Eat some bread, Lazo," exhorted Choma. "It will make you feel better."

Lazo began to eat the bread and the pain began to subside. "How in hell can you eat them?" he asked.

"They're very good," replied Fraino, as he placed a large pepper on a slice of bread and covered it with horseradish, then bit into it without as much as a grimace, and made short shrift of it.

"You must have an iron gut," said Lazo, who was becoming quite fond of this rather extraordinary gentleman. "Now, let's get back to Monsignor Stepan."

"Okay," replied Fraino. "It happened the year before I was to be ordained. On one rather hot summer evening, I was sitting in my room pouring over my textbooks. I was so engrossed that I was not aware of Father Stepan's presence, until I felt his lips pressing against my neck."

"You smell so good," he said.

"I was so repulsed by his attentions that I jumped up and without thinking, struck him with my fist. He was not a big man and the force of my blow caused him to fall back heavily, against the wall. He slumped to the floor and lay there, motionless. I rushed over to help but he was out colder than an anemic whore."

"Served the bastard right," uttered Choma. "What did you do then?"

"I tried to revive him but I couldn't. He appeared to be hurt quite severely. I rushed downstairs to get the rector and we brought him to the infirmary. It turned out that he was not badly injured."

"Did you tell the rector what happened?"

"Ya, I did, Lazo. I told him."

"And what did he say?"

"He told me that I must learn to control my temper. Can you imagine that! The son of a bitch rebuked me. I couldn't believe it."

"What happened to Father Stepan?" asked Choma.

"Father Stepan didn't even get a reprimand."

"What did you expect?" laughed Choma. "Hell, everyone knows that half of those short peckered bastards are queer."

Lazo laughed loudly. "Well, Choma," he said, "I guess that's the cognac talking."

"He's right, dammit! He's right!" yelled Fraino, slamming the crate with his huge fist, "and that's why I left the seminary. As far as I'm concerned, the priesthood is a perfidious conspiracy against the people and the sooner we rid ourselves of them, the sooner will mankind enter the Christian era."

"I'll drink to that!" yelled Choma, raising the bottle to his lips.

"Now wait a minute," exhorted Lazo, "we can't condemn the entire priesthood because of a few rotten apples. That's not fair."

"Fair!" yelled Fraino. "What the hell do you know? Where was the priesthood when Hitler marched into Vienna? I'll tell you where they were. They were in the front lines, saluting Hitler's triumph, that's where they were. And what are they doing about the slaughter of the Jews and the Gypsies?" he asked, his voice beginning to quiver with rage.

"I'll tell you what they're doing! Absolutely nothing. Hell, they're afraid that they might alienate that demented half-man, they call Fuhrer!" He was almost out of breath and had to pause to regain his composure. Then he took a large swallow of cognac, as if to wash away the bad taste in his mouth.

"Our 'Mother Church' believes in survival at any cost. And it works. It has surmounted every adversity, every travail and it has survived."

"The hell you say!" shouted Fraino. "Christianity died a long time ago. It was sacrificed on the altar of political expedience. It is drenched with the tears of moral cowards and buried under tons of rhetorical garbage. No, Lazo, an honest man can find no haven there. It has become a shelter for fools, cowards and knaves."

Lazo did not reply. He knew that Fraino was right and he was hanging on Fraino's every word.

"And then," continued Fraino, "there is the Ustashi. But I don't have to tell you about them, do I Lazo?"

Lazo had heard of the Ustashi, but he was not certain as to what Fraino was referring. Choma had been listening and not wanting to see Lazo compromise his true identity, remarked loudly, "Ya, those Croation bastards will have to pay for the nearly half million Serbs that they have slaughtered."

"And my brother-in-law was one of their victims," said Fraino. "Did I ever tell you about that, Choma?"

"No, you didn't or at least, I can't remember," replied Choma.

"They came to his house one evening and in the presence of his wife, beat him half senseless. Then one of them sat on his stomach, took out his knife and cut open his chest. Then the son of a bitch ripped his heart out. And for what? His only crime was being a Serb." Fraino grabbed the bottle, took a short drink, then toyed with the bottle.

"What happened to your sister?" asked Choma, quite solicitously.

"They raped her. There must have been twenty of them and they all took her. When they left, she went into her bedroom and hanged herself. My parents tried desperately to have her buried from the Church but the same priest that violated my other sister, said no. 'Suicide is a mortal sin'. He even refused to allow her to be buried in the family plot because it was on consecrated soil."

"Where did you bury her?" asked Lazo.

"My parents were so hurt and ashamed that I had to do something. I took the money that my grandfather had left to me and I went to see the good pastor. Of course, he demurred, at first. He was expected to. It took almost all of my legacy to assuage his pretended reluctance. Well, to make a long story short, my sister was buried in the family plot, with benefit of clergy and my parents were assured that her stay in Purgatory would be tempered by, in his words, certain pecuniary arrangements."

"The son of a bitch. How could he get away with it?"

"It's easy," replied Fraino. "The Church has always preyed on the ignorance and naivete of the masses. It will always be that way because there are none so blind as they who are not blind. Christ came into this world so that the blind might see. It would have been his greatest miracle, but he failed as have all others. It's hopeless."

"Why is that?" asked Lazo. "Are you suggesting that the Priesthood is devoid of any humanitarian impulse?"

"No, no," retorted Fraino. "Many good men enter the Priesthood but they are soon crushed by the weight of an institution grown ponderous by its own inactivity and wealth." He began to laugh very loudly.

"What the hell are you laughing at?"

"Well, you wanted to know how it was that I ended up in Budapest, didn't you?"

"Yes, of course, I did," replied Lazo, "but I thought you had finished your story."

"Not quite, Lazo. You see, I had to settle a score with that fat, baldheaded lecher, who called himself a priest. I went to his home one evening to settle up with him."

"What did you do?" asked Choma, who was now quite tipsy.

"We had a few drinks. He had one too many, I guess. He became quite drunk and was unable to walk. His housekeeper was out for the evening so I helped him to his bedroom which was on the second floor. He was a heavy bastard and it was with great difficulty that I finally managed to get him upstairs and onto his bed. I looked at the pathetic asshole, lying there and a tinge of compassion came over me. All of a sudden, the thought of harming him disappeared and I turned to leave. It was then that I saw the curling iron on the dressing table and the blood within me, began to boil. I hastily removed his clothing and with the drapery cords, I tied him firmly to the bed posts, belly down. Then I took the curling iron, turned it on, and rammed it up his asshole. A silly smile came to his lips and I thought that the instrument of my humiliation was defective. In any case, I turned and bounded down the stairs. When I reached the door, I heard this terrible scream and I knew that my sister had been avenged. Then, not wanting to be seen, I ran like hell. And that, Lazo, is how I ended up in Budapest."

"Did he die?" mumbled Choma.

"I don't know. Perhaps, someday when this war is over, I'll return and satisfy my curiosity. Who knows?"

"How about your parents?" asked Lazo. "Have you written them?"

"Neither of them can read, so it would be of no use."

"Well, in any case," remarked Lazo, "I'll bet that the good father, if you didn't kill him, can't stand the sight of peppers."

With that, they all burst into laughter and when the laughter finally subsided, Lazo stood up, grabbed Choma by the shoulder and said, "Let's go 'Stari'. We'd better get some sleep if we are to leave at daybreak." He turned to Fraino and said, "Thank you friend, for everything."

"You are welcome," replied Fraino, "and I hope you get to America some day, I really do."

"So do I. So do I," replied Lazo, as Choma and he disappeared into the darkness.

Fraino stood in the doorway until he was certain that the two merry makers were safely aboard the barge. Then he turned and walked slowly into his office. He fell back upon the bale of rags and with a smile on his lips, fell fast asleep. Lazo's laughter, it seems, had served as his absolution.

CHAPTER EIGHTEEN

The train pulled into the Hauptbanhof, just as the light was beginning to caress the rooftops of Dresden. The journey, though protracted by countless delays, was not unduly perilous. It seemed to Lazo that they had spent more time on the sidings than in transit. Human cargo was of very low priority on the Eastern Front. German valor was still unable to check the Russian armies that were advancing on the Vaterland. It was February tenth and as Lazo stepped out into the crisp morning, his thoughts, to be sure, were not occupied with the coming of lenten season. He followed the others toward the processing station. He had not shaved for several weeks and his clothes were in a rather shabby state. As he walked, his eyes were drawn to a long line of open railroad cars on one of the many sidings. Each of the cars was crowded with a host of pathetic looking men, women and children. Lazo stopped one of the yard workers and asked, "Who are those people?"

"Refugees from the East. They are running from the Russians," came the almost perfunctory reply.

"How far away are they?"

"Who?" asked the worker, somewhat bemused.

"The Russians."

"Rumor has it that Konev has surrounded Breslau and is even now, crossing the Oder."

Lazo thanked the man and was about to go on, when as an afterthought, "And the Americans? Where are they?"

"The Americans? They are still on the other side of the Rhine."

Lazo thanked him again and then ran to catch up with the others.

He felt quite safe. "It would be easy," he thought, "to lose oneself among the thousands of refugees who had poured into Dresden during the past several weeks. He also knew that the Germans, who were usually over zealous in checking identity papers, would be, because of the many refugees, less than scrupulous. And as anticipated, he experienced no difficulty whatsoever, in having his papers cleared. One hour after his arrival, he was on the streets of Dresden, bedazzled by the beauty of the Altstadt.

"How could these people create such wonders to behold and still be capable of committing such lamentable atrocities. It just didn't make sense," thought Lazo, as he whispered the words of Schiller, 'Bluhe deutsches Florenz, mit deinen Schatzen der Kunstwelt'."

He headed north on the Prager Strasse toward the Neustadt, hoping that he might find lodging of some sort. The city was quiet and so unmilitary in appearance, that in spite of the cold, Lazo began to feel warm. Off in the distance, he could see the mist rising above the Elbe

River and soon he was chuckling to himself as he thought of Fraino's avenging hair curler. By the time he reached the Ringstrasse, there was a marked increase in the number of people, milling about.

Hedda had told him of the wonderful shops in the Altmarkt but he paid no attention to them until he noticed a German soldier coming toward him. To avoid being noticed, Lazo turned and pretended to busy himself with the wares displayed in one of the shop windows. The German soldier, perhaps influenced by Lazo's example, stopped and likewise peered into the window. Lazo's heart began to race, but the German soldier stepped back and continued on his way. Lazo took a deep breath, relaxed and went on. He knew that he had to find the Augustus Bridge. Hedda told him that it would not be hard to find as it was near the Zwinger Palace and the Frauenkircke, two of the many historic landmarks of Dresden. Lazo did not find it as easy as Hedda had suggested. The maze of streets, some of them dating back to the middle ages, was too much for him. Bewildered and desperate, he finally stopped an old man and asked, "How can one get to the Frauenkircke?"

The old man laughed in disbelief. "It's right over there," he replied, pointing to the huge cupola which reached above the other buildings. "You can't miss it."

"Thank you very much," replied Lazo. "I am a refugee and I wanted to see the marvelous structure before the Russians destroy it."

"Well," the old man said, "it was here long before I was born and it will be here long after I'm gone. So there's no hurry."

"Well," rejoined Lazo, "one can never tell."

"You need not worry," insisted the old man. "This is Dresden. You are safe here. Nothing ever happens in Dresden."

Lazo bid him Aufwiedersehen, and the old man continued on his way. Lazo quickened his stride and hurried toward the Frauenkircke. A few minutes later, he was standing before the Martin Luther statue. He was transfixed by the spectacular beauty of the Church. So intent was his gaze that he did not notice the many people who passed by.

He was about to enter the Church, when he saw a woman, quite well porportioned, exiting the Church and walking toward him. When the woman was directly in front of him, Lazo, more through impulse than good sense, asked, "Pardon me Fraulein, but can you tell me, please, when this Church was built?"

The woman, somewhat startled by Lazo's question, paused, then replied, "I ... I believe it was built sometime during the eighteenth century. I am sorry but I cannot tell you the exact year."

"Danke, Fraulein," replied Lazo, "Aufwiedersehen."

"Wait! Haven't I met you somewhere before?"

"I don't believe that possible," replied Lazo, nervously. "I am a refugee from the East. This is my first time in Dresden."

She looked directly into Lazo's eyes, making him feel rather uncomfortable. "Oh, I am sorry. I didn't mean to make you feel uneasy. Her beautiful blue eyes became soft again and she smiled. "What are you doing here?" she queried.

Lazo paused briefly, then replied, "I am trying to get as far away from the Ruskies as possible."

"I know that. I mean, what are you doing here, at the Frauenkircke?"

"Oh, would you believe that I am studying to be an architect and this building holds a great fascination for me."

"So you want to be an architect, do you? My father was an architect."

Lazo smiled, he had said that just to gain time until he could think of a more likely reason. "I really came here to see if someone might help me locate a relative whom I haven't heard from since the beginning of the war."

"You're not studying to be an architect?"

"No, I'm not," replied Lazo, sheepishly.

"That's too bad. The world needs builders. God knows, we have enough destroyers." She paused briefly, then asked, "Do you have an address?"

"What?"

"The address, do you have it?"

"Oh, yes," replied Lazo. "I have already been there."

"And?"

"They weren't there. The landlord told me that they had moved in November of 1939, and left no forwarding address. It's rather quite hopeless."

"I wouldn't give up that easily. Perhaps I can be of some assistance."

"How could you help me? And why would you want to?"

"Well, for one thing, I work with the Department of Archives and have access to all kinds of records." Then without pressing, she asked, "Have you had breakfast yet?"

"No," replied Lazo, "and I am very hungry. By the way, my name is Lazo Krall and I am very pleased to meet you."

"And my name is Geli Bischof and I am very happy to make your acquaintance."

She removed the glove from her right hand and reached out to Lazo. He took the delicate, pale hand into his and shook it ever so gently.

"Good. Now let's get to my office. My immediate superior is a man of great influence and we always have good coffee and delicious pastries."

"May I carry your briefcase, then?" asked Lazo.

"It's not very heavy," replied Geli,"but if you insist." She handed it to him and they began to walk toward her office on the riverfront.

"Why are you carrying an empty briefcase?" asked Lazo.

"Oh," replied Geli, "it wasn't empty when I started out this morning. We use the basement of the Frauenkirche to store films. I had just dropped off several cannisters, when I met you."

"I see," replied Lazo.

The two walked along, making small talk. Lazo began to wonder why she was being so kind to him. "Afterall," he thought, "I am just another refugee among several hundred thousand. It just didn't make sense." Ah, but her smile was so disarming that Lazo had fallen victim to her pleasant demeanor and he became quite vulnerable. "How far is it?" he asked.

"Not very," replied Geli, as she put her arm into his, to reassure him. "There it is, the one with the large Nazi flag on the roof."

"I see it," replied Lazo, "but are you sure that your superiors won't mind my intrusion?"

"Don't worry about my superiors. They sleep very late. Afterall, rank has its privileges, you know."

"Yes, I know," replied Lazo, "but I will look so out of place. Just look at my clothing. I must smell like a pig."

"Don't worry about that. We have a shower in the building and I know that I can find you a razor."

"That will feel so good. Are you sure you want to go to all that bother for me?"

"It's no bother at all. As a matter of fact, Otto and I were talking about the refugee problem just the other day. We were wondering what we might do to ease the suffering of these poor people. They look so cold and hungry. It must be miserable for them."

"In that case, Geli ... May I call you Geli?"

"Certainly. It would please me very much."

"Then, Geli, I will be happy to accept your hospitality and I hope that some day I will be able to repay your kindness."

"Here we are," said Geli, as she ushered him up the steps.

"Good, I can hardly wait to get cleaned up."

The two entered the building and turned down the dimly lit hall that led to Geli's office. "Otto must already be here," she said. "The office lights are on."

They entered the office and Lazo closed the door. "Why don't you sit over there while I hunt up Otto. I won't be long."

As she left the room, she yelled, "Otto, where the dickens are you?"

"I'm in the dark room!" shouted Otto. "I'll be right out!"

"Hurry, I have something important to tell you."

"Ein moment. I'll be right there."

Geli paced back and forth before the dark room until the door opened and Otto emerged, wiping his hands in a soiled towel.

"Now, what's so important that it couldn't wait."

"Do you know whom I've got out there?" whispered Geli.

"Why are you whispering?"

"Because I don't want him to hear us, that's why."

"Who?"

"Heinz Frick, that's who. He's out there, posing as a refugee."

"The bloody Sweinhund! Are you sure?"

"I can't be certain, but as soon as he shaves I will be able to tell."

"Why did you bring him here?" asked Otto, as he threw the towel into the darkroom and closed the door.

"I didn't know what else to do. I was afraid that I might lose him."

"Well, what do we do now?" asked Otto.

"I told him that after he cleans up, we could have some breakfast." Then she smiled and added, "He doesn't suspect a thing."

"Are you quite sure? We can never be too careful, you know."

"Of course. Why else do you think he came with me?"

"I guess it's okay. What do you want me to do?"

"While he's cleaning up, I want you to go out and get some good pastry. Then after we have eaten, you can take him to the place." She paused, then said, "Remember to take your pistol."

"What if he refuses to come?"

"He won't. He needs a place to sleep and we will provide him with a very secure room. Now let's go back before he begins to suspect something," said Geli, grabbing his arm and ushering him into the office.

"Lazo, may I present my indespensible ally?"

"Hello, Otto, it's a pleasure."

"Likewise, H ... "

Geli, sensing that he was about to say Heinz, interrupted, "His last name is Krall. Isn't that nice?"

"Ja, that is nice," responded Otto, with a look that almost caused Geli to lose her composure.

Geli watched as the two shook hands. "Otto," she said, "would you please go out and get some pastries. While you do that, we'll try to make Lazo a little more presentable."

"Ja wohl, Frau Bischof!" responded Otto, clicking heels together. Then he left the office, slamming the door behind.

"He always slams the door like that. It rankles the Major and anything that irritates the Major, makes Otto very happy."

"But the Major isn't even present," offered Lazo.

"Force of habit, I guess," laughed Geli. She walked over to the large steel cabinet that stood next to the wall and flung the door open. "I think I can find some soap and a towel in here." She reached up on her tip toes and removed a large, field gray, military towel and a cake of soap. "Here,

Lazo," she said, "hold these, while I get a razor from the major's desk. He has so many of them that he won't notice that one of them is missing." She walked into the Major's office and soon returned with a shiny safety razor. "I told you that I could get a razor," she said, waving it before Lazo's eyes. "Now let's go to the shower room."

"Where is it?" asked Lazo.

"In the basement, of course. Where else would one find a shower?"

"Good," replied Lazo, as he followed her down the dark hallway.

"By the way, Lazo, what happened to your luggage?"

"I had an old suitcase when I started out but on the way, I met so many people more destitute than I, that I gave them what I had and then threw the suitcase away."

"That was so kind of you, Lazo." She opened the door at the end of the hallway. "Now be careful going down these stairs," she admonished. "They are not very solid."

"I see what you mean," said Lazo, as the stairs groaned loudly, under his weight. "How old is this building, anyway?"

"Over a hundred years, I guess," replied Geli, as she led him to a rather large gang shower, situated in the far end of the basement.

"Will anyone come down here?" asked Lazo, seeming to be a bit worried.

"No. No one ever comes down here. You need not fret."

Lazo removed his coat and sat down on the large, clumsy bench. He began to untie his shoes.

"Do you need anything else?"

"I don't think so," replied Lazo. I could use some clean clothes but I guess these will have to do for now."

"Good. I'll go back and make the coffee so that it will be ready when Otto gets back."

Lazo listened until the sound of her footsteps weakened. When he heard the door slam, he quickly removed his clothing and ran into the shower room. The warm water and the soap felt so good that soon he was humming the song that he had heard in Vienna. He didn't know the words but he couldn't forget the melody. It was so beautiful that it reminded him of Ilse. He was so engrossed in what he was doing that he didn't notice the return of Geli.

"Aren't you finished yet?"

Lazo was so startled by her voice that in a desperate move to cover himself, he dropped the razor. "No, I have not finished yet! Can't you see?"

"You're embarrassed, aren't you?" laughed Geli.

"Of course, I am. Wouldn't you be?"

"I guess so," replied Geli. She had not seen a nude, male body for such a long time that she kind of wished that he was not an enemy. As she turned, Lazo could not help but notice the red splotches on her face.

"Well, are you just going to stand there?" he asked.

"What do you want me to do, scrub your back?"

"That's funny," he replied, "By the way, what do you have there?"

"Oh these," she remarked, turning toward him, "these are some clean coveralls. I found them in the cabinet. I couldn't find any underwear, but you can put these on while we send your clothes to the laundry. It's just around the corner from here and the owner owes us several favors."

"That will be just fine," replied Lazo. "Just put them on the bench and turn around."

"What was the name of the song you were humming when I came in?"

"I don't know," replied Lazo, "but I like the melody very much."

"Where did you hear it?"

Lazo was about to say in Vienna, but he caught himself in the nick of time. "I don't remember exactly where. I guess I heard some of the refugees singing it. Do you know the words?"

"Yes, I know them."

"Would you teach them to me?"

"If we have time," replied Geli. "Now hurry, Otto will be back shortly."

"I'm finished. What do you think?"

She turned, looked at him, and said, "You are very handsome, aren't you?"

"And you," countered Lazo, "are a very lovely lady."

He put his hands on her shoulders and kissed her on her forehead. "Thank you, Geli. Thank you very much. I will never forget your kindness."

"Dammit," she thought, "why does he have to be so very charming?"

"Come, let's get back upstairs," said Lazo. "You lead, I want to look at your beautiful ankles. you know, you really do have beautiful ankles."

"Oh stop it," snapped Geli, smiling to herself. As they mounted the stairs she began to sing, "Hast du Heute Nacht, auch Lieb an mich gedacht."

"Geli, where are you?" thundered Otto's voice.

"We're coming, Otto. Just hold your horses."

"Oh, there you are."

"Yes, Otto, here we are. What are you trying to do, awaken the dead?"

"I was just worried about you, that's all."

"And why were you worried, old man?"

"You never can tell," he replied, "Afterall, he is ..."

"Hush, old man, before you say something that we both will regret."

168

"Ja wohl, Frau Bischof!"

Lazo laughed at the way Geli was able to cow the huge old man and said, "Otto, how can you permit this gentle little lady to push you around like that? Aren't you ashamed of yourself?"

"No, Lazo, Geli is the daughter, I never had and if it pleases her to push an old man around, so be it."

"Oh sit down, old man and let's have some breakfast," said Geli, pretending to be exasperated.

They sat down around Geli's desk and feasted on the exquisite pastries that Otto had procured. They were the best Lazo had ever eaten and the coffee was superb. He could not remember when food tasted so good to him and he ate until all of the pastries were gone. "I haven't felt this good for such a very long time," said Lazo, as he raised the cup to his lips and emptied it.

"Would you like some more coffee?" asked Geli.

"No, I've had enough," replied Lazo, returning the empty cup to the desk. "And now, I'm afraid I must go. It wouldn't do to wear out my welcome."

"Where?" asked Geli, somewhat astonished by the abruptness of his declaration.

"I must find a place to stay," replied Lazo.

"But you must stay until you get your clothes laundered," exhorted Geli.

"You two have done too much already. I'll never be able to repay you."

"You'll never find a place to stay," said Geli, "There are at least a half million refugees in Dresden. Tell him, Otto."

"Ja, Lazo, what Geli says is right, and they are still coming in."

"It's quite hopeless, then."

"Ach, nein! What a dummkopf I am! I know a place not far from my flat. It's not luxurious but it has a bed and it's warm enough."

"Where is it?" asked Geli, with pretended enthusiasm.

"On the Prager Strasse near the Augustus Bridge," replied Otto.

"Oh that place! Of course, that would be perfect. Why didn't I think of it?"

"Because I got all the smarts," replied Otto, pointing to his forehead.

"Then it's settled," said Geli. "Otto will take you there. Will that be alright?"

"I don't know what to say," replied Lazo. "I never expected to be treated so well."

"Think nothing of it," said Otto. "What are friends for?"

"Well, then, you take him there right now, Otto and I will see that his clothes get laundered before this evening. In the meantime, you can get some rest. Afterwards, Otto and I will show you the city of Dresden. We will show you a time like none you have ever experienced."

"Come," laughed Otto, "let me take you to your luxury suite."

Geli helped Lazo into his overcoat and bid him Aufwiedersehen. As the two departed she said, "See you this evening."

She closed the door and walked over to the window. She watched the two until they disappeared around a corner. Then she returned to her desk and sat down. "He doesn't suspect a thing," she whispered, as she gazed at the crack in the ceiling. "He doesn't suspect a thing."

CHAPTER NINETEEN

Geli and Otto departed the office later than usual that evening. The large clock on the Frauenkirke chimed six times. They had been quite preoccupied with preparations for the evening's session, and though they had conducted many trials in the past, this one was somewhat different. The only information that they had received were some photographs and a brief written description outlining the atrocity at Cherni Lukno. Heinz Frick or Lazo Krall, as he called himself, was somewhat of an enigma. Geli had searched through the files quite scrupulously to find more information so as to strengthen the case. She did not want to be accused of conducting a "kangaroo court". But search as she might, she could discover nothing further. It seemed that aside from his role at Cherni Lukno, Heinz Frick was non-existent. Yet here he was in Dresden. There was no denying that and he had to be dealt with. Justice demanded that the crime he committed be redressed in some fashion.

"What do you think, Otto? Do we have enough evidence to convict him?"

Otto did not respond immediately. He seemed to be preparing his words very carefully.

"Well, Otto, what do you think?"

"Ja, Geli, there is enough evidence. We must trust our instincts and our contact in Yugoslavia. He would not have sent the information if he had not considered it vital. Besides, Herr Frick will be given an opportunity to defend himself, and that's a helluva lot more than the Nazi courts permit."

"Ja, you are right, Otto. You are always right."

"No, Liebling, I am not always right but I know, deep down inside, that we must not let this crime go unpunished."

"Did you inform all of the others?"

"Ja, they have been notified."

"What time did you tell them?"

"Eight-thirty. Is that alright?"

"Ja, that's fine. That's just fine."

"We'll have to pick him up on the way, then," uttered Otto, as he unconsciously quickened his pace.

Geli tugged at his arm and asked, "Where's the fire? We have plenty of time." She stopped and put her finger to her chin. "Do you think he suspects anything?"

"No, Liebling. I'm sure that he doesn't. I think he trusts us. Poor devil." Then he chuckled and said, "You should have seen how happy he was with the room. He thanked me over and over again."

"Was his gratitude genuine?"

"As far as I could tell, yes, but who knows for certain? If it wasn't genuine then he is one fine actor." He put his hands to his mouth and blew on them. "However, something still troubles me."

"What is that, Old Man?"

"Well, if he is a member of the S.S., why didn't he seek shelter at S.S. Headquarters?"

"Ja," replied Geli, "it troubles me also. And why was he at the Frauenkirke at the same time that I was there? You don't suppose?"

"They may be on to us," remarked Otto with hushed voice. "The sons of bitches may be on to us."

"But how could that be? We have been extra careful and besides, the Major would have hinted if something was amiss."

"You mean old Major Fatbottom? Hell, they wouldn't tell him anything."

"But he is well connected at S.S. Headquarters, at least he tells me so," insisted Geli.

"He's just a big windbag," shouted Otto with a loud chuckle.

"Well, what shall we do?" asked Geli. She seemed somewhat perplexed. "Do we continue our efforts or do we call it quits?"

Otto did not reply immediately. Then he stopped and pulled Geli's arm. "What if, just what if the bastard had deserted from his unit and is heading west to meet up with the Americans."

"Ja, Otto and he knows what happens to deserters when they are caught."

"He knows that he could be hanged. That's why the son of a bitch is going along with us. Hell, he needs us."

Well, let's go and fetch the son of a bitch," declared Geli. There was a certain buoyancy in her voice and a renewed confidence in her stride.

"That's better," laughed Otto. "We don't have anything to worry about."

"Stop laughing" admonished Geli. "People might think that you have gone mad."

"Ja, Madame LaFarge! I am insane! You are insane! hell, the whole world is insane!"

"Ja," added Geli, "and the only sane person left is that little mustached shit in Berlin."

"Ja wohl, Madame LaFarge. You said a mouthful that time," laughed Otto.

Geli grabbed Otto's arm and said, "Come on. Let's find out what our charming young gentleman is up to. He is charming, isn't he?" Then she hit him on his arm and said, "And you quit calling me Madame LaFarge."

"Yes, he is charming and yes, I'll stop calling you Madame LaFarge."

"Well, I'll just bet that he'll scream, kick and cry like all of the other so-called 'supermen'."

"I hope so."

"So do I. It makes it so much easier to pronounce sentence when they turn out to be cowards."

Otto looked at his watch and said, "We still have time for a little supper. Can we stop somewhere and get a little bite?"

"Ja, but first let's pick up Heinz. He is entitled to a last meal, isn't he?"

"Ja wohl, Ma ...."

"You promised not to say that," interrupted Geli. "I don't want to be thought of as being a fanatic."

"Oh, Liebling, I was only jesting." He put his arm around her waist and pulled her over to him. "You are no fanatic. You are the most courageous woman I have ever known and God help anyone who says otherwise."

"Ah, thank you, Otto. You always know just what to say to make me feel good."

"It's the truth, Geli and don't you ever forget it."

The two continued until they reached the building in which Lazo was sequestered. It was by now, quite dark. The city was partially blacked out, not so much as a safeguard against enemy attack as to save fuel. And even though Dresden was situated in the midst of the Silesian coal district, the people were severely punished, if caught hoarding coal.

They entered the building and climbed the stairs leading to Lazo's room. When they reached the door, Geli looked at Otto and asked, "Do you think he is still here?"

"Of course he is," replied Otto, knocking on the door.

"Are you there, Lazo?" shouted Geli, "It is us. We have come to get you for supper."

"Ein moment," answered Lazo. "I'll be right there."

The two waited until the door opened and a well rested, Lazo appeared. "I'd ask you in but the room is a mess. He laughed as he handed his overcoat to Geli. "Would you give me a hand?" he asked. "These coveralls are a little tight and I'm afraid that they will split if I am not careful."

Geli helped him with his coat and asked, "Did you sleep well?"

"Oh yes," replied Lazo. "I slept like a baby, thank you."

"That's nice," uttered Geli. "Now let's go out and get something to eat."

"Yes, I am quite hungry. Is there a good place near here?" asked Lazo.

"Ja," replied Geli. "There is a place about ten minutes away. A lot of German officers frequent the place but they shouldn't bother us."

Are you sure?" asked Lazo, appearing concerned.

"Positiff!" replied Otto. "They have more important things to do now than watch a few loyal Germans." He laughed coarsely and slapped Lazo on the back. "Let's get going before those officers eat all the good food."

They hurriedly left the building and headed down the street. Geli walked between the two men, holding on to Otto's arm for support. The night was not especially cold, but she asked, "Are you cold, Lazo?"

"Not really," answered Lazo, "but I could use some warm underwear."

"Ach, mein Gott!" yelled Otto. "I completely forgot to go to the laundry. I promise you that I will do so the first thing in the morning." He covered his face with his arm, trying to conceal the large grin that graced his face.

The three began to laugh at Lazo's predicament and continued to do so until they turned into a narrow street, paved with cobble stones.

"It's right over there," said Geli, pointing to a building with a glimmer of light coming from the draped window. "It doesn't look like much but I assure you that the food is very good."

"Ja, Lazo, the food is Wunderbar."

They entered the restaurant and were cordially greeted by the head waiter.

"Guten Abend, Frau Bischof."

"Guten Abend, Dieter. Do you have a table for three?"

"For you Frau Bischof, I always have a table."

He led them to a table at the far end of the restaurant. The room was not overly crowded but the people who were present, seemed to be enjoying themselves very much. They seemed oblivious of the fact that the Russians were less than a hundred miles away.

"Don't they realize what's happening?" asked Lazo.

"Of course, they do," replied Dieter, "but after almost six years, they have become somewhat accustomed to war. Besides, they feel very secure in Dresden."

"Why is that?" asked Lazo.

"Because," replied Dieter, "the city, itself, is of no military significance. Oh, there are a few minor defense related industries but nothing that the enemy would consider vital. Ach, but you know that. You are just teasing me."

"Not really," interjected Geli. "You see, Dieter, my friend, Lazo, has come here from the East and that is why he seems to be overly concerned."

"I'm sorry, Lazo. I didn't know. Ach, but don't worry, you are safe here."

"Ja, I know," replied Lazo. "Nothing ever happens in Dresden."

With that, they all laughed and sat down.

"May I get you a drink?" asked Dieter. "We still have some very good cognac."

"What, no Schnapps?" asked Otto.

"Of course, we have Schnapps," replied Dieter, "but I thought perhaps, that you might crave something different tonight."

"Get the cognac," said Lazo. "It will be my treat."

"No, no! We couldn't allow that. Afterall, you are our guest," insisted Geli.

"But I do insist and there is nothing you could do or say that would change my mind."

"Very well," replied Geli, throwing up her arms in a gesture of futility, "have it your own way. Dieter, bring us a bottle of your very best cognac."

"And hurry," uttered Otto. "I am sooo thirsty."

As they waited, they listened to the music of the violinist who was making his way among the tables, trying to please the less than attentive diners.

"He plays quite well," commented Lazo.

"Yes, he does," said Geli. "He came to Dresden several years ago from Yugoslavia. He likes it here so much that he has made his stay permanent."

"Does he take requests?"

"Of course he does," laughed Geli. "Do you have one?"

"Yes, that song you were singing this morning."

"I'll ask him as soon as he completes this number."

The violinist had just about completed the number when Dieter returned, carrying a large bottle of cognac. He poured some into each of the glasses, clicked his heels smartly and was about to depart when Geli grabbed his arm and asked, "Will you have a drink with us, Dieter?"

"Danke no, Frau Bischof. You know how the boss feels about that." He winked and whispered, "Perhaps later, when he has gone."

"Good," replied Geli. "Will you please ask the violinist to play, 'Hear My Secret Call'?"

"It will be my pleasure," replied Dieter.

"Well, here's to us," said Lazo, raising his glass.

"Yes, here's to us and the causes we embrace," whispered Geli.

Otto downed the contents with one hasty gulp and returned the glass to the table. "That was soooo good. May I have another, please?"

"That's not the way you drink good brandy," admonished Geli. "You must sip it so that you can enjoy the full measure of its taste and pleasure."

"Ach," replied Otto, chuckling, "and now we have a poet at our table."

Lazo poured some more brandy into Otto's glass and said, "To each his own. To each his own."

"Ja, Lazo, I like that. Sipping is for women."
"Quiet, you two! The violinist is about to play your request."
"Would you sing it for me?" asked Lazo.
"I can't sing."
"Oh, yes she can."
"Shut up old man. You talk too much."
"She just wants to be coaxed," said Otto. "She has a good voice. She even took voice lessons when she was a young girl."
"That was a long time ago, Otto, a very long time ago."
"Please Geli. For me," pleaded Lazo. "I want to learn the words."
"Guten Abend, Frau Bischof. Guten Abend, Otto. And how are you this evening?"
"Never better, Boza," answered Otto and he downed his second glass of cognac.
"Boza, I want you to meet a friend of ours, Lazo Krall. Lazo, this is Boza Grabenc."

The two shook hands and exchanged niceties in the Slovenian language.

"I didn't know that you could speak Slovene," remarked Geli, somewhat astonished.

"I can speak fluent English also. Did you think that I was a dumb peasant?"

"No," replied Geli, as she winked at Otto, "but our suspicions of you are being confirmed. Right Otto?"

"Ja, Geli, they certainly are."

"What suspicions?" asked Lazo, somewhat bemused.

"Never mind," said Geli, with a sidewise swipe of her hand. "You will find out soon enough. Now drink up!"

"Would you like a drink, Boza?" asked Lazo.

"Ja, I would but first let me play your request." He raised the violin to his shoulder and began to play. Geli took a small sip of cognac and then very quietly, so as not to be heard beyond their table, began to sing.

> Horst du mein heimliches Rufen?
> Ofne dein Herzkammerlein;
> Hast du Heute Nacht,
> Auch Lieb an mich gedacht?
> Dann las mir in Traum bei dir sein.
> Las mich dich noch Einmal sehen,
> Zeig mir dein liebes Gesicht,
> Dann loesch aus das Licht,
> Mein Herz vergisst dich nicht.
> Schlafe, schlafe, ein.

"By the time she had finished the second verse, the room had become quite still with listening. Boza was about to put the violin down, when loud applause broke out and shouts of, "Noch Einmal," filled the room.

"Please, Geli, they love it. Sing it again," entreated Lazo.

"Ja, Liebling, go ahead," urged Otto.

"Oh, alright," replied Geli, whose face was now flushed with excitement, "if you insist."

Soon the room was filled with the sound of her lovely voice. One couple arose and began to dance in the narrow spaces between the tables. Others followed their example and soon most of the guests were up and dancing. Boza, caught up in the moment, continued to play the piece over and over again until the entire crowd was singing and humming along.

Lazo took Geli's hand and asked,"May I have this dance, gnadige Frau?"

Geli, transported by nostalgia and excitement, replied, "Of course. I would be delighted."

They joined the others on the floor, holding each other very closely. Geli closed her eyes and rested her head upon his shoulder. She had not danced since the death of her husband but she had not forgotten how and was indeed, enjoying Lazo's embrace. Then suddenly, she pulled away from Lazo and said, "Please, I want to sit down."

"Have I done something wrong?" asked Lazo, pained by the abruptness of her words.

"Nothing and everything," replied Geli, quite curtly. Then she turned and walked back to the table, leaving Lazo stranded among the host of other dancers. He slowly made his way back to the table and sat down.

"Well, Otto, it seems that I have somehow offended the lovely lady."

"Did he get fresh with you, Liebling?" asked Otto, very paternalistically. "If he did, I will see to him!"

"No, Otto, it's nothing like that. I just remembered that we are at war and we must never forget our enemies."

"And our friends," declared Otto.

Lazo, stung by the cryptic nature of their remarks, became quite sullen. He stared at the bottom of his empty glass. He could not hide the hurt expression on his face and he would have left the table, had not Dieter returned with their menus.

"Are you ready to order now?"

"Ja, Dieter," replied Geli. "What would you recommend?"

"The Sauerbraten is excellent. You must try it."

"Is that alright with you two?" asked Geli, quite politely.

The two men nodded their heads.

"Good. Then bring us the Sauerbrauten and would you please hurry. We have an important appointment at eight-thirty and that doesn't leave us much time."

"Very good, Frau Bischof. I will see to it personally."

"What appointment?" asked Lazo, pouring some cognac into his glass.

"There are some very important people who want to meet you, Lazo. I know that you must be tired, but I promised them. Do you mind?"

"How could I say no after all you have done for me," replied Lazo. "If it pleases you, I will be more than happy to accompany you."

"Good. Then it is settled," declared Otto, slapping the table with his hand. "Now, let's all have another drink."

They had no sooner emptied their glasses, when Dieter, true to his word, walked up with their dinners. The food was excellent and the three with their appetites whetted by the brandy, gorged themselves with the food, that Otto termed, "Wunderbar."

Otto was the first to finish and he experienced great difficulty, trying to muffle a belch, which in spite of his best efforts, surfaced in a kind of muted grunt.

"That's what you get for eating so rapidly," chided Geli.

"But I was so hungry and the food was so delicious. I just could not help myself."

"Well, shall we go?" asked Lazo, wiping his lips with the snowy white napkin.

"Ja, I think so," replied Geli. "We don't have very much time."

They paid Dieter and told him to give the remaining cognac to Boza. Then they left the restaurant and walked into the night. It was quite cold now. Lazo pulled the collar of his great coat over his ears and pushed his hands deep into his pockets.

"This way," directed Geli, as she pulled on Lazo's sleeve and ushered him down a narrow street leading to the river front. "It's only a few blocks from here."

"Good," replied Lazo, "I don't feel much like walking. I guess I ate too much."

"Me too," added Otto. "This is getting to be too much for an old man."

They continued at a rather brisk pace, none of them saying very much. When they reached the river they turned to the right and kept going until they came to an old building that seemed to have fallen into a state of disrepair.

"This is it," said Geli. "It doesn't look like much from the outside but the inside is quite well kept. You'll see."

Otto removed a bunch of keys from his pocket and fumbled with them until he found the one which unlocked the door. He opened the door and the trio entered the dimly lit hallway.

"Be careful," cautioned Geli, as she turned and descended the stairway leading to the basement. "There are some loose boards so keep your hand on the railing."

The smell of mildew penetrated Lazo's nostrils causing him to wonder about the kind of people who would take up residence in such a dilapidated building. It didn't seem at all habitable. Geli walked up to a large wooden door and knocked three times. Then she waited and knocked three more times. The door opened revealing a well lit and rather splendidly appointed room. There was a large oak conference table in the center of the room, around which sat no fewer than fifteen people, most of them quite old. A large crystal chandelier, which Lazo thought too bright, hung from the ceiling immediately above the table. The walls were panelled in dark mahogany giving the room a very official, almost sterile appearance. Aside from some quiet whispering, the atmosphere in the room was quite solemn.

"Hang your coat over there and then follow me," directed Geli.

Lazo removed his coat and followed Geli to the head of the table. He sat down, looked at the group, then shouted, "What the hell is going on here?"

"You'll find out soon enough," snapped Geli. There was no cordiality in her voice and Lazo became uneasy. Two of the men arose and walked up to Lazo, and without uttering a word, strapped Lazo's wrists to the arms of the chair.

"Is this some kind of a joke?" asked Lazo, wrestling with the straps.

"Believe me, this is no joke," replied Geli. Her voice was completely devoid of any compassion, Then she looked at Lazo, with eyes turned to ice and announced, "Heinz Frick, in the name of the 'German People's Retribution', we charge you with crimes against humanity."

"My name is not Heinz Frick," protested Lazo, tugging at the straps.

"Quiet! You will have an opportunity to answer the charges that have been brought against you, Heinz Frick or whatever you think your name is."

"I am not Heinz Frick!" yelled Lazo. "My name is Lazo Krall and I am an American agent working for the Offices of Strategic Services."

The room filled with laughter.

"Order!" shouted Geli. "We must have order if we are to proceed." Then looking at Lazo, "And you will be quiet or I will have your mouth taped shut. I told you that you would have an opportunity to speak, so until that time, you will remain silent. Do you understand? You will have an opportunity to defend yourself. And that sir, is more than you gave the people of Cherni Lukno."

"Oh, so that's it," thought Lazo, and for the first time he began to understand what was going on.

"And now, without any further interruption, let us proceed."

She walked up to Lazo and asked, "Would you please state your name and present occupation?"

"My name is Lazo Krall and I am an American Agent."

"Is that so?" asked Geli, quite sarcastically. "Then allow me to show you a photograph that was sent to me by one of our agents in Yugoslavia."

She placed the picture on the table immediately before Lazo and shouted, "Now tell me that this is not you in the picture with Major Karl Kranz! And tell me that you were not present at Cherni Lukno when all of its male population was wiped out."

She waited for him to respond and when no response was forthcoming, she remarked, "Well, do you have anything to say, Heinz Frick?"

Lazo continued to look at the photograph but made no reply. He kept wondering how a person like Geli could be so kind and gentle at one time and so cruel and vindictive at another. It just didn't seem to make any sense to him. It was almost like a charade.

"Perhaps," she continued, "these photographs of your handiwork will jar your memory."

She placed several photos on the table, in front of Lazo. They showed dead men lying on the ground in front of the low stone wall. He looked at them and felt a deep sense of shame. Then remembering Sam's last agonizing scream, he shouted, "You don't understand a damned thing, do you!"

"Oh, it is clear to us," replied Geli, with that certain smugness that comes to those who sense imminent victory. "It is as clear as these photographs." Then she took the pictures and waved them before Lazo's face.

He lowered his head, not in shame but in anger and disgust.

Geli turned to the group and said, "I place these photographs in evidence and I would like you, ladies and gentlemen to examine them very carefully. Our case against Heinz Frick rests upon these photographs and the sworn testimony of an eye witness." She surveyed the group and added, "After all of you have examined the documents, we will give our German hero an opportunity to defend himself."

She placed the pictures before the group. Each of them examined the pictures very carefully. Lazo watched them as they examined the evidence and from the expressions which shown on their faces, he began to sense impending disaster. He knew that his life depended upon their believing him and from the expressions on their faces, he knew he was as good as dead.

Geli waited until the group had completed their work, then she looked at Lazo and said, "Before you present your defense, let me assure you that if this group finds you guilty, you will be executed. We have, to date, executed no fewer than twenty-five war criminals, so please do not take your defense lightly. I also would like to caution you against the use of legal technicalities. There is not one trained lawyer in this group." Then she looked up at the ceiling and added with a large smile, "The lawyers have all joined the Fuhrer." The group responded with a burst of laughter.

"I am deeply sorry for my gratuitous comment. I did not mean to make light of such a grave matter. What I mean to say is that you will be judged on the merits of your testimony. You will be treated justly." She paused briefly. Then she sat down next to Lazo and said, "Now you may begin."

Lazo cleared his throat and began to relate how it was that he became involved in the disaster at Cherni Lukno. He weighed his words very carefully as he described in brutal detail, the murder of his friend, Sam Kaplan. He told them about the death of Vaso. He related everything to them, including his escape with Hedda. And not once did he lose his composure. He insisted that he had not killed anyone, not even Vaso. When he finished his testimony, he added, "And that ladies and gentlemen is the truth. I swear to you by everything that is sacred, that I am an American soldier. My name is Captain Lazo Krall and I am a member of the Office of Strategic Services."

The room fell into a deep and agonizing silence.

"Have you completed your testimony?" asked Geli.

"Yes I have," replied Lazo.

"You have nothing further to add?"

"No, nothing." Then he looked up at Geli and added "You might have one of your agents in Belgrade contact Hedda for corroborating evidence."

"We don't have time for that," snapped Geli. Then she turned to the group and asked, "Do any of you have any questions for the defendant."

"Why did you come to Dresden?" asked one of the jurors.

"I believed that it would be the safest way to meet up with the American army. I did not want to answer to the Russians."

Geli waited for a moment, "Any more questions?" she asked. "If not, would the recorder please pass out the ballots."

The ballots were distributed and Geli waited as each member of the group marked his ballot. When the balloting was completed, Geli asked the recorder, "What is the verdict, Frau Holz?"

"We find the defendant guilty."

"Were there any dissenting votes?"

"Just one, Frau Bischof."

Geli looked over the group and noticed that Otto's face was turned away from her. "It was Otto," she thought and her face turned to crimson.

She arose from her chair and in a voice somewhat subdued, said, "Heinz Frick, you have heard the verdict. Do you wish to make a final statement before I pronounce sentence?"

"No," replied Lazo. "This court had made up its mind before the proceedings even began. I do not think that anything I could say would dissuade them. You are not interested in the truth, you are only interested in vengeance."

"Very well. I will now pronounce sentence. Would you please unstrap him so that he might rise?"

Two men hastily removed the straps and then took up positions immediately behind Lazo.

"Would you please rise?"

Lazo shook his hands quite vigorously and then slowly stood up.

"Heinz Frick, this group finds you guilty of crimes against humanity and sentences you to death. You will be taken to the Elbe River this very night and drowned. May God show you the kindness that you refused your fellow man." Then with a sweep of her hand, said, "Take him away."

"Would you grant me one final request?" asked Lazo. "I am entitled to at least that."

Geli looked up at the chandelier and replied, "I see no reason that the request, if reasonable, should not be granted." She surveyed the group, then said, "Hearing no objections, I am disposed to grant you your request."

"Thank you, Geli. My request is a simple one. I would like a pen and some paper, so that I might write a letter. I also would like you to promise me that when this war is over, you will see that it gets to the proper address. Do I have your promise?"

"Ja," replied Geli, "but I don't see what good it will do." She turned and said, "Will you provide the defendant with some paper and a pen?"

"And an envelope," said Lazo.

"Ja, and an envelope," uttered Geli.

Frau Holz immediately furnished Lazo with the materials he had requested and Lazo began to write. The room was so quiet that one could hear the pen as it moved across the paper. When he had finished the letter, Lazo carefully folded it and placed it into the envelope. Then he sealed it.

"May I have it?" snapped Geli, quite rudely.

"May I address it first?" asked Lazo, quite defiantly.

"Yes, you may, but please hurry. We don't have all night."

He addressed the envelope and handed it to Geli. "Now remember you promised."

She grabbed the letter and with a voice barren of any human compassion, said, "Take him away and deal with him properly!"

182

Three men came forward. They bound his hands together, very securely and led him out of the room. He did not kick, scream or cry. Then the others left the room in groups of three, each group maintaining a precise time interval, so as not to attract attention when they departed the building. After the last threesome had left, Geli walked over to Otto.

"Why did you vote against us?"

"I didn't vote against you, Geli, I simply voted for him. I liked him and that is all there is to it. I liked him. There was something genuine about him."

"Did you think it was easy for me?"

"I know it wasn't," replied Otto, very tenderly. "I know." He took her hand and squeezed it affectionately.

"What shall I do with this letter?"

"You must do what he asked. It would be very wrong is you didn't."

"But why did he want me to wait until the war was over?" She turned the letter over and looked at the address. "Oh my God!" she cried. "You must stop them, before it is too late! Please hurry, Otto!"

"Where did they take him?"

"The Augustus Bridge!" shouted Geli, hysterically. "Please hurry! He was telling the truth! He wasn't lying. He wasn't lying!"

Otto moved with an alacrity that would have done honor to a man half his age. He didn't even stop to pick up his coat. As he ran out of the room, he shouted, "I will try, Liebling! I will try!"

Geli slumped into her chair. She was beside herself with emotion. Then she tore open the envelope and began to read what Lazo had written. Soon tears were streaming down her cheeks. Then with hands palsied with grief, returned the letter to its envelope and with shattered voice, whispered, "I'm sorry Ilse. I am so very sorry."

CHAPTER TWENTY

It was almost midnight when the door flew open and Otto, face purpled with cold, rushed in and shouted, "Rejoice Liebling! I have accomplished the impossible. I have lifted a man from the dead. I feel so good, Liebling, that I must hug someone."

Geli ran over to him and threw her arms around his neck. Her eyes, red with crying, sparkled as the warmth of her lips pressed against the grey stubble of his cold face.

"Oh thank you Old Man! Once again you have saved me! How can I ever repay you?" She pulled away and looked into the hallway. "Where is he?" she cried.

"Sit down, Geli and allow me to catch my breath. Afterall, I am an old man, you know."

"Alright, old man," she replied, sitting down beside him, "please tell me what happened."

"Well, Liebling, after I caught up with them, I told them what you had said. They untied him and departed, leaving Lazo and me all alone. It was so strange, the way he acted. He acted as if he didn't believe it. When he finally spoke, he asked why you had changed your mind. I told him that I was not quite sure but that it had something to do with the address on the envelope. Then he asked me if he was really free or if it was just another trick to humor Geli. I assured him that it was no trick and that we should hurry back because you were in a sorry state. He looked at me and with fire in his eyes said that he did not want to see you because and I quote, 'I don't like her very much'. I asked him what he was going to do and he just shrugged his shoulders and asked me if he could use the room for just one more night. I told him that that would be just fine and that he should not hate you. He made no reply. He just walked away and I came straight here to tell you."

"Oh Otto, I must see him." She paced back and forth. "We must go to him right now. I must explain. He will understand. I just know that he will. He must understand. Please Otto, help me."

"Alright, but this time I will take my coat."

"Ja, take your coat. I wouldn't want you to get a chill."

"I would like something more, to warm me up."

"Like what?" asked Geli, as she helped him with his coat.

"Like some good cognac," he replied. "Do you know what, Liebling? I think that I am acquiring a taste for good liquor."

"All right, old man. We'll stop by the restaurant and see if Dieter will sell us another bottle."

"Ach gut! Then perhaps the three of us can be together again."

"I hope so." She looked up, "It was fun wasn't it?"

Then arm in arm they walked out and headed for the restaurant. It was colder now and the brisk wind caused Geli's eyes to water. Otto could feel her shiver as she pressed against him to keep warm.

"What's the matter Liebling? Are you getting soft?"

"I guess so, Otto. It has been a very heavy night, you know."

They arrived at the restaurant just before closing time and Dieter was more than willing to sell them the cognac. Otto secured the bottle in the pocket of his great coat and the two headed for the river front, just minutes away.

"We didn't take any glasses," remarked Geli. "Shall we go back and get some?"

"No Liebling, we can drink straight from the bottle. After all, we are friends, aren't we?"

"Ja," laughed Geli. "We are friends," she hesitated. "At least we were."

When they reached the building occupied by Lazo, Geli stopped abruptly and with a quiet voice, said, "You go first and I'll follow. Don't let him know that I am with you. If he thinks that I am with you, he won't even open the door." She wrung her hands, "Oh, how he must despise me."

"Okay, I will do as you say."

They climbed the stairs and walked very quietly to Lazo's room. It was difficult, since the flooring, which had grown fragile with age, complained bitterly at the least provocation.

"Why am I walking on tippy toe?" whispered Otto, bringing his feet down mightily against the floor. "It's alright if he hears me." He walked over to the door and banged on it as hard as he could.

"Lazo!" he yelled. "Open up! I've got a bottle of good cognac and it's a very good night to get drunk! I think!"

"Go away!" yelled Lazo. "I'm not in the mood for company! Besides, you wouldn't want to drink with a war ciminal."

"Ach, Lazo! I don't blame you but please open the door. You don't want to disappoint an old man, especially after all the trouble he went through to get the bottle, do you?"

The sincerity of his pleas, caused Lazo to falter and acquiesce. "Oh, alright!" shouted Lazo, pretending to be irritated, "Wait until I get something on!"

"Okay, but hurry. I am sooo thirsty!"

"You are always thirsty!" shouted Lazo.

Soon the door opened and Lazo appeared. "Come in then but you can't stay too long. I must get an early start."

"I brought a friend," said Otto. "Is it okay if I bring her in?"

"Not Geli!" shouted Lazo. "I never want to see that bitch again!"

"Yup, Geli," replied Otto, "and there is no sense arguing because you are going to listen to her. After she has had her say, you can dismiss her. That is, if you still have a mind to."

"Hello Lazo," said Geli, almost in a whisper. "Now please allow me to explain."

Lazo made no reply. He turned away from her and walked over to the small window, pretending to look out. Otto ushered Geli into the room and closed the door. He jerked the bottle from his pocket and removed the cork. He took a quick swallow, replaced the cork and said, "Here, Lazo, catch."

Lazo turned just in time to snag the bottle in mid air.

"What! No glasses?"

"No, we forgot them," said Otto. "Go ahead, drink from the bottle."

Lazo removed the cork and set it on the window sill. He took a big drink. Then he looked at Geli and asked, "How about you? Aren't you drinking? After what you almost did, you ought to get stinking drunk. You have a lot to forget, Frau Bischof!"

"You have every right to be bitter and yes, I do have a lot to forget. But perhaps when you know who I am, you will feel differently."

"I doubt it," snapped Lazo, pushing the bottle over toward her.

"Here, have a drink with one who has returned from the dead."

Geli took the bottle and raised it to her lips. She took a small swallow, then handed the bottle to Otto.

"How is it that you know Ilse Krebs?" she asked.

"What the hell difference does it make?"

"Because, damn you," she shouted, "Ilse saved your life, that's why!"

."My life," replied Lazo, "was never yours for the taking! You had no damned business doing what you did. Who the hell do you think you are, God? Why the hell couldn't you have believed me!"

"Because," she replied, "you gave me no good reason to believe you."

"No good reason!" laughed Lazo. "That's funny!" "What do you mean?"

"At the restaurant. Did you actually believe that you were sitting next to a butcher! Did you not feel something pretty damned nice? Well, I did, damn it! I did! Give me the bottle, Otto. I think that I want to get drunk."

"Oh yes, Lazo. There was a moment there, when I had almost forgotten the war and the word enemy had no meaning for me. I felt like a young girl again." She walked over to the window and looked out into the darkness. "Ah, but then I remembered my husband and the promise I had made to him."

"And that's when you pulled away from me?"

"Ja. That's when I pulled away from you. Ah, but enough of that. Tell me, Lazo, how are Erika and Hermann? I haven't heard from them since the war began."

"How do you know them?" asked Lazo.

"They were my best friends."

"Then how come they never mentioned you?"

"I don't know." She took the bottle and put it to her lips. Then she handed it to Lazo. "Are you quite certain that they never spoke of Lev and me?"

Lazo scratched his head and said, "Well, I seem to recall Hermann speaking of a Lev, but his name was not Bischof. It was Goldberg, I think. Ja. Lev Goldberg and his wife, Geli."

"I am that Geli!" she whispered. "And Lev was my husband."

"No," whispered Lazo. "It can't be."

She moved toward him. "Can you forgive me, Lazo?"

"It's water over the dam, as far as I'm concerned," replied Lazo.

"Hell, we all may soon be dead."

"What's this water over the dam?" muttered Otto, who by now, had become quite tipsy.

"Oh nothing, Old Man," answered Geli. "It's just one of those silly American expressions."

Lazo stepped back and walked over to Otto. He put his arm around Otto's shoulder and said, "And now Old Man, I am ready to get drunk."

"I am already tipsy but if you insist, I will be happy to oblige." Then he looked over at Geli and added, "Providing, of course, that Frau Bischof doesn't object."

"I don't object, Otto. As a matter of fact, I feel, as they say in America, like hanging one on."

"But Frau, we have to work tomorrow, and you know how angry Major Fatbottom gets when we don't show up."

"The Americans have another expression which I have never used but am tempted to for the first time."

"Which one is that?" asked Lazo.

The words no sooner left his lips when he realized that he should not have inquired. Geli took the bottle, raised it upward and shouted, "Fuck Major Fatbottom!"

Then she took several large swallows and handed the bottle back to Otto. "Here Otto, drink and be merry for tomorrow we sleep in."

She looked at Lazo who was still laughing over her use of the American expression, and said, "It's ironic, Lazo, our court has tried several dozen Nazi butchers but at this moment, I feel happier at the saving of one life than I did after sending all of those bastards to hell. Can you understand that? I feel at peace for the first time since Lev's death. I don't feel like hating anymore. I want to kiss and make love and most of all, I want to forget. Can you understand that, Otto?"

"Ja, Liebchen, I understand. I understand."

Geli walked over to Lazo and gave him a kiss. Then she whispered, very softly into his ear, "I want you to give me a baby."

Lazo, blushing and bewildered, whispered, "Will you please repeat that?"

"I want you to give me a baby."

Lazo drew back, his face still crimson and grabbed the bottle from Otto. He took a huge belt then pointed his finger at Geli and said, "You and I, pretty lady, must have a long talk." Then he turned to Otto and said, "I think this lady has gone bananas."

"Bananas? What about bananas?" asked Otto, now more befuddled then ever.

"It is just another silly American expression," replied Geli. "It doesn't mean a thing." She looked at Lazo, "And we can have that long talk as you walk me back to my apartment."

"What about me?" asked Otto.

"You, Otto, can sleep here tonight. Give him the bottle. He can finish it."

"But I thought you said that you wanted to hang one on," protested Lazo.

Geli walked over to where Lazo had hung his coat. She took it and threw it over to Lazo. "Here, put this on mein lieber Herr, and then let's go and hang one on."

"You really have gone cuckoo, haven't you?"

"Yes, Lazo, for the first time in my life, I have gone cuckoo and what's more, it feels terrific." She laughed loudly and repeated, "I feel terrific!"

Lazo put his coat on but before he could do the buttons, she grabbed his arm and pulled him toward the door. They bid Otto a hasty good night and left the room. Neither spoke until they reached the street. She clung firmly to his arm as they hurried along the maze of dimly lit avenues. It was quite cold, but Lazo was too preoccupied to notice. The woman clinging to his arm had not only caused him to be muddle headed but excited as well.

"This is really crazy," he thought, and was about to tell her so, when Geli pulled away from him and began to run.

"I'm too happy to walk! Come on! I feel so much like a young girl again!"

Lazo ran to catch up. She took his hand and together, they ran up the street. When they reached the entrance of her apartment building, they were both breathing quite heavily. She removed the key from her coat pocket and unlocked the door.

"Come on," she said, as she pulled him by his arm.

"But ... "

Before he could complete the sentence, she whispered, "You have no place else to go. Now come on. Do you want to freeze?"

They ran up the stairs leading to her second floor flat. She handed him the key and said, "You unlock it, please."

He unlocked the door and stepped aside and allowed her to enter.

"Be careful," she said.

She had no sooner uttered the warning when Lazo, tripped over a table and let loose with, "God dammit, Geli, switch on the lights before I kill myself!"

"I can't do that until I draw the blackout drapes. Just stand there and don't move! It will only take a minute."

"Alright, but hurry."

Soon the room was bathed with a soft golden light. Geli removed her coat and asked, "Do you like it?"

"It's beautiful," replied Lazo. "I've never seen anything like it. Of course I like it. Did you do the decorating?"

"Yes, I did. Here, give me your coat and make yourself comfortable."

Lazo handed his coat to her and began to move about the room, studying the exquisite paintings that dressed the walls. She disappeared into what Lazo thought to be the kitchen and soon returned with a large bottle of champagne and two glasses.

"Now, let's hang one on!"

"Champagne?"

"Ja. Occasionally, Major Fatbottom shares some of his bounty with us. It makes him feel a little less guilty, I think. Come over here and sit down."

Lazo joined her on the sofa and made himself comfortable. "All I need now," he said, "is a good cigarette. I haven't had a smoke for over a week."

"I may have some," said Geli, getting up and leaving the room.

Lazo began to remove the cork from the bottle and just when he was about to congratulate himself on a job well done, he heard a loud pop and the cork sailed across the room. He quickly poured some into one of the glasses and watched the bubbles climb to the top of the glass.

"What was that?" shouted Geli.

"Just the champagne cork," replied Lazo.

"How does it taste?"

"I haven't tried it yet. I was waiting for you."

"I'll be right there."

Lazo filled the other glass and waited for Geli's return.

"I found some. Do you like Pall Malls?"

"I don't know. I never tried them. You'd better hurry before all of the fizz goes out of the champagne."

"Just a minute! I'm coming!"

"I'll be waiting!"

"Well, here I am. How do you like it?" she asked, as she appeared in the doorway wearing just the tops of a pair of pale blue pajamas.

Lazo, taken by surprise, arose and stared dumbfoundedly.

"Don't you like it?" she asked, handing him the pack of cigarettes.

"My God, but you are an attractive woman!"

"Do you really think so? It's been so very long since a man has told me so that I don't know how to respond."

Lazo took the pack and Geli watched as he removed the cellophane. Then she sat down, carefully crossing her legs so that the proper amount of thigh was exposed.

"May I?" she asked, reaching for one of the glasses.

"It's your champagne," replied Lazo as be finally wrested one of the cigarettes from the pack and sat down next to her. He lit it and took a long drag. "Oh, I'm sorry, I forgot to ask if you wanted one."

"I don't smoke."

She handed him the other glass and said, "Here's to us and a speedy end to the war."

"I can drink to that," said Lazo, raising the glass to his lips.

"It's good, isn't it?"

"Very good. The best I've ever tasted."

She put her glass down on the table and asked, "Do you really find me attractive?"

"Of course I do and I don't know how to deal with it."

"What do you mean?"

"You know that I'm in love with Ilse. I can't betray her. It just wouldn't be right. You can understand that."

"What about Hedda? Wasn't she a betrayal?"

Lazo blushed, but did not respond.

"I'm sorry. I should not have said that. Forgive me, please." uttered Geli, quite contritely.

"No harm done but you can understand my feelings, can't you?"

"Of course I can. Lev and I treated Ilse like the daughter we never had. I really care for her."

Lazo looked into her blue eyes and asked, "Then how can you even consider betraying her?"

"Listen, Lazo and listen carefully." She reached for her glass and said, "Maybe, just maybe, you will understand. Now fill my glass. Afterall, you said we were going to get drunk, didn't you?"

She took the glass in her pale hand and raised it to her lips. She did not put the glass down until it was empty.

"Once more," she instructed as she pushed her glass toward him. Then she folded her long legs under her pajama top and pulled her head back as though she was staring at something on the ceiling.

Lazo filled her glass and said, "Take it easy. We have all night, you know."

"The Russians," she continued, "will be here in a few months and you know what they will do to the German women. I have heard some of the stories and they are not very nice."

"I have heard about them also and no, they are not very pretty."

"They are barbarians, plain and simple." She looked directly into his eyes and said, "That is why I want you to get me pregnant."

"What has that to do with it. I don't understand."

"Oh," replied Geli, "I forgot. You are not a woman. How could you possibly understand?"

"No, I am not a woman, so please make me understand."

"If I am to become pregnant," replied Geli, "I would rather that the father be someone I know and like." Then she looked at Lazo for the longest time, causing him to become very uncomfortable. "And I like you very much."

"Oh, I see," replied Lazo. "A few hours ago, you were ready to kill me and now you want me to father your child. Am I supposed to make sense of that?"

"Would you rather see me ravaged by some slimy Mongolian? Don't you see, Lazo, if I am pregnant, they may even leave me alone."

"I wouldn't bet on that," replied Lazo. "What they are doing in Yugoslavia borders on the criminal." He sipped some champagne. "And the Yugoslavians are their allies. What do you think they will do to their enemies?"

"I know what they will do. I have read the reports and that is why I want you to sleep with me. I don't want to have some nameless Russian soldier getting me pregnant. I don't deserve that. I fought the Nazis too damned long to be treated like I was one of them."

"Well," mused Lazo, "why don't you find yourself a nice German gentleman."

"Because," snapped Geli, "the only German gentlemen I know are too old and the others are Nazis, and they aren't gentlemen. I couldn't betray the memory of Lev like that. Don't you see? It must be you and only you."

"It's not right," insisted Lazo.

"You don't even have to like me," pleaded Geli. "Just make love to me. I promise that I will do everything to make the exercise as pleasant as possible. And who knows, you may even enjoy it."

"But I do like you. How could I hate anyone whom Ilse and her family adore? You see, that's the problem. It would be much easier if I hated you."

She threw her arms around his neck and kissed him ardently. He pretended indifference, at first, but soon all reason disappeared in a wild torrent of passion which left no room for Ilse or Lev, he picked her up in his arms and carried her into the bedroom. Soon they were pillowed deep and she was on him and he in her. When they finally closed their eyes to sleep, the dawn was already brushing against the covered windows, but neither rose to the whisper of the new day.

CHAPTER TWENTY ONE

It was approaching noon when Lazo opened his eyes to the soft light of the February sun, streaming through the window. Several moments passed before he could recollect his whereabouts. He rubbed his eyes and making sure that he was not dreaming, shouted, "Where's the bathroom?"

"First door on the right! Now hurry! Breakfast is almost ready!"

Lazo sat up, stretched his arms toward the ceiling and yawned. Then he jumped out of bed and looked for something to put on.

"Where are my clothes?"

"I threw them out!"

"Why did you do that?"

"A German gentleman must attire himself in a fashion befitting his station."

"Don't be funny," he chided as he ran down the hall and disappeared into the bathroom.

"You'll find some pajamas hanging on the bathroom door. They were my father's but he won't mind. Now hurry before everything is burned to a crisp."

"Keep your shirt on! It will only take me a minute or two."

"How did you know that I had a shirt on?" she asked as he entered the kitchen.

"Oh, it's just another of those funny American expressions."

"Did you sleep well?"

"Just like a log. By the way, that outfit is very becoming."

"Danke, Mein Herr. It's one of my father's old shirts. I like it because it makes me feel warm and comfortable."

"It makes you look like a young girl."

"Well, thank you again. You are so very kind."

"Not at all. Now where do you want me to sit?"

"Over there," replied Geli, pointing to a chair on the far side of the table. She walked over to the stove and carefully picked up the frying pan and delivered it to the table. "Do you like bacon and eggs?"

"Oh yes, that will be just fine."

Geli emptied the contents of the frying pan onto a huge serving plate and returned the pan to the stove.

Lazo jumped up and helped her with her chair. She had pulled her hair over to one side, exposing her long graceful neck. Lazo could not resist the impulse and gently brushed his lips against the pale delicate skin of her neck. She turned and smiled. Then she took his face into her hands and gave him a very tender kiss.

"I'm so happy, I could burst," she whispered as she caressed his face with her hands, still warm from the frying pan.

"Oh, I almost forgot!" she cried.

"What?"

"I've got some rolls baking in the oven. I hope that they are not burned."

"I'll get them. You just sit there."

"Be careful!" she admonished. "I don't want you to get burned."

"Don't worry, I'm an old hand at this," he remarked as he opened the oven door.

"Use the hot pad!"

"Right," replied Lazo. "Now, how do you turn it off?"

"I'll do it." She jumped up and joined him at the stove. "There," she said, as she deftly turned the knob and watched the blue flame flicker and die.

Lazo reached in and removed the pan of rolls and dropped it atop the stove. Then he grabbed one of the rolls and tossed it into the air and kept it airborne, until he reached the table and allowed it to drop on his plate.

Geli tried to duplicate his feat, but the roll was too hot for her delicate hands and she instinctively caught the roll in her shirt but in so doing made herself quite visible.

"Beautiful, oh so beautiful," he whispered, as he again helped her with her chair.

Geli blushed and chided, "Hush up and eat before the food gets cold."

She smiled as she watched Lazo attack his plate. She had supplied him with what she considered to be a bounty but as he ate, she began to wonder if his appetite could ever be stilled.

"Another roll?" she asked.

"Ja, bitte. They are so delicious."

She went to the stove and returned with the pan. She put two rolls on his plate. "Danke," said Lazo, without looking up. "You are a splendid baker."

She raised her cup to her lips and at the same time ran her bare foot against his inner thigh. He pulled his thighs together, trapping her foot between them. She tried to pull it free but her efforts were quite futile. The harder she pulled the tighter he squeezed.

"Have you had enough?" he laughed. Then without warning, he released her foot. The abruptness of his move caught her unawares and she recoiled, spilling some coffee on her shirt.

"Now look what you've done!" she scolded, pulling the wet portion of her shirt away from her skin.

"What I've done?" protested Lazo. "Who started it anyway?"

"I was just being friendly," replied Geli, dabbing the wet spot with her napkin.

"Do you want some help with that?" he asked.

"Are you finished eating?"

"I guess so."

"Good. Then let's take a bath."

"Together?"

"Of course," replied Geli. "We must conserve fuel. No sacrifice is too great for the Fuhrer."

"Well, now that you put it that way, I guess I can make a sacrifice for the Third Reich. What about the dishes?"

"We can do them tomorrow." She got up and began to walk toward the bathroom.

"I need a shave but I don't have a razor."

"You can use Lev's straight edge. I saved it. I really don't know why."

"But I've never used a straight edge."

"Then I'll have to shave you," laughed Geli. "Do you trust me?"

"Do I have a choice?"

"I guess not but don't worry, I have a steady hand." Then she smiled softly and added, "You will be well compensated for each nick."

"And how, may I ask, will that be accomplished?" teased Lazo.

She just laughed and shoved him toward the bathroom. An hour later, they emerged, with Lazo's face covered with little patches of tissue paper, which Geli had used to stem the flow of blood. The nicks were not very deep and all things considered, she had given him a rather gentle shaving. She followed him toward the bedroom with arms wrapped around him and her face resting on his bare back. When they reached the bed, she loosened the towel which Lazo had draped around his waist and allowed it to fall to the floor. Lazo turned and undid her towel. He pulled her to him and together, they fell into the soft feather bed. She pulled the quilt up and nestled in his arms. The embrace was sustained for a very long time. Neither of them spoke or needed to. For the moment, at least, they were content to rest against each other, feeling the closeness of two human wills coming together, in remarkable confusion.

Finally, she whispered, "I have never felt so wonderful as I do now." Then she touched her lips to his. "And what's more," she added, "I don't feel any fickle sense of shame; just joy."

She drew her shoulders back just far enough to allow Lazo to caress her breasts. He watched as the dark crimson wreaths hardened into tight wrinkles, forcing her nipples upward. Then he caressed them with his lips. She rolled over, took his hand into hers and moved it downward, teaching his finger the way to her pleasure.

"Gently," she whispered. Soon the room was filled with soft moans and her hips began to move from side to side. She rolled him on his back and settled her body on top of his. The downward press of her body, caused Lazo to raise himself upward to meet her. "No," she whispered, "just lie back and relax." She rested her head on his shoulder and pressed her hips against him, gently at first and then more aggressively. Soon she was slamming her hips into him and just when he was about to lose control of himself, she screamed, "Now!" He raised his hips to meet her and erupted. He felt her teeth biting into his shoulder as swell followed swell, each more pronounced then the other, until spent, she fell upon him and became limp.

Soon they were asleep and as close as any two people could ever be. If a child was conceived at that moment, it would have been conceived with more joy, nay, more bliss than anyone could possibly imagine.

CHAPTER TWENTY TWO

It was Tuesday, February 13th. The alarm clock sounded and Geli quickly turned it off so that it would not disturb Lazo, who was still fast asleep. She quietly left the bed and tiptoed to the dressing table. She took one of her lipsticks and wrote on the large mirror, "Happy birthday, Lazo. I'll be home early so that we can celebrate."

When Lazo awoke, about mid-morning, he saw Geli's message, smiled and said to himself, "She's wonderful."

Geli was making his stay in Dresden, a happy one. She had acquainted him with every point of interest in the old city, and sometimes they just walked aimlessly through the Altmarkt, stopping now and again to peer into the shop windows. The only thing that made Lazo's stay in Dresden less than idyllic was the knowledge that the Russians were moving forward very rapidly and the Western Allies were still bogged down west of the Rhine. Lazo did not relish the thought of confronting the Russians while the American forces were still so very far away. To make matters even worse, Geli had told him that Roosevelt and Churchill had come to an agreement with Stalin at Yalta, calling for the Western Allies to stop at the Elbe River. Stalin agreed that he would not go beyond the Elbe, if perchance the Russians arrived there first.

Lazo thought about it and began to chuckle. "Fat chance that the Russians would stop at the Elbe. Those bastards will have their way in Eastern Europe and there isn't a helluva lot that Roosevelt and Churchill can do about it. There isn't a helluva lot anyone can do about it."

He jumped out of bed and walked over to the window. The sun was shining and there were a few clouds scattered along the horizon. "Nice day for a birthday," he thought. He slipped off his pajamas and walked over to the mirror. He picked up the lipstick, toyed with it briefly, and then wrote, "My heart quakes with joy."

He pulled in his stomach and flexed his biceps. He was putting on a little weight but he was not entirely displeased with what he saw. He smiled as he put down the lipstick and walked into the bathroom. He turned on the hot water and with utter contempt for the Fuhrer's proclamation regarding the conservation of fuel, filled the tub. He luxuriated in the hot water until the skin on his fingers began to shrivel. After toweling himself, he took the safety razor that Geli had procured, and gave himself a very close shave.

The phone rang, just as he had completed his toilet. He allowed it to ring the pre-arranged six times, then put the receiver to his ear.

"Are you awake?"
"Yes, I am."
"Did you like my message?"

"Yes, and thank you very much. You are so thoughtful."

"Look, Lazo, I'm just about finished here and after I drop some film off at the Frauenkirke, I'll come directly home. Is there anything special that you would like for supper?"

"Surprise me."

"Is it alright if I bring Otto? He wants to help celebrate your Geburtstag."

"Of course, it's alright. Tell the old geezer to bring some good schnapps. I want to get a little tipsy tonight."

"Good. I'll tell him that. He will appreciate it."

"I am sure he will. He does love his schnapps."

"I'll see you in a little while. Aufwiedersehen."

"Good. In the meantime, I'll tidy up around here so that you won't have to. Aufwiedersehen."

He hung up the phone and began to tidy up the flat. When he was satisfied that it would meet Geli's rigid standards, he poured himself a cup of coffee and settled down on the couch to listen to the radio. They were featuring the music of Johann Straus and when they played his favorite, "An dem Schonen, Blauen Donau", he closed his eyes and imagined himself seated in the club Laterne, in Vienna, where he had spent several evenings drinking with his friends. Then he must have dozed off because the next thing he heard was Otto shouting, "Wake up you Schafmutze! Are you going to sleep all day?"

Lazo opened his eyes with a start. "I must have dozed off. What time is it?"

Otto handed him a small glass filled with schnapps, then looked at his wristwatch and replied, "It is about three o'clock." He smiled. "A perfect time to start drinking." Then he raised his glass and shouted, "Prost!"

"Wait a minute!" shouted Geli. "Am I not included?"

"Ach, Schaztzie! You don't drink schnapps."

"I do now." She took Otto's glass and said, "Happy birthday, Lazo!" Then she raised the glass to her lips, and as the two gentlemen stared, wide eyed, downed the schnapps with one swallow. "Now," she continued, "let's all get tipsy."

Lazo had never seen her so carefree or so happy. "What's gotten into you? It's only my birthday. One would think from the way you are carrying on, that the Fuhrer had died."

"Oh no, Lazo, nobody has died. Is it a crime to be happy?" Then she turned to Otto, "Pour me another drink!"

"Are you quite sure?"

"Yes, I'm sure and while you are at it, you'd better pour yourself one."

Otto went to the kitchen to get a glass. While he was gone, she bent down and gave Lazo a kiss. "I know that it is wrong, Lazo, but I am in love with you. And furthermore, I have never been this much in love with anyone."

"Oh, you don't mean that. It's just the schnapps talking," insisted Lazo, becoming somewhat embarrassed but still liking what she had said.

"No, it is not the schnapps! I just can't seem to get you out of my mind. And do you know what else? It doesn't even matter that you don't love me. Crazy, isn't it?"

Lazo was about to reply when Otto returned and announced, "Now, let's all get drunk!" There was that devilish twinkle in his eyes and they knew that he meant business. He filled the glasses and declared, "To us!" and he threw the schnapps down his throat without a wince.

"Why aren't you drinking?" he asked, somewhat befuddled.

"We were one drink ahead," replied Lazo. "We were just waiting for you to catch up. That's all."

"Ach ja! That's right!" He took the bottle and filled his glass again.

"Now," said Geli, "to the three of us."

"To the three of us," echoed Lazo, and they touched glasses and drank the schnapps.

Geli looked at Lazo, winked and said, "And now, I must get back to the kitchen and prepare the food for our little celebration."

"It doesn't seem fair," said Lazo. "You shouldn't have to work on my birthday. Couldn't we go to a restaurant and celebrate?"

"No! I went through a lot of trouble to get the things I needed. This is going to be a dinner that you will never forget."

"Then I guess I'll have to bend to your wishes, but will you allow me to help?"

"No, you may not. This is woman's work and you will just be in the way. You visit with Otto and see to it that he doesn't get too drunk."

"I'll see to it but if you need anything, just yell."

"If I need you, I'll call. Now, don't drink too much," she cautioned and she disappeared into the kitchen.

Every once in a while she took time out from the kitchen to check up on the two men, to see that they weren't getting too drunk. Each time, she would pick up Lazo's glass, take a couple sips and return to the kitchen.

About seven o'clock, Geli entered the living room, carrying a bottle of champagne and three glasses. She had managed, somehow, to take the time to put on a beautiful black evening gown. She looked absolutely stunning.

Lazo jumped up from the sofa and helped with the tray. "I have never seen you look so beautiful! Nor so radiant!"

Geli blushed a little. "Stop it!" she said. "You are embarrassing me."

"No. He is absolutely correct," said Otto. "You look like the queen of the ball. Ach, if I were only twenty years younger."

"Will you remove the cork?" she asked, handing Lazo the bottle.

"I'll be happy to."

He took the bottle and with great dispatch, removed the cork and poured a little into each of the glasses.

Geli raised her glass and said, "Here's to Lazo. May this champagne serve to still his quaking heart."

Lazo blushed as he raised his glass and sipped some of the champagne.

"What is this quaking heart?" asked Otto.

"Oh nothing," laughed Geli. "It's just a little secret between the two of us. Here, have some more champagne."

"Don't mind if I do," said Otto, extending his glass.

She filled his glass, turned to Lazo and asked, "Shall we repair to the dining room?"

"By all means," replied Lazo, extending his arm to her.

She took Lazo's hand and said, "Come old man, let's have some dinner."

The three walked into the dining room. She had set the table with her best china and crystal. It was elegant. Lazo squeezed her hand then kissed her bare shoulder. "You have done yourself proud. you can be sure that I will never forget this moment."

"You sit here, Lazo and Otto, you sit over there. Now close your eyes and don't open them until I tell you to."

The two men did as she commanded and she left the room. They did not hear her return and were taken by surprise when she yelled, "Now!"

They opened their eyes and beheld the most wonderfully prepared duck. It had been roasted to perfection and from it, issued the most savory fumes. Otto and Lazo gazed in quiet disbelief.

"Well, what do you think?"

They made no reply. They just sat, wide eyed.

"What's the matter? Cat got your tongue?"

Lazo began to clap and Otto joined in. "Wunderbar!" peeled Otto, licking his lips.

"Will one of you please help me?"

They both jumped up at the same time, eager to render assistance.

"Just one of you. The duck isn't that heavy."

Lazo took the tray and set it down in front of Otto. "Here, Old Man, you may do the carving." Lazo then assisted Geli with her chair and when the three were all properly seated, Otto took the carving knife and began to cut into the bird.

"Where did you obtain such a fine bird?"

"I've got connections, Otto. You know that."

"I'll bet it was that fat Major Fatbottom, wasn't it?"

"Never mind. Just carve the duck before we all starve. And you Lazo, pour the wine."

And so they ate and drank until they had completely devoured the bird and all of the trimmings. They had been so busy eating and conversing that they barely heard the soft music coming from the radio. At about nine o'clock, the music was interrupted by a voice calling, "Achtung! Achtung! A small squadron of enemy aircraft is now flying over northwestern Germany."

"What does that mean?" asked Lazo.

"Oh, it's nothing," replied Otto. "It's just the usual warning. We get them quite often but as you can see, our beautiful city is still intact."

"Ja," said Geli. "Bei uns, nicht passiert." She arose and began to walk toward the kitchen.

"Where are you going?" asked Lazo.

"To get the cake. What is a birthday without a cake?"

"You went to all the trouble to make a cake?"

"Actually not," replied Geli. "I cheated. I bought it but it's a grand cake."

While Geli was in the kitchen, the two men continued to drink the delicious old wine which Geli had provided. Otto was by now, quite tipsy and in a very jovial mood.

"I wonder what's keeping Geli?"

"She's probably lighting the candles," replied Otto. "Women are such sticklers for formality."

Then the music stopped and only an ominous ticking issued from the transmitter. "What's that?" asked Lazo, not especially concerned.

"I don't know. I just don't know what to make of it."

Then the sirens began to howl and Geli ran in, shouting, "It's a full alarm! It's a full alarm!"

Then a voice cried out from the radio, "Achtung! Achtung! Kampfverbande!" Then his words became inaudible. The sirens were so loud that they couldn't even hear each other.

"Let's go down and look!" shouted Lazo, jumping up from his chair. He ran for the door with Otto following at his heels.

"I'll join you down there, after I change my shoes. Don't forget to take your coats! It's cold out there!"

"Okay, but hurry," implored Lazo, as the two left the apartment and bounded down the stairs. When they reached the street, they could scarcely believe what they were seeing. It was as if one Christmas tree after another was being lit. The city was becoming brighter and brighter, until it was almost as light as mid-day. From where they were standing, it appeared that the entire Altstadt was ablaze. The noise was deafening. The sirens and the thunder of thousands of airplane engines along with the exploding bombs, created a scene that was at once, terrible and yet awesome. The buildings were clearly visible and people could be seen leaving their homes and scampering into the streets. Children were screaming and women wept as they sought refuge, God knows where.

"Oh dear God!" screamed Geli, joining her two friends. Lazo embraced her, and tried to comfort her. Her body was shaking violently.

"Where are the shelters?" asked Lazo. "We'd better damn well get out of here. It's getting closer and closer."

"There aren't any shelters! Hell, there aren't even any anti-aircraft batteries in the city!" shouted Otto, with a cynical chuckle. He looked up and shouted, "Thank you, Herr Meier!"

"We'd better get the hell out of here, or we'll be dead," urged Lazo.

"The basement!" shouted Geli. "Any place is better than this! Let's go!"

She grabbed Lazo's arm and led him down the basement stairs. Otto followed close behind.

"Close the damned door!" came a loud voice from within. "Do you want to get us all killed?"

There were about thirty people crammed into the narrow basement. Mostly women, children and old men; all seeking refuge in this cavern of darkness.

"We're all going to die anyway!" shouted one of the old men. "We're all going to die!"

"Shut up!" came a loud chorus of voices.

Then all hell broke loose. Squadron after squadron dropped their missiles of destruction upon the unprotected city. The earth trembled as the huge bombs exploded, ever closer to their precarious haven. One of the bombs fell so close that it tore the basement door from its hinges. The blast was so powerful that it threw Geli to the floor. Lazo dropped down beside her. She placed her head against his shoulder and sobbed as the bright red light from the sea of fire, streamed into the basement, casting eerie shadows on the walls.

Otto rushed up the stairs so that he could better survey the damage. "It's all on fire! Everything is burning! We've got to get out of here!" he shouted. Even he, an old veteran, was losing his grip.

"No!" shouted Lazo. "It's safer in here!"

But it was too late. Several of the other people panicked and rushed up the stairs, trying to squeeze through the narrow doorway. Then a bomb, more powerful than any heretofore, exploded with such violence that it threw the would be escapees, including Otto, back into the basement.

For forty minutes, these frightened and abandoned human beings, endured a hell, like none, ever visited upon a people, anywhere. It was so horrible, so devasting, so cruel, that no man, no matter how perverted his sense of morality might be, could find justification for this wholesale destruction and indiscriminate carnage.

Then the engines of death departed, leaving in their wake, a burning city. Geli lifted her head from Lazo's shoulder and asked, "Are we safe now? Have they really gone?"

"No Geli," replied Lazo, "we are not safe. And what's more, nobody will ever be safe again."

Then he got up and helped Geli to her feet. "We've got to get out of here right now."

"Where will we go?" asked Geli, brushing the dust from her clothing.

"I don't know." Then he shouted, "Otto, where the hell are you?"

"Over here!" came Otto's reply. "I'm over here! Is Geli alright?"

"Yes, we're both fine, but we've got to get out of here."

"Hurry then!" he shouted. "Perhaps we can make our way to the Elbe meadows."

Together, they climbed the steps. Pieces of glass shattered under their heels as they carefully made their way upward. None of them was prepared for what they were about to see. It was a hellish nightmare that presented itself to them. The condemned city was blanketed with smoke, turned blood red by the flames of thousands of burning buildings. The charred sky was irritated by millions of sparks pushed upward by the winds ushering from the bowels of the inferno.

"My hat!" cried Otto. "I left my hat in your flat. I must go back and get it."

"You can't," pleaded Geli, half crying and half laughing. "Have you gone crazy?"

"The fires are closing in on us!" roared Lazo. "We've got to go right now."

Their pleas went unheeded by Otto, as he scampered toward the building.

"Shall we wait for the old goat?"

"We don't have time. Besides, he's old enough to take care of himself and he does know where the Elbe is."

Then they turned and began to make their way toward the Elbe. The heat was scorching and the acrid fumes tore into their lungs as they made their way through streets, piled high with heaps of brick and shattered masonry.

"Look!" cried Geli. "There's a broken water main over there."

"No!" shouted Lazo. "We don't have time. Hell you're becoming crazy like Otto."

"What difference does it make? We're all going to die, anyway."

"Dammit, don't say that. We are going to live." He looked back, lost his footing and fell into a huge crater.

"Are you hurt?" asked Geli, plaintively.

"No! I am not hurt!" There was anger in his voice, spawned, not so much by pain as by frustration. She took his hand and helped him up. But before he was half way out, he pulled her into the crater and threw her to the ground. Then he covered her with his body.

"What's the matter?" she shrieked. "Have you gone nuts?"

"Your dress is on fire!"

"Oh, goddamit!" she wimpered. "It's my best dress!"

Lazo quickly smothered the flames and then he tore about three feet from the hem of her dress.

"There, that's better. Now it won't drag over the hot rubble." He looked about to ascertain their whereabouts. "Where the hell are we?"

Geli searched for a landmark but the smoke was so thick that she could scarcely see anything at all. "It all looks the same," she sobbed. "There's nothing left. Dresden is no more."

Then they heard a series of pathetic screams. They turned and saw a line of people coming out of a basement. They were all aflame. Human torches, fanned by the rush of their retreat.

"We've got to help them!" screamed Gel, hysterically.

"No! We can't stop! There is nothing that we can do for them anyway. They're dead and what's more, there must be thousands of charred bodies under the rubble and in the basements. There's never been anything like this." Then he grabbed her hand shook his head and said, "It doesn't make any sense. I'm so sorry."

"I see it!" shouted Geli. "I see it!"

"What?"

"The Frauenkirke! It's still standing! Come on," she urged, "we can make it." There was a promise of optimism in her voice.

"Let's get going then," echoed Lazo, as they joined the thousands of others, making their way to the Elbe. He followed close at her heels as she made her way over and around the piles of smoldering rubble.

When they finally reached the Elbe meadows, she stopped and gave a sigh of relief.

"Why are you stopping?"

She ran up to him and threw her arms around his neck and gave him a kiss. "It's so good to be alive!" Tears were streaming down her blackened, beautiful face. Her eyes were almost swollen shut and her eyebrows were transformed by the heat into tiny specks of dust.

"Yes, it is good to be alive." He picked her up and cradled her in his arms, ever so tenderly.

"Oh for Christ's sake!" he cried. "Your shoes are on fire! The soles of your shoes are burning!"

He raced for the water and when reached it, he released his hold and allowed her to slip down until her feet touched the water.

"You little fool! Didn't you know that your shoes were on fire?"

"How could I tell? Everything is so hot! And besides, I was too damned tired and frightened to notice." She began to sob, uncontrollably.

"Why are you crying? You're safe now."

"I don't know. I'm sad! I'm angry! I'm tired! I'm happy and I'm alive and with you!" Then she looked up at him and murmured, "Hell, I don't know why I'm crying." She bent down and dunked her hands into the cold water. Then she splashed some of it on her face. "Do you think that it is safe to drink? My throat feels scorched."

"I don't know. A drop of water, a puff of smoke. What's the difference?" He reached down and scooped up some water and sipped it. "It tastes good. I don't think a little of it will kill us."

"I don't care if it does." She dropped her face into the water and began to drink.

"Enough!" yelled Lazo. He grabbed her arm and led her out of the water.

"That was good," she gasped. "That's about the best water that I have ever tasted." She tried to smile, but she couldn't. It hurt too much.

The night had turned cold but for the moment, at least, it didn't matter. They looked at the inferno and shook their heads. Flames were raging in the Altstadt, Johannstadt, Stossen and parts of the Neustadt. The Schloss, the Zwinger, the Hofkirke and the Opera, all appeared to be aflame. Nothing was spared.

As Lazo surveyed the destruction, his thoughts traced back to that first evening with the Krebs family and he remembered what Hermann said about the fragile nature of civilization. "He was right," whispered Lazo.

"What?"

"Nothing. I was just talking to myself."

"I wonder if Otto made it?"

"The old fool. What's so damned important about an old hat, anyway?"

"He'll be alright. I know he will survive." whispered Geli, trying to convince herself.

"Ja," echoed Lazo. "God always favors children and old fools."

They sat down and pressed together, as a defense against the cold February night. "What do we do now?" asked Lazo.

"Nothing," replied Geli. "We just wait and hope." Then almost as an afterthought, added, "And pray."

"What the hell for!"

"For another morning," murmured Geli. "Just one more morning and your warm embrace."

"Well," replied Lazo. "If there is a God, you will not find him among the ruins of Dresden. You must look for him elsewhere. This is the devil's night to dance."

CHAPTER TWENTY THREE

It was early morning, about one-thirty. The two, in spite of the turmoil and the chill, had managed to doze off. Geli was the first to stir.

"No, it just can't be," she whispered. "It's only a dream. They can't be coming back."

The sirens began to scream again and the ominous drone of airplane engines could be heard in the distance.

"They're coming back! Those sons of bitches are coming back!" yelled Lazo, as he jumped up and shook his fist at the heavens, still dressed in a scarlet mantle of fire.

"Where do we hide now?" asked Geli. "It's hopeless."

"We stay here. We're as safe here as anywhere."

Lazo remained standing as he waited for the approaching storm. He was angry. A look of defiance shown on his face and Geli became worried.

"Get down!" she shouted. "Do you want to get killed?"

"They won't have any trouble finding us tonight, will they?"

"No," answered Geli. She took his hand and pulled him down into the tall grass.

"Here they come! There must be hundreds of them. He covered her with his body, trying to shield her from the onslaught. "Don't worry," he whispered. "We'll make it."

Then all hell broke loose, as the bombers opened their bellies and disgorged their tons of fire bombs and high explosives on the already scarred and bleeding city. Geli closed her eyes and pressed the palms of her hands against her ears.

"One more morning. Just one more sunrise."

For half an hour, the city quaked, as the bombs slammed into the earth and rubble, tearing asunder, its very foundation; leaving it a mere fragment of its once glorious past. Then it was over. The airborne destroyers departed, leaving an inferno that could be seen for a hundred miles. The thousands of survivors that had collected on the Elbe meadows and terraces did not rejoice as the aramada slipped away into the darkness. They were too frightened, too tired, even to weep. Their faces, numbed by the grizzly ordeal, appeared gaunt and expressionless. They looked like unpainted mannequins existing on the edges of a shadow world. Many of the more fortunate had left the city after the first bombing and now, countless others were collecting their meager belongings and filling the streets leading to the suburbs. These walking corpses knew that safety lay elsewhere and not here.

"Why are they doing this?" asked Geli. "The war is over. It doesn't make any sense."

"Perhaps," suggested Lazo, "this display of might was contrived to warn the Russians. To show them what would be in store, should they become overly ambitious."

"That's silly," countered Geli. "Most of Russia has already been destroyed. You can't scare them anymore."

"Then why else? Look around. They didn't even destroy the Elbe bridges. If they had intended to disrupt German transportation, they would have destroyed the railroad bridge, at least." Lazo shook his head and mumbled, "I wish the hell I knew why."

"I know that we Germans must be punished. We deserve to be, but this is not chastisement. This borders on Sadeism."

"Well, there's no sense speculating about it. We've got more important things to do."

"Like what?" sneered Geli. "Do we form a bucket brigade?"

"No, we don't form a bucket brigade," snapped Lazo.

"Well, then what? Do we go back into the inferno and help with the rescue operations?" She shook her head and continued, "Perhaps you have not noticed but there are only a few men left in Dresden. There are mostly women and children left and what can they do. What can anyone do?"

"We'll wait until daybreak. Then we'll go back into the city and see what we can do. Perhaps it is not as hopeless as it appears to be. Hell, maybe your apartment building is still standing. Wouldn't that be something!"

"Alright," replied Geli, trying to appear hopeful. "We'll wait and perhaps Otto will join us." She looked up at Lazo and smiled, but the smile was short lived. Her lips cracked and began to bleed.

Lazo took his handkerchief, ran down to the river and wet it. Then he very gently moistened her lips.

"That feels so much better," she murmured. "Would you do my eyes too?"

"Of course."

But before he could do so, she shouted, "Look over there! They're passing out food and water!"

Lazo grabbed her arm and together, they ran for the truck.

"See!" shouted Lazo. "I told you that there was hope!"

They joined the long line of people and waited patiently as the long line moved slowly toward the truck. A young boy, he couldn't have been more than twelve, ran up to join the group. He was running so frantically that he could not stop and collided with Geli.

"Oh, excuse me, Fraulein. I didn't mean to hurt you."

"It's alright. You couldn't help it."

"Where are your parents?" asked Lazo.

"My father was killed at Stalingrad."

"And your mother?" asked Geli.

"She's dead. She went back into the house to get my scarf and that's when the terrible bomb hit. And just like that, there was no house. Nothing left." Then his eyes closed and tears began to slide down his darkened cheeks.

"Oh you poor child," said Geli and she took him into her arms and embraced him very warmly.

"What is your name?" asked Lazo.

"My name is Adolf Hensch. My father named me after the Fuhrer." He wiped his eyes with the back of his hand. "Father said that it would bring me good fortune, but he was wrong, wasn't he?" He looked up at the two of them and his big blue eyes glistened as they caught the light from the truck. His eyebrows were singed and his eyelids had been reduced by the heat into little sandy specks. His coat was covered with tiny holes caused by the thousands of sparks that filled the night.

"Don't worry," said Geli, trying to assuage his fears.

"Everything will be just fine. You wait and see."

"No, Fraulein. Nothing will ever be the same again and I don't know what to do."

"Do you have any relatives?" asked Lazo.

"My grandmother lives in the suburb of Nothitz. She must be terribly worried over us."

"Do you know her address?" asked Geli.

"Ja. It's right on the Berg Strasse. It's easy to find."

"When it's safe, we'll take you there," said Lazo. "Now let's get something to eat."

When they finally reached the truck, they were each given a cup of water to drink. The three were also given a loaf of bread to share.

"What a feast!" laughed Lazo. He led them away from the truck to a spot where they could sit down.

"Shall we eat it now or wait until morning?" asked Lazo.

"Please, may I have some now. I haven't eaten since noon."

Geli broke off a large piece and handed it to the young boy. "Here," she said, "you may have as much as you want. Lazo and I are not very hungry." She watched as the young boy bit into the bread. Then she turned to Lazo and whispered, "There is still hope, isn't there?"

"Of course, there is. We'll survive."

"I don't mean that," countered Geli. "I mean that if this young boy, who had gone through so much can act with such civility, then by God, we will build again, won't we?"

"Of course you will. It's crystal clear," replied Lazo, emphasizing the word, crystal. "And now," he added, "let's hunker down and wait for a new morning."

CHAPTER TWENTY FOUR

The rest of the night passed very slowly and when daylight finally arrived, it was hardly discernible. The smoke which blanketed the city was so dense that the newly risen sun did not have the power to unscramble it. The fire storms continued unabated and as they moved through the city they left broken skeltons where once beautiful old buildings held sway.

Geli raised herself to her feet and moved about, trying to rid her tortured body of some of its painful stiffness. "Are you going to sit there all morning?" she asked, gently nudging him with her knee.

"Oh God, I'm chilled to the bone."

"I know how we can get warm," remarked Geli, trying to smile.

Lazo jumped up, flailing his arms about quite wildly. Then he hopped around on one leg. "Oh, that feels so good!"

"Then why are you hopping about on one leg?" laughed Geli.

"Because the other one is numb, that's why." replied Lazo, trying desperately to still his chattering teeth. "Where's Adolf?"

"He had to answer nature's call."

"You mean to tell me that he has gone to find some privacy," retorted Lazo, with a cynical chuckle.

"I guess so. What's so funny about that?"

"It's not so funny as it is ironic. I didn't tell you this, but last night, while I was walking down to the river to get a drink, I heard what sounded like a puppy whining. I went over to investigate and what I found was not a puppy." He paused, almost reluctant to continue.

"Yes, go on," urged Geli. "What did you see?"

"It was a young woman. She couldn't have been more than seventeen. She was lying there with her arms folded tightly about her abdomen. I bent down to see if I might be of some assistance. I asked her what was wrong but she did not speak. She just shook her head and moaned. I took her hand as a gesture of compassion. Her hand was covered with sticky half-congealed blood. Then I noticed that her coat was also soaked through with blood. I pulled her coat back to see if I could do something to ease her suffering."

He shuddered and his voice began to tremble. He clapped his hands together quite vigorously and turned his head away from Geli. "Her belly had been laid open by a bomb fragment, and this girl, this pathetic creature, was trying to hold her intestines in place with her hands."

Lazo wiped his eyes with the back of his hand. He looked upward, trying to conceal his tears. "Then this girl, I don't even know her name, asked me if she was going to die. I reached down and re-arranged her tattered coat, so as to conceal the wound. I tried to reassure her, but I think that she knew that she was dying. I rested her head in my lap and stroked her forehead, until she dropped, exhausted, into death's thoughtless and welcome arms."

Geli took his hand into hers and tried to still his anger and calm his broken spirit.

"That sweet, beautiful, innocent, pale face. I'll never forget it. It will haunt me for the rest of my life." He looked directly into Geli's eyes and almost in a whisper, declared, "We live in one helluva world, don't we? A world that stamps a natural act, offensive and calls those who slaughter, maim and destroy, heroes. They give them medals and erect monuments to immortalize their infamies. And the others, those beautiful people who gather at the river banks to hold hands and make love. They who build cities and plant flowers, whose only magnificence lies in their gentleness of spirit, are scorned, ridiculed and despised. And that, my dear Geli, is the irony of history. The lesson we seem never to learn."

He pulled Geli close and embraced her. "But some day, Geli, those beautiful, gentle people will prevail and the steeled boots will hang from the rafters, where they will collect dust in the attics of the world."

Geli rested her head on his chest and said, "I so want to believe you but I'm not so hopeful as you are. We Europeans do not thrive so easily on frivolous fictions. We know of the darkness that dwells in the basements of our cities. The barking dogs that lurk there, will not be so easily stilled."

She stepped back and turned toward the Altstadt. Then without looking at Lazo, tightened her fists until her knuckles became ashen. "I have never told this to anyone but since you have so much faith in these gentle people, I feel I must at least caution you."

She put her arms around his neck and kissed him. "Do you remember Werner Krebs?"

Lazo taken quite by surprise, replied, "Of course, I do."

"Of course, you would remember him. How stupid of me. Well, anyway, on that November evening when they killed Lev, Werner was there."

"Are you sure?" asked Lazo, his voice hushed.

"Of course, I'm certain. He was like family to Lev and me. That's what makes it so damned painful. He was an active participant, this son of the two gentlest people I had ever known."

She paused and gently ran the palm of her hand over his cheek. "Now," she continued, "please tell me how it is possible for a young boy, so properly nurtured and loved could become so goddam vile!"

"I killed him," whispered Lazo.

"What did you say?"

Lazo backed away and repeated, "I killed him."

"But how? And why?" asked Geli, in utter disbelief.

210

Lazo then painfully recounted the whole story and when he finished, Geli just shook her head and said, "It must have been a nightmare."

"It was," replied Lazo, "but I've learned to live with it. And now it will be even easier."

"Have you told Ilse?"

"No, I haven't. I'm afraid that if I tell her, I will lose her. I just couldn't bear that."

"But you must tell her. If your love is as deep as you say it is, she will understand and forgive."

"Forgive what?" shouted Lazo. "He tried to kill me, for Christ's sake. The son of a bitch tried to kill me! No, Geli, I think it best to let sleeping dogs lie."

Geli thought it best not to pursue the matter any further and tactfully directed the conversation elsewhere.

"Look!" she shouted. "Over there!"

"What?"

"The Frauenkirke! Can't you see it? It's still standing!"

Lazo gazed at the smoke and flames. She put her arm next to his face and pointed toward the Church. "There now. Do you see it?"

"Yes, I see it. I wonder how they could have missed it. They've hit everything else."

"I wonder," remarked Geli. "Perhaps it's an omen."

"Yes, it's a sign alright. It stands there as an empty remainder of His failure; a monument to hypocrisy."

"I suppose you're right." She put her arm around his waist and said, "Let's take a walk. Maybe we can help someone and who knows, maybe we'll bump into Otto."

"He probably got himself killed," retorted Lazo.

"You don't mean that."

"Yes, I do. I don't know how anyone or anything could have survived that second raid."

"He'll survive, he always does," countered Geli, trying to convince herself of Otto's invulnerability.

And so they spent the next two hours walking along the meadows and terraces, rendering assistance where they could but most of all, their time was spent searching for Otto and their efforts were not in vain. It must have been about eleven o'clock. The sun's rays, though enfeebled by the dense smoke, touched Geli's face, bringing a slight blush to her sooted, blistered forehead. Lazo trudged at her side, awed and angered by a city in the throes of death. A deep sense of shame was beginning to tell on his face and he began to speculate as to what these people might do to him if his American identity were made known to them. Then he shuddered and whispered, "God forgive us."

"What?" asked Geli.

"Oh, nothing. I was just talking to myself."

When they approached the Augustus Bridge, Geli looked toward the Altstadt and began to run. "It's gone, Lazo! It's gone!"

"What's gone? Are you nuts?"

"It's not there! Oh, Jesus Christ! What happened to it?"

"What's not there?"

"The Frauenkirke!" shouted Geli.

"Of course, it's there," replied Lazo, trying his damnest to reassure her.

"It's gone. That beautiful old building has collapsed."

Lazo caught up to her. She was crying the way one cries when one loses an old friend. He looked toward the Altstadt and whispered, "It is gone. What a damned shame."

He took her in his arms and said, "What a stupid waste." He put his hands to her face and tried to wipe away the tears with his thumbs. Her tears had studied their way through the soot, leaving her cheeks etched with pale, jagged lines. He began to laugh.

"What's so funny?"

"You look terrible," he remarked, not with malice but with deep affection.

"So do you," countered Geli and she punched him in his belly. They dropped to their knees and embraced with such intensity that they lost their balances and fell into the tall, stiff grass. Geli ended up on top of him. He wrapped his powerful legs around her waist, in a tight scissors. Then they rolled over and over again, like a couple of children, playing and laughing during morning recess.

"What the hell do you think you two are doing? Have you no shame? The whole city is ablaze and you two take time out to make love or whatever it is you call that what you are doing."

"Otto!" shouted Geli. "You old fool! You've come back! We thought you were dead!"

"Of course, I'm alive!" he shouted.

The two jumped up and embraced him with unbridled enthusiasm.

"Where's your hat?" asked Lazo.

"What hat?" asked Otto. There was a big smile on his face.

"The one you went back to get, you old fool."

"The one you risked your life for," added Geli.

"Oh that one. It's right here," laughed Otto, slapping his pocket.

"That's a helluva place for such an expensive hat. Why didn't you wear it?" asked Geli.

"Oh," he replied, "the winds from the fire storms were so strong that they would have sucked the hat from my head and it would be no more." He scratched his head and became very serious. He looked at Geli and than at Lazo. "I don't know how I made it. The streets are covered with charred and dismembered bodies."

He looked up and his eyes became misty. "You know," he said, "I was at the Battle of Verdun during World War One and I thought that was hell, but Verdun was nothing compared to this." He shook his head and repeated, "It was nothing like this." Then he said, "Let's sit down. I feel very tired, very old and very sick."

They seated themselves in the tall grass. Geli put her arm around his shoulders. "You don't look sick," she uttered. "As a matter of fact, I have never seen you look so good."

"Not that kind of sick. I'm sick of the human race."

"Don't say that, Old Man," protested Geli. "You'll feel differently when this is over and the smoke clears away. We all will."

"Never!" exclaimed Otto. "I have seen many terrible things during my life time but none has ever moved me so deeply as what I saw earlier today, as I was making my way back here. It was so hot that the asphalt on the streets caught fire. I saw people devoured by this flaming asphalt. I saw desiccated bodies, if you can call them that, sucked dry by the heat. They were mummified and shrunk to half of their original size. I saw the copper on the roofs melt and drop down on the people who were running through the streets. I heard their screams as the drops of molten copper burned through their clothing and buried themselves deeply, in their pale, human flesh."

"How awful!"

"Ja, Geli, it was awful. But that was not the worst. Oh no, not by a long shot. I was running through the Altmarkt when I spotted this beautiful blonde head, protruding from a heap of shattered masonry. I went up to it to get a closer look. It was a little girl's head. Her big blue eyes seemed to stare at me, reproachingly. I will never forget those eyes. I bent down to close them and when I touched her eyes, the head became dislodged and tumbled down the pile of rubble and came to rest against the smoldering tire of a gutted fire truck. I screamed frantically and began to dig into the pile of masonry, trying to recover her body. But there was no body. Just a little girl's blonde head, and those beautiful blue eyes."

Tears were flowing down Geli's cheeks. She hugged him, but said nothing. She sensed that there was nothing anyone could say that might assuage his anger or his sorrow.

"So now it has come to this," he continued, with anger in his voice. "We slaughter women and children and call it war." He shook his head and added, almost in a whisper, "I will never learn to accept this kind of war. Never."

"Nor I," agreed Lazo.

"What a waste," uttered Geli, turning toward the Altstadt and watching the black smoke climb upward, rubbing itself out against the sky. "All of those beautiful buildings, obliterated. And now, the Frauenkirke, gone forever."

"Ja," said Otto. "They say that it was destroyed by an explosion caused by the films that were stored in the basement."

"Oh no!" screamed Geli. "That can't be!"

"Ja," said Otto, shaking his head. "One can never tell what an action may lead to, no matter how innocent it might be."

"Well, what do we do now?" asked Lazo.

"I don't know about you two, but I'm hungry and when one is hungry, one eats," declared Otto, as he reached into his pocket and pulled out a large piece of sausage.

"Where in hell did you get that?" asked Lazo, his eyes agape.

"When I went back to Geli's flat, to get my hat, I decided to plunder the pantry. A good soldier must take advantage of every opportunity. Is that not so, Lazo?"

"Ja wohl, mein Herr," snapped Lazo. "A soldier who knows how to steal, never goes hungry."

"Exactly," agreed Otto, "and I am a good soldier. Now Liebling, do you want a piece of this very fine sausage?"

Geli did not answer. The thought that she may have been partially responsible for the destruction of one of Europe's most cherished landmarks, was more than she could bear.

"Geli!"

"What? Oh, alright. I guess you can cut me a small piece," replied Geli, trying to smile through her tears.

Otto cut into the sausage with his pocket knife and was just about to hand Geli the slice, when Lazo jumped up and shouted, "They're coming back! Can't you hear them?"

"No, it can't be," cried Geli. "There was no alarm."

"The alarms are all kaput!" shouted Otto.

"Listen," urged Lazo. "Are you two deaf?"

"I hear them now," whispered Geli. "Maybe they are ours, coming to survey the damage."

"There are too many for that," suggested Lazo. "Let's get to the bridge before they get here."

"Why the bridge?" asked Otto.

"Because," replied Lazo, "they are obviously not trying to destroy the bridges. They are the only safe places left in Dresden."

He grabbed Geli's hand and pulled her upward. The two made a dash for the bridge, with Otto following close at their heels. They scampered by the hundreds of people who were lying down in the tall grass, thinking that they were safe from this yet another, onslaught. As they hurried toward the bridge, Otto stopped and handed a little girl, the piece of sausage that he had cut for Geli.

"Hurry, Old Man!" cried Geli. "Are you trying to get yourself killed!"

They reached the bridge just as the American Flying Fortresses flew over. They were so low that the tail gunners were clearly visible. There were several hundred of them, accompanied by a large number of interceptors.

"Where the hell are our Messerschmidts?" shouted Otto, shaking his fist.

Before anyone could answer, the P-51's swooped down on the meadows, their blazing guns kicking up chunks of earth and human flesh and sending them through the air. For over fifteen minutes, they rained death upon these people, who had sought refuge in the meadows. Helpless women and children, who had survived the previous night's ordeal, were now subjected to still another devastating and humiliating attack.

"Will they never stop!" sobbed Geli, her body trembling.

"I'll stop them!" shouted Lazo. He jumped up and dashed toward the uniformed body of a fallen soldier. When he reached the dead boy, he grabbed the rifle and began to fire wildly at the Mustangs, which were darting back and forth like giant mosquitoes, looking for a place to light.

"Lazo!" screamed Geli. "Get back here before they kill you!"

Then before Otto could stop her, she ran toward Lazo and with all the strength she could summon, threw her shoulder into the pit of his stomach and brought him to the ground.

"You fool! You damned fool! Do you think that you can stop them with that pea shooter!" She paused long enough to catch her breath and then began to beat him about his chest, with her fists.

"Stop!" shouted Lazo. "What the hell are you trying to do? Kill me?"

"No!" screamed Geli. "I'm just trying to knock some damned sense into that damned thick skull of yours!"

"Wait," whispered Lazo. "I think they're leaving. I think it's over."

They listened silently as the noise of the airplane engines began to soften against the distant horizon and Lazo's cautious optimism erupted into wild screams of joy. He jumped up, pulling Geli along with him. He took hold of her waist and swung her around and around, until he became dizzy. Then he released her and fell to his knees. She dropped down beside him and together, they celebrated the end of the ordeal.

"It's over now, isn't it?" murmured Geli, trying to reassure herself.

"Yes, it's over. They won't be coming back anymore," said Lazo. "I think that their blood lust has been satisfied. You'll be safe from now on."

"Ja, until the damned Russkies come." She kissed his forehead. "That was a brave thing that you did."

"What?"

"Shooting at those planes. You might have been killed."

"Brave? What a joke. There's a very fine line between stupidity and heroism." He began to laugh.

"Why are you laughing?" she asked.

"If the army finds out what I did, they are liable to try me for treason."

"Don't worry. We won't tell them." She took his hand and said, "Let's hope that the Fuhrer doesn't find out and gives you an Iron Cross."

"Don't even suggest something like that. I'm in enough trouble the way it is."

"Let's get back to Otto. Maybe he hasn't eaten all of the sausage yet, and I'm getting hungry."

"Ja," replied Lazo, "it's got to be way past my lunch time." He looked up to find the sun but there was no sun, just thick, dark smoke and the hushed whisperings of women treading softly through the meadows, not wanting to disturb the dead.

CHAPTER TWENTY FIVE

The days following the bombing of Dresden were, at once, horrible and hectic for Geli and Lazo. They joined the countless others in the clean-up operation. The search for survivors continued, even while squads of workers went about, trying to dispose of the thousands of dead bodies that had begun to putrify. The decomposing bodies posed a serious health problem for the Dresdeners and had to be quickly disposed of. The bodies were thus collected and stacked up like cord wood, then fired by flame throwers that had been provided to them by the military. The remains were then loaded into horse drawn wagons and carried off to be spilled into common graves. Time did not permit the identification of the bodies and even if there had been time, most of the bodies were so completely disfigured, that identification was rendered virtually impossible.

During the raids, many of the people had sought refuge in the basements of the buildings and when the fire storms raced through the city, they sucked up the oxygen from these places of refuge, causing suffocation among those who had gathered there. These basements had to be entered and the bodies removed. Lazo and several others, including Geli and Otto, formed one of these teams, whose unpleasant task it was to enter these basements and perform that function.

It was on the first Sunday after the raid that Geli returned to her residence for the first time. Dresden was still smouldering. Most of the heavy smoke, that had covered the city, had by now dissipated, permitting the sun's rays, though blunted by some low lingering clouds, to bump against the shattered walls of a city humbled by war. Twenty eight square kilometers were totally destroyed. The number of dead will never be accurately known, since the army of refugees that swelled the population of the city, can never be reckoned.

Geli's apartment was situated in the part of the Friedrichstadt that had been only partially destroyed and her apartment building, though damaged, was still standing and appeared to be habitable. She considered herself quite fortunate. It was almost noon when they approached the building. Geli stopped and seemed to despair of going on.

"Why are you stopping?" asked Lazo.

"Because I'm afraid to go on," she replied, her voice trembling.

Lazo ran his fingers through his hair and shook his head. "I'll never understand women, not as long as I live."

Otto stroked his chin, now covered with several days of grime and beard. "I discovered that a very long time ago." He laughed, as he was wont to do and said, "Let's go Liebling. I'm soooo hungry and who knows, maybe, just maybe, there's still some of that delicious roast goose lying around."

Geli tried not to laugh but the muffled giggle that slipped through her closed lips, caused Lazo to chuckle. "You always know how to cheer her up."

Geli put an arm around each of them and said, "Alright, let's go." She smiled and chided, "You two will be the death of me."

Their pace quickened as they neared the entrance of the building. The broken glass which covered the sidewalk, split and crackled under their feet.

"There, it's not too bad, is it now?" uttered Lazo, as he rushed forward and began to remove some of the debris that had fallen in the doorway.

"I wonder who left the door ajar?" asked Geli. She joined Lazo and removed some of the smaller fragments.

"I distinctly remember closing it," insisted Otto, pushing Geli aside. "Here, let a man do that."

"Oh alright, but hurry. I can hardly wait to see what happened to my porcelain figurines."

"There she goes again. Here we are, hungry and cold and she's worried about some damned figurines."

"You're right, Lazo. You don't understand women," chided Geli, gently nudging him with her shoulder.

"There," said Otto, "that should do it." He tried to push the door open but it wouldn't budge.

"What's the matter?" asked Lazo. "Are you getting weak in your old age?"

"I think that the damned thing is jammed." He put his shoulder against the door and pushed with all of his might. "It just won't budge," he insisted.

"Here, let me help you," said Lazo, joining Otto at the door.

"Together now, one, two, three, push!" he yelled.

They tried the maneuver several times but the door remained fixed.

"I guess you're right. The damned thing is jammed."

"What do we do now?" asked Otto.

"We break it down," muttered Lazo, somewhat exasperated.

"May I help?" asked Geli. There was that certain twinkle in her eye which suggested that she knew something that they didn't.

"What can you do, Liebling?" asked Otto, chuckling. "You're only a woman, but go ahead. Be my guest."

Otto stepped aside and Geli walked up to the door, and quite nonchalantly, gave the lower part of the door a severe kick. Then she nudged it with her shoulder and the door flew open.

"There," she uttered, "the portal now stands open and we may enter."

"How did she do that?" asked Otto, quite bemused.

"I don't know," replied Lazo, "but I have a nagging suspicion that she is going to tell us."

"Oh, it was nothing," replied Geli, brushing her fingernails against her shoulder. "It does that every once in a while." She smiled and asked, "Well, what are we waiting for?"

She bounded up the stairs, with the two gentlemen following. When she reached the door of her flat, she paused, reluctant to enter.

"Now, what are you waiting for?" asked Lazo.

"I'm afraid to go in. I don't want to see the mess."

"Come on. let's go in." he urged. "Anything will be better than sleeping in the hallway."

"Ja, Liebling. It can't be that bad. Afterall, there are three of us and we should be able to set things straight in a hurry."

"Alright, I'll go in."

She turned the knob and slowly, almost inch by inch, eased the door open. The black out drapes were still drawn, and though it was mid-day, the room was quite dark. Geli tried to assess the damage but was unable to. She made her way to the window and pulled the drapes back, allowing the afternoon light to enter the room.

"Is the window intact?" asked Lazo.

"What window?"

"You mean?"

"Yes, Lazo, the window panes are gone."

"I'll try the bedroom," said Otto, "maybe that one is in good order."

"You jest," said Lazo. "I doubt that there's a window pane left in all of Friedrichstadt."

"Lazo's right, Otto. But check it out anyway. Who knows? Maybe the gods are smiling down at us."

Otto went into the bedroom. Several seconds later, he yelled, "Ach du lieber!"

"What's the matter? Is it that bad?"

"No, it's not that bad, Geli. As a matter of fact, we still have half a window. Come on in and see for yourselves."

The two went into the bedroom. "What was all the yelling about?" asked Geli.

"Oh that. It was just a little monkey. He was hiding in the drapes. Trying to keep warm, I guess."

"Quit joking!"

"Who's joking, Liebling?"

But before Geli could respond, a little spider monkey jumped down from the chandelier and lit on Geli's shoulder. Her body became rigid and she screamed, "Take him off! Please take him off!"

Otto quickly removed the monkey from her shoulder and Geli ran over to Lazo.

"It's only a little monkey, a fugitive from the Tiergarten," whispered Lazo, trying to comfort her.

He put his arms around her and held her close, until she stopped trembling.

"Well, what are we waiting for?" asked Lazo. "We've got an awful lot of work to do around here so it's best we get started."

"We'll start in the living room," suggested Geli, "and while you're at it, get rid of that monkey."

"Oh, Liebling, he's such a little fellah, and besides, if we put him out he will freeze. You don't want that on your conscience do you?"

Geli smiled and said, "I guess not, old man, but you see to him and if he messes, you'll have to clean it up."

"I'll see if I can get the fireplace working," said Lazo. "It's so damned cold in here."

"And I'll see if I can find something to cover the window," said Otto.

"Try the basement," suggested Geli. "I'm sure there will be something down there."

"Ja wohl," snapped Otto. He put the monkey back on the chandelier. "I'm gone."

"And what will you do?" asked Lazo.

"I'll try to get rid of the broken plaster." She shrugged her shoulders. "There is so much of it that I don't quite know where to begin."

"It's a mess," agreed Lazo, "but at least, we have a place to sleep."

She smiled faintly. "I guess we are luckier than most." She turned to leave the room.

"Where are you going?"

"To get a pail so I will be able to carry out the broken glass and the plaster."

"You don't have to do that."

"What then?"

"Just throw the stuff out of the window. It will be a helluva lot easier. Before you do that, come over here and help me get this damper working. It seems to be stuck."

"Little wonder. It hasn't been used for over a year."

"I see. We'll probably burn the place down. Now, wouldn't that be ironic?" he chuckled.

"What do you want me to do?"

"I'll try to get the lever free and you look up the chimney and tell me when it's open."

"Okay," replied Geli, bending down and assuming a position which enabled her to look up the chimney.

"Ready?" asked Lazo.

"Yes, I'm ready."

Lazo jerked on the lever, pulling it back and forth with all of his strength. "This damned thing won't budge!" he shouted, becoming quite angry and swearing under his breath.

"Keep trying," urged Geli. "There seems to be something moving up there."

"I'll give it another try," said Lazo, breathing quite heavily. He reached down and grabbed one of the heavy andirons. He reared back and hit the lever with all of his might. "There," he shouted, "that should do it!"

"Stop! It's open!" yelled Geli, coughing and laughing at the same time.

"What's so funny?" He grabbed her legs and pulled her out. Her hair and face were covered with black soot. Lazo burst into laughter as she tried to brush away the grime.

"You think it pretty funny, uh?" And before he could reply, she reached down and grabbed a handful of soot. Then she rubbed it all over Lazo's face.

"There now, how do you like that?" Then she looked down at her dress which was now, completely covered with grime. "It's ruined. I'll never be able to get it clean again."

"It's alright," said Lazo, taking her into his arms and giving her an affectionate hug. "Now I'll get a fire going and you start cleaning this room."

"I've got to wash my face first," insisted Geli.

"You can do that later, after we get this mess cleaned up. Then, my dear, we'll burn that dress. I never want to see it again."

"Alright, if you insist." She picked up a large piece of plaster and flung it out the window. She continued until every piece of debris was gone. Then she dusted the furniture and swept the floor. While she was busy with the room, Lazo had cleaned out the fireplace and went in search of some coal or wood.

When he returned, Otto was already fitting the cardboard into the empty spaces where once the window panes had been. Geli had lit several candles which gave the room a kind of gentle glow.

"What kept you?" she asked, carefully dusting one of her prized figurines.

"I see you still have your figurines," remarked Lazo, setting the bucket of coal down by the fireplace.

"Where did you get the wood?" asked Otto.

"Oh, I managed," replied Lazo. "In the army, we call it midnight requisitioning."

"Where did you steal it from?" asked Geli, walking toward him. "You do know that looting is against the law."

"Oh yes," replied Lazo, "I know but it's like this." He set the wood down.

"Well?"

"Oh yes, the firewood. Do you remember the apartment on the first floor, south side?"

"Of course, I remember."

"It's not there anymore. The outside wall is gone. Kaput."

"Oh no, those poor people."

"Oh yes," replied Lazo. "So you see, we are luckier than most."

"And so you helped yourself to their firewood?"

"Yes, Otto, I helped myself to their wood. I don't believe that they'll be needing it."

"Well, what are you waiting for? Start the fire so that we can get warm."

Lazo quickly set the wood and started the fire. "There," he said, holding his hands over the weak flames, pretending to warm them. "That feels much better."

"What do we do now?" asked Otto, joining Lazo by the fire.

"We heat some water so that we can finally take baths," replied Geli. She smiled and folded her arms about her upper torso.

"Do you mean to tell me that we have running water?"

"Yes, Lazo, we have running water. There isn't much pressure but we do have running water."

"How about gas?" asked Otto.

"No gas," replied Geli. "Just water. Isn't that enough?"

"How about the bathroom?" asked Lazo.

"Everything works except the electricity," replied Geli.

"I'll bet it's cold as hell in there," suggested Lazo.

"Yes," replied Geli, "it is quite cold but I'll light a couple of candles and place them on the floor. That should take out some of the chill."

"Good, then let's fill some buckets and as soon as the fire gets warm enough we'll hang the buckets and wait for the water to boil."

"Sounds good to me, Lazo," said Geli. "I can hardly wait to bathe with soap and hot water. I can almost feel the exquisite pain of the soap, biting into my chapped, broken skin."

"That sounds good," echoed Otto, "but where do we get some good clean buckets?"

"The landlady keeps a couple of pails in the hall closet, but if they're not there, just empty the sand from the air raid buckets. I don't think that they will ever be needed again."

"Wunderbar! I'll check out this floor and you, Lazo, you check out the lower floors. The fireplace will hold at least three buckets, maybe four."

"And while you two are doing that, I'll get some glasses, if they are not all kaput, and the bottle of schnapps." She glanced at Otto, "You didn't drink it all, did you?"

"Nein, nein, Fraulein! I wouldn't do that. There should still be about half a bottle left." He looked at Geli, then at Lazo and added, "That is if the bottle didn't get broken in the raid."

Lazo was the first to leave and as he walked out, he turned and said, "I'll try to find a kerosine lamp. It will give us more light."

"Ja," laughed Geli, "but remember, they shoot looters."

"I'll try to remember," shouted Lazo.

"Well, what are you waiting for?"

"Nothing, Liebling. I'm on my way."

Geli laughed as they left the room and in spite of the hell that she had gone through, during these past several days, she began to feel warm and alive again. She walked over to the table and carefully picked up her favorite figurine, a little blonde, blue-eyed boy on a swing. She clutched it to her bosom and moved, almost unconsciously, toward the fireplace. She positioned herself as close to the fire as possible. The warm flames brought a flush to her face and a yearning for Lazo filled her thoughts. She drew her thighs together and pretended that Lazo was pressing his body against hers. She was so deeply engaged that she didn't hear the door open and Lazo enter.

"Look what I found," remarked Lazo, as he swung the lantern around and around. "I found two buckets."

She turned around so suddenly that she forgot about the figurine she was holding and almost dropped it.

"Careful," cautioned Lazo. "You wouldn't want to accomplish what the bombers couldn't, now would you?"

Geli returned the figurine to the table. Then she turned to Lazo and in a voice just above a whisper said, "Come over here."

Lazo set the pails down and walked over to her. She took the lantern and set it on the floor. Then she put her arms around him and gave him a passionate kiss. She pressed her body against his so closely, that their shadows on the wall became one. The sound of footsteps alerted them to Otto's approach, and they quickly separated.

She brushed her hair back and said, "I'll get the schnapps." As she turned, he gave her an affectionate pat on her seat. She stopped and without turning her head, said, "I love that old man, but right now, I would rather that he not be here."

"I found two buckets!" bellowed Otto, as he entered the room. "That's perfect," uttered Lazo. "Now we have four."

"Where's the schnapps?"

"Not so fast," admonished Lazo. "First, you've got to fill the buckets with water and hang them in the fireplace. While you are doing that, I'll clean the chimney of this lantern so that we can have some light."

"Good," said Otto, "then we can drink the schnapps."

"Ja, Otto. Then we can drink the schnapps."

Lazo picked up the cloth that Geli had used to wipe the figurines and began to clean the glass chimney. When he was satisfied that it was clean enough, he lit the wick and replaced the chimney. Then he stepped back and smiled.

"That's so nice," pealed Geli, looking around the room. "Where's Otto?"

"He's in the bathroom, filling the pails."

She set the tray down and said, "That will give us a couple of minutes alone, won't it?"

She took Lazo's face into her hands and kissed him, long and warmly. "I so want you," she whispered, rubbing her body against his.

"You wanton hussy. Have you no shame?"

"Not one little bit. In these times, I think it best that we live for the moment."

"I agree," replied Lazo, digging his fingers into her firm behind and pulled her even closer.

The sound of running water ceased and they knew that Otto was about to return so they disengaged and Lazo walked over to the fireplace. He picked up several pieces of coal and tossed them into the flames.

"There," he said, "it won't be long before we'll be able to hang the buckets over the fire."

"I can hardly wait," said Geli. "It seems like an eternity."

"Where shall I put these buckets?"

"Right there," instructed Lazo, pointing to the fireplace.

Otto put the two pails down and went back for the others. Geli filled the small glasses with schnapps and handed one to Lazo. He took a sip and toyed with his glass.

"It's hot enough, isn't it?" she asked.

"I suppose," replied Lazo. "Ja, I think we can hang the buckets now."

He set his drink on the mantel. Then he picked up the poker and stirred the fire, sending a host of sparks hurrying up the chimney. He reached in with the poker, pulled the metal arm out and hung both buckets on it.

"Is it strong enough to hold both pails?" asked Geli, leaning over his shoulder.

"It should hold," replied Lazo, pushing the arm inward until the pails were suspended directly over the flames. He straightened up and said, "That should do it. Now all we have to do is wait until the water boils." "Bravo!" She put her glass down, next to his and hugged him. "Here are the other two buckets," uttered Otto. He mopped his forehead with his handkerchief. "Now where's the schnapps?"

"On the table. Help yourself."

Lazo put the other buckets over the flames and tossed in some more coal. Darkness had settled over the shattered, shabby city but they were too busy to notice. As far as they were concerned, the war, at least for the moment, had slipped far, far away and together, they were alone.

"Otto, would you please bring some chairs over here by the fire?" asked Geli.

"Ja wohl! It will be a pleasure."

The three sat down and watched the flames dance around the buckets. The flames warmed their bodies and the schnapps rekindled their sensibilities and nourished their spirits.

"Do you know what I would like now?"

"No, Otto," replied Lazo. "What would you like now?"

"I would like some good Vienna sausages."

"So would I," echoed Geli, licking her lips. "Do you know where we can get some?"

"No. I was just asking."

"And dreaming." She got up and walked to the table. "I don't have any sausage but I do have several tins of meat in the pantry." She picked up the bottle of schnapps and returned to her chair. She filled the glasses and carefully set the bottle on the floor. "I was planning to have the meat after we have bathed."

She leaned over to see if the water was boiling. "Why is it taking so long?"

"Be patient," said Lazo. "Good things come to those who wait. Just try to imagine the sensation of hot, bubbling water cascading against your skin."

"That's all I've been thinking of these past several days." retorted Geli.

She sipped some schnapps. It burned her throat as she swallowed. She laughed and put her hand to her mouth. The hand that had been so pale and soft, was now rough and used, like that of a scrub woman. She looked at it, winced and quickly dropped it into her lap, where it disappeared in the wrinkles of her dirty, tattered dress.

"Now, I'm beginning to appreciate what the refugees must endure as they make their ways west. It must be a living nightmare."

"Well, Liebchen," said Otto, "there are thousands of them that will never feel pain again, nor hunger." He surveyed the bottom of his empty glass. "Their journey came to an end, right here in Dresden." He rubbed his bewhiskered face with the back of his hand and looked up at the shattered ceiling. Then almost in a whisper asked, "Who will weep for them? Who will even remember?"

"I don't know," replied Lazo. "All I know is that they died as they lived, anonymously."

"Oh don't say that," implored Geli. "You can't mean that. Their deaths were of more significance than the deaths of the cockroaches and vermin that were consumed by the flames. Oh no, Lazo, they've got to count for more than that. There has to be a lesson in this. There must be."

"What lesson?" asked Lazo, seeming to become angry. "They were just common folk, made from that common stuff which is not at all suitable for statues."

"They are the beloved of God!" protested Geli, she too becoming angry.

"And that God," remarked Lazo, "has now joined them on their journey. That God died long before these gentle folk were born. He was too heavy a burden and they, were just too damned tired to carry him any longer. For them, he was just an imposition." He leaned over to check on the water.

"Is it boiling?" asked Geli.

"Yup, it's boiling. Hot damn, it's finally boiling!"

"I'm so glad," mumbled Otto. "The conversation was getting too heavy and I don't much like to talk about those things."

"Sorry, old man," replied Lazo. "I didn't mean to upset you, but this damned war is beginning to piss me off."

"What does that mean, piss me off?" asked Otto.

"Oh nothing," replied Geli, "it's just another of those quaint American expressions."

"I see," muttered Otto, scratching his forehead.

"Well, what are we waiting for?" asked Geli. She jumped up and headed for the bathroom.

"Where do you think you are going?" asked Lazo.

"I'm going to run some water, while you two take the buckets from the fireplace. I can hardly wait," she shouted, as she disappeared into the bathroom.

"Don't run too much water," cautioned Lazo. "You want the water to be good and hot."

Then they carefully removed the buckets and carried them into the bathroom. They poured the water into the tub and watched as clouds of steam formed and began to fill the room.

"Now get out of here!" she ordered. I'm going to take the most important bath of my entire life." She smiled and hastened their departure with gentle pushings. Then she slammed the door and began to sing.

"She sounds happy."

"Ja," replied Otto. "It's good to hear her sing again." He paused, then asked, "What do we do now?"

"We fill the buckets. That's what we do." Then he laughed and said, "Then we'll wait for the prima donna to finish her bath."

"And while we are waiting, we'll finish off the schnapps. Ach, it feels so good to feel so good again."

It took longer to fill the buckets this time, due to the diminished pressure in the water mains. When the buckets were once again hanging over the flames, Lazo threw in a couple of pieces of coal and sat down. Otto filled their glasses and together, they waited for Geli to complete her bath. The room was quite warm and Lazo noticed that Otto was becoming drowsy.

"Don't fall asleep, Old Man," admonished Lazo, with a smile. "You don't want to miss the dress burning, do you?"

"No. I wouldn't miss that for all the tea in China." He smiled devilishly and added, "I don't like tea very much, you know."

About forty-five minutes later, Geli emerged from the bathroom. She was clothed in a snowy white, terry cloth robe, with a hemline that brushed against the floor. Her hair was wrapped in a bright orange towel and in her hands, was the old tattered dress. She looked absolutely radiant. She walked to the fireplace and without any hesitation, flung the dress into the flames. Then she stepped back and asked, "Where's my glass?"

"Right here, Liebling," replied Otto.

"Well, fill it up. I want to propose a toast."

Otto filled her glass and handed it to her. She took it into her hand and gazing at the dress, now nearly consumed by the flames, said, "May we always remember this moment; this moment of my triumph."

"What are you talking about?" asked Otto, somewhat bewildered. "We have lost the war. There will be no triumph."

"Not that, you old fool. I have personally triumphed over grime and I have never felt so clean in my entire life. Do you understand?"

Otto shrugged his shoulders and said, "Women, only women could transform a simple bath into a purification rite." He raised his glass and emptied it. "Now that," he said, "makes me feel good."

Geli laughed, raised her glass and with a deft flip of her wrist, threw the liquor down her throat. "And now," she asked, "whose next?"

"I am," peeled Lazo. "I'm afraid that if Otto goes first, he will fall asleep in the tub and I'll never get my bath."

"Okay," said Geli. "Is there anything that I can do to help?"

"No. You just sit by the fire. Otto and I can handle this."

They took the buckets and disappeared into the bathroom. Soon Otto emerged, carrying the empty buckets. He filled them and once again hung them over the fire. Then he sat down, neither of them speaking. They just stared at the flames and waited for Lazo.

One of the coals exploded. Geli winced and drew back. "What was that?" she asked.

Otto smiled. "No cause for alarm. It's just a hot coal, protesting in the only way it knows."

"Is there any more schnapps?" she asked, extending her glass.

"Ja, there is a little left." He picked up the bottle and poured a little into Geli's glass.

She studied the contents of the glass for the longest time. Then she raised the glass and took a sip. "What are you going to do when the Russians come?" she asked.

"I really haven't thought about it. There isn't a helluva lot I can do about it anyway." He looked at her for a moment, then asked, "How about you? Are you afraid?"

"Ja, I am frightened. If the stories I've heard are only half true, they would still be too horrible to contemplate. Ja, Otto, I am afraid."

"Don't be afraid, Liebling. I will see to it that no harm comes to you. Now quit worrying about the damned Russkies. We've got other things to worry about."

"Ja," said Geli, "like staying alive."

Just then the bathroom door opened and Lazo appeared. He was wearing one of Lev's bathrobes. It was of a heavy, rough wool texture, which suited him quite well. The greyish color went well with Lazo's bright green eyes. He walked over to Geli and smiled.

"Well, Otto," he said, "now it's your turn."

"The water is not quite boiling yet. Another few minutes should do it."

Lazo put his hand on Geli's shoulder. She looked up at his cleanly shaven face and winked. "You look good enough to eat," she remarked.

"I didn't know that you were that famished, but I'm quite sure that you can find something a little more nourishing."

She took his hand and squeezed it. "Sit down and make yourself comfortable."

He sat down next to her, his hand still in hers. "I feel just great. I tried to get my fingernails clean but I just couldn't." He held them up so Geli could examine them.

"They're not bad. A couple more hot baths and they will be as good as new." She laughed. "Otto," she said, "why don't you pour Lazo a drink?"

Otto raised the bottle, studied it carefully and said, "I guess there's enough for another drink."

He leaned over and filled the glass. Then he raised the bottle to his lips and emptied the bottle. "There," he said, as he put the bottle down. "Another dead soldier."

Then he slowly, almost painfully raised himself upward and checked the buckets. "It's boiling," he remarked, "now I can take my bath."

Lazo helped him with the buckets then rejoined Geli. "Shall we fill the pails?"

"Let's just fill two of them. That should be enough for a while."

"Good," replied Lazo. He took the two pails and headed for the kitchen.

"Hurry back!"

"Be right there. You might stir the fire a bit and add some coal."

"How about some wood? I like the smell of burning wood. It's so romantic."

"Go right ahead but don't put too much on."

She did as he suggested and when he returned from the kitchen, the flames were already leaping upward, into the chimney.

"That's some fire, you've got. He put the pails on one of the iron arms, then pushed the arm as far back into the fireplace, as he could.

"Why are you pushing them back so far?"

"I just want to heat the water, not boil it. Besides," he added, "I don't want those ugly pails interfering with the view of those romantic flames."

"Sit down and enjoy the fire."

He took his glass from the mantel and sat down.

"May I?" she asked.

"May you what?"

She did not reply. The smile on his lips told her that he knew, so she curled up in his lap and rested her head, towel and all, on his shoulder.

"It is at times like these, that one realizes how little it takes to make one happy and I am truly happy."

Lazo raised his glass, took a drink. Then he put the glass to her lips so that she might enjoy a sip. "How is it then, that the two of us can find such beauty and joy amidst this filthy, hellish war."

"Because," she replied, "I guess that in untroubled times, we allow ourselves to be distracted by all sorts of trivialities. We seem to lose ourselves in the tangled excesses of colliding moments."

She took another sip from his glass, then slipped her hand into his bathrobe and ran her fingers over his naked chest. "Then we wake up one morning and realize that we are mortal and that succession of colliding moments, that at one time seemed so bountiful, is now numbered and all joy is greyed by the shadow of death."

"And the antidote?" asked Lazo, as he turned his head and kissed her forehead.

"Do that again," she urged.

"Do what?"

"Kiss my forehead."

He lowered his head and was about to do her bidding when she raised her head and pressed her lips to his. He put his glass down, slipped his hand into her robe and gently ran his hand over her breasts. Soon his hand was brushing downward, his fingers whispering to her warm soft skin.

He looked into her eyes, smiled and asked, "Is this the antidote?"

Before she could reply, the bathroom door opened and out came Otto, clothed in a bathrobe that could scarce contain his bulging stomach.

"You two look awful cozy."

"We are," replied Geli. "You can just bet that we are."

"Well, now that I am clean, where's the food that you promised? I'm sooo hungry."

She looked up at Lazo, grinned and said, "And there, Lazo, is the antidote."

"Antidote? What antidote?"

"Never mind, Old Man," replied Geli. She slipped down from Lazo's lap and disappeared into the kitchen, leaving the two men sitting before the fire, one dreaming of food, the other, confused by the delicacy of the previous moment.

CHAPTER TWENTY SIX

It was Monday morning and Dresden still smouldered. Lazo walked to the window, carefully pulled the cardboard back and looked out. "It's going to be a nice day," he thought, replacing the cardboard. Then he turned and walked over to the fireplace. He moved very quietly, so as not to disturb Geli, who was still asleep before the fire. She had placed a feather bed on the floor immediately in front of the fireplace and that is where the two of them slept. Otto, in deference to his age, was given the bedroom.

Lazo put some wood on the glowing coals then settled down next to Geli. He tried not to disturb her sleep, but she was already awake. She turned and rested her head on his chest.

"That must have been some dream you had," she whispered.

"Did I scream?" asked Lazo, his face becoming contorted.

"Don't you remember?"

"No. I remember screaming in the dream, but ."

"Oh yes. You sat up and screamed over and over again."

"What did I say?"

"You covered your ears and screamed, No! No!, over and over again." She paused and kissed his cheek. "There were tears in your eyes."

Lazo ran his fingers across her brow. "I was dreaming about Sam. Oh God, it was so real! It was so real! He kept yelling, Lazo, help me! Lazo, please help me!"

"Have you had that dream before?"

"No. Never. I've thought about it many times but until last night, I had never really dreamed about it. It must have been the tins of beef."

He paused and unconsciously pressed his hand against her head. "Yes, that's what it must have been."

"The beef was that bad?"

"Oh no, not that. The beef was very tasty but the tins were exactly the same as the ones the Chetniks found in Sam's mussette bag." He paused once again and kissed her cheek. "Yes, that's got to be it. That's what triggered the dream!" he exclaimed, his voice becoming louder.

"Shhh, not so loud," cautioned Geli, putting her finger to his lips. "Do you want to awaken Otto?"

"I'm sorry. I must have gotten carried away but I do feel much better now."

He turned on his side and pulled her tightly to him. She melted in his arms, becoming completely and unabashedly his. They cleaved to each other with such intensity that any body motion was almost impossible. Still they achieved satisfaction, this time with such intensity that their bodies seemed to resonate, transporting them to a state of rapture.

"What was that?"

"That, dear Lazo, was the antidote."

"That noise. What was it?"

"Oh, that's just Otto, going to the bathroom." replied Geli. She pulled away and said, "It won't do for him to find us this way."

"Don't you think he knows?"

"Of course, he knows but he thinks that we don't know that he knows, so let's indulge him," replied Geli, her eyes sparkling.

"Okay, let's indulge the old man, but not too much. Afterall, if we treat him too well, he may just decide to stay with us and that would make things a little difficult."

"Ja," replied Geli, She took the orange towel that she had used to dry her hair, dipped a corner of it into one of the pails of hot water and scooted off toward the kitchen.

"Where are you going?"

"I'm going to clean up a little. Do you want to help?"

"Not especially," replied Lazo, his face, taking on a slight tinge of red. He raised himself to his feet and began to stir the fire.

"Do you want this now?"

Lazo did not hear her re-enter the room and he turned just in time to catch the towel that she threw at him.

"Do you need some help?"

"I'll manage."

"Well, what are you waiting for?" asked Geli, enjoying his embarrassment.

"I'm waiting for you to turn around. Then I'll begin."

"Begin what?" asked Otto, bursting into the room, his hair dissheveled and eyes quite blood shot. He walked over to the fireplace and held his hands over the flames.

"Did you sleep well, old man?" asked Geli.

"Just like a baby," he replied, with heavy emphasis on the word baby. "And now I think I am hungry." He looked at Geli and asked, "Do you have any hot coffee?"

"Not yet."

"Do you mean to say that you have some coffee? Real coffee?"

"Ja, Schatzie, I really do. As a matter of fact, I have a rather large quantity of coffee. Not ersatz, mind you, but the genuine stuff."

"How did you manage that?" asked Lazo.

She smiled smugly. "A good soldier takes care of herself. Afterall," she continued, "survival is the fundamental basis of all morality."

She walked up to Lazo, put her arms around his neck and asked, "And what else would you like for breakfast?"

Lazo blushed a little, then said, "Some bread to go with the coffee." Then he pinched her on her behind.

She winced and whispered, "I'll get even with you." Then added, quite loudly, "No, I don't have any bread but I'm sure that Otto could go out and get some."

"Who? Me?" asked Otto, pointing to himself.

"Ja," replied Geli, "You are the only one dressed."

"Ja, but where do I find this bread?"

"There should be a relief truck near by."

"Okay, I'll go," he answered, but the tone of his voice suggested that he was not overjoyed.

"And while you're gone, we'll get the coffee going and get dressed."

"Ja," added Geli, "and I'll try to find some good jelly to go with the bread."

"Do you have any sugar?" asked Lazo.

"Ja, Schatzie, I have some sugar for you." She winked and added, "working for the S.S., does have its advantages."

Lazo helped Otto with his coat and walked him to the door. Otto was about to open it, when Lazo whispered, "Wait, I'll be right back."

Lazo ran into the bedroom and returned with something hidden in his hand. "Here," he whispered, handing Otto some American money. "See if you can buy some eggs on the black market."

"American money! Ja wohl, mein Herr!"

"Shhh. Not so loud. I want to surprise Geli."

Lazo opened the door and ushered Otto out. Then he turned and went back into the living room, singing:

"There'll be bluebirds over
The white cliffs of Dover,
Tomorrow, just you wait and see.
There'll be love and laughter,
And peace forever after,
Tomorrow, when the world is free.

"That's pretty," said Geli. "Will you teach it to me some time?"

"Of course, I will. That is, if I can remember all of it. Now let's get busy so that the coffee will be ready when Otto returns."

"There's plenty of time. Now come here. I've got something for you," whispered Geli, as she undid her belt, allowing it to fall to the floor.

"Oh no you don't. I'm wise to you. You want to get even with me for the pinch I gave you, don't you?"

"Don't be silly. I've forgotten all about that."

"Then what?"

"We are alone. Let's take advantage of it."

"But we told Otto that we would be ready with the coffee when he got back."

"We will," she assured him, "but first, we have more important things to do."

"Can I make a suggestion?"

"Go ahead, but I still think that you are trying to avoid the inevitable."

"Let's get the coffee going first then we can play around to your heart's content."

"Oh, all right!" she retorted, screwing up her forehead and pretending to be irritated. "You stoke the fire and I'll fill the coffee pot."

"Good," replied Lazo, smiling victoriously. He knelt down before the fire and began to rearrange the coals. Then he added a few more pieces of coal to the fire and sat back, enjoying the flames. He was gazing at the fire so intently that he didn't hear Geli tiptoe up to him. "Well, here I am," pealed Geli, nudging him with her knee.

"Where's the coffee pot?"

"In the kitchen," replied Geli, kneeling down beside him.

"Is it too heavy for you to carry?"

"No, it wasn't too heavy."

"Then why didn't you bring it in?" asked Lazo, pretending to be irritated.

"Because, my sweet darling, we now have electricity and the coffee pot is on the hot plate," she replied with quiet nonchalance.

Lazo leaped up, took her into his arms and danced around the room, yelling, "We've got electricity! Hot damn, we've got electricity!"

As they danced around she tried every switch, shouting, "Let there be light! Let there be light!" Then they fell down on the feather bed, laughing loudly. She crawled on top of him, resting her body against his and they made love.

By the time Otto returned, the fragrance of coffee had already filled the room. Geli and Lazo were dressed and ready for breakfast.

"Open the door!" shouted Otto. "Open the door, before my arms fall off!"

Lazo ran to the door and threw it open. There stood Otto, both arms full and out of breath.

"Well, what are you waiting for? Take these so I can catch my breath!"

Lazo took the packages and carried them into the kitchen.

"Set them down on the table!" instructed Geli.

Lazo set the bags down and asked, "Can I do anything to help?"

"You can set the dining room table."

"I'll be happy to," replied Lazo, rummaging through the packages.

"What are you looking for?"

"He got them!" shouted Lazo. "He got the eggs! Damned if he didn't!"

"Eggs?"

"Ja, he got eggs and some ham. I can hardly believe it. The son of a gun."

"Well, how do you want your eggs?"

"Scrambled," replied Lazo, without hesitation. He licked his lips and said, "That's the way I like them."

"Okay then. I'll scramble them and mix the ham in with them. Otto likes them that way also."

Lazo set the table and by the time he had poured the coffee, Geli was ready to dish up the eggs.

"You two can sit down now. I'll be there directly!"

The two sat down and waited for Geli and when she entered, carrying the steaming bowl of ham and eggs, the two became utterly speechless. And no wonder. It was their first hot meal since Lazo's birthday party and they were famished. Otto's eyes widened as she heaped his plate.

"Save some for the two of you," he admonished, as he raised his fork and made ready to still his voracious appetite.

"Don't worry, there's plenty here for all of us," she replied.

When they had finished, there was very little left. The bowl was empty, the coffee pot dry, and they had dispatched two loaves of bread.

"Do you know what I would like now?" asked Lazo.

"No," replied Geli, "You're not still hungry, are you?"

"No, of course not, but I'd like a good American cigarette."

"So would I," chimed Otto, taking a deep breath. "I can almost taste it."

"Oh, you can, can you," laughed Geli, "Well, maybe just maybe, there's another pack of Pall Malls lying around."

"Quit taunting us and get them for us," said Lazo.

Geli left the kitchen and returned shortly. She was carrying two packs of cigarettes. She threw a pack to each of them and said, "Now you two can smoke to your heart's content but mind you, there aren't any more." Then as an afterthought, added, "And I doubt that there will be any more of these unless the Americans get here first."

They lit their cigarettes and sat back. Lazo inhaled deeply, pulled his head back and exhaled the smoke in a series of perfect rings. Geli watched intently, as the rings floated gently upward, uniting at the ceiling. She unconsciously moved her tongue back and forth against her upper lip and she began to blush.

"Well, while you two enjoy your smoking, I'll clear away the dishes. Then I think we'll have to go back and help with the clean up."

"I guess you're right," remarked Otto, "there's still a lot of work to be done but it's so damned depressing, even for an old man like me."

He drew heavily on the shortened stub and then with perfect aim, threw the butt into the fireplace.

"Nice shot old man," uttered Lazo, with a smile. Then he walked over to the fireplace, studied the glowing embers and dropped the dingy stub, that was once a cigarette, into the ashes.

"Do you think the Americans will get here first?" he asked, without turning his head.

Otto walked over to him and put his arm around Lazo's shoulders. "Who knows? In this damned war, anything is possible. For instance, whoever thought that the Allies would destroy the beautiful old city of Dresden, but they did."

"But the Yalta agreement ties our hands, doesn't it?"

"Screw the agreement," replied Otto, with a kind of cold vehemence. "I've been around long enough to know that treaties and agreements are made to be broken. Diplomacy is just a euphemism for bull shit and no matter how fine you slice it, it still stinks." He paused and then looked into Lazo's eyes. "I'm going to tell you something about myself that not even Geli knows."

He reached into his pocket and pulled out another cigarette and ushered it to his lips. Then he bent down, tore a page from a magazine and thrust it into the embers. He waited for it to burst into flame than used it to light his cigarette.

"After the last war, Lazo, I emerged alive and very angry. I saw thousands of men butchered in the battles of that war. It was the most senseless of all senselessness." He paused, took a long drag and continued, "Hell, we still don't know how it got started. I doubt that we ever will. Ah, but as I said, I came out of the war angry and if you can believe it, full of idealism. During the war I promised myself that if I survived, I would go to the University of Leipzig and study international law."

He laughed at himself, as he was wont to do. A mild form of self deprecation. Then he slapped Lazo on his back. "Can you believe that, Lazo? The son of a glass blower, wanting to major in international law? Ah, but I did. God, how I ached for it." Then he looked down at the dying embers and seemed reluctant to contiue.

"Well, did you go to the university or didn't you?" asked Lazo, becoming impatient.

"Ja, I went and as a matter of fact, I did quite well, but I quit after only one year."

"Why the hell?"

"Because I couldn't stand it any longer. That's why!" Then, in a whisper, added, "They kicked me out."

"They kicked you out!" exclaimed Lazo. "How in hell could they do that to you if you were making good grades?"

"Well," replied Otto, "it was partly my fault. One of my professors was a pinched nose, narrow eyed pedant, whom I didn't like very much. He specialized in pre-World War One diplomacy. I couldn't stand that son of a bitch. He kept insisting that the war was justified and no sacrifice was too great for the Vaterland. And do you know what Lazo? I think the fool actually believed it."

"Ja, I've met people like that," said Lazo.

"Well, one day he was lecturing to about forty of us and he was carrying on about the nobility of war. I bit my tongue and managed to maintain my composure until the bastard insisted that the German historian, von Treitschke's statement that war is the supreme court of history, was totally correct. When he said that, I saw red and recalling the horrible nature of war in the trenches, jumped up from my seat and yelled, at the top of my voice, Herr Professor, have you ever been blooded?"

"What did he say?"

"He did not answer my question but I could feel the chill of those narrow, beady eyes, glowering at me. The auditorium became as still as an autumn sunset. All eyes were fixed upon me. I began to feel dirty but did not capitulate. Perhaps I should have sat down and kept my mouth shut, but I couldn't betray the thousands of young men who died in the mud and slop of that war. Someone had to speak for them." He paused for a moment. Perhaps the recounting of the experience was too painful for him. He leaned against the fireplace and looked upward.

"What happened next?" asked Lazo, his interest piqued.

"Well, Herr Professor," I shouted, "I fought at the Battle of Verdun and I still bleed for the million young men who were destroyed in that senseless agony you choose to call a noble endeavor. Ah no, Herr Professor, I cannot allow you to make light of those brave men, thousands of whom could never be properly buried. They were turned into goo by the exploding shells and absorbed into the blood soaked earth. They disappeared without a trace, Herr Professor. I saw French soldiers rise up to meet our attack. Some of them had pieces of human intestines clinging to their faces and clothing. They walked into our gun fire and died like half crazed animals. I don't think that they even knew that they were dying. And why, Herr Professor, did so many of them die? I'll tell you why. Because people like you, who never stand in danger's path, continue to disguise the ugliness and futility of war with such finely embroidered words as, patriotism, duty, honor, nobility and Vaterland. Ach, Ja, Herr Professor, when everything else fails, then you appeal to the love of Vaterland. Is that not so, Herr Professor?"

"How did he respond?" asked Lazo.

"Well, Lazo, the Professor did not respond to my challenge and when I finally sat down, the room became absolutely quiet. Then my classmates began to clap, a few at first, then more, until finally they all rose and gave me a standing ovation. The professor, whom I had already embarrassed, became so incensed and flustered that he had no alternative but retreat, and retreat he did, right off the stage. The next day I was called into the rector's office where I was told that I was a threat to faculty morale and was no longer welcome at the institution. I tried to defend my actions but he would not listen. So I packed my bags and left. And that Lazo was when I decided to become a photographer."

Lazo was obviously moved by Otto's narrative but all he could say was, "Well, as they say in America, 'win some, lose some'. But if it's any consolation, I think that you would have made one helluva international lawyer."

"Are you two ready?' asked Geli.

"Ja, we'll be right there," replied Otto.

They put on their wraps and left the flat. The sun was shining brightly and a spring like breeze played on their faces. It was a very beautiful day, insulted only by the odor of decaying human flesh, too strong to go unnoticed.

"Will this smell ever be washed away?" asked Geli with a grimace.

"Oh yes, Liebling. The smell will be washed away and much sooner than you would think," replied Otto, "but let us hope that the memory of this nightmare will last a little longer than the smell."

"Ja, I think the smell will be washed away by the spring rains but the memory of it; now, that's something else," remarked Lazo, his voice expressing a marked degree of cynicism.

"What do you mean?' asked Geli, tugging on his arm.

"You know what I mean. You weren't born yesterday. All through history, nations and empires have committed horrible crimes and atrocities."

"Ja, I know that," said Geli, "but what has that got to do with this? This is the middle of the twentieth century."

"Nations," declaimed Lazo, "have a strong tendency to launder their crimes and tuck them neatly away in the farthest corners of their mental closets. And there, my dear Geli, they are very soon forgotten."

Geli turned to Otto and asked, "Do you believe that?"

"Ja, Geli, I'm afraid I do. The dead have no voices and no memories."

"Then I'll be their voice and I'll be their memory," she whispered, clenching her fists.

They proceeded to the heart of the Alstadt where the headquarters of the clean up operation had been temporarily established. Geli looked up at Lazo and asked, "And you, Lazo Krall, will you shortly forget me?"

Lazo put his arm around her waist and whispered, "To forget you would require that I become less than I now am, and that Geli, can never be."

CHAPTER TWENTY SEVEN

"Where the hell have you been, Lazo? We've been waiting for you for the past half hour."

"I didn't think we were that important," laughed Lazo, as he walked up to the old Volksturm sergeant and shook his hand.

"Sorry, Tomas," said Geli, "but we moved back into my flat yesterday and there was some tidying up that had to be done."

"I understand," said Tomas, "but now that you are here, I must put you to work."

"What do you have lined up for us today?" asked Lazo, screwing up his forehead.

"About the same as yesterday," replied Tomas, hiking up his pants and tightening up his belt. "No better, no worse."

"Who else will be coming with us?" asked Lazo.

"Well, let me see," he replied, scratching his chin. "All I have left are Helmut, Paul and Ute. Will they do?"

"Of course," replied Lazo. "They look healthy enough."

Tomas passed out the tools. Then he straightened up and arched his back. "Hell," he said, "it's tough getting old."

"Where do you want us to go?" asked Lazo, picking up a sack of lime and throwing it over his shoulder.

"I would like you to join some of the others who are making a sweep of the Comenius Strasse." He shook his head and said, "You won't find any survivors but I am told that there are a lot of bodies that must be disposed of."

The gruff old sergeant's grey eyes narrowed as he tried to conceal the film of moisture that had begun to cloud his vision.

Lazo repositioned the sack of lime so that his hands were free.

He walked up to Tomas, shook his hand, winked and said, "We'll see you later."

"Wear your face masks and for God's sake, be careful of those broken walls! They can be very dangerous."

"Ja Wohl!" snapped Otto, as he turned and began to walk toward the Comenius Strasse, some distance away.

When they reached their destination, several other teams were already removing the dead bodies from the basements, and laying them side by side in the rubble strewn street. These bodies would then be picked up by the disposal teams. It was not a very pleasant task but it had to be done and done without delay.

Lazo led his team up the street, making his way over the piles of rubble, always careful not to distrub the broken, charred bodies that lay there. He knew that the bodies would be picked up and unceremoniously thrown into carts and buried in common graves, but still he harbored a certain childish awe for the dead.

"Careful now, Ute! Don't step on any of the bodies!"

"I won't," she assured him, as she gingerly stepped over a pile of mouldering bodies.

Lazo smiled as she followed close at his heels. Though they had just met, she seemed to be taken with him, as were most people who met him.

"How old are you, Ute?"

"I will be nineteen," she replied, her face turning red at this unexpected attention.

"Are you still in school?"

"No, I completed my work at the Gymnasium."

"Do you plan to attend the university?" he asked.

"I had planned to but now I don't know," she replied, shrugging her shoulders.

"And your father, what does he say?"

She bent down on one knee and neatly tucked her slacks into her heavy woolen stockings. Then she looked up and said, "My father was with von Paulus at Stalingrad and since the surrender, we have heard nothing from him." Her voice quivered and she turned her head away from Lazo, trying to conceal her pain.

"What are you two waiting for?" shouted Geli. "We've got work to do."

Coming," shouted Lazo, as he helped Ute to her feet and hastened to catch up with the others.

"We didn't see you go by," he remarked.

"Well, let's get started," said Otto. "I'll take Helmut and Paul with me and we'll make a sweep of that side. The two women and you can take this side."

"Good," said Lazo, "then let's get at it. Remember," he shouted, "our primary aim is to check out the basements!"

Lazo stopped before the first basement door and dropped the sack of lime to the ground.

"What's the lime for?" asked Ute.

"Oh," remarked Geli, "then you haven't done this before?"

"No, I'm afraid not," replied Ute, somewhat embarrassed.

"We use the lime in those basements where the bodies are too decomposed to remove," said Geli, her face becoming contorted. The very thought of it, still made her shudder and squirm.

"I'll take the first one and Ute, you go with Geli and check out the next one."

"Must I? I'd feel much safer with you," pleaded Ute.

"It's alright, Lazo. Let her stay with you," insisted Geli, as she smiled and headed up the street. She went about ten paces, then she turned, winked at Lazo and shouted, "Be careful now!"

Lazo and Ute removed some debris from the basement door. Then Lazo pulled the door open and looked down the concrete steps.

"You wait here, Ute and I'll go down and have a look."

Ute, not wanting to be treated as a child, pulled at his arm and said, "Please, let me go."

"Okay," replied Lazo, "but use the flashlight and please be careful."

"Ja wohl, mein Herr!" snapped Ute, with a broad smile. "Now, I'll show you the stuff that a German Colonel's daughter is made of."

She switched on the flashlight and then carefully, very carefully, descended the stairs. Lazo watched her until she disappeared around a corner.

"There's another door here!" she shouted. "What shall I do?"

"Open it and see where it leads!"

She did as he instructed. Lazo waited and listened.

"Are you okay?"

"Ja, I'm okay. There seems to be a kind of ramp leading downward into a room. I'm going down now."

She had no sooner finished the sentence when Lazo heard a loud thud. Ute screamed, "Lazo, help me! Please help me!"

Lazo rushed down the steps, his flashlight on. When he reached the room, he found the stench almost more than he could stomach. He had to swallow several times to keep his breakfast down.

"Where are you?"

"Get me out of here before I die," came a desperate reply.

Lazo pointed the flashlight downward, in the direction of Ute's voice.

"Oh my God!" cried Lazo, his stomach churning. "Give me your hand! Quickly!"

She reached her hand toward him. He took it and jerked her up. Then he pulled her out of the room and up the stairs. When they reached the street, he shouted, "Geli, come over here! Please hurry!"

"What is this stuff on my clothing?" asked Ute, trying to remove her mask.

"Don't take it off!" shouted Lazo, tearing open the bag of lime.

"What's the matter?" asked Geli, running toward them. When she reached them, Lazo was already sprinkling lime over Ute's clothing.

"What happened?" asked Geli, trying to catch her breath.

"We've got to get her out of these clothes and into a bathtub."

Geli turned and headed for the basement door.

"Where do you think you're going?"

Before he could stop her, she was already descending the stairs.

"Put on your face mask!"

She didn't hear him. She turned the flashlight on and entered the dark room. She was not at all prepared for what she had to see. The stench was so bad that she had to hold her breath. There must have been forty bodies lying on the floor, in varying degrees of corruption. She screamed loudly and ran back up the stairs. When she reached the street, she put her hands against the wall of the shattered building and began to vomit. And even after all of her breakfast had been expelled, she continued to retch. Lazo walked over to her and put his arm around her shoulder. He tried to comfort her but she continued to sob and retch so violently, that Lazo became quite concerned.

He stepped out in the middle of the street and called out, "Otto! Come over here and bring Helmut and Paul!"

Geli had regained some of her composure. She wiped her face with her handkerchief and let the handkerchief fall to the ground.

"Do you feel better now?" asked Lazo.

"I guess so. I just wasn't prepared for that." Tears ran down her cheeks.

"Nobody could ever be prepared for that," he whispered trying to console her.

"What's the matter?" asked Otto, almost out of breath.

Geli turned to him and said, "There are about forty bodies in the basement and they are melting in their own soup."

She began to retch again, so Lazo continued, "She's right, Otto. The serum from their decaying bodies is at least six inches deep." He turned, pointed to Ute who was still sitting on the ground and said, "She fell into that stuff and we've got to get her out of those clothes."

"Is that what I've got on my clothes?" cried Ute, ripping at her mask. "Oh my God!" she cried, "I'll never be able to wipe it off! Never!"

She reached down and was about to undo her shoe laces when she noticed strings of yellowish slime clinging to the eyelets of her shoes. She jerked her hands back and began to scream hysterically. "It's all over me! That pussy slime is all over me! Will someone please help me? Oh God, how I must stink!" She began to sob uncontrollably.

"Geli, will you take her back to your flat and get her cleaned up?"

"Of course, Lazo. I think I could stand a good scrubbing myself."

Otto reached into his pocket and pulled out his pocket knife. "Here Geli," he said, "take this and use it to cut off her clothes."

"And whatever you do, don't go into the flat with those clothes on. Neither of you. Do you understand?"

"Ja wohl, mein General," snapped Geli, extending her hand to Ute. "Come my little one, let us repair to my flat and take to the waters."

Ute took her hand, and tried to smile. "You are all so very kind. I don't know how I will ever be able to repay you."

Geli smiled, then she winked at Lazo and asked, "And where, good sir, do you propose that we undress? In the street?"

"No, you brazen hussy, you might catch your death," laughed Lazo.

The two turned to leave. "Then where?"

Lazo slapped Geli on the behind and said, "You'll find a suitable place."

"How long will you be?" asked Geli.

"I don't know how long it will take us to clean up this mess but make sure that there is plenty of hot water. We'll need it after this."

Geli stopped in her tracks. "You're not going to remove those bodies, are you?"

"No, Geli. We'll cover them with lime and then we'll dynamite the building."

She closed her eyes and shook her head. "How horrible," she whispered, as the two began to walk away. "How horrible."

"I know," remarked Lazo, "but under these circumstances, there is nothing else we can do."

By the time the two had turned the corner, the men were already busy blowing lime into the basement and planting the charges of dynamite in such a way that the floor would collapse and the walls fall inward, entombing the nameless dead souls.

Meanwhile, the two women were making their way toward Geli's flat, with great dispatch and when they were within a couple of blocks of the building, Ute had already divested herself of her coat.

"Cut these shoe laces for me, will you?"

"Of course," replied Geli, and without any hesitation, knelt down and cut the laces on both of Ute's shoes. "There that should do it."

"Good," said Ute and she kicked her right leg as hard as she could, sending her hiking boot high into the air. Then she laughed and sent the other boot on its way. "I never did like those boots! I feel so much better now," she shouted and began to unbutton her shirt.

"Don't touch your clothing!" screamed Geli. "Have you forgotten what Lazo said?"

"Of course not, but I fell on my butt and not on my bust."

"Oh, I guess it will be all right but please be careful."

Before Geli could complete her sentence, Ute had already ripped the front of her shirt open and was running with her arms thrown backward so that the wind could catch the shirt and remove it from her back.

"There it goes!" she shouted, "and may it rest in peace."

When they reached Geli's address, Ute stopped and shouted, "Now cut these filthy slacks off!"

Geli opened Otto's knife, which fortunately was razor sharp, and slipped the blade inside Ute's belt. Then she drew the blade downward along the seam of her slacks. She did the same with the other leg and the slacks fell to the ground, the cuffs still neatly tucked in her woolen stockings.

"What do we do now?" asked Ute. "I can't stand here all day."

"I'll step on them and you pull your legs out, okay?"

Ute placed her hands on Geli's shoulders and pulled her leg upward until it was free. Then she did the same with the other.

"Thank God that's over." She pirouetted and asked, "How do I look now?"

"Just great. I love your underwear."

"Do you now? Well, they used to belong to my father. I don't think he'll need them anymore."

"Let's get inside," said Geli. She threw the door open and the two rushed up the stairs and down the hall, stopping a short distance from the door to her flat.

"Sorry, Ute, but I've got to do this."

"Do what?"

"This," replied Geli, as she inserted the knife blade inside the neck of Ute's underwear and cut down the length of her sleeve. Then she cut the other sleeve and the top of Ute's underwear fell away. Ute quickly drew her arms tightly over her breasts.

"Hurry!" she yelled. "It's cold out here!"

Geli had never seen such white skin and for a moment she could do nothing but stare and marvel. "Take your cap off!"

"Why?"

"Just do it!" insisted Geli.

Ute slowly raised her right hand and pulled her cap off and threw it to the floor. Her bright red hair fell down and came to rest on her shoulders.

"You are absolutely beautiful!"

"Do you really think so?"

"I most certainly do," replied Geli. "I have never seen such perfect contrast. Green eyes, red hair and white skin. No girl could ask for more."

"Thank you," replied Ute, who was now shivering, "but please hurry. I'm freezing."

"Oh, I'm sorry." She grabbed the front of Geli's underwear and pulled it downward.

Ute quickly lifted herself out of the garment and Geli opened the door.

"Now get yourself before the fireplace before you catch your death," admonished Geli.

Ute scooted in and Geli closed the door. Then Geli removed all of her clothing and ran in to join Ute by the fireplace. Geli quickly threw the last pieces of wood over the glowing embers and waited for the flames to erupt. Soon the flames were leaping upward and the two luxuriated in the wonderful warmth.

"I could stand here all day," uttered Ute, throwing her head back until her bright red hair brushed against the small of her back.

"So could I," concurred Geli, "but we've got to get cleaned up."

"Well," asked Ute, no longer embarrassed by her nudity, "who goes first?"

"Neither. We go together."

"Great," beamed Ute, "then you can scrub my back."

"And you can do mine."

"By the way," asked Ute, "are you and Lazo?"

"What?"

"You know what I mean. Are you lovers?" She seemed embarrassed by her question.

"No, we are not lovers but we do make love."

Ute seemingly confused by Geli's cryptic reply, ran the palms of her hands over her breasts and said, "Oh, I see."

It was obvious to Geli that Ute didn't see it at all and she was not about to enlighten her.

"Let's get going," said Geli. "You take one bucket and I'll take the other."

"Okay," replied Ute, reaching in to grab one.

"Hold it!" shouted Geli. "Do you want to burn your hand?"

"I wasn't thinking, I guess," stammered Ute, somewhat crestfallen.

"Here, take one of these hot pads."

Ute still somewhat embarrassed, took the hot pad and removed one of the pails. "See," she announced, quite proudly, "I didn't spill a drop and I didn't even burn a finger."

"Good," said Geli, "now follow me."

Geli then took one of the other buckets and headed for the bathroom. Ute followed close at her heels. They poured the water into the tub and Geli emptied a bottle of scented bath oil into the water. She turned on the tap and waited.

"Don't let it got too cold," exhorted Ute. "I like my water very hot."

"So do I," beamed Geli. She allowed the water to run for a couple of minutes then tested the temperature with her foot. "That feels good. Jump in and I'll get some soap and wash towels."

Ute did not hesitate. She stepped into the tub and sat down. The hot water lapped against her cold pale skin and she smiled as the water warmed her cold body.

"Catch!" said Geli, as she threw a wash cloth to Ute and handed her a bar of perfumed soap.

"Thank you. Thank you so very much."

Geli stepped into the tub and sat down behind Ute. She soaped her washcloth and began to rub it against Ute's back and shoulders. "How does that feel?" she asked.

"Magnificent!" cooed Ute, running her washcloth over her breasts and stomach.

"Now stand up!"

"Why?"

"Just do as I say!"

Ute grabbed the sides of the tub and pulled herself up. "How's that?"

"Perfect. Now spread your legs so I can slide under."

Ute spread her legs and Geli slipped between them. "Now do my back!"

Ute laughed loudly and began to rub Geli's back with the washcloth.

"You can do better than that," urged Geli. "Put some muscle into it."

Ute responded by scrubbing with such intensity that Geli's back soon turned crimson.

"How's that?" she asked.

"Terrific. Don't forget the shoulders," admonished Geli.

"I won't. You can be sure of that." Ute ran the cloth over Geli's shoulders

"What do we do now?" asked Ute.

"We wash our hair," laughed Geli.

"Not in this water, I'm not."

"No, of course not. We'll get some fresh water for that."

Geli jumped out of the tub, ran into the living room and returned with a bucket of hot water. Then she filled one of the empty buckets half full of cold water and added enough hot water to raise the temperature to an appropriate level. Then she stepped back into the tub and poured half of the water on Ute's head, and the remainder over her own. They shampooed their hair and used the remaining water to rinse.

"I never believed that I could feel this clean again."

"Nor I," echoed Geli, stepping out of the tub. She took two towels from the shelf and threw one to Ute. They helped each other dry off and went into the bedroom to find some suitable clothing for Ute.

A few minutes later they emerged, both dressed quite appropriately. Geli had managed to find a green woolen sweater and a pair of gray flannel slacks for Ute. They were a little big but not enough to notice. They sat down by the fire and toweled their hair.

"Would you like some coffee?"

"Thank you, yes," replied Ute, her eyes lighting up. "I would love a cup of coffee." She paused, then said, "That is, if it is not too much trouble."

"No trouble at all," replied Geli.

When Geli returned from the kitchen, Ute was busy brushing her hair, trying to undo the snarls.

"Here, let me do that for you." She took the brush and very gently, ran it through Ute's hair.

"What's it like?"

"What's what like?" asked Geli.

"Being in love, of course."

"Who's in love?"

"You are," replied Ute. "Why are you so evasive? I saw the way you looked at him."

"Oh, alright. Yes, I do love Lazo."

"I thought so," beamed Ute. "Are you happy?"

Geli looked into the fireplace. Her eyes sparkled and a smile came to her lips. "During the past several days, we have literally gone through hell and still, I have never been happier in my entire life. I cannot even imagine life without Lazo." She smiled wistfully and put the brush down. "There, that should do it. Your hair looks marvelous."

"Thank you," whispered Ute. She looked up at Geli and asked, "Will you be my mother?"

There was such sincerity and warmth in her expression that Geli became completely undone. She could not respond immediately.

"Well?"

"But you already have a mother," replied Geli, her voice faltering.

"Oh yes, but I need a mother that I can talk to. You know what I mean. I need a mother whom I can talk to about the things that really matter."

"Can't you talk to your mother?"

"Oh, heavens no. I wouldn't dare. She's such a prude."

Geli laughed and said, "Well, if I am to become your mother, I must know your last name." Then she winked and added, "I make it a habit never to adopt a person until we have been properly introduced."

"Oh, I'm sorry," stammered Ute. "I thought you knew. My last name is Jaeger."

"Do you mean to tell me that you are Ulrich Jaeger's daughter?" Geli slapped her knee and said, "I should have known. You bear a strong resemblance to him."

"Yes, I think I do."

"And your mother. What's her name?"

"My mother's name is Hilda. Did you know my father?"

"Oh yes," replied Geli, "but why do you refer to him in the past tense?"

"Because I am almost certain that he died at Stalingrad."

"You asked if I knew him. Yes, I knew him. He often came to my office. He was a true German gentleman."

Ute looked down at the floor. "I loved him so very much and now, because of this stupid war, I will never see him again."

"You musn't say that. You must never stop hoping. Do you understand?" Geli put her arm around Ute's shoulder and gave her an affectionate squeeze. "By the way," she said, "I now pronounce you, the adopted daughter of one, Geli Bischof. And yes, you can ask me any question about the things that really matter and I promise that I will answer as truthfully as I possibly can. Now let's have some coffee and celebrate the occasion."

Ute jumped up and threw her arms around Geli's neck, with such fervor and such warmth that Geli could scarcely get her breath. "Thank you! Thank you! You have made me so very happy!" Then as an after thought, asked, "Can I still call you Geli?"

"Of course you can. Now I'll get the coffee. They will be home soon."

Ute sat down and waited for Geli to return. "Are you sure that I can't help?"

"No, thank you. I'll be right there."

Ute was about to speak when Geli reappeared, carrying a tray with two cups of steaming coffee.

"I don't have any cream," remarked Geli, apologetically, "but there is some sugar."

"Splendid," replied Ute. "I don't use cream but I will have a little sugar."

Geli put some sugar into Ute's cup, stirred it and handed it to Ute. "Careful now. It's very hot." Geli took her cup and set the tray down on the floor. "And now," she said, "we can talk. We still have some time before the men get home." She sipped some of the coffee and asked, "What is it that you want to know?"

Ute did not respond immediately. She looked up at the ceiling, perhaps searching for the right words to deliver her from her embarrassment.

"Go ahead," urged Geli, "afterall, that's what mothers are for."

"Is it as good as they say it is?"

"What?" asked Geli, obviously stalling for time.

"An orgasm," she replied, almost in a whisper.

"Haven't you ever had one?" asked Geli, trying to appear as understanding as possible.

Ute's face turned crimson. It was obvious that she was becoming quite unravelled. "No, I haven't and I want to know."

"Yes, it is good. I can't begin to describe it. Words, whether spoken or written, could never do justice to the experience." She paused, weighing her thoughts very carefully. "Let me put it in another way, I don't believe that there are any words to describe that supreme joy which attends a perfect sexual union."

Ute sipped her coffee. "Thank you, Geli. That's what I wanted to know."

"You are a virgin, then?"

Ute seemed reluctant to reply. She raised her cup and turned her head.

"Come now," pleaded Geli. "We will have no secrets from each other."

With head still turned away, Ute replied, "No, I am not a virgin. I should be but I am not."

Geli moved her chair closer and put her arm around Ute. "Do you want to talk about it?"

Ute put her cup down and rested her head on Geli's shoulder. "It was early in the war. I was just fourteen years old. One day, during late summer, my father's commanding officer came to spend the weekend with us. He was a colonel and my father admired him very much." She looked up at Geli. "If only he knew what a complete louse the bastard really was."

"What do you mean?"

"He raped me," whispered Ute. "I tried to stop him but he was much too strong. And that, Geli, was my first and only encounter with a man."

"Oh, I'm so sorry." Geli embraced her ever so tenderly and stroked her forehead. "I do wish that your first encounter with a man could have been different, but please remember, all men are not beasts."

Ute wiped her eyes and said, "But that wasn't the worst. Oh no, when I told my mother what happened, she told me that it was my fault because I must have led him on. She also told me not to mention the incident to my father because it could only jeopardize his career. She made me feel so dirty and ashamed that I couldn't even look at my body without cringing, that is, until today."

"What do you mean?" asked Geli, somewhat mystified.

"It happened when you cut away my underwear and told me that I was so very beautiful."

"Ah, but you are beautiful and not only that; you are intelligent as well."

"But you were the first to tell me that and because of you, I no longer feel ashamed. Just look," she exclaimed raising her sweater until her breasts were exposed. "See," she declared, "I'm proud of my body. I'm proud to be a woman."

Just then the door flew open and Lazo shouted, "I'm home, I'm tired, I'm disgusted and I'm thirsty!"

He threw his hat on the floor and ran his fingers through his hair. Geli ran over and gave him a kiss. Then she stepped into the hall, looked around and asked, "Where's Otto? I don't see him."

"Oh, Otto. He's spending the night with Tomas, in the barracks."

Then he looked at Ute, scratched his head and asked, "Who the devil is that?"

Ute jumped up and said, "I'm Ute. Don't you remember?"

"My God but you're beautiful. I guess I didn't recognize you with all that red hair. Are you alright?"

Ute walked up to him, gave him a gentle squeeze and kissed his cheek. "Ja, I'm alright." She smiled. "As a matter of fact, I feel quite refreshed."

"How come you're so clean?" asked Geli.

"You should have seen me a couple of hours ago," laughed Lazo. "I wasn't fit company for pigs. Tomas took me back to the barracks. He allowed me to use the shower and did it feel good."

"And the clothes?"

"A gift from the Fuhrer and Dr. Goebbels." He looked around and asked, "Is there anything to drink?"

"There's some fresh coffee in the kitchen," replied Geli, "Do you want some?"

"I need something much stronger and I'll just bet that you two could use a good drink."

Geli ran her finger across her nose and said, "Well, maybe there is still a bottle of cognac in the pantry."

"Well, just don't stand there. Go and look."

"I'll be right back. You keep Ute company."

Lazo walked over to the fireplace. "Is all of the wood gone?"

"Yes," replied Ute. "We used it to heat the water."

"I'll have to get some."

"You won't need to."

"And why not?"

"Because I'm taking the two of you home with me, that's why. We have plenty of room and my mother won't mind. She could use the company." She stared at Lazo and whispered, "And so could I."

"Did you hear that, Geli?"

"Hear what?" asked Geli, as she entered the living room carrying a bottle of cognac.

"Ute has invited us to be her house guests."

"We couldn't do that," she replied, "Can we?"

"Of course you can," insisted Ute. "You can stay as long as you wish."

"Then it's done," pealed Geli. She laughed and shouted, "Let's do it!"

"Yippee!" shouted Ute, all of her youthful exhuberance rushing forth. "Now, let's drink to it. Hold this, Lazo, and I'll get the glasses."

"Glasses, hell!" shouted Lazo. "There's no time for formality." He removed the cork and shouted, "Here's to us, the survivors! They can try but they can't kill all of us." He raised the bottle to his lips and took a huge swallow. He wiped his lips with the back of his hand. "Here Ute, now it's your turn."

"But I've never done this before." She looked at Geli, then at Lazo. "Will it be alright?"

"Of course it will be alright," said Lazo, trying his best to reassure her.

"Well, here goes then." She raised the bottle and said, "Here's to old 'blue nose' and all of the other self righteous bastards in this world. May they all rot in hell!"

She put the bottle to her lips and paused, as though reluctant to drink. Her brilliant green eyes sparkled as she gripped the hem of her sweater with her left hand.

Geli rushed over and moved Ute's hand away from her sweater, trying to be as unobtrusive as possible. "Musn't do that," she whispered, her teeth slightly clenched.

Ute winked at Geli and then with a devilish smile, said, "I had you worried, didn't I?" Ute took a swallow. "Oh, that burns, but I think I like it." She looked at Lazo and repeated, "I really do."

She was about to take another swallow, when Lazo stayed her hand and said, "Easy now. We've got all of the rest of the day."

He put the cork back in the bottle, scratched his neck and asked, "Who in hell is this 'blue nose'?"

"It's just a family secret," replied Geli, taking Ute's hand, squeezing it gently.

"How far is it?"

"It's not too far. I'll show you," replied Ute, "but we'd better get started. I don't wish to walk in the dark."

"What about Otto?" asked Geli, "Should I leave him a note?"

"No," replied Lazo, "we'll see him tomorrow."

"Do they know what they've done?" asked Ute tugging on Lazo's sleeve.

Lazo turned and with a bewildered expression asked, "What do you mean?"

"Those who dropped the bombs," replied Ute. "Do they know? Do they know about the people in the basements?"

"Ja," whispered Lazo. He paused briefly. "They know that they drop bombs, but to them, we are not people. We are the enemy! We are the Nazis! We are the Boche! We are the Huns! But we are not people."

Ute did not reply immediately. She just shook her head as if unable to comprehend what Lazo had said. Then she whispered, "But I will remember that they were people. I will never forget and on those days when I am alone, I will remember them." She looked upward. "And, and I will cry for them."

The three left the flat. Lazo carried the bottle and when they reached the street, he took a drink and began to sing, "Vor der Kaserne, vor dem grossen Tor."

The women each took one of his arms and joined in. When they turned the corner, Geli pulled on Lazo's arm and cautioned, "Not so loud. Do you want to awaken the dead?"

Lazo turned to her, winked and whispered, "If only I could. If only I could."

CHAPTER TWENTY EIGHT

It was March thirteenth, and a month had slipped by since that horrible night of death. Frau Jaeger had received them quite cordially and though she could be over bearing at times, she was not entirely without charm. There were instances, though not frequent, when Lazo found her to be quite engaging. The Jaeger home, or should I say villa, was situated in the suburbs, not too distant from the Ringstrasse. Lazo and Geli were comfortably installed in the servant's quarters above the carriage house. Geli offered to pay rent but Frau Jaeger would not hear of it. Lazo attributed this gesture more to Ute's devotion to Geli, than to Frau Jaeger's generosity. All in all they were quite happy with their new accommodations. To be sure, Geli was still somewhat troubled but when Otto agreed to take up residence in her old flat, Geli's misgivings vanished. She was quite certain that Otto's presence would deter any prospective looter from carrying off her prized porcelain figurines.

One evening, shortly after their arrival at the Jaeger residence, Geli spoke to Lazo about her figurines and how very precious they were to her. Lazo responded by reminding her that the Russians would eventually take them and being unschooled and uncivilized, use them for target practice. Lazo had not intended to make light of her plight but he did want to prepare her for the worst.

In the meantime, Geli had gone back to work for Major Fatbottom. The old office building had been destroyed and a new one had been procured in the Newstadt. The Major had helped Geli obtain a ration book for Lazo so that the two would have sufficient food. He also provided them with such scarce items as soap, toothpaste, and coffee. Her association with the Major, though precarious, did have its advantages, and though she felt guilty at times, she did not want to alienate the source of this largesse.

On this particular day, Lazo had finished his chores early and decided to take a walk, not realizing that Ute, whom Lazo now regarded as a sister, was following him. He had not gone more than a kilometer, when he heard a voice shouting,

Lazo recognized the voice but pretended not to hear it.

"Are you deaf?"

Lazo turned and yelled, "No, I am not deaf! And what are you doing here anyway?"

"Mother went into town and I am bored. Can't I come with you?" she pleaded. "It's such a lovely day."

"Oh, come on then, but remember, I walk very rapidly."

"Haven't you noticed?" she asked.

"Noticed what?"

"My long legs, of course," she replied, pulling the hem of her skirt upward to reveal more of her thighs.

"Don't do that," chided Lazo, turning his head to hide the blush that had marked his face.

"Do I have nice legs?" she asked, deliberately trying to embarrass him.

"You know that you have beautiful legs," he muttered.

"Then why are you afraid to look at them?"

Lazo turned toward her and said, "I am not afraid to look at your legs. As a matter of fact, I have always considered myself to be a leg man."

"Then let me lead. I know the area better than you."

"Oh alright, but keep a brisk pace." He pretended to be exasperated.

She scooted ahead of him and said, "Follow me and I will take you to a place overlooking the river. The view is quite overwhelming." She turned her head, smiled saucily and asked, "Are you looking at my legs?"

And indeed, Lazo had been looking at her long slender legs. She was wearing white, woolen knee socks and a gray, pleated skirt, made out of very heavy wool. As she walked, her long red hair, made brilliant by the afternoon sun, rushed back and forth, across her shoulders.

"Am I going fast enough for you?"

"Do you walk a lot?"

"Why do you ask?"

"Because you do it so well."

"Papa always took me with him when he went mountain climbing in Bavaria."

"You climbed with him?"

"Oh yes," she replied, "ever since I was seven years old."

"Wasn't that dangerous?"

"No, not really. Papa is a very good climber and he taught me well." She stopped and turned toward him and her green eyes sparkled like emeralds. "Perhaps when this stupid war is over, you and I can go climbing together."

"I've never climbed," replied Lazo.

"Then I will teach you," she replied. "Yes, I think I would enjoy that very much." She turned and began to walk. "And I won't take no for an answer."

"Did your mother climb with you?"

"No. Mother didn't like the mountains," She paused, wrinkled her forehead and continued, "I don't think that she likes me or Papa very much, either."

"You can't mean that."

"But I do," insisted Ute, and she began to walk faster.

"How far is this place?" asked Lazo.

"About another kilometer. Are you getting tired?"

"No, I am not getting tired but Geli will be home soon and she will worry."

"Do you love her?"

Lazo was caught completely off guard and it took him a few seconds to fashion a response. When be finally recovered, he said, "Geli and I like each other very much."

She smiled. "Then you do love her, don't you?"

"I didn't say that," replied Lazo, becoming more embarrassed and somewhat irritated.

"Well, if you don't love her, why do you live together?"

He did not reply. He hoped that his continued silence would put an end to the subject. When she reached the top of the hill, she stopped. The expression on her face which had been so sanguine, suddenly dimmed. "Don't come up here," she cried.

"Why not?"

"They've spoiled it," she replied, her voice trembling. "It will never be the same!" Tears filled her eyes.

Lazo ran up and embraced her. Her tears touched his neck, sending shivers up and down his back.

"Please," she whispered, "let's go back. I'm so ashamed."

Lazo kissed her forehead and said, "Ashamed of what? Ashamed because you are gentle enough to shed tears? Ashamed because you believed that the face of humanity was blemish free?"

Lazo sat down and rested his back against a large gray rock that projected from the earth. He took her hand and pulled her down beside him. "No Ute, it's not your fault that the face of humanity is stained and pocked. It has been that way for a very long time."

"I know that," insisted Ute, "that's not what I'm ashamed of."

"Then what?" queried lazo, somewhat perplexed. He slipped down and rested his head in her lap.

"I don't know quite how to explain it."

She paused and ran her fingers through his hair. Then she said, "It's kind of like when I was a child and I did something that I shouldn't have and was spanked. I always felt ashamed. Not because I was spanked but because I deserved to be spanked."

She leaned forward, looked directly into his eyes and asked, "Does that make any sense to you?"

"I think so," replied Lazo.

"Oh, how I will miss the beautiful old buildings and the sun reflecting off the copper roofs." She bent down and kissed his forehead.

He smiled and whispered, "It must have been so very beautiful."

"Oh yes, it was, especially after an early morning rain. I would always make a special effort to come up here after it rained. The moisture would deepen the green color of the copper. If you only could have seen it then? The sun's rays ricocheting off the roofs, in streams of yellow and green."

Then she paused, as if transfixed and whispered, "Sometimes, not always, the colors would intersect and produce shafts of purple light. It was spectacular."

Lazo looked up, smiled at her and said, "You are quite spectacular, yourself but I think we'd better start heading back."

"May I kiss you?" she asked.

"May you what?"

"May I kiss you? I've never kissed a man. I never wanted to." Her voice cracked and she paused, "That is, until this very moment."

He pursed his lips playfully as she lowered her head until her lips touched his. She pulled back and scolded, "That's not fair. You're not helping any."

Lazo jumped to his feet and pulled her up. He took her face into his hands and kissed her very gently. "Was that better?"

"I'm not sure. Do it once more. This time with a little more conviction."

He put his arms around her waist and pulled her very close. Then he kissed her fully and intentionally. Her arms, which were at her sides, began to inch upward, with palms open. Soon her palms were moving in a circular motion against his back and she began to press against him.

"Was that better?" he asked.

She did not reply. She threw her arms around him and kissed him several times. "I love you! At least, I think I do."

Lazo took her hands and slowly removed them from his shoulder. Then he looked directly into her beautiful eyes and slowly and deliberately said, "No, you don't love me. I'm just the first man you have ever kissed. There will be others. Just wait and see. You are much too beautiful to go unattended."

She shook her head and sat down on the rock. "Can't you love me just a little bit? I have never felt like this and I don't want it to stop."

Lazo leaned down and very gently pulled her up. "Now you lead, I'll look at your legs."

She leaned forward and kissed his cheek. "Alright, but I do love you."

She turned and began to run down the hill, her flaming red hair fighting the wind. Lazo waited for a moment, then he began to chase after her, marvelling at the beauty and grace which accompanied her every stride. When they reached the courtyard, she turned and headed for the villa.

"See you later!" she shouted.

"Ja, see you later!" echoed Lazo, running toward the carriage house. When he reached it, he bounded up the stairs. Geli had seen him coming and met him at the door.

"I've got good news! The Americans have crossed the Rhine and are well on their way to Kassel!"

"That's wonderful!" shouted Lazo. He took her into his arms and danced her into the living room. His joy was so over flowing that he swung her around and around until he became so dizzy that he stumbled to the floor, she on top of him.

"How far away are they?" he asked, his voice fighting for air.

"About two hundred miles but Patton's army is advancing very rapidly. They should be here by the end of the month. Isn't it wonderful?"

"They might beat the Russians afterall."

"Ja," replied Geli. "Major Fatbottom told me that the Americans could shake hands with the Russians a good fifty kilometers east of the Elbe, if they wanted to."

"What do you mean? Of course, they want to. Hell, they'll be in Dresden before the Russians and you know what that means?"

"No," replied Geli with a puzzled expression on her face. "Tell me, what does it mean?"

"It means that the Russkies won't get your figurines afterall."

"Why must you always tease me about my figurines?" she blurted and then pretended to pout.

Her contrived gesture had, as she intended, disarmed him so completely, that he did not see her reach for one of the large pillows which adorned the couch. And before he could defend himself, she was buffeting him about his head. As she did, she kept repeating, "Say you are sorry! Say you are sorry!"

Lazo finally succeeded in wresting the pillow from her hands and flung it across the room. Geli had not noticed but during the melee, several buttons on her shift had become undone, revealing a considerable portion of her female anatomy.

"Oh my God!" she shouted, "I'm coming apart," and she hurried to restore her dignity.

Lazo never reluctant to exploit the vulnerability of an adversary, rushed up and began to tickle her. She began to laugh uproariously and tried her level best to squirm out of his reach but the more she squirmed, the more resolute he became. Finally she grabbed his wrists and pulled herself free. By this time, he was laughing so uncontrollably that he became incapable of mounting a defense and consequently, she was soon on top of him, her knees digging into his biceps.

"You are not wearing anything under that shift, are you?"

"No, I am not. I just got out of the tub when I saw you coming through the courtyard."

"Well," he whispered, "you're going to get it now."

"Am I now!" she retorted, rolling her knees back and forth across his biceps, causing him to wince. "How do you like that?"

"I like it very much."

"Well, maybe you'll like this even more," she whispered, moving herself forward on his chest as far as she could. She was just about to close in on him when she heard footsteps.

"Someone's coming."

Lazo moved his head forward and ran his lips against her inner thigh. "Dammit!" she muttered, as she jumped up and ran toward the bedroom.

"Who is there?"

"It is I, Ute. May I come in?"

"Please do," replied Lazo, trying his best to conceal his indignation.

She opened the door and walked in.

"What is it you want?" asked Lazo, without getting up.

"I thought that maybe we could have a party." She surveyed the room and asked, "Where's Geli?"

"She's in the bedroom. She'll be right out. Now, what's this about a party?"

"Mother thought that you might like these."

"Like what?" asked Lazo, sitting up and resting his back against the couch.

"She wants you to have some of this Russian vodka," replied Ute, removing two bottles from the bag that she was carrying.

"What else do you have in the bag?"

"Some Danish cheese and believe it or not, a very large Polish ham."

Lazo jumped to his feet. "You've got to be joking!" he shouted, as he rushed up to get a closer look. "You're not kidding!" He took the bag and set it on the table. Then he took Ute into his arms and gave her a mighty squeeze.

"What's all the commotion?" asked Geli, entering the room.

"Come over here and see what we've got!" exclaimed Ute, her voice quivering with excitement.

Geli smiled but Lazo noticed a certain harshness in her expression, causing him to become uneasy. She walked over and looked into the bag. Her eyes widened as she reached in and pulled out the ham.

"Mother said to be careful with the vodka because it is over one hundred fifty proof."

"Let's try some," suggested Lazo. "I've never tasted vodka."

"Nor I," said Geli, still holding onto the ham. "Are you two going to cling to each other for the rest of the day?"

Lazo noticed some hurt in her voice and removed one of his arms from around Ute. "We were just rejoicing over our good fortune. Come and join us."

"Ja, come on," pleaded Ute, pretending to be hurt by Geli's rejoinder.

Geli put her arms around them and embraced them very tenderly and though she held Lazo very closely, she began to realize that her hold on him was so very tenuous, and Lazo felt her body tremble.

"Well," said Lazo, "I'll get the glasses and then we will drink vodka like the Russians do."

"How is that?" asked Ute.

"Straight up," replied Lazo, "and then, straight down." He laughed, as he headed toward the kitchen.

"I'll remove the cork from one of the bottles," said Ute.

"And I'll put the ham into the oven so that it will be ready for supper." She took the ham and dashed into the kitchen, almost colliding with Lazo, who was returning with three small glasses balanced precariously in the palm of his band.

Ute rushed up, just in time to rescue the glasses. "You men are all so reckless. It's a wonder that there is anything beautiful left in this world."

"You're right, you know," replied Lazo. "Man the destroyer and woman the curator. Now that's a precarious balance."

"Thank God there are more of us than there are of you!" shouted Geli from the kitchen.

"Well," rejoined Lazo, "I guess that is the cross we men must bear." He looked at Ute, winked and said, "And what an awesome burden it is."

Ute carefully filled the three glasses and painstakingly reset the cork. "Shall we wait for Geli?" she asked.

"I think we had better."

"Ja," whispered Ute, "I think she is a little irritated with us. Do you think that she is jealous?"

"Perhaps," replied Lazo, very softly. "We are quite a bit younger than she and I suppose we remind her of her age, especially when she encounters one so beautiful and so young as you."

"Oh, but she looks so young and pretty," insisted Ute.

"She is old enough to be your mother," said Lazo, "and she knows it."

Geli walked into the living room. "What are you two talking about?"

"Nothing important," replied Lazo. "We were just waiting for you."

"Good. Now let's drink to that precarious balance." She walked to the table and took one of the glasses. Then she looked at Ute and asked, "Are you certain that you want to drink this vodka? It's awful strong, you know."

"Yes, I know and yes, I want to. I think I can handle it."

"What if you can't?" queried Lazo.

"Then," she replied, "I'll have to spend the night right here."

"Well, alright," remarked Lazo, "straight up and straight down! All together now. One, two, three, nozdravia!"

The three downed the vodka and set their glasses down.

"How was it, Ute?" asked Lazo, waiting for the grimace that did not come.

"I thought that it would burn much more. Actually, I feel none the worse for wear," insisted Ute.

"How about you, Geli? Was it to your liking?"

"Yes, I think I like it. As a matter of fact, I think I like it very much."

"Well then," said Lazo, "let's pour another round."

Ute filled the three glasses and replaced the cork. Then they picked up their drinks and hurriedly quaffed the robust liquor.

"Straight up and straight down," laughed Ute. "Shall I pour another round?"

"You had better not," cautioned Geli. "Let's sit a while and give the vodka a little time to settle."

They sat down on the couch, Lazo in the middle. He kicked off his shoes and rested his feet on the table. Then he put an arm around each of them and pulled them close.

"I could get to like this very much," remarked Lazo. He looked up at the ceiling and whispered, "but I am beginning to feel very guilty."

"Why, in heaven's name, should you feel guilty?" asked Geli.

"I don't know why. It's just a feeling and I can't put my finger on it."

"It's just the vodka," laughed Ute. She kissed him on the cheek, smiled and said, "Let's have another."

"Oh, alright," declared Geli, "anything to raise Lazo's spirits."

Then she turned to Ute, who was already standing and cautioned, "But this time, fill the glasses only to half."

"Alright, if you insist."

"Ute seemed to be holding her liquor very well," thought Lazo. And though her face had become slightly flushed and her demeanor a little less constrained, she seemed to be in complete possession of her faculties. Lazo was becoming more and more impressed with her beauty, perhaps because she didn't even suspect that she was beautiful.

Ute picked up the bottle and was about to pour when she stopped and put the bottle down.

"What's the matter?" asked Lazo. "Are you becoming tipsy?"

"No, not that," replied Ute, shaking her head. "I just remembered something that mother said."

"Well, what did she say?" asked Geli.

"Mother said that the Russians can put away a lot of vodka because they always have something to eat after each drink. Does that sound right?"

"I heard that too," remarked Geli, "I'll slice up some of that Danish cheese."

"Do you have anything to go with it?" asked Lazo.

"I have some crackers. Will they do?"

"Wait a minute!" shouted Ute. "I just remembered something!" She slapped the table and rushed to the door.

"Where are you going?" asked Lazo.

"I'm going to get something and don't worry. I'll be right back." She slammed the door and bounded down the stairs.

"Now what?" asked Geli, slapping her forehead with the palm of her hand.

"Don't ask me but you can bet that it will be good, whatever it is."

There is no sense worrying about it," remarked Geli, "so we may as well go and get the cheese."

"Let's have a drink first," urged Lazo, pouring some vodka into their glasses.

"Just a little," she cautioned. "We've got all night."

"Here's to us," whispered Lazo, handing Geli her glass.

"I'll drink to that," said Geli, as they crossed arms and downed the vodka. "Now let's get the cheese before Ute gets back."

The two went into the diminutive kitchen and Geli began to slice the cheese. "There's a very large tray on the top shelf of the cupboard. Can you get it for me?"

"Certainly," replied Lazo. "My pleasure. Where are the crackers?"

"Bottom drawer, left," replied Geli without looking up.

When they carried the tray into the living room, it was replete with cheese, crackers and pickles. Geli set it on the table. Then she turned to Lazo and asked, "I wonder what's taking her so long? It's almost five o'clock. You don't suppose?"

"Suppose what?" asked Lazo, munching on a cracker.

"You don't suppose that her mother made her stay in, do you?"

"No," replied Lazo. "She's much too spirited to give in to her mother."

He paused. "Listen, I think I hear her."

He had no sooner finished the sentence, when a loud voice cried out,"Open the door!"

Lazo ran to the door and threw it open. There stood Ute with a large paper sack, filled with God knows what, in one arm and holding a portable phonograph in the other. Lazo took the sack from her arm and carried it to the table. Ute paused for a moment to catch her breath, then entered. She gave the phonograph to Geli and plopped herself down on the couch.

"I'm quite warm," she declared, fanning her brow with the palm of her hand. "I could use a drink."

Lazo handed her a glass. She toyed with it, then downed the vodka.

"What do you have in the bag?" asked Geli.

Ute jumped up and ran to the table. She reached into the bag and said, "You could never guess what I've got, not in a million years!" She drew out a large flat tin and held it up. "Russian caviar!" she exclaimed, her face beaming with happiness. "Now, we have some Russian caviar to go with the Russian vodka!"

"What else do you have?" queried Geli, obviously impressed with Ute's liberality.

"I've got Spanish olives, pickled herring from Norway, Danish crackers, Bulgarian peppers and a bottle of Greek Ouzo for afterward. Is it enough?"

"Of course, it's enough," replied Geli, "you've brought enough to feed an entire army." Geli took the tin of caviar and went into the kitchen. In the mean time, Ute and Lazo helped themselves to the cheese.

"Do you like caviar?" asked Ute.

"I only tasted it once and I didn't really care for it."

"You'll change your mind when you taste the kind I brought. It's the best in the world."

"I'll take your word for it." Then he picked up the jar of peppers. "Do you like these?" he asked.

"I've never tried them but I'm willing to give them a try."

Lazo pulled the rubber ring from under the lid and unscrewed it.

"They smell terrific." He reached into the jar, removed one and handed it to Ute.

"You first," laughed Ute.

Lazo pulled his head back, lowered the pepper into his mouth and bit off a piece. "Now it's your turn," he said, holding the pepper over her mouth.

She opened her mouth and Lazo lowered the pepper. She bit into it. "It's not bad," she remarked, as she began to chew the pepper. She had no sooner spoken when she let out a scream and spit the pepper into her hand.

"Some water! Please get me some water!" she screamed, running into the kitchen.

Lazo began to laugh and though he kind of regretted tricking her, he could not help himself and soon he was doubled up with laughter.

When Ute returned from the kitchen, she was holding a glass of water. Her green eyes sparkled through her tears. She walked up to him, pointed her finger and said, "You are some friend." She emptied the glass and set it down. "And I thought I could trust you."

"But I thought you knew that the pepper would be hot," he protested, as he sat down and pretended to be stung by her reproach.

"It's alright," she countered, with a smile. "I should have known better." She sat down next to him and kissed him on the cheek.

"Geli, what's keeping you?" shouted Lazo. "We're getting hungry!" He was obviously bothered by Ute's proximity.

"I'll be right there!"

"You're afraid to be alone with me, aren't you?" whispered Ute, moving a little closer. "Why?"

"Don't be silly. Why should I be afraid of you?"

"Because I'm young and I'm beautiful." Then she winked and added, "And I'm going to get you." She took his hand and said, "And now I want to dance."

"But I don't know how."

"Then I'll teach you," replied Ute, getting up from the couch. She pulled him to his feet and led him to the phonograph.

"Do you have to wind it up?" asked Lazo, with a smile.

"Don't be funny," she chided. "We do have electricity in Germany, you know." She opened the case and pushed back the lid to an upright position. Then she carefully undid the electrical cord and handed the end to Lazo.

"Plug this in somewhere!" Then she removed one of the records from its compartment and lowered it on to the turn table.

"What did you put on?" asked Lazo.

"Voices of Spring by Johann Straus. It's one of my favorite waltzes." She turned the switch and waited for the turntable to reach the proper speed, then lowered the arm. Soon the room was filled with the cheerful and enchanting music from Vienna.

"May I?" asked Lazo, reaching out his hand.

"Oui," she replied, batting her eyelashes in a delightfully coquettish manner.

Soon they were spinning and whirling about through the narrow spaces with such elegant precision that one may have thought them trapped in an eddy of velvet mist. The sun which was now leaning against the horizon, sent forth its last rays of shimmering light, giving the room a warm rosy glow.

Then the music stopped. Ute rested her head against his shoulder. "And you said you couldn't dance."

He smiled, "So I lied a little."

"Let's do it again," urged Ute, not aware of Geli's presence.

"You two dance marvelously," she declared, as she walked in carrying a large tray of delicacies. She set the tray on the table and said, "There, now let's have some food." She looked at Ute, smiled and said, "Then we can dance and play."

"And make merry," laughed Lazo. They positioned themselves around the table. Ute took one of the crackers and covered it with a thick layer of caviar. She took a bite, swallowed and then licked her lips. "It is absolutely the best I have ever eaten," she beamed. She turned to Lazo and said, "Here, you try some. I'm certain that you will find it delicious."

Lazo, not wanting to disappoint her, did as she requested. Soon his eyes widened and a smile came to his lips. "It is marvelous! Damned if it isn't!" He took the rest of the cracker from Ute's hand and made short shrift of it.

Lazo filled the glasses with vodka and the three ate and drank until the tray was quite empty.

"It's getting a little chilly," observed Geli. "Why don't you start a fire?"

"Yes," chimed Ute, "it will be so cozy."

Lazo got up and said, "Sure, just when a man gets comfortable, the women find something for him to do."

"Oh, you poor thing!" laughed Ute. "Now don't over exert yourself."

"And you, Ute," admonished Geli, "you pick up around here and I'll go into the kitchen to check up on the ham."

"I'll be happy to help," replied Ute, quite enthusiastically.

Geli could not help but marvel at Ute's agility. Ute had consumed a large amount of vodka, yet she showed no signs of becoming tipsy.

Lazo was now kneeling before the fireplace. He turned and said,"You're not going to bring in the ham, are you? I couldn't eat another bite."

"Of course not," replied Geli. "I'm going to turn the oven down so the ham won't burn."

Soon the room was aglow with the warm soft light issuing from the flaming logs. Ute was about to turn on the phonograph, when the quiet was interrupted by a loud clamor, coming from the kitchen.

"What happened?" shouted Lazo.

"I fell!"

"Are you hurt?" asked Lazo, very much concerned.

The two rushed into the kitchen and found Geli, trying desperately to stand up. "I guess I drank too much," she mumbled, with a silly grin on her face.

"I'll help you up," said Lazo, reaching down.

"You'd better not. I think I'm going to be sick."

"Get a cold towel," instructed Lazo, "and I'll carry her into the bedroom."

He cradled her in his arms and carried her into the bedroom. He set her down on the bed. Then he removed her shoes and covered her with the quilt.

"Here's the towel," whispered Ute, handing it to Lazo.

"Good," remarked Lazo. He placed the towel on her forehead and gently pressed it downward.

"I'm sorry," whispered Geli, her words scarcely audible.

"It's alright," said Lazo, trying to comfort her.

They remained with her until she was asleep. Then they returned to the living room and stood before the fireplace.

"Can I turn on the phonograph?" asked Ute.

"Go ahead, but softly."

Ute brought the phonograph closer to the fireplace and turned it on. "Is Lili Marlene, alright?"

"Yes," he replied, "it's one of my favorites."

He walked over to the couch and picked up one of the pillows. Then he returned to the fireplace, settled down on the thick carpet and rested his head on the pillow.

"Would you like some Ouzo?"

"Is it any good?"

"I've never tasted it. They say it is very strong."

"I'll try anything once."

Ute filled the glasses and handed one to Lazo. She dropped to her knees and sat down, without spilling a drop.

"Well done," remarked Lazo, "but how is it that you are not tipsy yet?"

"May I?" whispered Ute, resting her head on his chest.

"Be my guest."

"Well," she continued, "my mother told me that I should take several tablespoons of butter before I drink vodka, so I did as she suggested. It seems to have worked."

"It sure did," remarked Lazo, as he took a sip of the ouzo. "This tastes just like licorice."

"Of course it does. It's flavored with aniseed."

"I like it."

"Be careful!" admonished Ute. "My mother said that it is very potent."

"Shall I play it again?" asked Ute.

"Yes, please do," replied Lazo, running his fingers through the softness of her hair.

She reached over to reset the arm. "I wish it could be like this forever," she whispered.

Lazo kissed her forehead. "Nothing is forever." He took another sip of the ouzo and then set the glass on the floor. "And life is just a handful of tomorrows, that as if by some sleight of hand, are quickly and silently transformed into memories."

She put her glass down and raised herself to her knees.

"What are you doing?"

"Oh nothing. It's getting warm in here."

"Its just right," insisted Lazo. "The ouzo must be getting to you."

But before he could utter another word she was sitting on his stomach, her knees pressed against his sides.

"Am I too heavy for you?" she asked, her hands reaching for the hem of her sweater.

"Don't do that!"

"Why not?"

Lazo grabbed her wrists and held them firmly but she was stronger than he anticipated. Her arms moved upward and soon her sweater flew across the room and came to rest on the sofa.

"There," she said, "that feels much better."

Lazo became speechless as he beheld the most perfectly formed breasts he had ever seen. He wanted to reach up and caress them but before he could move she fell forward and kissed him passionately. "Did I do it right?"

"Of course, you did it right." He slowly eased her over until she was resting on her back. He kissed her warmly then put the pillow under her head. The flickering light from the fire played on her breasts as he began to move his lips over her firm body, leaving no area of her upper torso, unexplored. She raised her hips and undid the buttons of her skirt. Then she pushed the skirt downward until all of her body was available to him.

She pressed her hands against his face and whispered, "I had no idea that there could be such exquisite joy in this world." She leaned forward and kissed him over and over again, with an abandonment he had, hitherto, never experienced.

"Easy now," he cautioned. "We've got all night."

"I know, but I have waited all of my life for this moment and I don't want it to end. She took the pillow and placed it under his head. She climbed on top of him and pressed her body down against his. "Ouch!" she cried.

"What's the matter?"

"Your belt buckle is hurting me."

He reached down and undid his belt. Then he pushed his trousers down below his hips and kicked them off. "Is that better?"

"What do I do now?"

Lazo caressed her back and she nuzzled against him, her lips against his neck. Together, they listened as the dying embers protested with an occasional anemic sputter. The turntable of the phonograph continued to turn against the needle, creating a rhythmic tic, a tic, tic a tac.

When they arrived at the summit, they were together, consumed by the same fire and the only sound to be heard was the scratching of the needle against the record's sterile grooves.

CHAPTER TWENTY NINE

It was the eleventh of April and Lazo was already becoming weary of his stay in Magdeburg. Eight days had come and gone since his arrival and he began to think that Geli had been mistaken. She had told him that the American armies would not take Dresden and in all probability, elements of the American Ninth Army would be the first to reach the Elbe, somewhere near Magdeburg. So with the help of Major Fatbottom, she had procured the necessary papers and a train ticket.

Lazo was, of course, reluctant to abandon the city of Dresden and the women who had become so dear to him but the prospect of being captured by the Russians, tipped the balance, leaving him no choice but to quit the city. Time weighed heavily on his hands and when he wasn't reading, he usually walked through the suburban markets on the west bank of the Elbe. On this particular day an unusually large number of civilians were milling about. Lazo stopped an old man.

"Excuse me kind sir, but could you tell me the time?"

The old man reached into his pocket and carefully, almost reverently, removed his watch. "The time," he replied, "is exactly ten minutes past five."

"Thank you very much. Aufwiedersehen!"

The old man turned and was about to walk away, when he paused and asked, "Tell me please, why is such a strong young man like you not in the army, defending the Vaterland?"

Lazo pretended not to hear the question and continued on his way. When he turned the next corner, all hell broke loose. There, in the middle of the shopping district was a platoon of American reconnaissance scout cars and armored vehicles, trying to make their way through the crowded streets. This platoon had broken through the German defenses and were now stopped, not by German guns but by German shoppers and pedestrians. Some of the American soldiers fired bursts into the air to clear the way. Women began to scream and run in all directions. Some of them fainted and were run over by the terrified civilians.

Lazo decided that it was time to make his move. He dashed up to the lead car and shouted, "My name is Captain Lazo Krall of the O.S.S.! May I join you, sir?"

The young major removed his pistol from its holster, nervously pointed it at Lazo's head and shouted, "Jump in!"

Lazo jumped into the back seat just in the nick of time. Some German soldiers, alerted by the gun fire, ran up and began to fire, quite wildly, at the Americans.

"Let's get the hell out of here before we get our asses shot off!" screamed the Sergeant, who was driving.

The platoon, somehow, managed to disentangle itself and with throttles wide open, sped away.

"Where in hell are we going?"

"Well, Captain, if that's who you really are," shouted the Major, "we're going to take the airfield and then the Autobahn to Berlin."

"Then may I have a weapon?"

"How do I know that I can trust you?"

Lazo, becoming impatient, snapped, "I've been behind the German lines for the past six months and if I'm going to get killed, I'm going to die with a weapon in these hands!"

The Captain reached down and came up with a Thompson Sub Machine gun. "Here, take this but if you make one wrong move, I'll blow your fuckin head off."

"If it is all the same to you Sir, I think it best that we save our anger for the enemy!"

A short while later, they were driving full speed, down the tarmac of the enemy aerdrome, firing their guns at the planes that were desperately trying to become airborne. Lazo seemed to be enjoying the moment. At last he was doing exactly what he wanted to do, ever since he entered the army. He was standing up and firing at everything that moved. He seemed to love it.

"More ammo!" he shouted, reaching his hand toward the Major.

"Get down, you damned fool! Do you want to get yourself killed?"

"I will get killed if you don't give me another clip."

The Major threw him another clip and Lazo quickly inserted it and began firing at an old Stuka that was lumbering down the runway. He fired the entire clip into the engine. The plane left the ground, lurched clumsily, then plummeted, nose first, into the asphalt, and was soon engulfed in a bright red mantle of fire.

"Just like the fourth of July!" he shouted gleefully. "Throw me some more ammo!"

"I don't know who the hell you are or where the hell you came from," shouted the Major, "but you can fight with me any damned day of the week!"

The Major threw him another clip but before Lazo could insert it, the driver turned the vehicle to avoid some debris and Lazo was almost pitched out of the car.

"God damn, that was close!" he shouted.

"Oh, oh!" yelled the Major.

"What the hell's the matter?"

"We've got company! A helluva lot of company!"

"Where the hell are they?" asked Lazo, inserting another clip.

Before the Major could reply, the platoon was greeted by an intense rifle and mortar fire, that seemed to be coming from all directions at once.

Lazo instinctively dropped down. He could hear the bullets whizzing by, some of them coming awfully close.

"Are you hit?"

"Hell no! There isn't a German alive who can kill me!"

"There are too damned many of them!" barked the Major. "Let's get the fuck out of here!"

Lazo resumed his standing position and was about to fire when a mortar shell made a direct hit on the armored vehicle to their immediate right. The force of the explosion was so brutal that it overturned the vehicle and catapaulted one of the occupants out onto the tarmac.

"Stop!" shouted Lazo. "He's still alive!"

The driver, accustomed to following orders, slammed down on the brakes, placing the vehicle in peril. Lazo jumped out and ran, hell bent, toward the burning vehicle. He quickly picked the man up and began to rush back. He could almost feel the bullets rushing past him, some of them ricochetting against the asphalt, just ahead of his steps. When he reached the car, he threw the man in and jumped up on the running board.

"Now, let's get the hell out of here!" he shouted, as the Major pulled him in. Soon they were out of range and heading toward the American lines.

"Is he still alive?" asked the Major.

Lazo bent over the injured man. "Are you alright, soldier?"

"I think so. I'm bleeding a little and my arm feels broken, otherwise, I'm okay." He squinted at Lazo and said, "I don't know who the hell you are but thank you very much for saving my life. I'll never forget you."

"That was the dumbest thing I have ever seen!" exclaimed the Major, shaking his head. "So awful dumb that I'm going to recommend you for a medal."

"Just doing what I'm getting paid for, Major. Besides, I told you that no German could kill me." He laughed and handed the machine gun back to the Major. "I don't think I'll be needing this any more, so you'd better have it."

The Major took the piece and set it down. Then he turned and extended his hand to Lazo. "My name is Domian."

Lazo took the hand and shook it cordially. "What's your last name?"

"That is my last name," said the Major. "My first name is Marty."

"It's been a pleasure doing business with you, Marty," remarked Lazo, noting for the first time, Marty's face, which though covered with grime and several day's growth of beard, was quite handsome. "You're my kind of guy," continued Lazo, "and if it were at all possible, I would gladly transfer to your command."

"Well, thank you, Lazo, and you can bet your damned life that I would do anything to have you in my outfit." He chuckled and added, "You're damned good for morale."

"Do you have a cigarette, Major?"

"You bet I do," replied Marty, reaching into his pocket and pulling out a pack of Camels. "Keep them," he said, as he threw the pack to Lazo. "You've damned well earned them."

Lazo lit up. "Thank you! You are an officer and a gentleman."

"I've been called worst," laughed the Major.

"May I have a smoke, please?"

"Are you old enough?"

The soldier turned his face to Lazo. "Please, sir. I need a smoke real bad."

"Major," shouted Lazo, "I need some sulpha and a compress."

"Are you hurt?"

"No, I'm not hurt, but this young gentleman doesn't have any skin left on the side of his face and we'd better cover it before it becomes infected." He put the lighted cigarette to the soldier's lips.

"Thank you, sir."The young soldier took several quick puffs and asked, "Is it bad?"

"I really can't tell. It probably looks worse than it is."

"Here," said the Major, handing Lazo a packet of Sulpha. "Make sure you cover the entire wound," he cautioned.

Lazo did as the Major directed and then he carefully covered the wound with the large compress and tied it. "There," he said, "out of sight, out of mind."

"Thank you, again," remarked the soldier. "By the way, my name is Paul Shober and if you are ever in Medford, Oregon, look me up." He took another puff and added, "That is, if I'm still alive after the war."

"You'll survive," said Lazo, reassuringly. "Anyone who can survive a mortar blast and the belly flop you took on the tarmac, is a genuine survivor. So yes, if I ever chance to be in Medford, you can be certain that I will give you a call."

They were travelling about fifty miles an hour, so it did not take them very long to reach the battalion aid station, where they dropped Paul off. Then they continued onto Regimental headquarters, where Lazo was questioned by a Colonel York, of G-2. Afterward, he had a phone call placed to O.S.S. Headquarters in Caserta, Italy.

"Well, gentlemen, what say we have a drink while we wait for the call to go through."

"Sounds like a splendid idea," replied Marty. "Is the smoking lamp on, Sir?"

"By all means," replied the Colonel, removing a bottle of French cognac from his desk drawer. "Make yourselves at home." He threw the bottle to Lazo and said, "Have a swallow and as you can see, we are a little short of glasses and formalities out here."

Lazo removed the cork and placed it on the desk. He took a generous swallow and handed the bottle to Marty.

"By the way, Colonel, I'm, putting Lazo in for a D.S.C." He took a large swallow and handed the bottle back to the Colonel.

"Is that so?"

"Ya. You should have seen him fight. Hell, he's not afraid of anything, I've never seen anything like it."

Lazo's face turned crimson. "He's exaggerating considerably, Sir."

The Colonel took a drink and handed the bottle back to Lazo. "By the way," he asked, "what are they saying about our Russian allies?"

Lazo took another swallow. "Not much. I managed to get out of Yugoslavia in the nick of time but the stories I was told by some of my friends, did nothing to endear the bastards to me."

He set the bottle down. "Why do you ask, Colonel?"

"We just received orders that we are not to go to Berlin."

"Why the hell not?" stormed Marty. "We could be in Berlin in a couple of days!"

"I know, Goddam it!" shouted the Colonel. "You know as well as I, that orders are orders!"

"This is some fuckin war!" grumbled Marty. He raised the bottle and took several swallows, "Well, Colonel, where the hell do we go from here?"

"We stop at the Elbe and then we head south," replied the Colonel. "They expect the Germans to make a last ditch stand at the Alpenfestung."

Lazo scarcely believing what he was hearing, jumped up and shouted, "They can't be serious! There is no Alpenfestung! There is no national redoubt! There is no southern fortress! The Germans are beaten! They've got nothing left! They are all used up, Colonel, all used up!"

Lazo walked over to Marty. "Give me that bottle. I think I want to get stinking drunk."

"How can you be sure?" asked the Colonel. "Our intelligence indicates that there is a national redoubt."

"Where the hell do you think I've been for the last half year? No disrespect intended, Colonel. The Germans want us to cross the Elbe. They want to believe, that together we can drive the Bolsheviks back to the Urals."

The Colonel's face turned beet red and he was about to respond when the door opened and a sergeant entered. "Your call to Caserta is ready, Sir. A Colonel Featherstone is on the other end."

"Thank you, Sergeant."

The Colonel picked up the phone, "Colonel York, here."

The two exchanged pleasantries, then got down to business. "Yes, Captain Krall is right here. Do you wish to speak to him?"

The Colonel paused briefly then turned to Lazo. "He wants to know the whereabouts of Sam Kaplan."

Lazo's face became contorted. He looked up at the ceiling. "Tell him that Sam is dead. He was killed by the Chetniks in a little village called Cherni Lukno."

The Colonel relayed the message, then waited. Then he said, "I see. Yes, I understand and I'll tell him immediately. Yes, thank you, and goodbye."

He put down the phone. "You're a lucky devil, Lazo. The Colonel is sending you home, post haste. He will arrange air transport to Frankfurt and will join you there. Then the two of you will fly to Washington, D.C."

The Colonel grabbed the bottle, took a drink and scratched his head. "Hot damn, I didn't know that you were that goddam important. How do you fit in the scheme of things?"

"I don't Sir," insisted Lazo. "Sam Kaplan's father has a lot of political clout in Washington and I'm sure that he's been trying to find out what happened to his son. I'm the only one who can tell him and that's the reason and the only reason they're sending me back."

"Here, have a drink, Lazo."

"But it's almost empty," replied Lazo.

"Never mind," insisted the Colonel, "there's plenty more where that came from."

Lazo poured the remnants of the bottle down his throat and dropped the bottle into the waste paper basket. "Tell me, Colonel, how do you tell a man that his only son was hung up by his balls and then shot?"

Lazo walked over to the chair and sat down. Then he looked at Marty and said, "Now you know that I'm no damned coward, but tell me, how do I explain to this good man that I watched his son's final agony and listened as he screamed and begged for mercy. How do I tell him that I could do nothing but watch? How do I tell him that, Marty?"

Marty said nothing. He knew that there was nothing he might say that could ease Lazo's anguish. The Colonel uncorked another bottle, took a couple of swigs and handed it to Marty. He walked over and put his hand on Lazo's shoulder. "Maybe," he said, "just maybe, we can try those bastards as war criminals."

"No need for that, sir. They're all dead." Lazo looked down at the floor and whispered, "I took care of that."

Lazo grabbed the bottle and took several healthy swigs, then he laughed and said, "I shot that bastard's balls off with a German machine pistol."

"Whose balls?" asked Marty, not certain of whom Lazo was speaking.

"The Chetnik leader, of course! Who the hell else?"

Marty burst out laughing and soon the Colonel joined in. Soon all three were laughing uproariously.

"That's what I call poetic justice," shouted the Colonel, between fits of laughter. "That's poetic justice!"

"Poetic justice, hell, That's what I call ballistic justice!" roared Marty, with heavy emphasis on the syllable, ball.

They were well into their third bottle of cognac, when the revellers finally decided that it was time to hit the sack. Lazo and Marty bid the Colonel, good night and were about to leave when the Colonel tossed the bottle to Lazo and said, "Here, you two can make better use of this than I can. I'll see you tomorrow morning, before you leave." He watched the two stumble down the road and disappear into the darkness. Then he turned and whispered, "Ballistic justice." He chuckled, shook his head and retired.

CHAPTER THIRTY

It was late in May and the war in Europe had been brought to a successful conclusion. Lazo was slowly walking down the dusty country road, which led to the Krebs' domicile. He had been detained in Washington for several weeks and was treated with great kindness and respect. He had written several letters to Ilse but since he had no idea how long he might be detained, he instructed her not to write until he had a permanent address.

As he walked along the country road, his attention became nailed to the tall pine trees and their new green that was unfolding itself in bended streams of brilliant turquoise. And for one moment, just one moment, he could have sworn that he had seen a purple shaft of light filtering upward, toward the sun. A torrent of pleasant memories brought a smile to his face. Suddenly the happy expression disappeared and his face became visibly contorted and pained. He kicked at a small stone that lay in his way thinking perhaps, that this gesture might somehow divert his thoughts to more genial memories. But it did not help. Nothing, at least for the moment, could erase the memory of that first brief encounter with Sam's father.

Lazo quickened his pace, attempting to leave that memory behind. He turned his head and looked back but all he could see was the iron red dust drifting upward from the newly graded gravel, and Saul Kaplan's tears splashing against the beautifully finished mahogany desk top.

When he reached the mail box bearing the name of Hermann Krebs, he stopped and looked across the quiet blue lake. Then he smiled and began to run down the path, toward the beautiful old cottage that held such pleasant memories for him. He was so excited and agitated that he almost tripped as he bounded up the steps and onto the porch. He knocked on the screen door and shouted, "Ilse! I'm home! I'm home!"

But it was not Ilse who appeared at the door to greet him. It was Erika and she seemed so terribly distant that Lazo became unnerved.

"Where's Ilse?" he asked, his voice cracking.

"She's not here," replied Erika, with a coldness that Lazo could not believe possible.

"Where is she?"

"She's not home to you, Lazo, and what's more, she will never be home to you." She looked directly into his eyes and asked, "How could you do that to her? To us? Have you no honor?"

She turned and began to walk back into the living room.

"Please, Erika, tell me what's wrong. What have I done that has so upset you? Tell me, please."

Erika turned and in a voice that was very mean, said, "You know what you've done. How could you not know?" She wrung her hands. "And to think we all loved you so."

Lazo was in a desperate state. He didn't know quite what to think. Then it struck him. "Of course," he thought "they've found out about Werner's death. Oh God, that's why she hates me. That's why they all hate me."

He dropped his head, turned slowly and began to walk away.

"Are you going to marry her?"

"What?" asked Lazo, without turning.

"Are you going to marry this Virginia Lee?"

Lazo turned toward her and began to laugh.

"We don't find anything funny about it," she yelled, losing most of her equability.

Lazo, stung by her rebuke, stopped laughing and asked, "How do you know Virginia?"

"She came to see us."

"What? She couldn't have been that stupid."

"From all appearances, I'd say that she was about seven months stupid and that, Lazo is why she came to see us."

"I still don't understand," insisted Lazo.

"You can't be that naive," retorted Erika. "She told us that you were the father and that she fully intends to marry you."

"And you believed her?"

"Of course, we believed her. She was very persuasive. How else could she have known all those dates and places?" Erika opened the door and walked out on to the porch. "Are you suggesting that you don't know her?"

"I know her. Of course, I know her. Her father was the officer who organized my mission, but that doesn't mean that I slept with her." Then he looked directly at her and said, "I didn't, you know."

He was so sincere that she was almost persuaded. "How can we believe you?"

"You must," snapped Lazo, who was losing his patience. "I know who the father was." He looked into her eyes and said, "My God, but you're beautiful! I had almost forgotten."

Her face became red. "Oh, now, as they say in America, you're giving me a snow job."

"No snow job," insisted Lazo. "I had honestly forgotten just how beautiful you are."

"Well, now that your attempt to disarm me has failed, will you please tell me what you meant when you said that you know who the father was?"

"I meant," replied Lazo, "that he is dead. he was killed in Yugoslavia."

"How convenient for you," retorted Erika, as she leaned back against the railing. "Your word against his and he is in no position to defend himself. I find that quite bothersome."

"What do you mean? Do you believe that I could lie about something like that? Hell, Sam was my best friend. I could never betray his memory. You've just got to believe me. You've got to."

She watched him as he paced, uneasily, from one end of the porch to the other. "I would like to, Lazo, but the young lady was very convincing. She even knew that we had not taken out our final papers."

"What has that to do with anything?"

Erika did not respond immediately. She seemed troubled. Finally she spoke, "We have found a home in this country and we have found happiness and peace, in this cottage by the lake." She looked up at the ceiling, perhaps searching for the correct words. "She, Virginia, suggested that if Ilse continued to see you, her father, who is now a general, would see that we were deported." Erika looked at Lazo and with trembling voice, said, "You understand our predicament. We have no choice. You must leave us alone. We do not wish to be sent back to Germany. Do you understand?"

"You really are afraid, aren't you?" He stopped pacing and his manner became almost austere. "Well, let me tell you something." He leaned against the railing and declared, with anger, "You will never be sent back to Germany. I can guarantee that you and your family will never have to leave this place. This is not the Third Reich! This is America!"

"Oh, so now you are a big shot!"

Lazo was hurt by her sarcasm and he paused briefly. He did not want to hurry his words. Then he said, "No, I'm not a big shot but I know a big shot in Washington, who will be the happiest man alive, when I tell him that he will become a grandfather, afterall."

Erika, now more confused than ever, asked, "What are you talking about?"

"Sam," shouted Lazo, "is the man who slept with Virginia and his father is a very powerful man in Washington."

"But Sam is dead," insisted Erika, "and you'll have as much success convincing Sam's father as you have had convincing me."

She turned and walked to the far side of the porch. "I want to believe you, Lazo. God knows that I do but it's going to be difficult trying to convince Sam's father. It's just your word against Virginia's and she seems to be holding all the cards."

"Oh, he'll believe me alright, but that is not my immediate concern."

"Then, what is your immediate concern?"

"Trying to convince you and Ilse. That's my immediate concern." He turned and began to walk toward the steps.

"Where are you going now?"

"I've got to do some thinking and I do that best alone." He bounded down the steps and began to run up the path. Then he stopped abruptly and shouted, "Tell Ilse, I'm home!"

Erika watched until he disappeared among the trees. Then she turned and was about to go indoors when she heard, "Wait a minute! I just thought of something!"

"What?"

"Call 887-4145!" shouted Lazo, running back toward the cottage.

"What did you say?"

"Call 887-4145, and ask for June Janesek!"

He leaped on to the porch, took her in his arms and swung her around and around with such excitement that the much weathered timbers which supported the porch, screamed loudly as they gave way to his enthusiasm.

"Put me down!" she screamed. "What's come over you? Have you gone mad?"

"No!" he shouted. "I will not put you down! Not until you promise to call June!"

"Alright, I promise. Now put me down!"

"Not until you say please! Besides, I kind of like this." He laughed and squeezed her even more tightly.

"If you don't put me down, I will scream!"

"Go ahead! Tell the whole world that you were carrying on with your future son-in-law!"

"Please put me down and I will call this girl you call, June."

Lazo, sensing that she was becoming very embarrassed, released his hold and eased her down until her feet made contact with the floor. She blushed as she pulled her skirt down and smoothed out the wrinkles. Then she looked up at him and asked, "Did you really mean it when you said that I was beautiful?"

"Of course, I meant it but I do have a confession to make."

"And what is that?"

"I lied when I said that I had forgotten how beautiful you were." He turned away and almost reluctantly, added, "I could never forget that."

"Will you do me a favor?"

"Of course."

"Will you kiss me?"

Now it was Lazo who blushed. "You're not serious?"

"But I am."

Lazo put his arms around her and was about to kiss her when he drew back and said, "I can't do this. It just wouldn't be fair."

"Oh, go ahead," she urged. "I just want to find out something about myself."

He lowered his head until their lips made contact, then he quickly retreated.

She smiled and seemed to be enjoying his discomfiture. "Is that the best you can do?" She threw her arms around his neck and kissed him quite vehemently. Then she turned and ran into the house, allowing the screen door to slam at her heels.

Lazo was very puzzled by what had just transpired. He looked at the screen door for a moment then turned and began to walk down the steps. When he reached the path, he turned and looked back. She was standing in the doorway.

"Where are you going?"

"I'm going for a walk."

"May I come along? It's so lonesome here."

"No," he replied, trying not to sound too abrupt. "Besides, you promised to make a certain telephone call."

"To what city?"

"It's a Georgetown number."

"And what do I ask her?"

"Just ask her if I slept with Virginia."

"And what if she's not in?"

"Just keep calling until you reach her," he yelled, running up the path. "I'll pay for the call!"

She waited until he disappeared among the trees, then she too, disappeared among the shadows. When he reached the gravel road, he stopped and looked in both directions, as if trying to establish his bearings. Then he turned and began to walk down the road but this time he was not going to pick berries. He began to reflect on all of the things that had happened to him since last he walked this way and wondered why his life had become so very complicated.

"Thank God, we have the capacity to forget." he whispered.

He reached into his pocket, took out his handkerchief and mopped his forehead. He walked quite slowly, not wanting to miss the path that led to the Krebs camp site. When he finally spotted it, he returned the handkerchief to his pocket and began to run. He didn't stop until he reached the spot overlooking the beautiful, crystal clear lake. It was even more beautiful than he had remembered. He walked over to the spring to refresh himself. The birchbark vessel was still hanging on its peg. He filled it with the cold, clear water and drank until his thirst was quenched. He wiped his lips with the back of his hand and returned the vessel to its peg.

"And now, Lazo Krall," he whispered, "you have nothing to do but wait."

He walked over to where the grass was unusually thick and sat down. The forest was arush with the sounds of birds and other wild life. He settled back against an old weathered log and listened as the water waged its gentle war against the rocks below. As he listened, he began to wonder why these most vulnerable of God's creatures were betraying their very presences with their squawkings, squealings and chirpings. "How vainglorious of them," he thought.

Then his musings were interrupted by what sounded like some one smacking a tree, repeatedly with a hammer. He looked around, endeavoring to ascertain the whereabouts of this brazen tympanist.

"Ah, just as I thought," he whispered, as he spotted the large Pileated Woodpecker, chiseling into the withered skin of a dying Oak tree. He gazed at the feathered drummer for a long time, then settled his head against his Musette bag and was soon fast asleep.

It was already late afternoon when he was awakened by the persistent efforts of an illusive deer fly, that had nothing better to do than trip callously over his ear. When he could bear it no longer, he jerked his head around and found himself looking directly into the eyes of Ilse. She was kneeling at his side, holding a sliver of grass in her hand.

"Oh God!" he shouted. "If this be a dream, may I never awaken."

She leaned over and kissed him, very gently on his cheek. Her long soft hair brushed against his face as she drew back and smiled.

"It is no dream, my love. Mother sent me to get you."

She raised herself to her feet and extended her hand to Lazo. "Here, give me your hand."

She helped him to his feet and he whispered, "I missed you so very much. I didn't believe it possible but you have become more beautiful than you were when last I saw you. He looked directly into her blue eyes and said, "I love you. Oh, how I love you."

He took her into his arms and kissed her like he had never kissed anyone before.

"How I wish I could remain here, in your arms forever, but mother told me to get you back as fast as my feet could carry me."

"Well, let's get going then," uttered Lazo. "We musn't disappoint Erika."

She took his hand. "But first, I've got something to show you."

"What?"

"You'll see." She began to run, pulling him behind. She didn't stop until they reached the place where the brook tumbled into the deep, clear pond. She paused to secure her breath, then asked, "Do you remember?"

"How could I ever forget."

"Do you see that log over there?" she asked, pointing to an old gray log that lay half hidden in the grass.

"I see it."

"Roll it over for me."

Lazo rolled the log over and waited.

"Is it there?"

"Is what there?"

"It must be there," she insisted, running over to the log.

"Oh, you mean the brown package?"

"Yes, I mean the brown package," retorted Ilse, bending down and carefully picking up the package.

"Here, unwrap it for me."

Lazo removed the brown paper and there pressed between two blocks of wood, was a cellophane envelope containing the Indian Paintbrushes. They were dry but still completely intact. "How beautiful," he remarked. "Are these the ones you picked on that last day?"

"Yes," she replied, "the very same. A little worse for wear, but the same."

Lazo looked into her eyes. "We must find a way to preserve them. It is the second most beautiful flower in my life."

"And what, pray tell, is the most beautiful flower in your life?" taunted Ilse.

Lazo blushed and whispered, "You are and you always will be."

"Danke, Herr Hauptmann," she replied. "I already knew that but I wanted to hear you say it."

Lazo repositioned the flowers between the two blocks and carefully tucked them into his Musette bag. "They shoud be safe in here for the time being."

"And now my brave soldier, see if you can keep up with me!" She gave him a quick peck on his cheek and darted down the path.

Lazo tucked his Musette bag under his arm like a football and raced after her. "I'll catch you!" he shouted. "I'll pass you before you get to the road."

"That's what you think," she yelled, as she reached down and without breaking stride, pulled the hem of her skirt upward, allowing her to lengthen her stride.

Lazo could easily have overtaken her but there was no good reason to, so he ran just fast enough to make it a good race. When she reached the gravel road, she stopped and waited for him to catch up.

"Did anyone ever tell you that you have elegant legs?"

She blushed and put her arm around his waist. Then they began to walk down the road.

"How come they made you a captain?"

"It's a long and boring story," he replied. "Perhaps, when we are all together, I can tell you about it. Then you see, my darling, I'll only have to tell it once."

"How long can you stay?"

He put his arm around her waist and said, "They've given me ninety days. After that, who knows?"

"That means that we can be together most of the summer." Her eyes lit up. "Just think," she beamed, "I can have you to myself for ninety days!" She removed her arm from his waist and with an almost childish disregard for propriety, leaped and danced down the dusty road, punctuating her graceful leaps with several high pitched yipees. When Lazo finally caught up to her, he kissed her on her cheek.

"Not exactly. I will have to spend some time with my family."

"I know that, but we'll still have a lot of time together."

"You bet we will," he assured her, "and what's more, I've got over three thousand dollars back pay in my wallet."

Ilse's mouth fell open. "Did you say three thousand! I've never seen that much money in my entire life!"

"Nor I," laughed Lazo. "Nor I."

"I'm so happy I could burst!" she yelled and once again, she was off and running, leaping upward after every few steps, as if reaching for the sun.

"I didn't realize that money was so important to you."

"It's not," replied Ilse. "It never was, and now," she shouted, "it's even less!"

"What do you mean?"

She stopped and waited for him to catch up. She put her arms around him and kissed him fervently. "Did you enjoy that, my handsome young hero?"

"Oh yes! Of course, I did."

"And how much is a kiss like that worth?" she asked, smiling quite devilishly.

"You can't buy a kiss like that."

"I rest my case. Papa said that too much money weighs down the human spirit and rivets it to the earth. We must exchange it for a higher currency."

"And what, pray tell, is that?"

Her eyes lit up and she appeared happier and more beautiful than he had ever believed possible.

"Love is the most precious of all currencies. Papa said that it can be likened to an aerostat because it buoys up the human spirit and allows it to soar and become one with the immediate object of that love. Not only that," she continued, "but it also makes it possible for that spirit to unite with the universe. Love is man's victory over himself."

Lazo shrugged his shoulders. "If to love is to surrender," he asked, "then why is it not a senseless capitulation?"

"Because, my dearest, in love we lose the self in order to know the other."

"Oh, I see," replied Lazo, "and to know the other is to become one with the other."

"Precisely!" remarked Ilse. "It is a kind of transmigration. It is this intermingling of kindred spirits that leads to ecstacy. To be beside the other is, at the same time, to be beside oneself!" Then she smiled and said, "No pun intended."

Lazo ran his fingers through his hair. "It's amazing," he said.

"What's amazing?"

"How someone so young can be so wise."

"Just blame it on papa. He wants me to go to college and become a professor of philosophy."

"And you, what do you want?" asked Lazo, taking her hand and caressing it gently, with his lips.

"I want to be beside you for the rest of my life. I want you to love me as I love you."

"Okay professor, I've got just one more question for you."

She leaned over and kissed him. "Is it a good question?"

"If your father is correct and love is the ascent of the human spirit, why pray tell, did we fall in love so precipitously?"

He took her in his arms and said, "I fell in love with you because you were the most beautiful young woman I had ever seen." He paused and looked upward, searching for the right words.

"And if I had been ugly?"

Lazo kissed her forehead and replied, "If you had been ugly, I doubt very much that I would be here, with you, this day."

She turned her head away from him to hide her blush. "Am I really beautiful?"

"You know that you are. Now tell me why you happened to fall in love with me."

"Because you were the most handsome and clumsiest man I had ever met." She smiled and squeezed his hand.

Now, it was Lazo's turn to blush and blush he did.

"You're embarrassed, aren't you?" she teased.

"Yes, I am embarrassed and I don't know why, I should be." He paused for a moment. "Yes, I do. I know why and I'll tell you. We are just afraid to admit that we love each other because we are physically attracted to each other and by God, I am physically attracted to you. I lust for you and I want to explore and know every inch of your body and if my spirit soars, so much the better but for now, I'll settle for pure sensuous joy that I feel when I'm near you, when I touch you, when you touch me. I want to make love to you and I want to do so unabashedly." He paused to catch his breath. "And if that is love, then I love you more than any man has ever loved a woman."

She put her arms around his waist and kissed him ardently. She pulled his hips against hers and whispered real tenderly. "I don't think that I'd want you any other way, but I'm selfish and I must have you exclusively." She smiled. "And now my ardent young lover, I think we'd better hurry before mother sends out a search party." She took his hand and together, they ran down the path. When they reached the cottage, she stopped, looked into his eyes. "Lazo," she asked, "if what you said back there is true, then why wouldn't any other beautiful, young woman serve your needs as well as I? How can I know that you really love me?"

The suddenness of her question caused Lazo to squirm a little. "I could never fall in love with a woman who could not ask that question, no matter how beautiful she happened to be."

She smiled and squeezed his hand. "There is something beside my physical beauty that attracted you to me, isn't there? Papa was right afterall," she beamed, as she bounded up the steps, shouting, "We're here! We're home!"

"Welcome home, Lazo," pealed Hermann, rushing to the door. He took Lazo's hand and shook it heartily. Then shedding his usual Spartan equanimity, embraced Lazo excitedly.

"It's so good to be home, Hermann. You will never know how much I looked forward to this moment."

"Ilse, get some wine and you Erika, come over here and give our young soldier a proper welcome."

Erika had never seen him this excited for such a long time and caught up in the moment, she rushed over and embraced Lazo with unabashed enthusiasm. "I talked to June and she assured me that what you told me was the truth. Can you forgive me for the way I treated you earlier today?"

"Of course, I can. I would have felt the same way under those circumstances."

"June referred to you as an officer and a gentleman and I assure you that from this moment on, in this house, you will always be treated as such. Please forgive me."

Lazo felt her body tremble and knew that she was sincerely contrite, yet it seemed to him that she was much more agitated than she had cause to be. He put his hands on her shoulders and said, "There is nothing to forgive but if it will make you feel better, I do forgive you." He leaned over and kissed her forehead. Then he added, "Please do not treat me as an officer and a gentleman, but as a member of this very dear and remarkable family."

Erika walked over to Hermann and kissed him fully on his lips. Then she turned to Lazo and said, "Welcome home and welcome to the family."

Lazo smiled appreciatively and said, "I thank you and may I never do anything that would bring dishonor to this family."

"Where's your duffle bag?" asked Ilse, as she entered the room, carrying a tray upon which she had neatly arranged four glasses around a large bottle of wine. "Did you forget it again?"

"No, I didn't forget it but I did almost forget something else," he replied, feverishly reaching into his musette bag. "This is for you, Erika," he said, handing her a small, carefully wrapped package.

"Oh, thank you, Lazo. Do I open it now?"

"Of course," said Lazo.

She carefully undid the wrapping and opened the box. Her eyes turned misty. "Oh Hermann, come and see. It is the most beautiful wrist watch I have ever seen." She nervously put the watch on her wrist and carefully secured it. Then she extended her hand so that she might further admire it. "Isn't it elegant? Thank you, Lazo. I will treasure this for the rest of my life, but you shouldn't have. It must have cost ever so much."

"I hope that you will get as much pleasure from my gift as I have just now experienced." He turned to Hermann. "And this, good friend, is for you." He handed Hermann a box. "I didn't have time to wrap it, but I knew that you would understand."

Hermann opened the box and removed a pair of binoculars "Oh Thank you, Lazo! But how did you know? Oh! They must have cost a fortune!"

"You are most welcome, Hermann. I know how much you love the outdoors and I thought that these would enable you to enjoy it even more."

He turned to Ilse and said, "And now it's your turn." He reached into the bag and very carefully removed a rather large box. He handed it to her. "I hope you like it. It has been on a very long and arduous journey."

Ilse carefully opened the box and began to remove the many layers of crumpled paper that was used to protect the object. Her eyes sparkled as she removed the last layer of paper and came to another box.

"Is this a joke?" she asked, her face reddening.

"No, I assure you that it is not. Now please open the box."

She removed the lid and there, reclining on a soft bed of cotton batting, was a beautiful porcelain figurine. A little blond, blue eyed boy, on a swing. She slowly removed it from the box and held it up so all might see.

"It's exquisite! Oh, thank you, Lazo! I will always treasure it!"

"May I see it?" asked Erika.

"Of course, you may," replied Ilse, handing the figurine to her mother.

Erika examined the figure carefully, then handed it to Hermann. "Where have you seen this before?"

Hermann examined the figurine and said, "I have seen it somewhere but I just can't seem to remember where."

Erika walked over to Lazo. "You were in Dresden, weren't you?" She looked at Hermann. "Do you remember now?"

"This is one of Geli's Meissens, isn't it? But how did you get it?" he asked, his voice expressing a profound disbelief.

"Geli's alive!" cried Erika, as tears of joy filled her eyes. "She is alive, isn't she?" she asked, waiting for Lazo to reassure her.

Lazo smiled and said, "Yes, she was alive the last time I saw her, but that was over a month ago."

"Oh Gott sei dank! Oh, Hermann," she continued, "our Geli is still alive! Isn't that wonderful!"

"Ja, Liebling, it is wonderful news, but I still would like to know how Lazo acquired this piece."

"It's a very long story, Hermann, much too long to relate at this time but Geli asked me to give it to Ilse. She was not certain but she thought that it might be one of Friedrich Meyer's works and she didn't want it to fall into Russian hands."

"Was she well?" asked Erika.

"Yes," replied Lazo, "she survived the bombings but I don't know how she will face up to the Russian occupation." He walked over to Ilse and put his arm around her. "I can tell you this though," he continued, "she is a survivor and the Russians would have to be damned clever to get the best of her."

Hermann handed the figurine to Ilse and said, "Be very careful with this. It is not only beautiful but priceless as well."

"Yes, papa, I know," she replied, clutching the figurine to her bosom.

"Is it really that valuable?"

"Ja, Lazo, it is a genuine treasure," replied Hermann.

"Oh my God!" exclaimed Lazo. "I've got to sit down!"

"What's the matter?" asked Ilse. "Do you feel ill?"

"No, it's not that." He rubbed his forehead with his hand. "If I had known it was that valuable, I never would have taken it with me."

He took his handkerchief and mopped his forehead. "Hell," he continued, "I had it with me in Magdeburg, where I was involved in a real shooting war."

He put the handkerchief back into his pocket and said, "It may have been destroyed."

"But it wasn't," beamed Ilse, "and now it is safe with us."

"How did you manage to get it here in one piece? Even under the most hospitable of circumstances, it would have been nearly impossible."

Lazo did not respond immediately. He seemed a little hesitant. Finally he replied, "I think it will have to remain our little secret, Geli's and mine."

"Just like the glasses," laughed Hermann.

"No, Hermann," replied Lazo, "Geli told me how they hid the glasses."

"She didn't," protested Erika, her face becoming crimson.

"Yup, she really did, but I won't tell Hermann. She made me promise."

"What a relief," sighed Erika. "Now let's have a little wine." She turned to Hermann, "Will you pour?"

"Ja, Liebchen, it will be my great honor and pleasure."

"Oh, wait a minute!" shouted Lazo. "I almost forgot. Hand me my musette bag, please."

Ilse picked up the bag and handed it to Lazo.

"Thank you." He reached into the bag and pulled out a small box. "Here," he said, handing it to Ilse. "That other gift was from Geli, this one's from me."

Ilse took the box and began to undo the wrapping. She unconsciously pressed the tip of her tongue against her upper lip, a sure sign of her repressed excitement. She placed the lid of the box on the table. Then she raised a corner of the protective layer of cotton and beheld a beautiful diamond pendant lying on a bed of blue satin, She gazed at the blazing gem and became completely dumbstruck.

"You don't like it."

"Like it? Of course, I like it, Lazo! I have never seen anything so grand! I, I just can't seem to find the right words to express the joy that I now feel. I'm totally overwhelmed."

"What is it?" asked Erika.

Ilse pinched the exquisite golden chain between her fingers and raised it upward. The diamond spun dizzily on its chain, casting streams of multi-colored light about the room.

"It's beautiful!" shouted Erika. "It must be more than half a carat!"

"It is very beautiful," observed Hermann.

Ilse walked over to Lazo and said, "Please."

Lazo took the pendant and carefully arranged it around her long graceful neck.

"Make sure that you secure the clip," she cautioned, "I would die if it ever became lost."

"Don't worry. I'll make sure," said Lazo. "Now turn around so I can see."

She turned slowly and said, "Remember, an old sweatshirt is not a proper background for such an exquisite gem."

Lazo was the first to speak. "When I purchased it," he said, "it was simply a crystalline form of carbon, but you, you give it a beauty, an extravagance that it never had. You give it life. you give it class."

"Oh, thank you, Lazo!" she exclaimed. "I'm the happiest girl alive!" She threw her arms around his neck and kissed him.

"And now can I pour the wine?"

"Ja, Hermann, you can pour the wine," declared Erika, who had become extremely pleased with the way the day was progressing. She looked at her watch and a shocked expression came to her face. "My God! It's almost six o'clock! I'll have to start thinking about supper. I didn't think that it was that late." She wrung her hands. "Where does time go?"

"It isn't almost six o'clock," remarked Lazo. "I think I set the watch on eastern time. It's only five o'clock."

"Gott sei dank!"

"Here, Liebling, take this," urged Hermann, "it will settle your nerves."

He handed each of them a glass of wine. then he raised his glass upward and proclaimed, "We have received some very fine presents today, but Lazo's safe return, is the greatest gift of all. Here's to Lazo."

They drank the wine and Hermann filled the glasses again. Thus began the celebration that would continue well into the night and when they were ready to retire, Hermann reminded them that the next day would be spent at Hermann's place by the lake. And so they went to bed that night with a certain gladness of heart, but for Hermann, the best was still to come. Once under the bed clothes, he was besieged by an Erika, whose sexual passion was so aroused and overwhelming, that she literally tore off his pajamas. Her ardor continued, unabated, until the darkness began to loosen its grip on the world. Then they fell asleep in each other's arms. The cause of Erika's romantic excitement would forever remain a mystery for Hermann, but the joy of that night, would impress his memory forever.

CHAPTER THIRTY ONE

Lazo slept well that night and might easily have slept until noon, had he not been awakened by a loud banging on his door.

"Are you awake?" came a loud voice from the other side of the door.

"Is that you, Ilse?"

"Yes. There's an urgent phone call for you."

"Who is it?" asked Lazo, still half asleep.

"He calls himself Colonel Featherstone."

"Tell him I'll be right there!" shouted Lazo. He scratched his head and mumbled, "How in hell did he know that I was here?"

He quickly jumped into his trousers and ran donwnstairs. Erika was making breakfast and as he picked up the phone, she handed him a cup of hot, steaming coffee.

"Thank you," he said, taking the cup. "My, don't you look radiant this morning."

He picked up the phone, took a sip of coffee and said, "Lazo here. What's up Colonel?"

He listened for a few moments, then in a voice somewhat elevated but still deferential, replied, "But Colonel, I was promised a ninety day furlough. Hell, Colonel, I haven't even been home yet."

Lazo paced back and forth as he listened to the Colonel's reply. "Oh, I see, Sir. Yes, I thought I smelled a rat." He paused for a second, then added, "No disrespect intended, sir, but you must understand how I feel, and I do intend to go over his head."

Ilse walked over and put her arm around him.

"Yes, Colonel, I do understand the magnitude of the situation in Yugoslavia and yes, Colonel, I know that I'm the one best suited for this mission, but hell Colonel, a few weeks can't make that much of a difference."

He gave Ilse a peck on the cheek and said, "Yes sir! An order is an order! Goodbye to you too, sir."

He hung up the phone and said, "That son of a bitch! I'll fix him."

"What's the matter?" asked Ilse.

"General Lee has cut new orders, calling for my immediate return to Washington. That's what's the matter."

Ilse looked up at him. Her eyes began to glisten. "How soon is immediate?" she asked, her voice trembling.

"In the army, Ilse, immediate means yesterday."

"What are you going to do?" asked Erika.

"I've got a few cards up my sleeve and intend to play them."

"Then," stammered Ilse, "you won't be able to come on the picnic."

"Don't count on that," replied Lazo. "I've got a few calls to make." He dashed upstairs shouting, "I've got to get dressed!"

Ilse's eyes were now overflowing with tears. "It's not fair," she remarked, walking over to her mother.

Erika put her arms around her and held her very close. "No Ilse, life is not always fair, but it has its moments."

"Oh, mother, but I do love him so much."

"I know, Liebling. I know."

Then the bedroom door slammed loudly and Lazo came dashing down the stairs.

"Where are you going?" asked Ilse, wiping her eyes. "You're not going back right now, are you?"

"No," laughed Lazo, "I'm not leaving yet. Not by a damned sight!"

"Then where's the rush?" asked Erika.

"I have a few phone calls to make and I'd best make them from town."

"Why can't you make them from here?" asked Ilse. "It will save you some time."

"I want to play it safe. God only knows what that bastard might do."

"You will have some breakfast before you go, won't you?"

"No, Erika, I'm not very hungry." He took Ilse into his arms and said, "Now you help your mother prepare the picnic and I'll see you later today, at Hermann's rendezvous."

He kissed Ilse and smiled. Then turned and left. "I'll bring the wine!" he shouted, as he ran up the path, leading to the road.

They watched as he disappeared among the trees. Then they embraced and returned, misty eyed, to the kitchen.

"Was that Lazo I saw running up the path?"

"Yes," replied Erika. "Where have you been?"

"I was just trying out my new binoculars. It is such a lovely morning and I thought it a shame to waste it." He walked up to Erika and gave her a kiss. "Now, will someone please tell me where he has gone?"

"He has gone into town," stammered Ilse.

"What for? Have you two gentle women frightened him away?" He chuckled and walked over to the stove. "When will breakfast be ready?"

"Is that all you can think about, papa?"

"What's the matter with her?"

Erika went over to him, took his hand and squeezed it quite gently. "Lazo must return to Washington immediately."

"What?" He stepped back, scarcely believing, what he was hearing. "There must be some mistake!"

"No mistake," replied Erika. "He received a telephone call this morning, notifying him of his new orders."

"And he left without even saying goodbye to me! How could he?"

"No papa. He hasn't gone yet. He went into town to make a few telephone calls. He said something about some cards up his sleeve, whatever that means."

"If I know Lazo, it means that he will find a way to stay. That's what it means. Now come over here and give me a big hug for good luck."

Ilse threw her arms around his neck and hugged him intensely.

"There, there, that's much better. Everything will be just fine," he assured her. He turned to Erika. "And now, let's have some breakfast. I have never felt so alive for such a long time and I am very hungry."

Erika put her arms around them and ushered them to the table. "Now sit down and I will bring you your breakfast."

"No, you sit and I will fetch!"

"Have you gone mad?"

"No," laughed Hermann, "I have not gone mad." He attended to Erika's chair, then kissed her behind the ear. "Sometimes I think that we forget too little and remember too much."

"You really have lost hold," chided Erika, but the smile on her face indicated that she was very pleased by his display of affection and concern.

He went over to the stove, turned and said, "This morning, when I was out there, watching the birds, it suddenly came to me."

"A bird came to you," laughed Ilse.

"No, Ilse," he replied, shaking his head. He picked up the coffee pot, returned to the table and filled their cups. He looked at his wife and softly but firmly said, "I want you to be more than a Hausfrau."

"But I like being a Hausfrau," she protested. Then a strange expression came to her face. It was almost as if she was in pain. "What else could I be?" she asked, her voice cracking.

Hermann put the pot back on the stove and returned with the eggs and bacon. He sat down next to Erika and said, "Hell, you can be anything that you want to be. Anything! You can soar with the birds!" He passed the eggs and bacon to them and began to sip his coffee.

"I'm much too old to fly and besides, I like what I am doing."

"That's fine," he replied, filling his plate with bacon and eggs. Then he pointed his finger at Ilse and said, "But will that be enough for her?" He shook his fork, then making certain of the correctness of his stand, said, "For the past four thousand years, western man has crippled western woman and now he mocks her because she limps." He paused and lowered his head.

"And you learned all of that from the birds?"

"Ya, Erika, I did. Birds, you see, are free to be birds, so why can't we be free to be what we are?" He looked at Ilse and with a deep sincerity, said, "I would be very hurt and embarrassed if I thought that I had in any way, intentionally or otherwise, thwarted your aspirations."

"You haven't papa." Then with a kind of diabolical grin, added, "Afterall, it was you who said that Werner could no more help being Werner than Ilse could help being a young woman. Do you remember, papa?"

"Ya, I remember," replied Hermann, somewhat embarrassed by Ilse's acuity. He ran his fingers against his forehead and reached for his pipe, as he was wont to do whenever he was engaged in the unraveling of a puzzle. "I believe it was Pinder who said that we must win through to being what we are."

"Ya," laughed Erika, "and I believe that it was Nietzsche who said, 'Du sollst werden der du bist'."

"I'm sorry. I didn't realize that I was in the presence of two such remarkable women."

"You have taught us well, papa. And when I am ready to soar, I will do so, but only because I have you in my blood."

He smiled and seemed to become embarrassed. "It was just," he continued, almost apologetically, "that for the first time since I arrived in this country, I truly feel like an American. I guess it was Lazo who made me feel this way and I just wanted to express that feeling to the ones I love. Freedom is such a wonderful fulfilment."

"Do you want some more eggs, papa?"

"No Ilse, I'll just have a little more coffee and my pipe. Then I think we'd better get a move on it. Afterall, we are still going on a picnic today, aren't we?"

"Of course, we are," replied Erika. "I'll get you some coffee."

"No, I'll get it," insisted Hermann. "You just sit there and relax."

Ilse looked at her mother and said, "I guess old habits do die slowly."

Hermann filled his cup and sat down. "I guess it is true what they say."

"What's that?" asked Erika.

"That illness comes in pounds and leaves in ounces."

Ilse raised her cup to her lips but she did not drink. She had been trying ever so desperately to retain her composure, but now her resolve gave way to tears and soon she was sobbing quite pathetically.

"What did I say? I didn't mean..."

"It wasn't anything that you said," whispered Erika. She put her around around Ilse's shoulder and tried to comfort her.

"Oh, Mutti! He's not coming back! I just know that he isn't! I'll never see him again!"

"He'll be back. Just you wait and see," uttered Erika. The soft tenderness of her voice was so soothing and reassuring that soon Ilse's shoulders stopped shaking and she became more composed.

"Ya, Liebchen, he'll be back. I have never seen a man so star crossed, not in my entire life." He lit his pipe and took a few puffs.

"Are we to wait here for him?"

"No," replied Ilse. She wiped her eyes. "He said that he would meet us at Hermann's Rendezvous. And oh yes, he said that he would bring the wine."

"Wunderbar! I'll be on the porch if you need me." He walked out on to the porch, without turning, for indeed, he did not want them to see his misty eyes. He leaned against the railing and whispered, "Old habits do die slowly." Then he rubbed his eyes with the back of his hand. "Yes, indeed."

CHAPTER THIRTY TWO

When Lazo reached the road, he turned and began to run toward town. He couldn't have gone more than a mile when he heard the sound of a car, coming up behind him. He moved on to the shoulder and waited for the car to pass. The car sped by and the driver honked his horn. Then he slammed on his brakes and pulled over.

"Do you want a lift?" He shouted.

Lazo ran up to the car. "Oh, it's you, Otto. Yes, I would like a lift into town, if it's not too much trouble."

"Well, jump in, then," said Otto.

Lazo, noting that the back seat was occupied, jumped into the front seat and dropped his mussette bag onto the floor.

"By the way, Lazo." He suddenly became uneasy and then said, "It is Lazo, isn't it?"

"You have a good memory, Otto. Not many people would remember a name like Lazo."

"Well, anyway," he continued, "I want you to meet my daughter, Jenny and her friend, Louisa Schneller. Girls, this is Captain Lazo Krall, the soldier that I talked about."

Lazo reached back, shook their hands and said, "Es freut mich sehr."

The girls giggled and replied, "Pleased to meet you, sir."

"I see they promoted you, Lazo." He shifted the car and eased back onto the road.

"Ya, Otto. They do some funny things in this man's army."

"Did you have a good time in Europe?"

"Not exactly," replied Lazo, "but I want you to know that you may have been right about the Russians. They're going to give us a helluva lot of trouble."

"Well," replied Otto, scratching his chin, "when we finish off those bloody Japs, maybe we can have a go at those damned Bolsheviks." He laughed loudly, slapped Lazo on his back. "Where do you want to get off?"

"Anywhere in town, where there is a public telephone. I've got to make a couple of calls."

"There's one in front of Schuler's drug store, papa."

"Ya, Jenny, that's probably the best place. I'll drop you off there, Lazo."

"Good," remarked Lazo. He picked up his bag and set it on his lap.

"Can you drop us off first, papa?"

"Why in heaven's name?" queried Otto. "It wouldn't be that you want the other kids at school to see this fine American officer, would it?"

The girls giggled and made no reply.

"I thought so," said Otto. "Well, if it's alright with Lazo, it's alright with me."

"That'll be just fine," remarked Lazo.

When they reached the school, Otto parked the car and said, "Okay, girls, you can get out now."

"Would you please walk us to the door, Lazo?" asked Jenny.

"Now, why would you want him to do that?" scolded Otto. "He has more important things to do."

"We want to make that snooty Barbara Jean Sutherland jealous. And besides," she added, "it will be so neat."

"It's alright, Otto. I'll do it."

The three got out of the car and began to walk toward the school. "It will really make Barbara Jean jealous if you each take one of my arms," whispered Lazo, with a smile.

They drew closer to him and did what he suggested. Then they walked slowly, very slowly toward the door. They stopped occasionally for the benefit of the host of students, who were milling about in the school yard. When they reached the door, he gave each of them a hug and said, "Aufwiedersehen, Jenny! Aufwiedersehen, Louisa!" Then he turned smartly and walked back toward the car, little knowing that this small gesture of kindness would make Jenny and Lousia the envy of all of the other girls for weeks to come.

"That was nice of you," beamed Otto, as Lazo reentered the car.

"It was nothing, and besides, I kind of enjoyed it," laughed Lazo.

"Well, thank you anyway," said Otto. "And now, I'll drop you off at the drug store."

Lazo reached into his pocket and pulled out his wallet. Then he took out the card, upon which he had written Saul Kaplan's telephone number. He examined it very carefully then placed it in his shirt pocket where it would be easily accessible.

"Here we are, Lazo."

Lazo opened the door and stepped down. "Danke vielmals, mein Herr!" He shook Otto's hand and said, "Aufwiedersehen!"

"The pleasure was all mine, Lazo. If I can be of any further help, please feel free to call on me. Aufwiedersehen!"

Lazo slammed the door and watched as the car moved away from the curb and headed down the street. Then he reached into his pocket and pulled out some loose change. He walked into the booth and closed the door behind. He took up the receiver and dropped a coin into the slot, waited a few seconds and then dialed the operator.

"Yes, operator. My name is Captain Lazo Krall and I would like to make a person to person call to Mr. Saul Kaplan in Washington, D.C. The number is Union, five, four, five, four, five."

As Lazo waited for the operator to dial the number, he studied the many scribblings which adorned the fragile walls of the booth. He looked upward and there in large letters, were the words, 'Barbara Jean S. is a snotty brat'. He smiled, took his pen in hand, and immediately below the word, 'brat', scribbled, "ditto." Finally, a voice on the other end said, "Hello Lazo! To what do I owe this singular honor?"

"Hello Saul. I'm so glad that I was able to reach you. I've got some good news for you." He hesitated, then continued, "At least, I think it's good news."

"Well, go ahead," urged Saul. "Don't keep me in suspense."

"I think that you are going to be a grandfather."

"What?"

"You're going to become a grandfather!" shouted Lazo.

"Are you sure?"

"As certain as anyone can be about paternity," replied Lazo, with a chuckle.

"When did all this happen?" asked Saul, his enthusiasm becoming more pronounced.

"It was in Tokra and the mother to be, is the daughter of Brigadier General Lee. Her name is Virginia."

"Well, why in hell hasn't she contacted me? I know her father quite well."

"It's a long story, Saul. Are you sure that you want to hear all of it?"

"Of course, I do," insisted Saul. "If what you say is true, you will have made my wife and me, the happiest people on the face of this earth. Now please continue."

Lazo related the whole story, being very careful not to omit anything and when he completed the story, he waited for Saul's response, but none was forthcoming.

"Are you still there?" He waited for a few seconds, then repeated, "Are you there?"

"Yes, Lazo. I'm still here but your story is so damned bizarre that it leaves me flabbergasted. I just don't know what to say."

"I know that you will need someone to corroborate my story."

"Yes," replied Saul, "not because I doubt your integrity but because I'll need someone or something to support your story. Otherwise she could deny it until kingdom comes. Do you have someone in mind?"

"I wouldn't have bothered to call you unless I did. Her name is June Janasek and she can be reached at 887-4145."

"How do you spell that last name?"

Lazo spelled it out for him and added, "She is an officer in the United States Army and was with us at Tokra. She knows what happened and will corroborate my story."

"That's terrific, Lazo. I haven't felt this good for some time now. How can I get in touch with you if I should need to?"

"Just call the Hermann Krebs residence in Pine Center, Wisconsin, but before you hang up I have a favor to ask of you."

"You know that I will do anything I can, that is, if it is within the scope of my influence, as meager as it is."

"Sam told me about your influence with the Washington moguls. As a matter of fact, he said that it was quite far reaching."

"How may I help you?"

"As you know, I was given the customary ninety days furlough to which I was entitled."

"Yes, I was aware of that."

"Well, I received word today, that my furlough had been cancelled by General Lee and my new orders call for my immediate return to Washington."

"I wasn't aware of that. Do you know why?"

"I'm not certain but I think that Virginia is involved in it someway. She has her old man wrapped around her little finger."

"Do you think that it has something to do with her pregnancy?"

"I'm sure it does. Hell, she came all the way out here to Pine Center to warn Ilse's parents that if Ilse continued to correspond with me, her father would see to it that the family is deported."

"That takes a helluva lot of guts."

"She scared the hell out of them and for a while, I was personna non grata at the Krebs household. She even told them that I was responsible for her pregnancy and that she intended to marry me."

"And they believed her?"

"You bet they did!"

"How did you convince them that you were not responsible for her delicate condition?"

"They wouldn't believe me, so I had them call June."

"The name you gave me?"

"Yes. I wasn't privy to the conversation but June's story must have been convincing because I am no longer persona non grata."

"Well look, Lazo, I'll make a few calls and get back to you in an hour or so. Will you be available?"

"You bet I will, and say hello to your wife for me."

"I'll do that and if what you tell me can be proved, my wife will be the second happiest person on this planet. Talk to you later."

"Goodbye," said Lazo. He hung up the phone and began to walk back to the cottage. He hadn't gone more than two blocks when he turned and began to walk back up main street. He had forgotten all about the wine and he now had to find a liquor store. He was able to find one without much difficulty and purchased four bottles of their best champagne. He carefully arranged them in his bag and resumed his trek. He glanced at his watch, shook his head and quickened his pace.

"Hell, I should have allowed myself more time," he whispered. "Well, maybe someone will give me a lift."

He looked back and saw an old Model A Ford, coming up behind him. He stepped to the side of the road, hoping that the driver would stop and offer him a ride. The car did stop and the driver leaned over and yelled, "How far are you going?"

"To the Krebs residence!"

"Jump in!"

Lazo got in and said, "Oh Thank you. You are a God send."

The old man nodded his head, shifted and headed back up the highway. "I am the rural route man and you just don't know how happy I am to see you."

"Me?" asked Lazo, somewhat startled. "You don't even know me."

"That's where you are wrong, young fellah," he retorted. He winked, then said, "Hell, you're Lazo, Ilse's boyfriend."

"Yes, I am," replied Lazo, "but why are you glad to see me?"

The old man spit a stream of tobacco juice out of the window and wiped his chin on the sleeve of his faded, winter underwear. He cleared his throat and said, "It's like this, young fellah. I have delivered their mail ever since they settled here. Ilse was just a scrawny string bean, then."

"I'll just bet she was," remarked Lazo, with a smile.

"But she was prettier than a button, she was. And now she's just about the prettiest girl in all of Burnette County." He turned toward the open window and another spray of tobacco juice collided with the wind and was swept back into the rising dust. "It's like this, Lazo. I just wanted to meet the man who could.." He paused, searching for the correct word. He spit once again, "inspire such undying devotion. Since she met you, not one single day has gone by when she hasn't waited at the mail box for me." He spit another stream of tobacco juice and repeated, "Not a single day. Can you believe that, young fellah? Nine months without a single letter from you. Still she came, every single day." He shook his head, then almost reverently added, "I doubt that any man could ever be worthy of such affection."

Lazo became uncomfortable. He began to wonder if he, could be worthy of her love. "A man can only try," he replied. "He can only try.

"Well, here we are, young fellah. It's been a pleasure."

"What do they call you?" asked Lazo, as he opened the door and prepared to exit.

"When I am late with the mail," he laughed, "they call me everything under the sun, but Slim Johnson will do just fine."

Lazo extended his hand and said, "Thank you very much, Slim and I know that I will see you again."

They shook hands and Lazo jumped out. He waved to Slim and began to run down the path, toward the house. When he reached the cottage, he stopped to look at his watch. He smiled and whispered, "Plenty of time."

He knocked on the door, just in case they had not yet left. He waited and when no response was forthcoming; opened the door and entered. He walked into the kitchen, hoping that Erika had left some coffee for him. He picked up the pot and smiled, then poured himself a cup and waited for the phone to ring. He paced back and forth, looking at his watch. Finally the phone rang. He picked up the receiver and shouted, "Hello! Lazo here!"

"Hello Lazo," came the reply. "This is Saul again. You'll be happy to know that I was able to get your orders rescinded."

"Terrific," uttered Lazo, his voice becoming more buoyant.

"I was able to get you thirty days and a promise that when you came back from Yugoslavia, they would give you the additional sixty days."

"That's great Saul! Thirty days will do just fine! Thank you very much. I owe you a big one."

"By the way, Lazo, I found out that there were no ulterior motives involved. They really need you."

"Did they say why?" asked Lazo.

"They know all about your connections in Yugoslavia, especially your friendship with the daughter of a very prominent statesman."

Lazo blushed and said, "I guess I'll have to go back there, then."

"By the way, Lazo, I would like to go with you."

"And why is that? You must know that there will be certain risks involved."

"I know," replied Saul, "but I want to bring my son's body home and you're the only one who can help me."

"We'll find the body alright," replied Lazo. "It will be painful for me but I would consider it an honor to help you."

"Good. Then I'll see you in about thirty days. By the way, Colonel Featherstone will verify what I have told you."

"Did you call June?"

"Yes, I did and she confirms your story and she promised to swear to it, in court if necessary. She has nothing but the highest regard for you, Lazo."

"That's great! That should make your wife very happy. Have you told her yet?"

"No, I haven't and I won't, not until I have had an opportunity to speak with Virginia."

"I understand," replied Lazo. "I'll see you in thirty days. Goodbye for now and I will always be indebted to you for the kindnesses you have shown me."

"It was my privilege. See you soon."

Lazo hung up the phone. "Hot damn!" he shouted, as he ran up stairs to clean up. He shaved and showered. Then he put on his favorite pair of well faded, olive green coveralls, stepped into his heavy leather mocassins and bounded down the stairs.

"Musn't forget the champagne," he reminded himself. He picked up his Mussette bag and walked out into the late morning sun. He felt very warm and safe again. When he neared Hermann's rendezvous, he saw the three sitting on the cliff overlooking the lake. They did not hear his approach, so he began to sing,

"Es war ein Tag,
Ein treuer Hussar,
Der liebt ein Madchen,
Ein ganzes Jahr.
Ein ganzes Jahr.
Und noch viel mehr.

Ilse was the first to hear him. She jumped up and ran to meet him.

"Can you stay?" she asked, her voice cracking with excitement.

"They have given me thirty days!" he shouted, his voice echoing through the forest.

She threw her arms around him and kissed him passionately.

"There, there!" chided Hermann. "You don't have to smother the poor boy."

Hermann embraced the two lovers then asked, "Then where do you go?"

"Back to Yugoslavia, but they promised me a sixty day furlough after my mission was completed."

"Wunderbar!" shouted Erika, caught up in the frenzy of the moment.

Lazo looked at Hermann and displayed an uneasiness that Ilse had hitherto, not seen. His right mocassin dug into the reddish soil, causing the dust to settle on the leather, giving it a burnished cast. Then in a voice, a full octave above normal, said, "Hermann Krebs, I would like your permission to marry your daughter when I return from Yugoslavia."

Hermann put his arm around Erika and replied, "Of course you have my permission and welcome to the family." Then he paused, scratched his chin and asked, "Have you asked Ilse?"

Lazo looked into Ilse's eyes and without hesitation, asked, "Will you marry me and make me the happiest man on this planet?"

"Of course, I will." She laughed and said, "If you hadn't asked me, I would have asked you."

"You shameless hussy," chided Lazo, having difficulty restraining a giggle. "Have you no pride?"

"Quite the contrary! I am now the proudest woman on the face of this planet."

"This calls for a celebration," beamed Erika, embracing the young couple affectionately.

"Did you bring the wine?" asked Ilse.

"Yes, my love. I brought four bottles of the best champagne in Pine Center. They're in my Mussette bag."

Hermann opened the bag and pulled out one of the bottles. He ran his hand over the bottle. It's a little warm but it will do just fine. Get the glasses!"

"I'll get them mama."

"They're in the green basket."

Hermann removed the cork very carefully but his efforts were for naught. The cork burst forth, sending a loud report through the forest. The champagne erupted and soon Hermann's hands were covered with cascades of foam.

"Hurry with the glasses before all of it disapppears!"

"Coming," replied Ilse.

Hermann filled the four glasses. Then he raised his glass and proclaimed loudly, "Here's to Ilse and Lazo. May the whisper of their love be as gentle as a summer breeze."

They touched their glasses and drank the warm champagne. Then they all embraced and for several moments, their silent display of affection smothered all of the other sounds that usually shower this splendid wilderness.

"And now I will prepare the lunch," said Erika, "and you, Hermann, you had better find a place to cool the champagne because I plan to get very tipsy."

Ilse smiled, took Lazo's hand and said, "And I've got something to show to Lazo."

"Don't be too long," urged Erika, "lunch will be ready in no time at all."

Ilse began to run, pulling Lazo along.

"Where are we going?"

"Where do you think?"

He smiled gently, then picked her up, cradled her in his arms and began to run, as if unencumbered, toward the crystal, clear pool and the promise of summer.

END, BOOK ONE

NORMANDALE COMMUNITY COLLEGE
LIBRARY
9700 FRANCE AVENUE SOUTH
BLOOMINGTON, MN 55431-4399